'Wise and funny . . . Catherine Fox knows that daily life is never trivial. Her characters' big experiences take place in the ordinary world of COVID, cake and kindness, but – like our own – they are no less significant for that.'
Gillian Cross, winner of the Carnegie Medal and the Whitbread Children's Book Award

'By innovatively laying her characters onto real-time, month-by-month events, Catherine Fox reminds us of the vital narratives of our own lives, and asks us to pay attention to the human stories that pulse beneath the headlines.'
Andrew McMillan, poet and Professor of Contemporary Writing, Manchester Writing School

Also by Catherine Fox (all published by Marylebone House)
The Lindchester Chronicles
Acts and Omissions
Unseen Things Above
Realms of Glory
Tales from Lindford

Angels and Men
The Benefits of Passion
Love for the Lost

'Catherine Fox's glorious Lindchester series is the twenty-first-century answer to Trollope's Barchester – but Trollope was never so funny, so fundamentally kind or so mischievously attentive to grace.'
Francis Spufford, author of *Golden Hill* and *Light Perpetual*

'These books are utterly unputdownable, gossipy, subtle and wise. What's astonishing is that, despite Catherine Fox's sharp awareness of the feet of clay under surplices, she somehow makes you believe several cheering things that most modern fiction doesn't: that the natural world is endlessly beautiful, that most people aspire to

goodness even if they fall flat on their faces and that the attempt to live a good life is worthwhile.'
Maggie Gee, novelist and Professor of Creative Writing, Bath Spa University

'Unsure what to buy the Trollope devotee in your life for Christmas? Look no further than Catherine Fox's *Acts and Omissions* and *Unseen Things Above* for a refresher course not only in cathedral politics but also a set of profound, although lightly drawn, insights into the contemporary Anglican Communion.'
Janet Beer, *Times Higher Education*

Angels and Men

'As original as its abrasive but engaging heroine.'
Pat Barker in the *Sunday Times* Pick of the Year

The Benefits of Passion

'Fox . . . writes this provocative and witty story as if she were on springs, her exuberant style happily combining with religious argument . . . thoroughly enjoyable.'
Good Housekeeping

Love for the Lost

'Catherine Fox is brilliantly skilled as a novelist.'
Penelope Fitzgerald

catherine fox

the company of heaven

First published in Great Britain in 2023

The Record Hall
16–16a Baldwins Gardens
London
EC1N 7RJ
www.marylebonehousebooks.co.uk

Two of the bonus material stories, 'Changes and chances: A Lindchester story for Christmas 2018' and 'One more river: A Lindchester story for Easter 2019' were first published in the *Church Times*.

Extracts from The Book of Common Prayer, the rights in which are vested in the Crown, are reproduced by permission of the Crown's Patentee, Cambridge University Press

Extracts from the Authorized Version of the Bible (The King James Bible), the rights in which are vested in the Crown, are reproduced by permission of the Crown's Patentee, Cambridge University Press.

British Library Cataloguing-in-Publication Data
A catalogue record for this book is available from the British Library

ISBN 978–1–910674–67–3
eBook ISBN 978–1–910674–68–0

Typeset by Fakenham Prepress Solutions, Fakenham, Norfolk NR21 8NL
First printed in Great Britain by Clays Ltd
eBook by Fakenham Prepress Solutions, Fakenham, Norfolk NR21 8NL

Produced on paper from sustainable forests

For the Steel City Choristers

Contents

Dramatis personae

Bishops

Steve Pennington	Bishop of Lindchester
Matt Tyler	Bishop of Barcup

Priests and deacons

Cathedral clergy

Marion Randall	Dean of Lindchester (the boss)
Giles Littlechild	Cathedral Canon Precentor (music & worship)

Lindchester clergy

Martin Rogers	Borough (and Churches) Liaison Officer
Dominic Todd	Rector of Lindford Parish Church
Wendy Styles	'Father Wendy', Vicar of Carding-le-Willow, Cardingforth
Virginia Coleman	'Mother Gin', Diocesan Officer for Social Justice, Associate Priest at Lindford Parish Church
Ed Bailey	Rector of Gayden Parva, Gayden Magna, Itchington Eposcopi, etc.

People

Gene	Husband of the dean
Freddie Hardman-May	Tenor, Lay Vicar of Gayden Parva
Ambrose Hardman-May	Alto, Lay Vicar of Gayden Magna
Ellis Gray	Owner of Gray's reclamation yard
Paver	Artist, Ellis's cousin

Dr Jane Rossiter	Lecturer at Linden University, married to Matt
Kat	Bishop Steve's EA
Neil Ferguson	Father Ed's partner
Andrew Jacks	Director of the Dorian Singers
Becky Rogers	Ex-wife of Martin, mother of Leah and Jessica
Leah Rogers	Older daughter
Jessica Rogers	Younger daughter
Chloe Garner	Street pastor, lawyer, lay member of General Synod, cousin of Ambrose
Madge Williams	Retired midwife, parish nurse
Miss Clarabelle Sherratt	Retired nurse, philanthropist, heir to the Sherratt fortune
Jack	Lives in Miss Sherratt's summerhouse
Carrie Logan	Wedding planner

All Creatures Great and Small

Cosmo	Chloe's labradoodle
Pedro	Father Wendy's rescue greyhound
Lady	Father Dominic's golden labradoodle
Bear	Neil and Ed's golden labradoodle
Alfie	Ambrose and Freddie's golden labradoodle
Andy and Theo	Alpacas

Prologue

———◆•◆———

Each time I finish blogging a volume of the Lindchester Chronicles, I vow it will be the last. But here we are again, dear reader, about to set off on a new adventure. 'As a dog returneth to his vomit,' says the proverb writer, 'so a fool returneth to his folly.'

I've never had a dog, but I'm guessing most owners haul the dog away and swiftly clear up the mess to prevent any canine foolishness. We must not collapse the distinction between vomiting and regurgitation, however. Regurgitation is a natural and wholesome process in the animal kingdom. We have much to learn from the ordering of the natural world. It behoves us to remain humble, and recall that God does not make mistakes.

If we are going to argue from nature, we cannot do better than contemplate emperor penguins. Everyone loves emperor penguins, with their monogamous heterosexual lifestyle, so unlike those gay zoo penguins that one reads about. The male emperor penguin incubates the egg, while the female goes off foraging for food. This may at first sight look like a troublesome example of gender role reversal, but we would do well to remember that if an activity is undertaken by the male of the species, it is de facto more arduous and perilous. The mother penguin returns from two months at sea with a belly full of fish, which she regurgitates for her newly hatched chick to eat. Such a normal and beautiful thing! I imagine mothers reading this find themselves wishing they could do the same for their own children. Images arise unbidden of foraging through the aisles of Sainsbury's, cramming their maw with doughnuts, before returning home to their clamouring brood.

We will leave the Antarctic wastes and bring things closer to home by wandering through the fields of Lindfordshire. What could be more soothing than the pastoral image of Daisy placidly chewing her cud? As you may recall from school Biology lessons, this is really Daisy regurgitating a bolus of food into her mouth, which she re-chews and re-swallows. Cows have a quite terrifying number of stomachs and digestive enzymes, the details of which need not detain us here. I will skip nimbly from cows to dogs, and conjure a picture of a golden labradoodle (let us call him Bear) retching behind the sofa – and thence to the proverb writer. 'As a dog returneth to his vomit.' Vomiting in dogs is caused by 'dietary indiscretion' (in Bear's case, rotting badger). Bad boy! Leave! I would argue that a dog returning to its *regurgitation* is less problematic, as this is probably just hastily gobbled food that never made it as far as the stomach. Not being picky eaters, dogs are fine with that idea. Hey, most of it still smells like food, and besides, they haven't finished with it yet.

All this is by way of an apologia. Revisiting Lindchester may look like folly. I daresay (*caveat lector*) there will be parts of this narrative that leave you grimacing with disgust. But I keep going back because there's stuff there I haven't finished with yet. Interestingly, if you read the next proverb in the Bible, it's this: 'Seest thou a man wise in his own conceit? There is more hope of a fool than of him.' The hope of this fool is that she knows she's a fool. She may yet listen, change her mind and amend her ways. The man wise in his own conceit is beyond the reach of hope. Armoured in the tower of his conviction, he will defend to the last any assaults on his rectitude.

It is not the business of this narrative to make the reader relive the first quarter of 2021. Let other laptops dwell on Capitol riots, inaugurations and impeachments. We will rejoin our Lindchester friends on Easter Monday, just as the third lockdown in our COVID winter of discontent draws to a close. The new paschal candles have been lit. The endless snowy ghastliness of January, February and March is behind us now. We trudged for three months on short rations of hope, with nothing to look forward to. Or so it felt. You'd think our spirits would have risen with every day that passed, every extra minute of daylight, every dose of vaccine administered. For once, the government's flightpath out of lockdown is holding firm. 'Flightpath' is not the right word. The right word has vanished, like a picture from a wall. We stare gormlessly at the space where it ought to be. Oh well. We'll have to make do with flightpath, until the correct word reappears later on when we no longer need it. COVID brain fuzz. It's as though some well-meaning buffoon has been tidying up our mental desk and misfiling half our vocabulary.

It feels as if this whole year hasn't really happened. How can we still be here, twelve months on from the first lockdown when it was all Zoom and Zumba, and weirdly exciting? Surely we drove a stake through the heart of 2020, so it could never come back? We stood by our windows at midnight on New Year's Eve as fireworks flickered in the clouds like sheet lightning. Near and far we watched as red stars, green sprinkles and white flowers crackled across Lindfordshire, declaring it was finally over. How can it *still* be like this? What if it replays endlessly and we never move on? Like that film, *Warthog Day*.

(Is that right? It sounds wrong.)

But the end of lockdown 3 is in sight now. In another week, non-essential shops can reopen and we will be permitted to sit shuddering in pub gardens enjoying a pint with pals we haven't seen for months. Many of us have had the first dose of the vaccine. The worst is over and spring is here. Look! Daffodils and primroses. Listen! The chiff-chaffs are back. Why so glum? We need not enquire why the long hair; but why the long face, people of Lindfordshire? Are we not an Easter people? Is hallelujah not our song? Hallelujahs famously get cold and broken. We are hosanna people these days: hosanna, in the sense of 'save us now!' Hosanna at 3 a.m. when we lurch awake in dread. Hosanna when we can't face another day. Hosanna when we are going under. Let all our panicked hosannas clatter up to the highest heavens like pigeons, with SOS tied to their tiny pink legs.

And we will fly too, dear reader, as is our custom. This time we take things in a more dignified manner, a month at a time. We will not proceed like a sparrow with a hawk locked on its tail. Instead we will aspire to the dignified wingbeats of a heron.

Roadmap! That's the word – not flightpath.

A heron flying over is a fairly common sight in Lindfordshire, along the Linden and its tributaries. You might even spot one in suburban areas, scouting for a nice peaceful garden pond where it can stand on one leg and think deep thoughts before eating your koi carp.

So come, dear reader. Let us take to the air once more, and fly through these hosanna-riven Lindfordshire skies, towards the village of Turlham. This is one of the rural hamlets of which Father Ed is vicar, and where Neil is revamping Turlham Hall boutique hotel, with the help of Freddie Hardman-May. We will catch up with them in due course. But first, we will be making some new friends.

APRIL

Daisy and diamond

icture, if you will, a cross-stitch sampler worked entirely in red thread, in a simple wooden frame. It was sewn by Alice Greatrix, aged 12, in New Orphan House, Lindford. Red might have been her favourite colour, but I think it more likely that a local draper donated a box of surplus crimson skeins. Embroidery was clearly an educational tool. The alphabet, upper and lower case, and the numbers one to ten, occupy the top section. Then comes the Bible verse 'Thou God Seest Me'. But perhaps when the business of letters, numbers and Bible was out of the way, Alice was allowed to exercise a bit of choice over the flowers and birds that border the rest of the sampler. I like to think that the hymn in the centre was a personal favourite, rather than something Matron or the rector's wife thrust at her and told her to copy.

> When He cometh, when He cometh
> To make up His jewels,
> All His jewels, precious jewels,
> His loved and His own:
>
> Like the stars of the morning,
> His bright crown adorning,
> They shall shine in their beauty,
> Bright gems for His crown.

Readers who enjoyed an old-fashioned chapel upbringing are probably humming the tune by now. They will know that little children who love their Redeemer are the precious jewels, his loved and his

3

own. The sampler is dated 1867. I'm trying to imagine what was going through Alice's head as she bent over her sewing, minute by minute, stitch by stitch. The orphanage has gone; demolished to make way for the ghastly brutalist 1960s shopping precinct that I cannot find it in my heart to love, any more than the town planners of the 60s could admire the ghastly florid Victorian orphanage. Lindford cemetery is still there, though. We can go and look at the gravestones listing the dozens of orphanage children who died in the cholera epidemics of 1832, 1849, 1854 and 1866. Fenton, Fenton, Fenton, Dobson, Dobson, Dobson, Dobson, Greatrix, Greatrix.

> He will gather, He will gather
> The gems for His kingdom;
> All the pure ones, all the bright ones,
> His loved and His own.

Why wasn't I gathered when so many other children were? Wasn't I pure and bright enough? Perhaps questions like these ran through Alice's mind. Thomas Greatrix (aged 14) would have been a brother or a cousin. Was she the only one left now? I hope the hymn consoled her, because she couldn't have realized that the outbreak of 1866 would turn out to be the last to ravage Lindford; that she was safe. From cholera, at any rate.

The sampler now hangs on the kitchen wall of the Old Barn in Turlham. If you are picturing an ancient tithe barn with medieval roof timbers full of endangered bats, I must stop you at once. The Old Barn is early twentieth century and made of corrugated iron. This was the smart building material *du jour* when it first appeared; vastly preferred to thatch, which had connotations of rural squalor and deprivation. How the wheel of good taste turns! Imagine the outrage in a picturesque village today if a cottage owner replaced the thatch with tin.

That said, vintage corrugated iron is enjoying a renaissance. Our good friend Neil is a fan, and I know of no sterner arbiter of what we are permitted to like than Mr Ferguson. He has been hankering after a tin tabernacle to renovate for years. If the adult voices of your childhood dismissed rusty sheds as eyesores, this trend may surprise you. Do you remember them? Beached in nettle seas like decommissioned ships, with smaller wrecks nearby, ancient Citroëns perhaps, wheel arches like leaping dolphins. That kingdom behind a wonky gate, which only children entered. A hot June day, hot and still, the nettles firing puffs of pollen into the dappled air, scent of elderflower, and a train rattling south through the fields in the distance.

This was the scene waiting for Ellis Gray thirty years ago, when he drove his converted transit van down the narrow lane, parked and fell in love. He put in an offer straightaway on the plot with its trees and tumbledown buildings. The locals rejoiced. At last, someone was going to smarten up this shabby bit of Turlham. There was already planning permission for a tasteful four-bedroom house. Instead, Ellis lived in his van while he renovated the barn and converted it into a home. Not content with one tin ruin, Ellis constructed a second out of salvaged materials, and established a small reclamation business. All this took the best part of five years – Ellis works Entishly with the grain of things – and you'd better believe that the villagers had a thing or two to say about their disappointment. The word 'eyesore' cropped up again.

Of course, that's long forgotten. Images of the Old Barn are all over Pinterest, and before COVID, people drove miles to visit Gray's reclamation yard and craft centre (in a third tin building). This was where Neil bought that load of perfect teak block parquet flooring salvaged from an old church hall. (It's still stacked in the vicarage garage waiting for the general resurrection.) You went to Gray's to potter among butler's sinks and stacks of 1970s chicken tiles; or to browse the craft barn, coveting the upcycled chalk-painted furniture, local ceramics and jewellery, while the kids played in the semi-wild garden.

Oh, the garden! Worth a trip for its own sake. A free theme park with winding mown paths and willow tunnels, sand pits, tyre swings, tree houses, and tiny fairy doors set in the roots of the giant copper beeches and horse chestnuts. Afterwards you could buy coffee and homemade cake from the converted horsebox coffee bar and sit at one of the picnic tables. Doesn't it sound like heaven? If Ellis proposed now to demolish it all and build that tasteful four-bedroomed house, there would be uproar.

Gray's will remain closed until non-essential shops can reopen next week, so the good people of Lindfordshire must find other ways of amusing themselves this Easter Monday. I catch myself longing to go there, although I know that none of it exists. Yet even as I write this, it feels as though Gray's has been there all along (didn't Neil buy his parquet there?) and that by following the line of words, I am merely discovering it for the first time. All writers will tell you this. I suppose it can be reduced to the creative interplay of left and right hemispheres of the brain, synapses firing, signals travelling down neural pathways and so on. But no explanation quite does justice to a deep sense that there are more things in heaven and earth than are dreamt of in neuroscience. My soul, there is a country.

But come, I want you to meet Ellis. He's standing in his kitchen staring at the sampler, improvising a tiddely-pom song like Winnie-the-Pooh as he waits for his kettle to start warbling. Medium height, stocky, with a grizzly beard and short hair, he's wearing his customary work boots, jeans and lumberjack shirt. For the avoidance of doubt, he's a bear (according to Neil). Ellis was born in 1959, the surprise only child of delighted parents in their forties, and he has thrift running through his veins. Not a stingy thrift; theirs was a loving thrift that nursed old appliances back to life, that patched, darned and sides-to-middled, that composted, reclaimed, improvised and saw beauty in old lino. Practically everything in the Old Barn is pre-loved.

'Thou God *seest* me.'

Like most solitary people, Ellis is capable of repeating things half a dozen times without realizing he's speaking aloud.

'Thou God seest *me*.'

No matter how he says it, this verse always strikes him as menacing. A God of surveillance, tracking every movement. And that hymn! It makes Jesus sound like a Victorian gem collector. Poor Alice.

Ellis sets the table for breakfast. Over the years, he has fallen into the habit of thinking of Alice as an ancestor. He remembers that jolt when he came across the sampler propped in the corner of a Lindford junk shop. He can picture her vividly, sewing by a window with light angling down.

'Hey Ellis.'

Ellis turns. There's Paver (a genuine relative), standing on one leg in the doorway. Cousin Anne's youngest. As always, Paver's pale skin and hair seem to be lit by an unseen source, a skylight on to another

6

world. That tiny twenty-six-week scrap in an incubator. Ellis remembers staring through the glass partition into the Special Care Baby Unit, heart clenched in love and fear. Twenty years ago now.

Paver's dark eyes roam round, counting. The mugs on the draining board, the blue-glass poison bottles along the windowsill. Ellis knows not to interrupt. There needs to be an even number of things. Unless it's a single thing. One is exempt. The panes in the sash window are problematic. Three in the top half, three in the bottom. But six in total. Six is safe.

The kettle starts whiffling. Ellis makes tea in a big brown teapot. He checks out of the corner of his eye. Good. Paver has both feet on the ground now. 'Morning. Sleep well?'

'So-so. At least I didn't have The Dream.'

'Well, that's good to hear.'

The Dream, apparently, is that you've committed some unspeakable crime – only you cannot remember what. It squats on your stomach like Fuseli's nightmare, paralysing you with guilt and terror. The more you reason with yourself that it's not real, the more it sounds as if you're trying to cover up the truth and rationalize it away. *You* would *say that, wouldn't you?*

Paver reaches a hand round the doorframe, turns the light off and on again twice, then finally comes and sits at the blue Formica-topped table.

'It was snowing earlier, Ellis. I was laid up there in bed looking out through my round window, and there was snow whirling everywhere, and suddenly in my head it was like the garden was actually inside a massive snow globe. Ever think our world might actually be in a snow globe, with giants watching us – or is that just me? I mean, how would you even know?'

Thou God seest me. 'Hard to say. Toast?'

'Am I . . . weirding you out?'

'Not at all. You know I like to hear you talk.'

'You're the best.' Paver moves the enamel mug so that it lines up properly with the tip of the knife. 'So Mum had a vintage snow globe, I think it was Granny's, with snowy trees and an angel and a fawn in, maybe 50s, 60s, only most of the water had leaked out, so it looked like the angel was paddling in a forest with the baby fawn, maybe rescuing it after a flood. I don't know what happened to it. The snow globe, I mean, not the fawn. The angel would've saved the fawn. For sure. For sure it would. Angels do that, save things, guardian angels – I kind of believe in them. I used to think thistledown was tiny angels. I was convinced someone told me that, same as I was convinced if it wasn't raining outside, it was raining inside, fine rain, and if you squinted your eyes you could see it. For years I thought everyone knew that.' Paver laughs. 'Came as a total surprise to learn it wasn't true.'

'Life's one long surprise,' says Ellis.

'True, true.'

There's a pause. Paver's talk comes in super-charged bursts, like wren trills followed by silence, with the song still echoing. That's how Ellis thinks of it. If you'd asked him any time in the last thirty years, he'd have told you he was never lonely living by himself. But he would be now, without Paver, without that husky voice riffing, and the silence teeming with wonder.

'So you know Boneflower, Ellis? As in the hardcore band from Spain?'

Ellis shakes his head.

'No worries. Turns out bone flower's another olden-days name for daisy? I mean, think about it – a hardcore band called Daisy!' Paver laughs. 'So anyway, they used daisies on broken bones.'

'Like comfrey? Interesting. One for your April book?'

'Probably. Yeh. Probably. Daisy aka gowan and bruisewort. So April's daisy and diamond. I'm looking into diamonds as of today. Diamonds are like three billion years old and here's a thing – did you know graphite and diamonds are the same thing in and of them-selves – i.e. carbon? It just depends on what happens to the carbon how it turns out. Immense pressure makes diamonds. So engagement ring or pencil, depending. What I don't get is how you cut diamonds, if diamonds are the hardest thing in the world? What kind of knife could cut a diamond?'

Ellis knows about lasers and bruting machines. But he also knows Paver mainly wants his company, not his solutions. He shakes his head. 'You'll have to Google it.'

'Yeah, but I kind of like not knowing, so I can still wonder about it?'

Ellis smiles. 'That's how we lived before the internet. In a state of idle wonderment, until we could get to the library and look it up in a book.'

'Idle wonderment. I love that.'

Ellis puts slices of his homemade sourdough in the toaster (1970s four-slice Dualit, still going strong). He's humming 'Daisy, Daisy' now. Wasn't that a 60s schools' TV programme? He remembers sitting with the other children in the dining hall watching through the snowstorm of the big black-and-white TV screen.

He opens the top half of the back door and looks out. A bee buzzes past. It's a bright morning now. He leans his elbows on the lower door. The wind blows and powdered snow winks down from the trees like diamond dust. There's a wood pigeon brooding. Paver's doing breathing exercises at the table. *In*-two-three-four. *Out*-two-three-four. Good. Each week has been a little calmer. There have been ups and downs since January, but the general direction of travel is good. Fewer panic attacks. No longer checking the skip twenty times a day for accidentally killed and concealed bodies.

He shuts the door. 'Any plans for the day?'

'Maybe the May garden?' Paver hesitates. 'Except now I need to work bones into April. Maybe bird skulls among the daisies? Or will that freak out the little kids? I mean, if they're neurotypical. I kind of struggle to gauge that stuff.'

'Well, I'd say most children are fascinated by creepy things.' Ellis gets the toast out and brings it to the table. He sits and pours the tea.

'That's what I thought,' says Paver. 'Like *Horrible Histories*. In Juniors, history wasn't, you know, *real* for the NT kids, to them it was just another bunch of pretend stuff in kids' books with happy covers same as *Goosebumps*. *Goosebumps*? Kids' horror? Never mind. So you know how people have this cliché that you can't empathize if you're "on the spectrum"? My observation, it's the NT kids that can't empathize, they have to literally learn to join the dots that hang-drawing-quartering isn't like *Goosebumps* and if you cry in History it's what you *should* do it's not because you're lame and weird because I mean God this was *actual* people doing this unbelievably cruel thing to *actual* people while massive crowds watched and cheered and—'

9

'Paver? Look.' Ellis places his right hand on his own chest and holds it there. Paver copies him. Odd how this simple action helps; how it grounds you and soothes the fluttering bird in its cage of ribs. 'It's OK.'

In-two-three-four. *Out*-two-three-four. 'OK. I got it.'

'Good. How about some toast?'

'Thanks, Ellis.' Paver cuts the slice into quarters and reaches for the butter. 'That was close! But to my point, how can you *un*-learn over-empathy? That's the question. Everyone my whole life: Shush! Stop talking. Stop crying. Dial it back, you're over-reacting! Me: Like I'm not trying to not over-react? But then I'm like, wait, I still want to be *me*. Maybe *the world* needs dialling back? So anyway, maybe a better thought is, is there body armour against over-identifying – soul armour, if you will? Unless my meds are soul armour, of course.'

'And CBT maybe?'

'And CBT, yeh, a bit. And your people, you got to find your people.' Paver nods. 'Yeah. To finally know you're not the only one? And the right language and vocabulary obviously. Talking of which, bone garden is slang for cemetery. So April could be like a tiny graveyard. Plus, thinking ahead, how are we going to get carnations to flower in January?'

We will leave them to discuss the twelve birth flower plots that Paver is creating around the grounds. The idea is to form a little treasure trail. This prompted Paver's other project – to make tiny books to fit in decorated matchboxes, all about the birth flowers and gems for each month. If you're looking for a quirky one-off present for a new baby, why not browse them on Etsy? They will also be available from the craft barn when it's open again.

Since dropping out of art school in January, Paver has been living with Ellis and making miniatures. Old tobacco tins containing woodland scenes or Gothic interiors, and eerie landscapes on pebbles. To say nothing of tiny glass cases displaying weird creatures constructed out of watch parts and fragments of dead beetles and moths. Paver's work always reminds me of those febrile fairy paintings by Richard Dadd and John Anster Fitzgerald, with their uncannily real flora and fauna, and beasts fresh from medieval marginalia and Bosch paintings. You're uncomfortably aware of your own intrusive gaze, as though you've lifted a paving stone, or you're spying into a bird's nest. Those Victorians. One glug too many from the laudanum bottle, if you ask me.

But I'm getting caught up in the fascination of new lives, reader, while you are hankering for tidings of old friends. How are they all faring? We abandoned them at the close of last year, in a welter of fireworks, dancing on the grave of 2020. Little did they know that the portcullis of a very long, bleak lockdown was about to descend – before they'd got round to having their hair cut, even!

Our friends have survived these months as best they can. January to March is always grim in these northern climes, even without COVID. Some have lost weight after a dedicated regime of diet and fitness. Others have gained weight after a dedicated regime of late-night boozing and snacking. (As the White Witch herself observed, it is dull for the Sons of Adam to drink without eating.) Either way, my characters have been united in finding this lockdown the hardest and most miserable. It felt as though there was nothing on the horizon to look forward to. No parties, no concerts, no football matches. No point in booking a foreign holiday. The UK variant of COVID ripped round the world, with other variants hot on its heels. For those who compulsively check graphs, the jagged mountain ranges of death and infection rates reared endlessly, peak after peak.

But winter is over, at least, and miraculously the vaccine programme has been efficiently rolled out – it actually has. All across Lindfordshire church halls, fire stations and leisure centres were repurposed. Text and email invitations went out. Lindchester Cathedral opened its venerable doors as a mass vaccination hub. You may have seen footage on the news: people sitting waiting in the nave as the organ sounded, or volunteer musicians sang and played and were rewarded with leftover vaccinations at the end of the day (some of our old friends among them). Over twenty-two million doses administered in the UK, which means the majority of those in the 80+, 70+ and 60+ categories have now received a first shot.

Gradually the grandiose claims of 'Best' and 'World-Beating' have stopped sounding like a six-year-old boasting about their dad. Remain voters graciously concede that the EU is bungling vaccinations, and it's lucky we extricated ourselves. Leave voters magnanimously refrain from crowing – because COVID has chastened us all, and taught us that there is more that unites than divides us! Yeah, right. You will have observed a similar outpouring of peace and goodwill across the ruinous divides of Anglican Twitter. *In a world where you can be anything, be kind!* And if you can't be kind, at least be quick to point out the unkindness of others in a vicious subtweet.

So, theoretically a corner has been turned, even if we still feel numb and wretched. A year ago, we talked endlessly about the virus, whether we'd had it, how badly, with what symptoms. Now we talk about the vaccine. Have you had your first dose yet, second dose? Pfizer? AstraZeneca? Any side effects?

The roadmap out of lockdown has held so far. Schools have reopened. People can now meet outdoors in groups of up to six (or two households). Perhaps our spirits will pick up soon. In a few more days, the doors of Lindfordshire's barbers and hairdressers will open. Stylists will once more display the skill of trimming around ears without snipping through their client's mask elastic. We will spot women in disposable gowns sitting on benches in front of the salon, heads bent over phones, with the April sunshine winking off their colour foils.

I mention this because we will forget. These details will slip away, all the qualia of COVID. Just as we've already forgotten that cargo ship jammed sideways across the Suez Canal. Our numbscape pandemic memory is as holey as Swiss cheese. It's collective trauma, I suppose. Sometimes I don't care. Other times I fret about all the things I'm failing to gather up and salvage in this rusty listing barn of a narrative.

But you are getting frustrated. So I will flop my heron's wings and get us airborne. Come with me, all the way from Turlham to Lindford. We will find somewhere convenient to land, peer in through a window, and I will stop discussing hair in general and zoom in on the hair of Freddie Hardman-May in particular.

This Easter Monday morning, Freddie is standing in the heavenly blue kitchen of his 1960s house. If we listen closely, we will hear the hens chook-chook-chooking in the garden. They've started laying again now that the days are lengthening. Alfie the golden labradoodle is on high alert. The bacon and eggs are cooking. The cinnamon buns are warming. The sourdough bread is toasting. Unlike Ellis, Freddie has not baked the bread himself, but he did get up early to do the carb run. The loaf and pastries are fresh from Lindford's Mister Bun the Baker, a new business that has done rather well during the pandemic.

Prepare yourself for something you might not want to hear, dear reader. Freddie's raggedy blond hair is now so long that he has taken to wearing it in a man bun. I know. I can't leave my characters alone for three months without them getting into mischief. He's also grown back the hipster beard he shaved off in 2016, after his mentor smirked in lofty derision. Freddie now resembles a smoking-hot Viking off to pillage a gay sauna (Neil's verdict, not mine). Have no fear, Freddie is a reformed character. He has no such plans. (And in any case, saunas and other indoor venues won't be open until 17 May.) Freddie is innocently doing lip-buzz exercises while he practises his juggling.

Hmm. Didn't think that one through?

He ponders his exit strategy. It's one thing to start juggling fresh eggs, quite another to stop without breakage of some kind. Fortunately, Ambrose has just come in.

'Catch? Whoa! Awesome. Reflexes of a cat, my dude.' Freddie sets the other two eggs down on the counter.

Ambrose stares at the egg he caught, as though it might hold a clue to why his husband is a nutter. Then he shrugs, and puts it with the others, before picking up a Sharpie and writing the date on this morning's clutch.

You will want an update on Ambrose's hair too, I daresay. It's short and neat. He looks like the accountant he is, rather than a Viking – or worse, a member of the Shelby family. Chloe wielded the clippers this time round, thank goodness. In a moment, Chloe will come through from her little apartment in the extension and join them for breakfast. We will discover whether her long dark hair is still in its swishy ponytail, or if she's decided she's too old for that and has had it cut off in a stylish bob, or even a pixie cut. Can you bear the tension?

Enough with the hair, I hear you cry. What about the baby? Oh, very well.

We left this unorthodox household of three with their hopes of parenthood pinned on a faint blue line, a line that appeared rather wonderfully in the middle of the night of Christmas itself. O night divine! What happened next?

The road forks here, reader. Which direction shall I take? Baby, or no baby? The art of serializing a novel in instalments turns out to be rather like the art of living. With hindsight, we might wish we'd done it all differently; but there's no going back and changing things. We make a decision and a course of action follows. All other options promptly fall away. From now on, we must travel along *this* road, not another. This is not *The French Lieutenant's Woman*. If you want alternative endings to choose between, you'll have to imagine them yourself.

Here we go.

Look at the fridge door. There it is, beside the weekly meal plan (held in place by a 'You shit rainbows' gay fridge magnet) – the image from the twelve-week scan. Huzzah! It was taken six weeks ago. This means that the due date of Baby Garner-Hardman-May (good grief – they're going to have to decide on a family name at some point, so the poor child doesn't grow up triple-barrelled) is 4 September. If Baby comes four days early, Baby will share a birthday with daddy Freddie! Yay! Like all scan pictures, it resembles a peanut in a snowstorm. Naturally, it has been pored over and WhatsApped to the suite of grandparents. All manner of family likenesses have been magically inferred.

But is it a boy or a girl, you ask? For the purposes of consumer capitalism, the road forks here too: Daddy's Princess, or Future Boss. I don't know what your opinion might be, but I resent this meat-cleaver division into pink/blue stereotypes. So I'm going to tick the 'Prefer not to say' box for now. Besides, Freddie, Ambrose and Chloe aren't telling people yet either. This is not because they are planning a big gender-reveal party. Nor are they intending to bring Baby up without imposing gender at all (although Ambrose is amusing himself by leading Freddie's father to believe this). No, they've simply decided not to tell people yet. And why should they?

Here's Chloe now.

'Morning, boys!' Ah, her hair is still in its long ponytail. Baby will enjoy tugging that. Sideways on, she now has a small mound of a

14

bump. It's just big enough for tactless people to ask when she's due. Cosmo is with her. He skids to a halt in front of Ambrose and wags his tail eagerly.

Ambrose pours dog food into both bowls, and Cosmo and Alfie tuck in. Approximately thirty seconds of golloping later, they turn their starving orphan eyes on Freddie, knowing there's a good chance he will – oops! – drop some bacon while he's dishing up.

'Er, remember we talked about this, babe?' says Ambrose.

'I know! Jeez. Gimme a break here.' Freddie hands round the plates and sits beside Chloe, opposite Ambrose. The dogs crowd close and prop their chins on his leg. He shrugs at them. 'Dudes, I don't know what to tell you. Brose says no.' He turns to Chloe. 'So what fruit are we at today?'

'OK. So today . . .' Chloe consults her phone. 'It's sweet potato! Five point nine inches, six point seven ounces. "Baby's tiny fingers now have unique fingerprints." Aw.'

'Thank you, sweet potato!' sings Freddie, face up close to the bump. 'Unique fingerprints? Cute.'

'How are you doing?' Ambrose asks her.

'A lot, lot better.' She starts her bacon and eggs. 'Still tired, but I keep reminding myself at least I'm not sicky. I'm telling you, though, if this is meant to be the *blooming* phase, then I want a refund.'

'Have YOU been mis-sold a pregnancy?' asks Freddie. 'You could be entitled to—'

'I saw that,' Ambrose cuts in.

'Dude, it was just the rind? Don't wanna eat rind. You'll get pigs growing in your stomach.'

Ambrose puts his fork down and leans forward. He waits for Freddie to stop clowning around and meet his gaze.

Chloe picks up her phone again and starts scrolling.

We find ourselves, like Chloe, wishing we were somewhere else. It's an old argument: Freddie is casting Ambrose in the role of Killjoy Dad again, while he showboats in the Fun Dad role. They've got five months to get this unhelpful dynamic addressed.

We hold our breath. Life bristles with moments like this. To be a dick, or not to be a dick? The poor dogs stare up at Freddie. Their doggy foreheads rumple. Alfie begins to whimper.

15

Freddie sighs and raises his hands. 'OK, fine. Sorry. My bad.' He strokes the dogs. 'C'mon, it's OK, guys. We're cool.'

'It's OK,' Ambrose tells Chloe. 'We're cool.'

'Thank God for that.' Chloe puts her phone down. 'You know I don't do rows.'

'Nor did I until I met him,' says Ambrose. 'But unlike you and me, he comes from a plate-throwing background.'

'Hey, hey, hey! *He* is in the actual fucking room, excuse me very much?' Freddie shoves his mug towards Ambrose. 'Can I get a coffee here?'

Ambrose plunges the cafetiere and pours.

'Ooh, *I* know! We should buy a round table,' says Chloe. 'Then we won't have to choose sides.'

Ambrose and Freddie both turn to her and stare.

'Know what?' says Freddie. 'We should so do that. That's a seriously good idea.'

Ambrose nods. 'For a girl.'

There's a dangerous pause.

'Uh-oh,' says Chloe. 'You blew it, oinker. I'm playing my "Trip to IKEA" card. We're going table shopping.'

Freddie punches the air. 'All r-i-i-ight!'

'And we're doing it properly,' says Chloe. 'No looking up the warehouse shelf location online and sneaking in through the exit when someone comes out.'

Freddie gasps. 'You'd *do* that?'

'Oh, he's done it,' says Chloe.

Ambrose nods. 'In, straight to item, buy, out. Ten minutes max.'

'Whoa! Serious whole-ethos-of-IKEA violation, dude! You're gonna have to turn in your gay badge now.'

'Happily.'

'No,' says Chloe. 'We're all going, and we're doing it properly.'

Ambrose mutters something about cruel and unusual punishment.

'Nuh-uh. You totally brought it on yourself, babe.' Freddie shakes his head. 'Better get your sexist ass in gear before Baby comes, is all.'

We will leave them to finish breakfast – noting that Ambrose has the scant consolation of knowing the café won't be open, so at least he'll be spared the meatballs – and take a swift tour of the rest of Lindchester.

Come, let us do the best we can with these heron wings. We will proceed with whoomphing wingbeats like a flying patio umbrella, harried and worried by jackdaws. If we look down, we will see that the blackthorn is out. Hazy clouds of white along the hedges. The magnolias in suburban gardens, the daisies in the grass. Lambs skipping. Joggers jogging. Delivery vans delivering. 'Thou God seest me.' Every me in Lindfordshire. Every me in the world. We cannot pretend to that level of omniscience. I confess, I had wanted to show you everyone and everything, so that nothing would be lost. (Lindford, Lindford! I'm half crazy, all for the love of you.) But I can see that we are going to have to make do with one April day, chosen as representative of the whole month. Pressed and framed in a glass case, or prong-set in gold – take your metaphorical pick. All other days promptly fall away.

Where are we going now? Martonbury. This is where we will find the Rogers family. The two girls are jogging round the reservoir, while Becky and Martin walk very slowly hand in hand, looking for a bench where they can sit and wait while Jess and Leah complete the 5k loop. The sky is bright blue and the wind is keen. It sends shivers of glory zithering across the water. The bursting sticky buds gleam as though wet.

Martin looks up and sees the tracery of beech twigs against the blue. The buds shine like constellations of stars. He's never noticed this before. He was always too busy in his previous life. Today this feels like a small silver lining to his COVID cloud. On other days – the concrete duvet days of crushing fatigue – he notices nothing at all.

'Will this do?' asks Becky. 'It's out of the wind.'

'Perfect.'

They sit in the shelter of the boathouse, and Becky opens up the brown paper carrier bag from Mister Bun, and hands him his coffee and pastry. This is permitted, because all the packaging is recyclable, and they remembered to take their own reusable bamboo coffee cups.

He raises his cup. 'Cheers.'

'Are you warm enough? You're shivering. Here.' She unfolds the blanket she's brought and spreads it over his knees. Long COVID seems to have fritzed his body thermostat.

'Thanks. So, what about this Kai?' says Martin. 'Are we OK with this? She's only fourteen.'

'She's fifteen next month. And with the best will in the world, she's hardly going to carry on mooning after Freddie till menopause, Martin.'

'I know, I know. It's a dad and daughter thing. Maybe I should just punch him, pre-emptively.'

Becky laughs. 'Except he's a karate black belt.'

'Hmm. There is that.' He gazes out across the water. 'Look, there they go.'

On the opposite side, the two girls are slowly jogging past. Jess looks across the water and waves.

'Look, Leah,' she pants. 'There's Mum and Dad!'

'Focus!' barks Leah. 'If you've got enough energy to wave, you're not working hard enough!'

'Sor-ree! Oh look – a bluebell!'

'Don't stop!'

'Yes, but it's quite early for—'

'Keep going! You're six seconds faster than your PB!' Leah bounces up and down on the path. 'Listen, I'm going to sprint for a hundred metres, then do burpees until you catch up, OK? *Don't* slow down.'

'OK.' Jess waits until Leah's disappeared round the curve in the path, then slackens her pace. What is even the point of killing yourself and not enjoying anything, like for example the bluebells, which are super-early this year for some reason? Oh! Violets! And celandines, *not* buttercups FYI. Leah thinks she's world expert on everything, but Jess knows the difference, from Flower Fairies, which Leah despises obviously.

Jess jogs round the corner. And there's Leah up ahead doing burpees. If Jess never caught up, would Leah literally carry on doing burpees for, like, ever? Like an evil older sister in a fairy tale put under a spell for bullying the sweet kind sister who was nice to cats and old ladies and ended up with gold coins falling out of her mouth when she spoke, not toads. Ew. Jess can almost feel what it would be like to sick up an entire toad, a slippy bump coming up your throat and filling your mouth, ew ew ew!

'Are you OK?'

'Bit sick!' pants Jess, doubling over.

'That's because of reduced blood flow to the digestive tract. Here.' Leah hands her a bottle. 'Sports drinks are a total scam. Kai texted me his recipe.'

'Cool! What's in it?'

'Organic honey and orange juice.'

Jess takes a couple of swigs and spurts them back out. 'Bleah!'

'Oh yeah. And salt,' adds Leah. 'To speed up rehydration. Ready?'

They set off again. Jess's glasses keep slipping down her nose. Sweat's getting in her eyes. But she keeps on going.

Someone else is keeping on going. It's Jane. She'd normally be jogging round the reservoir too, but she's broken a toe. There was a time when her injuries were badges of sporting honour – black eyes, broken collarbones. Not a fractured toe caused by walking across the bedroom floor barefoot – something she's been doing with impunity ever since she could walk at all. Was this the first in a depressing catalogue of stupid injuries, until her quotidian world was nothing but tripping hazards, which she inched her fearful way through, groping for handrails?

Jane is walking slowly round Martonbury's golf course. This lockdown, the golf club has put up mean-spirited signs warning that this is private land, and instructing the public to keep to the one official right of way that crosses the second fairway. *Risk to staff from COVID-19.* Bullshit. This would all have been common land before the Enclosure Act. She'd have been pasturing her cows up here pre-1604, so the golf club can do one.

Her toe twinges, so she pauses. Sixty this June. Bloody Nora. Mum was only sixty-four when she died! What if Jane only has four more years left? Admittedly, Jane isn't a chain smoker who does zero exercise. Pretty dismal gene pool, though, in terms of longevity. Her dad had died aged sixty-two. But again, Jane hasn't spent her working life breathing asbestos fibres.

It comes to her that she doesn't much care. About anything. Dying. Living. Looks as though the old full-spectrum daylight bulbs in her study aren't doing the trick. Even today, with the sun shining and the chiffchaffs singing, she's looking out through rainy windows. It's raining in her head the whole time. She's so waterlogged with sorrow, there's nowhere left for it to go.

19

That sinkhole of dread and guilt opens in her mind. She skirts round it. *It wasn't your fault. You did nothing wrong.* Turnitin lit up like a Christmas tree. Sixty per cent similarity. Stuff lifted from Wiki, rehashed from earlier assignments. You had no choice.

'Oh Jesus!'

Jane glances round. Nobody within earshot.

Well, that set the tone for 2021. Coming back to your work inbox to find that waiting. Poor kid. There had been other suicides in the faculty over the years, but never one this close to home. At least Jane's still basically functioning. She can get up, do stuff, plod on. Unlike her colleague, signed off with stress. Coran had been one of Elspeth's personal tutees.

Jane checks her watch and heads for home. Matt's cooking lunch. Then they'll go for a drive, come back, try to find a feel-good film. Drink too much wine (in Jane's case). Go to bed. Crash out. Lurch awake forty-five minutes later. Go twelve rounds with insomnia. Fall asleep at 5 a.m. Rinse, repeat. Such a sweet funny kid. Quiet but bright. Bowler hat, dungarees, eye make-up. All the gender queer folderol that wasn't on offer when Jane was an undergrad. Jesus, Coran, why didn't you just ask for another extension? Or throw yourself on the mercy of the plagiarism panel – we aren't monsters! It's a global pandemic, for God's sake. So you made a mistake, kid. So it was poor judgement. It wasn't the end of the world.

Maybe if I'd dropped you an email, or . . .

Shit shit *shit*. Jane dashes away the tears. Leave it alone. Let be.

She limps through suburban streets, past skips full of ripped out bathrooms and kitchens, and portaloos standing on drives. If you can't go on holiday, may as well build that extension.

Sixty years. Was that diamond? Never coveted them – perfectly happy with trashy diamante. She hopes to God Matt won't take it into his head to buy her an eternity ring. No, too expensive, probably. Except this is the man who once splashed out on a thousand red roses, so who knows?

She turns on to their road. Can I sleep through the rest of this pandemic, please? Sleep through history in the making. The Chauvin trial. Northern Ireland burning. Is there no end to this waterlogged blood-soaked Empire legacy landscape we are all wading through?

Telling ourselves, over and over, we did nothing wrong, we had no choice.

Music drifts from an open window in their house. Matt's playing Nina Simone again. 'He's got the whole world in his hands.' Ha. She smiles to remember Danny aged four, adamant it was 'He's got the little bits of baby in his hands'. She smears away the tears again. Danny. God, I miss you. I'll swap the eternity ring for a trip to New Zealand. She passes the wagging pampas grass and limps down the drive. Maybe Danny's version is reassuring, come to think of it, rather than grisly. All humanity's little broken bits gathered up and held.

I wish I could gather it all up for you, dear reader. But as godlike narrators go, I'm pretty rubbish. My hands are nowhere near big enough to hold it all. The sun goes down on Lindfordshire this Easter Monday. Leah grudgingly admits that there's a difference between one teaspoon and one tablespoon of salt. Becky and Martin exchange glances. It must be serious if Leah would rather admit she made a mistake than allow Kai to take the blame for the non-potable sports drink. On the other side of Lindford, Chloe hides in her flat until the yelling stops. Behold, how good and pleasant it is when two men assemble a flat-pack table together.

It is the blue hour. The garden at Gray's reclamation yard is still. Everything white seems to give off a pale glow – the painted doors and fence, the circle of fifty painted pebbles where Paver kneels in front of the April garden. It's crammed with daisies dug up from grass verges around Turlham. The heads are closed now. There are twenty-eight plants. So no matter how many flowers open on any given day – maybe thirty-seven, forty-three – Paver can choose to say it's OK, nothing bad will happen, because underneath it all, out of sight, there's an even number of plants.

Paver's lips move.

'Don't you love how they grow low and stay under the mower blades and even if they get mown they grow back? *Bellis perennis*. Bairnwort. Bairn as in child. They follow the sun. It means day's eye.

'So I'm thinking, before long, maybe these tiny gravestones will look like they've always been here? Lichen will grow on them, moss. In my head, this one here's yours, this one with the blackbird skull.

Yeah, I know, I get how the daisies look kind of freaky and giant beside it, and maybe that would make you feel small. But it's OK to be small, Corie. It's the flower of childhood. It means innocence. It means you can sleep safe now.'

In the Old Barn, a light comes on. Paver turns. It looks like a bright picture hung in a dark gallery. Three panes at the top, three at the bottom. Six. It's OK. Everything's safe. Paver can see Ellis standing there, and behind him on the kitchen wall, the old sampler. *Thou God seest me*. To feel *seen*? By actual God? Paver kind of loves that idea.

MAY

Lily of the Valley and Emerald

What a miserable month for Maying in Lindfordshire. Late frosts nip at new growth. The sun comes out then goes in abruptly, as though someone keeps turning May off and on again to see if that sorts the weather out. Roadmap Step 2, 12 April, saw blanket-wrapped groups huddled under umbrellas in pub gardens. Gardens, indeed. Repurposed car parks in many cases, with wooden tables on crazy slopes, drinks at crazy angles, and some School-of-Charlie-Chaplin manoeuvres in the tiny coned-off space remaining for cars. If you were lucky, you'd find gazebos and patio heaters, but mainly you had to tough it out if you wanted a drink with friends. The rule of six came back into play, and two households could meet outdoors, including in private gardens.

The rain falls. Far away, the pale horse rides through India. Far away unless half the family lives in Delhi, that is. Then those crowded hospital corridors erupt into our Lindfordshire kitchens and living rooms. The distraught search for oxygen is our search, the scramble for funeral slots, a healthcare system overwhelmed – these things are not remote news items. It's unfolding inches from our faces, on the phone in our shaking hands, as we check moment by moment on relatives, praying, waiting, waiting to see who's next.

Day and night planes land at Gatwick, Heathrow, Manchester. We wake at 3 a.m. and hear the rumble overhead, or stand by the window and see the tiny lights travelling across the sky. All those people.

Where have they come from? The wind stirs in the trees. There's a siren in the distance. At the edge of everything, just out of earshot, the drumming of hoofbeats. Surely the horseman is done with us and ridden out of the UK now. The race between vaccine and variant is neck and neck, but we must be out of the woods now. All over Lindfordshire the optimists are perking up. Roll on 17 May when we can drink indoors. And thank God the end is finally in sight. It's not long till Freedom Day on 21 June, when we will shrug off all these COVID shackles for ever!

Lindfordshire seethes with cow parsley and hawthorn blossom. The signature scent of the exam season (remember exams?) hangs in the air. Days start gloriously bright, then cloud over. High on candled horse chestnuts, song thrushes repeat, repeat, their jewel-bright fragments. *Quick fall, quick fall? True, true, true, true! It'll do. It'll do.* Warm days finally come, when rain threatens but never falls. Children go to school, or get sent home because someone in their bubble has tested positive. Parents work from home, or scramble childcare. They are dogged by guilt whichever option they choose.

The engine of spring throbs away regardless. In woodlands, a bluebell mist has risen and lingers ankle deep in the dappled light. Wildflower mix flourishes along municipal verges (heavy on the oxeye daisy), and pathways meander through suburban lawns this #NoMowMay. Tall grasses wave in gardens, and blown in from who knows where, lady's smock appears, and herb robert, and early purple orchids.

This is the weather the cuckoo likes. Well, apart from the ferocious twenty-minute hailstorms, when all the new growth of Lindfordshire is fretworked from the peppering. You would not believe the racket if you live in a corrugated iron house.

During one such storm, Paver and Ellis watched through the open kitchen door.

'Have you ever seen hailstones the size of golf balls, Ellis? Does that actually happen or is that just a saying? I'd say it's the size of Arborio rice or maybe polystyrene beads, like that time me and Josh unzipped the beanbag in our bedroom to make Narnia. Mum was not happy. It stuck to literally everything.'

'Yes. I remember advising on the cleaning-up process.'

'I hope this won't trash the May garden. Lily of the valley's so delicate. The flowers could be wafer-thin porcelain bells for fairy funerals, if you will. But maybe they're tougher than they look because the stalks and leaves are flexible. You know that fable in the Bible, or maybe Aesop? We used to get it in school assembly. The reed and the oak tree, and the reed doesn't resist the wind, it bends with it, but the oak tries to be strong and it gets blown over? So go with the flow, I guess that was the message, don't be proud and think you're stronger than you are.'

The hail roared on and on.

'Wow, this is like a white noise app turned up too loud,' said Paver. 'It looks like it's jumping. If you didn't know, you'd think there were invisible peashooters in the grass firing the hail upwards. Did you know it's poisonous? Lily of the valley, I mean. So the Anglo-Saxons used it to make hand salve, that's why it's called glovewort. But wouldn't you be worried you'd end up poisoning yourself? Do you know how many times a day you accidentally touch your mouth? Nor do I, but I'm guessing a lot. You know when you've sanitized your hands and then you're eating kettle chips? And, bleurgh, I forgot – sanitizer! Imagine if sanitizer was poisonous – that would be the situation with glovewort lotion, as in lily of the valley, also known as Mary's tears, Jacob's ladder and ladder to heaven.'

The stones gathered like white frogspawn in the puddles. Avalanches rumbled with a whoosh from the barn roof. Then the thunder started.

'Ellis, oh my God – are we, like . . . standing in a giant lightning magnet? I mean, is it safe?' Paver's eyes darted around, starting to count things.

'We're safe. Metal doesn't *attract* lightning. It's much more likely to hit one of the tall trees.' Ellis placed his hand on his chest. 'Paver?'

Paver stopped the knuckle-cracking routine and copied Ellis. 'And . . . breathe. Thanks. But what if it *does* hit us, Ellis?'

'The charge would travel straight down the walls harmlessly into the earth. We're grounded.'

'Grounded.' Another flash. A rip of thunder overhead. 'Oh God, that's so close, Ellis!'

'It'll blow over.'

They both stood, hand on heart, looking out. Paver was trembling.

Ellis began talking over the shingle-shore roar of hail. Positive and negative charges. Cloud-to-cloud bolts. Rapidly expanding air that creates thunder. How his aunty Hilda always left the back door open in a storm, so the thunderbolt could get out if it came down the chimney. The infinitesimally small chance of being struck if you're caught out in the open, alongside a cheery nine out of ten survival rate if you are.

'We're much safer inside than out, Paver. Much. In fact, metal roofs are better than other kinds. They never catch fire. It's safe in here.' Another flash. They waited. Then the rumble. 'There you are. Further away now. Tell me about emeralds.'

'So emeralds are the May birthstone. Did you know emeralds are twenty times rarer than diamonds? They all have inclusions, aka flaws, only it turns out that's actually desirable for emeralds, it's called "*le jardin*" – is that how you say it? Cool, I wasn't sure because I did Spanish not French GCSE. It means garden. I love that, the idea that any given emerald has a miniature garden inside it, and the flaws are what make the garden – maybe trees and vines and pathways – so the flaws aren't a problem, they're what makes it so precious, and you'll like this – it actually *increases* the value because no two stones are the same.'

'You're right. I do like it.'

'You're the best, Ellis. You never make me feel stupid. I could always download to Coran as well. It was, like, finally I've found someone who gets it. I still keep going in my head, oh I must tell Corie, he'll love that. Then I remember. How can he be just . . . gone? Do you ever get over it, Ellis?'

'Well, I think you gradually get used to it. And it stops hurting all the time.'

'I don't want to get used to it.'

'No.'

'So that's the takeaway thought I put in the May book. Like in April, it was: Diamonds polish diamonds, sometimes it hurts, but in the end we help each other shine? So for May, it's: Don't ever give up. Your very flaws are precious.'

'That's beautiful.'

'I wish he could've believed that.'

This, then, is May in Lindfordshire in 2021. Drifts of hail lingered in the shadows the next day like heaps of dirty salt, but the storms have passed for now. I've been circling, looking for somewhere to land. Perhaps in your mind's eye the heron is a solitary bird. For most of the year, this is true. However, even introverts must mingle if they wish to pass their genes on. Listen. Can you hear those hoarse *cronk-cronk* sounds? Come with me, over this full-throttle emerald spring, over towns and villages, busy dual carriageways and trading estates, past the vast hangars of Mammon, schools and hospitals, cherry-lined surburbia, landfill sites with circling gulls, fields full of lambs and calves, turbines turning, cooling towers rearing. And, meandering and feathering out across it all, the Linden and its tributaries.

You see that broad river bend below us now? The racket intensifies, and we start to pick out a rapid *chack-chack-chack* as well. We are approaching Lindfordshire's largest heronry. There it is, in that stand of mature trees on the far bank of the river, at the edge of Shotton Hall Farm. It's made up of around thirty shaggy nests in the treetops, still visible among the young oak and ash leaves. Adult birds descend, legs dangling, with fish to regurgitate (see how we return to our theme, like dogs to their vomit!) for their chicks. If ever you doubted that birds are descended from dinosaurs, a quick peep in the nest would convince you.

There are other songs in this teeming soundscape: bees everywhere, chiffchaffs and willow warblers, blackbirds and black caps. High above us, the first swifts circle, crying *few, few*. Oh, there's a cuckoo! The little wooden door of the heart flies open and nostalgia pops out like a sob. England! England!

Let's not get carried away. This is Shotton Hall Farm, remember. The alpacas are singing in less tuneful accord this May midday. Freddie's Christmas presents (two male cria) are play-fighting again in their enclosure down beside the river. The noise is frankly excruciating. Freddie, being Freddie, has taught himself to replicate their gargling screams. He will give you a pitch-perfect demonstration if you ask him (and occasionally if you don't).

It's Tuesday 18 May, another of those days of sunshine and threatened rain. This is the day after Step 3 in the government's roadmap. The 'cautious but irreversible' easing of lockdown went ahead despite the Delta variant laying waste to India and stowing away to the UK on multiple flights. We wait to see what Humpty-Dumpty flexibility the government will retrospectively apply to the word 'irreversible', but for now we doff our blankets and enjoy meals inside pubs and restaurants. Cinemas, galleries and children's indoor play areas are open. Sports events with up to half-capacity crowds can go ahead. The rule of six/two households now extends to indoors and includes overnight stays.

Above all, our eighteen-month respite from social awkwardness is at an end: we may hug one another again. This Yes is caveated with the usual No. We *may* hug, but we are advised *not* to. Or if we do, we are to avert our faces, avoid breathing on one another and keep it brief. It begins to sound more like gut-barging than hugging. But we will navigate the morass of conflicting advice as best we can, armed with the legendary 'Common Sense of the British Public' that has served the nation so well in these difficult times.

From hugs in general to hugs specific. One is about to take place at Shotton Hall Farm. Two friends are meeting for the first time since February 2020. Both are double-vaccinated and happy that the risk is low. It was all negotiated in detail, in advance. Included within the hug package is the possibility of an air kiss, or an Italianate cheek buss (to clarify, in the conventional sense of that word, without recourse to Urban Dictionary or young person patois). There will be no snogging, and clothing will stay in place at all times. I trust that is clear.

By now, readers of my earlier works will have a fair idea of who articulated these ground rules. His silver car pulled up punctually ten minutes ago in the lane beside the alpaca enclosure. He wanders up and down, checking his phone and his (tastefully understated) Frederique Constant watch, and rubbing his thumb over the birthstone signet ring he's not quite used to yet. Now and then, he glances loftily at the alpacas, rather in the manner of a *comte* surveying the appalling prospect of his peasants through a lorgnette. The other hugger is late.

Ah, here he comes at last, thrashing the ancient Volvo over the cattle grids, leaping out to open and shut the gates. He parks behind the first car and runs, arms wide.

'Yo, Andrew! Sorry-sorry-sorry! Swang by for petrol and there was a massive queue? Hey, c'mere! Aw, so good to see you! Missed you so *much*!'

'Mr Hardman-May. A joy, as ever.'

There it is. The hug. Chest to chest. Eyes closed. Time stands still. Or time zips past. There's no saying. But somehow the past eighteen months concertina down into a crazy-normal nothing. Squeeze, pat-pat and release. They look into each other's eyes and laugh.

'Omigod, soooo good to see you! This is so . . . I dunno, weird but not weird?' Freddie shrugs. 'How the hell *are* you?'

'I'm well.' He considers. 'Surprisingly.' The pale serial-killer eyes scan Freddie, taking in the beard, the hair, the painty work clothes. 'Well, well. Look at you.'

'Yeah? Look at *you*. I mean, dude, look at *us*? How hot are we?' Freddie shakes his head. 'Can't believe we never got it on. Man! Just imagine—'

'Let me stop you there, Frederick. As the poet says, heard melodies are sweet, but those unheard are sweeter.'

'Totally fair. Moving on, how's the half-naked guy? Am I allowed to ask?'

'No. How's *la famiglia*? The mother- and fathers-to-be? Congratulations again.'

'Aw thanks. So yeah, I mean obviously we're all super-super-excited for the whole deal? Like, I've wanted this my entire whole life? Long as I can remember, I've wanted to be a dad?'

'I'm happy for you. When's it due?'

'September fourth?'

A semi-quaver rest. 'What, *this* September?'

'Fucking yes, *this* September, Andrew! Whaddya think she is, a blue whale— Gah!' He sighs. 'OK. Got me. Funny guy. So I guess, yeah, awesome, but . . . kind of scary? Make sense? I mean, part of me's all, omigod, what if I turn into my dad?'

'You won't.'

31

'God, I seriously hope not?' Freddie shakes his head. 'So yeah no, all good?' He suddenly registers the silver car. 'Wait. Is this yours? Dude, what happened to your Aston Martin?'

'Sold.'

'No!'

'I confess, it cost me a pang, but the time comes in a man's life when climate guilt overtakes vanity.'

'Yeah, right, vanity. Except I can't help noticing this here's not exactly a second-hand Leaf.' Freddie runs his hand along the paint-work, and ducks to look inside. 'Whoa, look at the screen! So, nought to sixty in what, three, four seconds? Can I self-drive it?'

'No.'

'G'wan, why not? Listen though, you *so* should've got the Model X. Why didn't you get the Model X?'

'Well, let's see, Freddie. Possibly a desire not to look like a tragic old queen?'

'Dude, it's got falcon-wing doors!'

'Exactly.' He checks his watch. 'I didn't come here to talk cars. Introduce me to my namesake, please. Frankly, I can't tell one llama from another.'

'Alpacas. Llamas are— Tsch!' Freddie throws up his hands. 'Fucksake. Would you stop that? You're as bad as Brose for ripping the piss out of me.'

Andrew smiles. 'Your *ingénuité* is an endless provocation, I fear.'

'Whatever. So Andy and Theo aren't here? Can't put them in with the sheep. They'd be all, Well hellooo, little short-neck ladies! Have some hot alpaca loving!'

'Dear God. Then what are those ones doing in there?'

'Those? They're lady alpacas. Plus a couple of wethers?' Freddie mimes a snipping action.

'Ah. Castrati. Poor fellows.'

'I know, right? So Andy and Theo are way down there, where they can't see all the booty. Oh yeah, so he's called Theo, coz that's the name of Brose's ex-life coach from City days? Like, both our ex-mentors? Case you were wondering. Theo's totally the alpha, ha ha.'

'Yes, very droll, Frederick.'

'Sorry, what now? That a problem?' Freddie takes in his expression. 'Hey, whoa! Brose's idea, not mine.'

There's an assessing pause. Andrew narrows his eyes. 'The endlessly lovely Brose. I see. Well, let's get this over with so we can have lunch.'

They set off along the lane towards the river in the sunshine, ambling side by side, ex-mentor and ex-mentee, the light of that historic torch flickering all over Freddie. Must've wasted, like, fifteen years crushing on this dickhead? Sometimes their knuckles accidentally graze, but Freddie's got it reined in – no love-spamming. Oh, but still? So. Much. LOVE.

So he talks. The scary state of the English choral tradition, how he's longing for 21 June and choirs, his voice, how things are going with La Madeleine his teacher, what he learnt on the coalface of fucking *Winterreise*, how Brose is such a brilliant accompanist, intuitive, how he makes Freddie sound better than he is, plus he actually *prefers* not to be centre stage (I know, weird, huh?). Freddie keeps trying to make it a two-way street, but he's deflected every time, and here he's talking about himself again? His crazy job portfolio (painting and decorating for Neil, volunteering, singing in care homes, his YouTube channel and TikTok, the girls' choir, lay clerking); what the future might hold for his career when things open up fully; what life will look like then, when Baby arrives; how he's hoping, hoping, hoping by then the rules will have changed, and he and Brose can both be there for the birth?

It will take them a while to reach the river, so I suggest we visit some of our other friends.

At this moment, our lovely Father Wendy is sitting in her facemask in church, waiting. This is not your 'R. S. Thomas' waiting, where the meaning is. She's waiting to be called through for her second jab. This is St John's Renfold, where Father Dominic was once vicar. The GP surgeries of Renfold, Cardingforth and Carding-le-Willow hold their vaccination clinics here. Sunlight casts patches of turquoise light on the shiny wooden floor, and on the people sitting in their socially distanced chairs. (St John's is a 1950s build, so there was no bloody Battle of the Pews waged between the vicar and people who never came to church.)

The main doors are open to keep the air circulating. It's chilly, but Wendy is warm in her puffy pink gilet. People arrive in a steady stream. They assure the masked volunteer they have no COVID symptoms; that they have not been in contact with anyone who has COVID. They receive like supplicants a squirt of alcohol gel, before going inside to give their details to another volunteer sitting at the table with a laptop. Then they are directed to a third volunteer, who gives them a number and invites them to wait.

Wendy studies her raffle ticket: 42. The meaning of life, the universe and everything. Number 41 is called. A man in his 40s goes through to the church hall, where ten separate socially distanced tables are set up. He's probably getting his first dose. There's a much wider age range this time round. Good. More and more people are getting some protection. The volunteer sanitizes the empty plastic chair with an anti-bac wipe.

Is it selfish to pray she won't be knocked sideways for three days this time? Wendy gets out her little blue and white NHS vaccination record card. *Make sure you keep this record card in your purse or wallet.* Rather than in your back pocket, where it will end up getting laundered. Oops! But she ought to have checked his trousers before sticking them in the machine, so she can relieve poor Doug of at least half the blame. She studies the details that were filled in carefully in black ballpoint last time. Name: Wendy Styles. 1. Name of vaccine: AstraZeneca. Batch no: 413Z007. Date vaccine given: 18.3.21.

In a few moments, details of her second dose will be added and she'll be done. What a long haul it's been from those first distant rumours of a new virus in Wuhan, she thinks. Back when we thought it was impossible this could ever happen to *us*. Are we nearing the end now? A tide of wobbly gratitude surges up. She gazes towards the sanctuary and the wooden cross on the wall. Thank you. Thank science. Thank the NHS networks that have made this possible. And the government? Yes, in all fairness, she's thankful to them for getting this part right. She will make another donation to Christian Aid when she gets home. Paying it forward. It won't really deal with her survivor's guilt (so many funerals! and look at India!), but Wendy knows it's not all about her feeling good about herself. There's no point in chasing the rainbow of a clear conscience, she's decided. Conscience isn't a load of laundry. It's more like a child terrified of the dark. But she's learnt that even if it's still night, the child can be consoled by a loving embrace.

'Number forty-two.'

Wendy gets to her feet and smiles behind her mask, then nods and over-crinkles her eyes, because she thinks the volunteer might not be able to see she's thankful. She's wrong about that. Nothing could mask the beauty of ordinary gratitude.

All over Lindfordshire people are getting vaccinated, or waiting to get vaccinated. A small proportion are vowing never to get vaccinated, because you don't know what's *in* the vaccine, do you? It gives you blood clots, and anyway you don't want Bill Gates or the Chinese implanting their nano-tech to keep track of you, control you and manipulate your data. We won't bother pointing out that your mobile phone is doing that already, without a cunning plan of mass vaccination. Reason will gain no traction here. This is just our old friend Gnosticism in modern guise, touting the centuries-old promise of bestowing special status on its initiates. After all, the most likely explanation for things is very dull. Much more glamorous to live in a world where if it looks like a duck, swims like a duck, quacks like a duck, then it probably is a clever hologram of a duck made by a cabal of satanic cannibalistic paedophiles.

Meanwhile, ducks swim on the River Linden this May lunchtime. On ponds and lakes and reservoirs they enact their rough wooing in various indiscriminate configurations of duck and drake. So unlike emperor penguins, alas.

Oh, it's all happening somewhere in Lindfordshire this spring. A hearse drives slowly towards the crematorium. Eggs hatch in nests. A partner waits in a hospital car park until labour is sufficiently advanced for him to be allowed into the labour ward. People visit the foodbank. The post arrives. A skip is delivered on to a driveway. Someone foolishly clicks on the link in a scam text. A mother cries as she takes her son's toy guitar to Cash Converters while he's at school, because the electric has run out and there's no money. Someone is remanded in custody, someone is released. A man gets an old push mower out of the garage and starts to mow the camomile lawn. *Whir, whir*, like the sleepy wheeze of a greenfinch call. An old woman has her lunch on the terrace. Two pupils slip out of school illegally and meet in Lindford Arboretum to continue their tentative romance. The girl throws the remains of her Greek-style vegan wrap into the lake, and tells the boy, 'Birds need a varied diet to stay healthy.' He nods and offers her his homemade sports drink.

Two other people are meeting up, though not for romantic purposes. It's Jane and Dominic. They were on the phone this morning. It emerged that Jane was keen to escape from her marking, and Dominic was keen to escape the vicarage (he has the decorators in). Dominic suggested somewhere equidistant from Lindford and Martonbury. He could not *believe* she had never been to Gray's before. Pish and tosh! She would LOVE it. Of *course* she was interested in a barn full of old rubbish. She was to stop being so grumpy and get in her car immediately.

'And by the way, they serve Wood's of Lindford pork pies.'

'Now you're talking,' said Jane.

We will join them after they've finished a happy forty minutes of browsing and are seated at a wooden table under the copper beech. They have their pork pies and Fentimans ginger beer, bought from the converted horsebox, and there's the happy prospect of Bakewell tart and tea to follow.

In case you are wondering how Dominic has escaped on a jolly without his mum, or what the decorators are up to in Lindford Vicarage, let me tell you at once that the two things are connected. Mrs Todd moved into a care home at the end of February. It took Dominic a long time to get accustomed to this change, and to stop feeling like a heel and a cad, but he has now reached the point where he feels comfortable transforming her empty room into a gentleman's snug. Nay, a smoking room! Not that he will actually smoke in it, but he will sit in a velvet armchair in a velvet jacket, with a glass of vintage port at his elbow, and feel like a very raffish devil.

After some eye-rolling derision over his paint choice (Farrow & Ball Paean Black, a *red-based* black), Jane entered fully into the spirit of the snuggery and has been egging him on. The table is piled with purchases from Ellis's barn. Dominic could have stowed it all in the boot of his car, but they both wanted to gloat over the swag. There are some jewel-coloured velvet cushions, an old box file disguised as a leather-and-marbled-paper folio volume, with 'Admiralty Charts' embossed on the spine. On top of these sits a vintage leather collar box. Jane insisted on buying this for him, because it will be perfect for storing his clerical collars. On top of that is an empty wooden cigar box from Havana. At the pinnacle of this bric-a-brac tower of joy a Murano green-glass cigarette lighter sits gloating, like a fat emerald from Brobdingnag.

Jane's haul is meagre by comparison: two wooden dolls. Dominic insisted on buying them for *her* when she gasped, 'Oh my God – I remember those!' They have hand-painted faces and stand about seven inches tall on their big red wooden feet. The girl doll has a yellow dress and hat, and long yellow plaits. The boy is in stripy knee-britches and a blue waistcoat. He has clumps of glue in his hair, as though he once had a hat too. There's a handwritten brown luggage label attached to his leg: '1960s Polish. Mass-produced figures, probably individually dressed as part of cottage industry.' Most of the items in the barn have similar interpretation labels attached. Jane approves. It turns the barn into a hybrid jumble sale/museum of social history. See? Father Dominic *told* her she'd love it here!

'I used to buy these,' she says through a mouthful of pork pie, 'if an uncle gave me a ten-bob note or something. They were always disappointing. The arms broke off and you couldn't undress them, because the clothes were glued on. And their hair was scary.'

'What do you mean, scary?'

'Well, it could be celluloid, couldn't it? Highly flammable. Mum warned me about celluloid toys.' Jane laughs. 'For years I thought that meant they'd spontaneously combust. Sitting innocently by your bed, then one day, whoomf!'

'Dear Lord! That sounds like a horror movie,' says Dominic. 'No wonder you're so traumatized and peculiar.'

'Says the man who was terrified of hair bats.'

Dominic gives a little scream. 'But they nest in your hair if you leave the window open at night!' Then he leans close and whispers, 'And then the doctors have to shave all your hair off, *to find out what's doing it.*'

'Your mum never said that!' scoffs Jane.

'No, it was Mrs Bytheway, relating what happened to her niece. I was in my pushchair listening. Mum said, "Ooh dear, how worrying for you!" and off we went to the shops. *Obviously* she knew it was a load of tarradiddle, but she never thought to explain that afterwards to three-year-old me!'

'Poor lamb. How is Mum?'

'Really well. Chirpy,' says Dominic. 'She's got past the stage of being terrified of losing her marbles.'

'Does she recognize you?'

He shakes his head. 'Sometimes she thinks I'm my dad and asks where I am and starts fretting. I tell her, "Dommie's fine, don't worry." But mostly she's genuinely delighted that the nice vicar has come to visit.' His eyes brim. 'Every single time, I'm a lovely surprise.'

'You *are* a lovely surprise, sweetums. Always.' Jane squeezes his arm. 'And she's lovely too. A different woman would complain every single time that nobody ever visits her. Does she still think she's away on holiday?'

Dominic blows his nose. 'She's decided she's at some sort of college or summer school. They do craft activities and whatnot, and there's a book club.'

'And Freddie goes in and sings his cheesy Last Night of the Proms numbers.'

'He does. I sing with her too. Sea shanties. Gilbert and Sullivan. Old music hall numbers. Funny how songs unlock the memory.' He laughs. '"Shame and scandal in the family".'

Jane pauses, last bite of pork pie in mid-air. 'Hah! Not thought about that for years. I only ever knew that one line. My mum refused to tell me the rest because it was "nasty".'

'Well, it is mildly risqué, I suppose,' says Dominic.

'I'm going to Google it.' She wipes her fingers and picks up her phone.

But then someone appears with the tea and Bakewell tart.

'Ooh, here's our cake! Goody-good!' Dominic glances at Jane. She's bent over her phone, face hidden.

Something's happened.

'Thank you so much.' Dominic unloads the cardboard plates and cups from the tray. He waits till the figure has disappeared. 'Janey? Everything OK, darling?'

'We should go.' She stands.

'Oh! Well, yes, of course. Let me just—'

'No, it's OK.' She sits again. 'I'm being daft.' She bows her head and shuts her eyes. 'Shit.'

Dominic puts a hand over hers and waits.

She sits up and draws a breath. 'Sorry. That was a friend of Coran's. I recognize them from the funeral. And possibly from around campus.'

'Oh, darling.'

They sit for a while without speaking. There's a blackbird singing. A train goes drumming by in the distance.

'I'm thinking of retiring,' says Jane. 'I was going to hang on till sixty-five, but . . .'

Dominic nods.

'I've spent my whole life fighting, Dommie. For something. Against something. And now this fatuous "war against woke". God, it's like trying to engage with a jellyfish the size of Wales, flailing its toxic tentacles at anything that threatens its ego. If being a responsible historian gets you death threats for "doing Britain down" . . .' Jane throws up her hands. 'I'm too old.'

The blackbird carols on.

'I still feel responsible,' she says.

Dominic nods again.

'I know I'm not. But I feel bad. I feel old. Outmoded and irrelevant. Like a TERFy old brontosaurus feminist who still thinks there's something basic and primary about biological sex, and something to be said for viewing biological women as a political entity done down by the patriarchy. I listen to my genderqueer students and sometimes I feel like I just don't *get* it any more. You realize you don't even count as queer? You're a cis gender assimilationist suburbanite.'

'I am *affronted*!'

'Exactly. I don't want to choose tribes. I just want to lie low. I haven't the energy for the mental graft,' says Jane. 'That's why I feel bad.'

'Well, we're all a work in progress. I expect you're kind to your students,' says Dominic. 'You don't go around mispronouning and dead-naming them.'

'Of course not.'

'There you are. So long as we always err on the side of inclusion, not exclusion.' He pats her hand. 'Here – have your tart, you old tart. Then we'll load the car and have a quick wander round the grounds.'

Paver sees them later, stooping over the May garden to smell the lily of the valley. A tall woman and a priest. Just strangers.

Ellis sees them too. One of those heart-lurch moments earlier, when they approached him at the till with their purchases. Of course, Jane wouldn't know him from Adam now, let alone from Oxford days. But he doesn't fully unclench until he sees them hug goodbye and drive off in their separate cars.

The rain is still holding off. All across Lindfordshire, parcels are delivered and photographed on doorsteps. Hens scratch in the coop. People try to be kind. The Bishop of Lindchester asks his PA to book him into a London hotel for General Synod in July. Somewhere, a dropped mask blows into a gutter. A drill whines in a dental surgery. The girl choristers of Lindchester Cathedral are isolating again, because someone tested positive.

All this is happening while Freddie and Andrew are walking towards the river. There's the cuckoo again, but his call is drowned by the herons' racket.

Look – they've arrived at the alpaca enclosure. They lean on the fence. Freddie calls the alpacas, but they won't come. Later, he and Andrew will go to Gray's for lunch too, missing Jane and Dominic by ten minutes. This is where Freddie will finally notice the emerald signet ring and leap to a wild conclusion, which Andrew will deny. All that is still in the future. For now, we remain grounded in this particular moment, on this particular May day, when rain threatens but has not yet fallen.

'So basically, since *Winterreise*gate, I've realized how much I always just busk my way through stuff, sightreading? Like, it's still out *there* in the score, not in *here*. So now I'm revisiting all the stuff I think I know, the repertoire I've sung to death, and trying to relearn it, like, from new?'

'Good. Sing me something.'

'Yeah, so good example – Tom Bowling? I read up, and it turns out it's really problematical? Dibdin wrote it for his older brother who, wait for it, was a captain on an East India trader? Those guys, whoa! I mean, colonialist or what? But the thing is, it *still* gets me every time? Not sure what I'm saying here? Maybe, what stuff are *we* doing that's really morally dubious, only we can't see it? We are still all, Oh, he was such a good guy, his heart was kind and soft, when actually he did these terrible things, or he was part of this oppressive system?' Freddie shakes his head. 'Sometimes I don't get how God ever could love humanity? Anyway, here goes.'

So he sings. And as he sings, the alpacas prick up their ears. For a moment, it seems as though they will come running. But no. The herons still shriek and clack across the river. Rain still threatens. But while Freddie sings, it's possible to believe that our inclusions will be what matter in the end.

JUNE

Rose and Pearl

Man plans, COVID laughs. Sometimes I can hear him, hunched over on his pale horse, snickering. Other times there's silence. Like the day when there are no recorded COVID deaths in the UK for the first time since the pandemic reached our shores. Nurses on the ICU COVID ward in Lindford General Hospital post pictures on social media: 'We're empty!!!' More than 39.4 million people in the UK have received their first dose of the vaccine now. That's 74.9 per cent of adults. We tell ourselves it's all going to be fine.

Then comes the jingle of a harness and another snicker. Infection rates start to climb again, and mirth gives way to coughing. Like an old man on a park bench, as Jane's mother used to say. She knew a fair bit about that, listening to her husband hawk his lungs up every morning in the bathroom. She was a forty-a-day cougher herself, who died young of chronic obstructive pulmonary disease. The sound hacks away at the edges of Jane's earliest memories. Creaky wheezing laughter. *Cough-cough-cough.*

Spitting strictly prohibited. Jane is drifting towards consciousness from a dream, or perhaps a memory, of buses. Her mum lights up on the swaying top deck. They're going home from a shopping trip to Nottingham – her ninth-birthday treat. She's spent the money she's been given on a wooden doll with long yellow plaits. If only her own hair was like that! 'I don't know why you want that cheap rubbish, Jackie. Why not buy yourself a nice book?' But Jackie unwrapped two nice books from Mum this morning. *A Dog So Small. The Oxford*

Book of Wild Flowers. Books, books, books. So she bought the doll, and a pair of white socks from Woollies, knee-high, with little blue daisies up each side like the other girls had, not ankle socks, not beige, not grey. ('Hur hur, Jackie's wearing boys' socks!') *Mind your head when leaving seat.*

'Jackie? Are you up?' It's Mum, calling from the foot of the stairs.

Jane drifts, unmoored. She's in her council house bedroom, under her yellow-rose eiderdown. Then a buzz yanks her awake. She gropes for her phone. A gif from Dominic: male strippers flexing their pecs.

Happy birthday to you, squashed tomatoes and stew! Have a lovely day, you old trout. xxxxx

Hah. My sixtieth year to heaven, she thinks. Rain patters against the window. The dream clings like Bri-Nylon sheets. Sixty! How is that possible? She tests the perimeter fences of her psyche for threats. Just the pale horse cropping grass in a field and, on the horizon, the end of the world. She lets out a long sigh. It's over, the whole *annus horribilis academicus* (or whatever the proper ending is – they stopped teaching Latin at her Comp the year she arrived). But as always the mirage of wellbeing retreats as she approaches, because she brings her woes with her. Drags them clanking along behind, like the penitent tugging a load of armour and weapons in that 80s film, with whatsisname playing the Jesuit missionary.

She's spent months trying to bootstrap herself into self-acceptance. *You're not responsible for Coran's death. You did nothing wrong, Jane.* But this only short-circuits the problem. If she's done nothing wrong, then there's no possibility of absolution. And sometimes she thinks – atheism notwithstanding – that this is what she needs: to be absolved. If she'd been able to go to his funeral in person, not just log in and watch from her desk, maybe that would have helped. But even the Duke of Edinburgh only had thirty mourners at his funeral service. Jane pictures the queen alone in her pew, and the piper slowly receding down the long tunnel into the light at the end. Seventy-three years married. That's longer than either of Jane's parents lived.

Where does the time go? A year back, we were in the thick of #BlackLivesMatter, Jane thinks. Colston tossed overboard,

Poundstretcher University frantically decolonizing, everyone having difficult conversations and mending their ways. Presumably Coran was at the protests, in Lindford if not in London. And you stayed at home through weariness, Jane. (As if you, a white middle-class academic, know anything about weariness.) Stop. You're just wallowing. Maybe the tide really did turn with George Floyd's murder. Derek Chauvin was found guilty, wasn't he? The accusing pixies in Jane's head sneer and go to ground. For now. At Matt's suggestion, she's taken a couple of days' birthday leave, so that she can legitimately ignore her inbox. He's organized God knows what frisks and festivities for her.

Aaargh! It's about to kick off. She can hear him coming up the stairs now, with the careful tread of a man bearing a loaded breakfast tray. Jane shoots up a desperate prayer to the white elephant god that she will like whatever special gift he has bought her (please, not a diamond eternity ring!). She heaves herself up, punches her pillows into shape and adopts the brace position.

We will leave Jane to her misimagined vistas of ghastliness – you'd think after nearly eight years she'd trust Matt to know her taste – and go on a tour of Lindfordshire this solstice morning, this non-Independence Day of dashed hopes (or tears of relief) when everything was supposed to be back to normal. Weddings have once again been downsized. Fresh rows break out over the proper definition of #staycation. Kat, the Bishop of Lindchester's PA, has cancelled the ordination hospitality marquee for the second year running. Today she will cancel the bishop's London hotel reservation and train tickets, for General Synod is reverting to Zoom at the eleventh hour. Singers and choral directors gnash and rage that the rule of six *still* applies to non-professional musicians. Madness! The Lindchester Community Choir must postpone rehearsals of *Elijah* until after 19 July, while drunken flag-draped England fans can gather with impunity to watch Euro 2020 matches and bawl like a cow with a foghorn that 'It's coming home'.

Could the fans possibly be right for once? Nourished by a chunk of 2–0 Schadenfreude bierwurst, our starving hopes revive. Maybe, like the prodigal in a far land, football is finally coming to itself. We glimpse it while it's still far off. Oh, how we will run out to meet you and fall on your neck and kiss you, football! How we will call for the best robe and kill the fatted calf!

Miserable weather seems fitting today, to mark the fact that COVID has comprehensively rained on the government's roadmap parade. Early June brought a few hot days of shorts under cassocks, of bare legs and strappy tops. There was sun-spanked flesh blazing on our streets, and BBQs blazing in back gardens. I conclude that a new memo must have gone out from Fashion Central, for shorts are shorter this year. Freddie Hardman-May has updated his look from skins to three-inch-split shorts. Neil Ferguson has gone for a more dignified five-inch, with liner. No, he's not *shy*. Excuse me? He actually *prefers* the compression-like feel provided by the advanced breathability of seventy-five per cent recycled polyester fabric, he'll have you know.

We are now in the last mad emerald days before the foliage of Lindfordshire settles into a measured green. There are chartreuse fields where early silage has been cut and no larks sing. If you look up into the blighted chestnut leaves, you will see tiny conkers prickling like medieval weapons. Rhododendrons continue their scorched-earth march across Lindford Common, and papery seedpods flutter from doomed elms.

But be of good cheer. The air fills as ever with the scent of roses. In all the lovesome spots across the Diocese of Lindchester, petals unfurl. Tea, climber, rambler, shrub, moss, musk. Out in the country-side, dog roses and field roses scramble pink and white, and we can believe that England is green and pleasant. Wren song fairly rattles the eardrums. Spiderlings drift upside down from gossamer kites. Who knows where they are ballooning to as they meander on air currents through electrical fields we cannot see.

Oh, we've had interminable double Maths in stifling classrooms this June, and wild swimming in Martonbury Reservoir beyond the signs warning that *Cold Water Kills*. On days like that we hear the *poc* and *thoc* of tennis balls on the rundown courts in Lindford Arboretum. We sweat into our masks in offices and classrooms, on hospital wards and buses, in foodbanks and charity shops. People queue outside Mister Bun's in Lindford for Turlham Farm ice cream, or they buy the kids an icepop each from the corner shop while they are topping up the gas, because who the hell has £2.95 to spare for a scoop of lavender ice cream in a gluten-free sugar-waffle cone? The weed-mobile drives jangling round the Abernathy estate. Every teddy bear who's been good is sure of a spliff today.

Oh June, with your strawberry moon. How I love you, how I love you, my dear old Lindford. Why does everything take on such a yearny nostalgia the minute we look back through rose-tinted spectacles, when at the time it was nothing special, just another numb day to be got through as best we could, part-muffled by carbs or booze or sport?

Day by day, volunteers stand outside the old Victoria Hall, hailing passers-by. 'Can I interest you in a free COVID test?' We shake our heads and smile Englishly, as though they're asking if we're satisfied with our internet provider. Cars drive over the faded rainbows and Thank Yous painted outside the hospital. A young man wasted on spice approaches stranger after stranger to see whether they will change his limp £50 note for five tens. Pink e-scooters buzz legally about the roads and cycle lanes of Lindford (and illegally on the pavements), as part of the government trial.

There are e-scooters in far-off London too, of course, where the wheels on the red buses go round and round and the liars on the Westminster bus go lie, lie, lie, all day long. Whatever. In a world where all pants are on fire, we've become inured to the smell of scorching. There's no point dancing up and down in frustration, Sméagol my friend (thinks Jane, never a big fan of Cummings), if the trusty sword of truth turns to cardboard in your hand. You're the one who hocked the original weapon in exchange for £350 million a week to fund the NHS.

We must shake the cosmopolitan dust from our heron wings and lollop instead through the drizzle to our old stomping ground, the historic cathedral city of Lindchester, where five minutes ago a silver Tesla pulled off the Close. Don't get too excited – it is not driven by Mr Dorian. We will glide down and get a closer look and discover which of our other friends has been splashing the cash about as they decide to go down the electric car route.

'You may now look at your card, Deanissima,' says Gene.

Marion opens the envelope. It's a kitsch sacred heart postcard. She turns it over. *I hereby grant you permission to enjoy your minibreak.* Signed *Jesus*. She laughs. 'Thank you, darling.'

'I forged his signature,' whispers Gene. 'But all in a good cause. My aim is to short-circuit your customary start-of-holiday anguish, as you labour to lay down the cathedral church of Lindchester, ever perched upon your shoulder like a pirate's parrot.'

'Well, let's hope it works. It *might* help my stress levels if I knew where we're going . . .'

'Are you scared I've chartered a private jet to whisk us away to Bora Bora?' he asks. 'Not this time. No, today *je te propose* a trip to fairyland.'

'Oh God,' mutters Marion.

'Tilly-vally! It's all COVID-secure.'

'That's not what's worrying me. Fairyland? Please tell me it's not some theme park.'

Gene begins warbling 'Trust in me' from Walt Disney's *Jungle Book*. They have just reached a stretch of dual carriageway, so he turns his hypnotic gaze on her while the car works its autopilot magic.

'No no no no!' cries Marion over the escalating beeps of the car. 'You're meant to be attentive at all times!'

Gene puts his hands back on the wheel. The bleeping stops. 'Here's a theological question for you. Did Jesus dance at the wedding at Cana?'

Marion thinks for a moment. 'Yes. Almost certainly.' She smiles. 'In fact, I can almost picture it. Like those Israeli circle dances at our youth fellowship back in the 70s.'

'A spot of boisterous grapevining with his disciples, you mean?'

'Something like that,' she says.

'Good. Second theological question: was he drunk?'

'No.'

'My, my! Not a moment's hesitation there. Why not? He was fully human.'

'He was also fully divine, Gene.'

'And the divine never gets rowdy?' Gene leaves the dual carriageway at the next exit. 'I concede that the Son of God wouldn't have passed out paralytic. Heaven forfend! He wasn't *English*, after all. No, he was mortal without getting mortal. See what I did there?'

'Yes, Gene.'

'And so I ask, was Jesus three sheets to the wind at a village wedding? Of course he was! It makes perfect sense of that exchange with his mother. And the industrial-scale over-catering of the miracle itself.'

Marion purses her lips. 'Where are you going with this, exactly?'

'I'm merely expanding your repertoire of answers to WWJD?' He takes the turning to Gayden Parva. In a mile or so, there's another junction and the lane becomes narrower. Hedges rear on either side, and grass grows down the middle, tinkling against the underside of the car.

'I hope we don't meet a tractor,' says Marion.

'Oh, the car sprouts wings if it detects a farm vehicle approaching.' He switches from *The Jungle Book* to *Chitty Chitty Bang Bang*. At the next crossroads, they follow the sign to Turlham.

'You're excited,' she says.

'Well, it *is* my first night away from the Close since all this started.'

'And you're sure it will be all right?'

'Stop fretting and study your permission slip.' He pats her knee. 'I'm double-jabbed. We're going to a small boutique hotel, where we'll be the first guests since it was refurbished. The hosts are aware of my frailties. We can take our meals in our room, so fear not.'

Gene doesn't know it, but by booking the Titania's Bower honeymoon suite at Turlham Hall, he threw a spanner in Bishop Matt's birthday extravaganza plans. Matt is no Shakespeare buff, but he did *Midsummer Night's Dream* for O-level back in the day. He knows that the whole fairyland shebang with a four-poster 'over-canopied with luscious woodbine', complete with ass's head on the wall, would tickle Janey pink. He clocked it on Trip Adviser, but when he came back to book it ten minutes later, he'd been pipped at the post.

Still, that simplified the old designated-driver dilemma. They'll stay in the Lindford Excelsior tonight. Not very glam, admittedly, but on the plus side they can walk there from the gem of a family-run Italian place his search threw up. He's done a recce. Nothing much from the outside, but inside it's proper old school. Red-checked tablecloths, candles stuck in those raffia-covered bottles. Speakers belting out 'That's *amore*'. And they've only got a vintage brass espresso machine in the corner, like a chuffing steampunk diving suit with a little brass bird perched on top. Right up Janey's street. Can't believe he never discovered it in all his archdeaconing years.

Then tomorrow morning they'll pootle out for Night Two on a narrow boat. It's moored up on a quiet stretch, just down from the pub where they had their first date. Matt's pretty pleased with the schedule, under the circs. Shame he had to stand down the B-list guests, but he'd warned them from the off that the roadmap was looking dicey. Provided none of the four guests invited for tonight's surprise party tests positive, everything should be peachy.

Everything in the birthday-related category, that is. Matt's at his study desk now [see query below], after watching Janey open her cards and presents. The necklace from the craft barn seemed to tick all the right boxes. Quite pleased with that find. He'd steered clear of diamonds (after a couple of hints) and went down the birthstone route. Strands of seed pearls, and a socking great red rose in the middle – genuine, sealed in resin, apparently. It shouted Janey the moment he clocked it.

Project Birthday might be on track, but he's up to his axles in other crap. He could do with a chuffing recorded message: *All our fans are currently busy, but your shit is important to us. Please hold until one of the diocesan fans becomes available.* There are days when he thanks the Lord he's only the deputy; that Head Boy Steve gets the brunt of it. Still, the senior staff team makes a pretty effective nettle-grasping outfit. There are other dioceses in worse bother, financially and otherwise.

That said, the mother of all nettles has been quietly flourishing for the last eight years. *Almost* off Matt's radar. But now, like football, it's coming home. Matt relives that speeding-over-a-humpback-bridge lurch back there.

'And finally, here's a lovely, lovely card from Susanna Henderson,' Jane said. 'God, now I feel bad. I never remember her birthday. Wow, Paul's retiring. How old is he? Sixty-six? Isn't that a bit young? Anyway, they're coming back this autumn. I guess they'll be living close by, in the bolt-hole. How lovely.' Then she saw his face. 'What's wrong?'

'Nothing. The inbox calleth. Enjoy your day.' He gave her a kiss and went downstairs to his study. [He is in his study a few sentences earlier]

In a moment, he'll get to the emails. Once his blood pressure's a tad closer to normal. He laces his fingers behind his neck and leans back. Safeguarding good practice has moved on in the last eight years. There's no way Matt would take it upon himself to tidy up a mess like that now. Nope. Total no-brainer – refer it straight to the Diocesan Safeguarding Adviser.

He closes his eyes. Unlike Jane, he has never been able to tell himself he did nothing wrong. He knew at the time the whole thing smacked of cover-up. Top priority – airlift Freddie out of it, make sure Paul stepped back from the York job, and keep a lid on the whole sorry affair for everyone's sake. Complete no-no by today's standards. Not his place to decide. But back then he believed it was.

Matt groans. Good intentions aren't enough. If Paul's coming back, he'll want permission to officiate in the Diocese of Lindchester, won't he? Matt's going to have to fess up to what, in the intervening years, has grown into a pretty hefty blemish on his safeguarding record. If he squeaks through without going another twelve rounds with the Clergy Disciplinary Measure, he'll count himself lucky. He shakes his head, not optimistic about how this will play, given that the CDM process has all the fine-tuning of a steamroller. Not optimistic at all.

He sits up and cracks his knuckles. No point getting his knickers in a twist now. On with the day, Tyler. Emails, school visit, then Janey's birthday bash followed by a day's annual leave. He can contact the DSA later. His heart squeezes tight. When to tell Janey what's in the offing? Not before the birthday jolly, that's for sure.

Rain trickles down his study window. Bishop Bob will have sat at this very desk, he thinks. There will have been times when he looked out of the same window, at the end of his tether too. It's starting to feel like a good shout, early retirement. Ah, well. Matt logs on. For a moment he half senses something. Bob's presence, almost. He remembers all those hands laid on him in the holy red scrum of his consecration. And all the hands laid on them, and so on, and on, back through history. Saints and sinners alike. All the motley crew of heaven, he thinks. Something shifts in his soul and he feels a bit less alone.

Rain falls over at Gray's reclamation yard. Paver sits at the kitchen table. The air is full of the smell of fresh-baked sourdough bread.

Paver can hear the tiny ticks of the crust as the loaf cools on the rack and the surface crazes. A happy sound, like something from the natural world, not the kind of noise that drives you mad. Ellis has taken the kitchen clock down.

Paver focuses. The daylight bulb in the Anglepoise lamp illuminates a circle of the Formica table, lighting the tiny book. The different watercolours are mixed in mussel shells, the spectrum, left to right. Richard of York gave battle in vain – problematic, because that's seven. Some say seven is the number of completeness and perfection. Paver's tried hanging loose to seven, but it just won't sit right. Seven's still panic-inducing and that means your hand isn't steady. Bad news for a miniaturist! So, first thought: indigo and violet *could* maybe share a shell? Which you'd have to talk yourself through, because that feels wrong, like it's disrupting the pattern. No, no. Alternative solution: leave a bigger gap between the indigo shell, and violet, then it's six (even) and one (safe). Obviously, you have to line up the ultrafine brushes in category – script liner, spotter, dagger striper – *and* in order of thickness. It all takes time, but it's worth it.

Paver works with a magnifying glass. It's a vintage nautical one Ellis found. *The pearl blesses new life beginnings.* Is that too cheesy? Paver wants the book to channel positivity, in case someone buys it for a child. All the stuff you *could* put in, but don't. Is that legitimate? To edit stuff out, to keep quiet? Paver isn't sure about pearls any more. You'd think they were all about innocence and simplicity, but when you research into it, no. Pearls can really creep you out. Like figs, when you Google how come they grow without blossom, and you find all this stuff about a tiny wasp shedding its wings to crawl inside to lay eggs, which pollinates the insides of the fig (which turns out is actually a whole bunch of tiny flowers) and the wasp dies and gets absorbed, and the eggs hatch and maybe that crunching is bits of wasp larva when you eat a fig. Oh God.

Paver has to pause and count the brushes.

But remember, fortunately there are sterile figs according to Ellis, which don't require wasps, so in all probability the crunching is just seeds, and nobody's *making* you eat figs, are they. Deep breath. It's fine. Paver counts the brushes again, then starts on the next sentence. *In ancient times, people believed pearls were teardrops from heaven, or formed in the brain of a dragon.* This is definitely the kind of cool fact Paver would have wanted to read as a child. OK, so pearls aren't as freaky as figs, but still pretty freaky.

'You know the biggest pearl ever found?' Paver looks up from the tiny magnified world to say this. The real world of the kitchen comes into focus and Coran isn't there. Lost deep in your work, in your zone, that's when you momentarily forget, and it still feels like you're both working companionably at the same table, Coran writing his journal, or maybe reading. What if in a way he *is* still here, like in a parallel universe side by side with ours?

Paver can hear Ellis outside, shifting a load of old chimney pots from the trailer to the barn. One of them is earmarked for the October garden. Hopefully they can persuade some kind of marigold to bloom late in the autumn. *One garden at a time, Paver. That's all you have to do.* It could almost be Corie saying that. June garden's done, July's nearly done. It's all going to be OK.

Ellis looks across at the June garden as he shifts the pots. It's a big section of concrete drainage pipe that came with the plot when he bought it. He levered it on to its side and planted some old-fashioned climbing roses – pink, yellow, apricot – to scramble over it. It's half hidden now. He walled the back with reclaimed wood many years ago to make a nice hidey-hole. Later, when he'd had a moment, he installed a good solid bench seat made out of an old railway sleeper. It had – to Ellis's mind – a kind of austere urban chic. But Paver wanted to paint the inside pale blue and add some faded linen cushions. Which means it's a bit shabby chic for Ellis's taste now. There are strands of copper-wire fairy lights wound through the roses. But, as a concept, it works. Paver's happy and the customers love it. One of his regulars identified the shade as Pantone 'Cerulean' (or possibly 'Teapot'). Which reminds him. Ellis sets the last chimney down, gets out his phone and takes a picture. He texts it to Neil, who's been after a couple for his potagerie:

Any good?

He heads back to the kitchen in the old barn. His heart sinks a bit, because Paver's not been in a good place for a couple of days. The

Dream. Checking the skip for bodies again at 3 a.m. Ellis opens the back door gently, so as not to startle Paver and ruin the work in progress. But Paver's taking a break.

'Pearls are creepy, Ellis. I'm fast coming to that conclusion. I wish I'd gone with moonstone or alexandrite, also June birthstones. Did you know some alexandrites are known as "emerald by day, ruby by night"? It depends on the type of light, I guess.'

'Probably does.' Good. Sounds like Paver's ready to use him as a sounding board at last. Ellis reins in the scientific explanation for colour-change gems. He washes and dries his hands, then fills the kettle and puts it on the hob.

'OK, talk me through pearls.' He sits down at the table. 'If that helps.'

'Sure. Thanks, Ellis. So to start with, if you're vegan I'm guessing you could never wear pearls, especially cultured pearls, where they deliberately introduce a nucleus into the oyster and force it to produce a pearl. You've got to think that whole industry's cruel. But balance that against slave labour and the human cost of pearl-diving for natural pearls in olden times, drowning, shark attack, decompression, which to my mind makes it equivalent to conflict diamonds. The wealth never goes to the ones who risk their lives, does it?'

'The way of the world.'

'The way of capitalism, I'd say. But does it have to be like that? I mean, are market forces just there, like the weather? Even if it *is* like the weather, you have to factor in metaphorical financial climate change too, driving the weather, and is that situation really beyond our control and not our fault? I want to say not. So yes, pearls are beautiful, but I don't know, I don't know.' Paver draws breath. 'People talk about "the grit in the oyster", like something irritating can be the catalyst for character development. But it's normally not grit, it's more likely damage of some kind, or a parasite. The shell secretes nacre, like an immune reaction, like our white blood cells reacting to an invasion. Did you know there are pearls in the Bible, Ellis?'

'Yes. Pearls before swine.'

'Right. That's one I found. And the pearl of great price, which could either be a message about how we should be prepared to give up everything to get to heaven, or the opposite, as in God gives up

56

everything for us. Maybe it's both/and? I like how birthstones have their origin in the Bible, from Aaron's breastplate – that's twelve stones for the twelve tribes – and then the twelve foundations of heaven. So I should probably stop. I know you're not a fan of the Bible.'

'I wouldn't say that, exactly. I just don't like being clobbered with it.'

'Sorry.'

'No, no. Not you, Paver. The hardliners. The "God doesn't make mistakes" brigade.' Ellis leans across to the dresser for some mugs. 'You've remembered the pearly gates, of course.'

'The pearly gates. Turns out I've been picturing them all wrong. In my mind they were like golden gates encrusted with millions of pearls.'

'They aren't?' Ellis pauses in surprise, then puts the mugs down.

'Seemingly no.' Paver adjusts the mugs until they're lined up with the brushes. 'There are twelve gates, and each gate is one massive single pearl. I know, right? Even the world's biggest pearl isn't big enough for a gate, being only thirty by sixty centimetres. It was found by a Filipino fisherman when a giant clam got tangled in his anchor. He kept it under his bed for a lucky charm.'

'I read about that.'

'Have you seen the pictures? It looks like a giant deformed tooth, or maybe bracket fungus. So for a gate, imagine how big the clam would need to be to make the pearl. Maybe thirty metres wide, minimum?'

Ellis smiles. 'Well, I guess the vision was more about beauty and imagery than the practicalities.'

'I guess. They'd have to scoop out the inside to make a passage through, a bit like *James and the Giant Peach*, where he lives inside a hollowed-out peach. That always icked me out as a kid because think how sticky it would be. Oh God, I keep thinking about figs again, Ellis.'

'No-o-o!' Ellis laughs. 'Not the figs, Paver!'

'Yeah, the figs.' Paver colours and grins. 'I'm just not good at living things with other things living inside them. Taking mammals out of the equation, obviously. But parasites?' Paver shudders. 'Anyway. To my point: how would they tunnel through a pearl? Maybe angels with a diamond drill? And what would they do with all the debris? Oh yeah – maybe use it in a garden, like a pearly gravel path. Cleopatra drank pearls dissolved in wine, allegedly, but your average wine isn't acidic enough to do that. It would need to be vinegar. Maybe you *dissolve* a tunnel through to make a pearly gate. Is there vinegar in heaven? I want to say no, because vinegar's basically sour wine, and you'd hope the wine in heaven never goes off.'

'You'd hope.' The kettle starts to warble. Ellis gets up and warms the teapot, then makes tea. 'I like the idea of a pearly footpath.'

'Me too. Ellis, I know beautiful things can come from bad things. But you've got to think bad's still bad, even if beauty comes out of it,' says Paver. 'What would be your takeaway message from this?'

Ellis stops to think. 'Something in the region of character, I suppose. Slow growth and endurance. How we respond to our environment, to the things we have no control over. Like rings in tree trunks. Another year, another ring. Another layer of nacre round a pearl.'

'Thanks, Ellis. So, keep at it, you're saying?'

'Yes. Keep at it.'

All this year Neil has been keeping at the renovation project at Turlham Hall hotel. He's been hampered by paint and timber shortages. Everyone and his dog's got a DIY project on the go! Firms going bust, disrupted supply chains. Thanks for that, Brexit – but let's all pretend it's the pandemic and the prime muppet's oven-ready turkey is cooking nicely. Och well, they're closing in at last. One room to go.

Freddie ought to be on his way to Turlham to join Neil, but he's running late. He and Brose have been giving the duet a run-through for Jane's party tonight so that Chloe and Baby can hear it.

'You guys are amazing!' Chloe wipes her eyes. 'Sorry, sorry, sorry! Everything makes me cry right now!' She gets her phone out and checks the baby growth as fruit app.

'So listen,' Freddie is saying, nose to the bump. 'Papa Brose was singing in his chest voice there because this duet's for tenor plus baritone? Normally he screams like a girl.'

'"Your baby, at twenty-eight weeks, is about the size of a large eggplant,"' reads Chloe.

'We'll get properly into the whole *passaggio* deal in detail when you're bigger,' explains Freddie.

'Eggplant is American for aubergine,' explains Ambrose, nose to the other side of the bump. Freddie pushes him away.

'"Baby now weighs about two and a quarter pounds,"' Chloe continues, '"is almost fifteen inches long from head to heel, and can blink their eyes (which now sport lashes)."'

'Eyelashes?' Freddie straightens up. 'Yay!'

'And Mummy is now the size of a small hippo, can't sleep, has heartburn and needs a wee every time Baby stomps on her bladder,' says Chloe. 'And she still has twelve weeks to go. Yay!'

'Aw, babe. You're such a star.' He gives her a hug. 'Gotta go. Take care today. Don't try and walk those lunatics. They're wa-a-y too strong. Promise?'

The lunatics wag their tails and pant.

'I won't.' Cosmo and Alfie are in the doghouse (as it were) for chasing a squirrel and pulling Chloe over in the arboretum. Just grazes and bruises, but it gave them all a scare.

'And you . . .' Freddie stabs a finger at Brose. 'Make sure you swing by at lunch to walk them.'

'I'm on it.'

'You better be. I'm still mad.'

'Oh, don't be mad,' cries Chloe. 'You know I can't do anger!'

'Yes, Freddie. Think about Chloe's blood pressure, for God's sake,' says Ambrose.

Freddie flips him the bird and leaves for work.

Ambrose, dear reader, is also in the doghouse for yet another piece of fucking control-freaky withholding secretive ass-hattery. It has emerged that Brose knew back last spring – last spring! – who Andy's half-naked guy was. Theo. That's right. Brose's former mentor. Not only did Brose *know* they were now an item, and for *no good reason* chose not to tell Freddie (thus blindsiding him and making him look like a dickhead when he and Andrew met that time), Brose was totally the one who set it up? As in, he was matchmaking? Hello? He better not have any more secrets he's not sharing, is all.

'There are good secrets and bad secrets, Freddie.'

'Uh-huh. And *you're* the one who always gets to decide which is which in this marriage? Why's that? Wanna walk me through that again?'

Jane is sitting by the hotel window with a mug of hotel coffee. She's waiting for Day 2's schedule to be revealed. Matt's just quickly swatting away some work stuff that can't wait. Once that's off his plate, he's all hers. She can hear him tapping away at his laptop.

We're both doing our best, she thinks. Me trying to keep my mood up, so he knows I'm grateful for all the effort he's put in for my sixtieth. And he's trying to compartmentalize and shield me from whatever work crap is currently raining down on his big bald head, bless him.

She gazes over the almost empty car park. The puddles shiver in the breeze. There's a mass of sycamores and hawthorn, and a yellow crane towering above some hidden construction site. Behind that, a glimpse of the dual carriageway flyover with traffic whizzing past. She can just hear the muffled roar.

Well, the hotel's Grab'n'Go COVID breakfast box might have been a poor substitute for a full English, but last night was perfect. Just the right number of them round the table. Infinitely preferable to Plan A, which apparently was some tithe barn somewhere packed with guests and a live jazz band. Instead, just her and Matt, Dommie, cousin Elaine, Spider from Poundstretcher, and lovely Freddie, her surrogate son, standing in for Danny.

She needs to keep hold of the memory and store it. Her hand goes to the necklace. Preserve the night intact, like this rose. When had she last flung on her glad rags? End of 2019? The restaurant had been empty, other than the six of them. Monday in a pandemic. Excellent food and, miraculously, Jane managed to hit the alcohol sweet spot for once – just enough booze to make the world glow, but not enough to trigger the Pixies of the Apocalypse at 2 a.m. and a blinding headache for breakfast. The age-old fear that people from different facets of your life will hate one another proved groundless. Right now, everyone's just too tearily happy to be together at last to bother with personality clashes. Ambrose turning up during dessert, he and Freddie singing the Pearl Fishers duet. Corny, yes, but perfect.

For a moment she catches an olfactory memory of the torched sugar on the Italian lemon meringue pie, of espresso and limoncello. The song's soaring phrases play again in her mind.

Her eyes brim. Save it, save it all. Save the tears and laughter. Save Danny FaceTiming her from Queenstown over the antipasti. Save Elaine's anecdotes from childhood (stripping all of Mrs Underhill's lupins and posting the flowers through her letterbox). Save Spider's Poet Voice rendition of the birthday doggerel he'd composed for her. *Sixty years have passed away/since your joyful natal day/On that sunny summer morn/when a darling girl was born.* Save Matt's speech, and Dommie finally treating her to the full version of 'Shame and scandal in the family'. Hah! Compared with Jane's repertoire of rugby songs, Mum's bête noir lyrics turned out to be disappointingly innocuous.

A heron flies over. Jane watches it go. They used to be rare in her childhood. She remembers Mum taking her to see a dead one, miles out along the canal towpath. The yellow crane has started working. She can see the cables swaying very slowly, but the load is out of sight behind the trees. Her hand goes back to her necklace. She thinks of the other roses from the same shrub. Long dead now, not selected, not preserved. The mildew and greenfly, slugs, rain, withered leaves – all edited out, just as Jane's been busy curating last night by editing out COVID and the whole sorry state of modern Britain. She knows her party would have looked different from the outside, if you were peering in from the rainy street with no money and nowhere to sleep.

Half the year gone. Way more than half her life gone. For a moment it makes her feel giddy, as though she's on the brink of a deep drop. It feels as though this will never end, and yet it's all racing by so quickly. Behind her, she hears Matt logging off and packing away his laptop. The crane lets out the cable slowly, slowly. All this will be in the past. She watches the pulley descend. The task continues out of sight, and the dual carriageway traffic streams by.

JULY

Larkspur and Ruby

'Morning, Paver. Not quite so hot today. On pest patrol?'

Paver straightens up quickly. 'Oh hey, Ellis.'

Ellis approaches the July bed where the delphiniums are growing. He steps round a slug coiled on the path like a ginger turd. 'Shall I relocate this monster?'

'No worries, I'm on it.' There's no eye contact.

'Fair enough.' Broad beams of light angle down golden through the trees. A wood pigeon calls. 'What do pigeons say these days,' wonders Ellis, 'now "tak two coos, Taffy" sounds like a racist football chant?'

'So some people say "my toe bleeds, Betty",' says Paver. 'But I'm not hearing that myself.'

'Nor me.' Still no eye contact. Ellis knows to wait. He breathes in. Elderflower, mock orange, roses, lime. There's some thrashing in the leaves overhead, then silence. A feather drifts down.

Suddenly Paver smiles and turns red.

'What?' asks Ellis.

'Aw, it's probably really dumb and icky, but I kind of always think they're saying, "I love you, Paver."'

'I think that's lovely, not icky. We all need that message. Can I adopt it?'

'Of course. Thanks for not laughing, Ellis. I told Coran once, and oh my days trust me, big mistake, because from then on anytime we ever heard a wood pigeon, he'd join in? I mean do you even know how often you hear a wood pigeon? *A lot*, a lot. They're everywhere. And now it's like a constant reminder, happy-sad. Like, I hear his voice, but at the same time he's not here.'

'I wish I'd known him.'

'Yeah. Talking of pigeons, by strange coincidence – synchronicity, if you will – "pigeon blood" is the colour of the most valuable rubies,' says Paver. 'I was going to put that in the July book, but I don't know. It's kind of weirdly specific, like did they discuss it in ancient times, what colour shall we say this type of ruby is, so everyone will get it? I mean, who knows pigeon blood from, I don't know, chicken blood, horse blood?'

'Good question.'

Paver draws breath and is off on another riff. 'So regarding birth flowers for July, did you know the name for delphinium comes from the Greek, *delphin*, meaning dolphin, because the shape supposedly resembles a dolphin's back? Which doesn't compute, because the other name is larkspur, derived from the horn-shape part of the flower head, which supposedly resembles the spur on a lark's foot, though to be fair, as far as I can tell most passerine – as in perching – birds' feet look similar, they have that spur, so why lark? I don't know, and interestingly there's also a flower called bird's foot trefoil aka eggs and bacon. So lark's foot, dolphin, could be either. Take your pick. Apparently, larks partly sing as a predator deterrent, so the hawk knows they can sing and fly at the same time, thus they're strong and healthy and hard to catch. So keep singing, I guess, would be the life hack there if you were looking for one.'

'Works for me.' Ellis watches the thistledown glide. 'There go your angels, Paver,' he says. 'Busy with the day's angelic errands.'

'For sure. Always busy.'

There's that heavy July stillness Ellis loves, dense with scent. The leaves are darker now the tannins have built up. A pause in the year, almost, he thinks. School is about to end. Hangman and videos instead of lessons. Or whatever they do nowadays. In the big copper beech, a juvenile chiffchaff pegs away, mastering its song. Ellis looks back at the delphiniums in the shade. They seem to glow against the wall that hides the skip. Absorbing light, emitting different light, he guesses. They'll change when the sun's on them. He wonders how they appear to insect eyes. Gaudy, with UV landing strips, maybe.

'Actually, you got me, Ellis,' says Paver abruptly. 'I was checking again. Sorry. I know it's dumb to think you could kill someone and hide the body and then forget. Sadly, the phenomenon of selective amnesia means you can't rule it out, so you have to just quickly check even though you know it's dumb. Scary how I suddenly escalated from checking I'd locked the door to this.'

'Well, it's a way of accounting for your feelings, maybe,' suggests Ellis. 'You feel terrible, so logically you must have done something terrible.'

'Yeah, I guess. So to my point, as regards the timing, maybe it's linked to the question: how is it possible to not spot your best friend is suicidal? If you can miss that, maybe you can miss anything.'

'Not forgetting the global pandemic.'

'Not forgetting the global pandemic. True, true. So anyway, sorry.'

'You don't have to apologize.' Ellis bends to take a closer look at the flowers. 'Well, they seem to have survived the storm.'

'They symbolize cheerfulness and goodwill; also they commemorate loved ones who have passed, so . . .'

There's another pause. The chiffchaff song limps on. Then a wood pigeon calls. *I love you, Paver. I love you, Ellis.*

'This is another month that doesn't have Corie in, Ellis. I'm doing all these gardens for him, I guess.'

'Yes.'

'So anyway, I was reading that next spring there might be lots of new little plants growing round the outside of the clump,' says Paver. 'In which case, you can replant those, and get this: you have to "discard the hard old heart".'

'Hah.' Ellis smiles. 'You knew I'd like that.'

'I did, I did.'

'Discard the hard old heart,' repeats Ellis. 'Words to live by. Anyway, I just came to remind you Neil will be here in a few minutes, if . . .' Paver flinches. 'Well, see how you feel.'

'I should, but . . . I don't know, I don't know, now's not a good time, seemingly. Plus he has a dog, I'm not good with dogs. Can you talk to him for me, Ellis?'

'More than happy to. I'll ask him to keep Bear in the car.' They hear tyres scrunch into the gravelled yard. 'That'll be him now. We'll be in the kitchen having coffee.'

'Oh God. So tell him yes, I'll do it, I just can't . . . Sorry. Me and social interaction? Mum's forever on my case. Like, just try. If you're brave once, you can build on that, and next time it won't be so bad. Which literally never works, because every time there's the same horrible silence and everyone's focused on you, waiting for you to answer?'

'I know. Don't worry.' Ellis turns away to hide his grin. Horrible silence, ha. Unlikely to be a problem this morning. Neil is usually more 'transmit' than 'receive'.

We will break off here, dear reader, to ask ourselves where the year has gone, and shake our heads over the state of our poor world. The Delta variant rips through communities round the globe. There's catastrophic flooding in Germany, wildfires in Cyprus. The sea itself is ablaze after an underwater gas leak in the Gulf of Mexico.

But the sun shines over Lindfordshire. Lime and elder blossom bless our land. The long bleak lockdown of the first quarter feels a long time ago now. It's Thursday 22 July. On the 19th we celebrated the Feast of Normality (transferred from 21 June) – the lifting of all remaining COVID restrictions (apart from isolating if you test positive). This final landmark on the government's roadmap bristled with so many dire warnings – not to mention 51,000 new infections and the 500,000 people contacted by the NHS app and told to isolate – that most of my characters felt like rural schoolchildren dumped in a hostile urban wasteland and told to go and play. Is it safe? You go first. No, *you* go.

Unless you were clinically vulnerable, the first tentative forays into Back to Normal proved reassuring for the most part. After all, nobody was *forcing* you to go out clubbing. The pinged workers mainly stayed at home and resisted the urge to delete the app from their phones. Many people still considerately wore masks in shops and on public transport. No lunatic rushed up and licked your face (if you discount Bear, whom Neil should have trained better). When you ventured out, you found that Perspex screens remained in place between tables in restaurants. Outdoor dining options were still available in the marquees and plywood booths of pub gardens, or else on busy pavements outside coffee shops – even if there was no food actually being served because all the kitchen staff had been pinged.

After eighteen months of high alert, small wonder we're still nervously asking ourselves whether it's safe. No queuing outside shops any more. No social distancing or mandatory masks. Buying drinks *at the bar*, rather than ordering from the table after scanning the QR code for the menu. Crowds at sporting events. Choir practice! Yikes. Time will tell whether we can trust to these newly restored freedoms, or if they will be snatched away. Weren't we more or less here this time last year? Thinking we were out of the woods, and then bang, another lockdown. Still, the vaccination programme means it *feels* as though we have passed the watershed at last.

The watershed! If, like the Bishop of Lindchester's wife, you've spent your life imagining a structure housing some sort of pumping equipment, then you'd pass it with barely a glance. I know Sonya would be astonished to learn about the area of high ground where the streams shed either into one river or, on the other side, a different river. The decider. This way or that way, and no going back. I will now put on my sermon face and propose that every moment is a tiny watershed, and this is why, potentially, every moment matters. Every micro-decision, every act that is *this*, not *that*. Good, bad or indifferent, it is what it is now. We must stand by it or repent, resign from office and rectify things as best we can.

This used to be the consensus. Now, apparently, there is the option of boldly saying in the face of incontrovertible evidence, 'That never happened.' Or of emulating Lady Macbeth before she lost her marbles: 'A little apology clears us of this deed.' I confess such strategies stagger me into open-mouthed silence. Like Elizabeth Bennet witnessing the shamelessness of Mr Wickham, I can only resolve henceforth to draw no limits to the impudence of an impudent politician. Until common decency and falling on your sword is enshrined in law, there's not much we can do about people who are prepared to double down and shoot the rapids of national indignation in their old school swimming trunks. What if a true despot came along, with a real political agenda beyond self-interest? Scary times for democracy. Let us take refuge in Holy Writ, reader. We have psalms for people like that. (Evening Prayer Day 7: 'Yet a little while, and the ungodly shall be clean gone . . . Their sword shall go through their own heart.')

We will now rise above all this sordid scurrility. Come with me instead and see how the heronry out at Shotton Farm has fallen quiet now. The younglings have fledged and departed to seek out their own territory. Herons everywhere can revert to their solitary ways. We will join one such bird as it flies slowly above the diocese this July morning. Look – there is the Linden down below, looping gently round the cathedral city of Lindchester. Gresham's Boatyard is just opening for business, and before long tourists will be punting and rowing under the trailing willows in a faux-Oxbridge vignette of Englishness. We will swoop in and land among the bankside rushes. Moorhens dab by with their brood of chicks. A swan glides under the old bridge. There are swallows and dragonflies. Trail a hand in the water, and don't think about the flooding in Germany and Belgium. Banish that footage of floodwater smashing through streets as if they were nothing but a balsa-wood model in a disaster movie set, over-turning cars, swirling them away like paper cups along a gutter. It could never happen here.

Meanwhile, I am dithering on a tiny patch of narrative high ground, wondering which way the water will shed. I can't tell whether Paver will go and join Neil and Ellis in the kitchen, or whether Neil will come out and hunt Paver down in the garden. The issue is this: Neil wants to commission a cabinet of curiosities for the reception area of Turlham Hall, which will form the gem in the crown of the renovation project. Does it matter whether Paver goes in or Neil comes out? It's only a small decision, but it will reveal things about character and set up certain trajectories. Is Paver on a path towards overcoming social anxiety, for example? I had better leave the action on this tiny knife-edge and see how my other characters are faring.

The lovely Misters Hardman-May have gone on holiday. They took the dogs, so that Chloe wouldn't have to worry about exercising them. The run-up to departure was tense – would one of them get pinged? Would they have to isolate for ten days and miss the entire holiday? This is a long-deferred Hardman clan gathering on the ancestral lands in Somerset, made possible at last by the lifting of restrictions. The timing is good: a final unencumbered frolic for Freddie and Ambrose before parenthood. The location is good too: not so far away that Freddie will spend the whole holiday catastrophizing about the impossibility of getting home in time if Something Happens. Chloe will drive down in the middle weekend, to attend the jamboree in the big barn with the other members of the wider family.

Everything will be fine. Chloe will hold the phone against her bump so Freddie and Ambrose can still sing to Baby every night, just like they always do. True, they will miss feeling Baby kick, and that strange ripple under their hands – whoa! – of a little elbow or knee knuckling round whenever this *highly active singleton* wants to get comfortable.

If only poor Chloe could get comfortable too. She's now thirty-two weeks pregnant, and Baby is 'about the size of a jicama'. If we knew what the heck a jicama was, we would be better placed to sympathize. At any rate, Baby is 'taking up more and more space in the uterus, weighs about 3¾ pounds, and is roughly 16¾ inches from head to heel'.

'I swore I wouldn't waddle, but *look* at me! I'm so FAT!' wailed Chloe as they were saying goodbye. 'Even my ankles are fat!'

'Aw, babe.' Freddie hugged her. 'No way are you fat!'

'No way,' agreed Ambrose. 'You look like a snake that's swallowed a beach ball.'

'Hey!' Ambrose swerved out of Freddie's range. 'And that's meant to make her feel better how? Don't listen to him.'

'I never do,' said Chloe. 'He's always been a pig.'

'You gonna be OK feeding the hens and stuff?'

'Of course. Go. See you at the weekend.' She kissed them both and shooed them out of the house. 'Have fun.'

'Talking of beach balls,' said Ambrose as they headed for the ring road.

'Red card!'

'Talking of inflatables, she'll enjoy floating in the new swimming pool.'

'Say what? Swimming pool? For real?'

'Yep. Dad's had one put in behind the barn.'

'Awe-SOME! How come, though? I mean, aren't farmers every-where totally going down the pan from COVID and Brexit?'

'There's basically two kinds now,' said Ambrose. 'Barely surviving and millionaires. It's all about diversifying. My folks have converted

71

the stables and barns. They were already sub-letting most of the land for grazing, just doing a bit of rare breed cattle and poultry stuff. So essentially they'll run it from now on as a luxury holiday and hospitality venue. Next up is a farm shop and café.'

'Oh great. So that's *both* sides of the family. No pressure. Being as how my dad's, what, a bazillionaire, the way he talks?'

'Fact of life. Money makes money.'

'And here's us.' Freddie sighed. 'You, a small-town accountant. Me, still pissing away the advantages of my expensive education. Oh *sorry*, no return on investment there, Dad. Living in our quote, ugly house, baby on the way, in quote, the middle of bumfuck nowhere, going nowhere? Earn it, son. You millennials are soooo entitled. Yeah, maybe we are, Dad, maybe we are. But here's a question – who told us you can be anything you want, just follow your dream? Um, that would be *you* guys, I'm guessing. With your no-loan degrees, your paid-off mortgages and final salary pensions and shit.'

Ambrose laughed. 'And based on my City experience, there's nothing on God's green earth as entitled as a white guy in his fifties whose career's not going according to plan.'

'Omigod, you can't *say* that, you reverse-racist! Straight white fifties guy is like a protected characteristic?' Freddie mimed a tiny violin arpeggio. 'Hey, maybe I'll diversify too? Set up, I dunno, my own nude housework company? Wait, wait, wait – I got it – Yas Clean? Awesome! Ha ha ha! I'd smash being a millionaire in year one with that concept.'

'You hate housework.'

'Oh yeah. Hmm. How about millionaire alpaca farmer? Man, I'ma miss Andy and Theo soooo much this holiday. Reckon they're gonna tie the knot?'

'No.'

'No? Dude, you shoulda seen the ring, the "it's not an engagement ring" ring, with the fucking mahoosive big fuck-off emerald? They are *so* getting married.'

Ambrose shook his head. 'Still not legal for alpacas.'

'Tsch!' He knuckled Ambrose's thigh. 'Are *our former mentors* planning on getting married?'

'I don't know.'

'And if you *did* know, you'd totally tell me?'

'I totally would.'

'You totally better, that's all.' Freddie let loose his hideous alpaca battle cry. The dogs joined in from the back of the car. Ambrose started singing 'We're all going on a summer holiday' in that particularly piercing way male altos seem to have at their disposal.

My ears! Goodbye, Misters Hardman-May. Enjoy your break.

Jane and Matt are also going on holiday tomorrow. Two weeks on Holy Island. I hope they will be able to relax with those twin thunderheads bubbling up on the horizon: the next academic year and Matt's safeguarding record. They will probably spend most of the first week downloading a year of stress in the form of terrifying dreams. A few days of peace will follow, before they have to bundle their angst back into the metaphorical cupboard, ready for the return home. Ah, annual leave! So restorative.

Today, Jane is informally cashing in some of the numberless hours of unpaid overtime she's accrued. She's meeting up with her former nemesis, Dr Elspeth Quilter (who must never again be thought of as the Quisling). We will join them as they enjoy coffee and warm cinnamon buns in the sunshine. They are perched on turquoise chairs, at a tiny turquoise table, on the pavement outside Mister Bun the Baker. Jane is in her colonial linen trousers and farting Birkenstocks. Elspeth is in a yellow floral cotton dress and trainers; a sartorial combination Jane considers herself too old to embrace. The two have been colleagues for donkey's years, but they've never gone out for coffee together before. It was Elspeth's suggestion. Jane is doing her best. She may have discarded her hard old heart, but sadly this does not seem to have rendered Elspeth any less annoying.

'Well. Lovely and warm, anyway,' Jane tries.

'Not really,' says Elspeth. 'It's very close.'

Don't you know the weather rules? You're supposed to *agree*. 'Yes, it's pretty humid, but—'

'*Too* humid.'

Jane presses her lips together and says nothing.

'So,' says Elspeth. 'Have you finished for the year?'

73

'Leave starts tomorrow,' says Jane. 'I'm bunking off emails and calling this work. A working brunch.'

'I'm still signed off, so this is socializing,' says Elspeth. 'For me.'

Give me strength. 'Well, we're historians. We don't need to privilege one account over another.' Jane looks at the pattern on her coffee. 'Is it just me, or does this look like a cock and balls? I reckon they know I'm the bishop's wife and they do it on purpose.'

Elspeth cranes her neck to look. 'I think it's meant to be a heart and ferns.'

Yes, Elspeth 'Barrel of Laughs' Quilter, I do realize that. 'There you go. It's both. There *is* no grand narrative.' She takes a bite of her cinnamon bun. 'So how are you doing?'

There's a long pause. 'I don't know. Still not too good, really. If I'm honest.'

Jane nods sympathetically. 'And your phased return to work starts when?'

'Next week. Do you ever think about retirement, Jane?'

'Yep.'

'There was an email about voluntary severance.'

'I saw,' says Jane. 'The sector's in freefall and management would be more than happy to shake loose a few old dinosaurs like me. Not you, though. You're still young.'

Elspeth tuts, as though Jane's paid her an off-colour compliment. She stirs her coffee, ruining the latte art. Her hand trembles.

'You're young!' repeats Jane. 'Look at you, rocking the frock-and-trainers combo.'

Is she meant to offer some old-dinosaur-type advice here? Is that why Elspeth wanted to meet? *Don't try and make a major decision while you're off with stress.* Jane gazes across the road at the buildings opposite. There are a couple of shirtless roofers up there against the sky, hammering some blue plastic between joists. The sound lags fractionally. It gives the scene a lazy summer feel. A few swifts are circling.

Elspeth is stealthily blotting tears under her sunglasses. If things had panned out differently, thinks Jane, I might have been sitting here in a dog collar, brimming with pastoral advice, knowing what to do, what to say. She hesitates. Then reaches out and puts a hand on her colleague's arm.

'Look, Elspeth, for what it's worth, and at the risk of sounding like a motivational poster, be kind to yourself. The past eighteen months have been totally shite. Your mum died and you couldn't be with her at the end, we've lost a lovely student to suicide, and we've all been under unprecedented pressure at work. My guess is you're disproportionately conscientious, so it's affected you disproportionately.' God, listen to you – this is terrible! 'And you're a lovely person,' she adds. Argh! Now *I'm* crying.

But apparently, woo-woo though this feels, Jane has said the right thing. They both weep a bit, laugh a bit, then eat their cinnamon buns. Pigeons limp round the tables on broken pink feet.

'I can't seem to let go of it,' says Elspeth. 'The guilt. I still feel like it's my fault.'

'Me too,' says Jane.

'Really?' Elspeth stares.

'God yes!' Jane hesitates again. Is this going to sound as though she's asking Elspeth to invite the Lord Jesus into her heart? 'Listen, I don't know if you're a person of faith at all?' Elspeth shakes her head. 'Nor me, really. But I've found it helps if I go and sit in an empty church for a bit. Don't ask me why. Liminal space? Sense of the transcendent Other?'

'Well. It's a thought.'

'Anyway, I hope the phased return isn't too bumpy.'

'Thanks, Jane.' Elspeth blows her nose. 'You're a lovely person, too.'

Jane laughs her filthy laugh. The pigeons scatter. 'We both know that's not true.'

Elspeth turns pink and grins. 'Well, you're kind, then. Sometimes. I admit I always resented you for not pulling your weight in the department, but I still admired your . . . confidence?'

'Chuztpah, my dear,' says Jane. 'The word is chutzpah.'

'That's it.' Elspeth points at her. 'That's exactly it. *Are* you Jewish, out of interest?'

'Nope. Just arsy.'

There's a pause while they both scan this comment with their academic soundness Geiger counters. Implied anti-Semitism? Inconclusive. Then Jane finishes her bun and crumples her napkin. 'What would you do if you left Poundstretcher?'

'Work for my neighbour's cut flower farm.'

'Wow.' She looks at Elspeth over the top of her sunglasses. 'You really have been thinking about this, haven't you?'

'I really have, Jane. But with my sensible head on, I know it's just escapism.'

'Why is it? Tell your sensible head to go fry its face. You could go down to point five and do both, couldn't you?'

'Maybe.' Elspeth drains her coffee. 'What about you?'

'Oh, God knows. It's much more fun telling other people what to do. Anyway, thanks for coffee.' They get up. 'Look, you take care of yourself.'

They dither, then bump elbows.

'You too. Thanks.'

Jane walks back to the station. Well, that was weird. Morphing into the Revd J. Rossiter like that. For a moment, she considers detouring to Dom's church for a top-up of transcendent Otherness herself. But that would mean having to fill most of another hour in Lindford before the next train to Martonbury. Too depressing. Empty shops. Debenhams gone bust. She heads through the cut towards the footbridge by the Fergus Abernathy building. She'll be back soon enough, assuming campus teaching goes ahead in the autumn. And in any case, you don't get much more liminal and thin-place-y than Lindisfarne.

In a moment, we will take the road less travelled by Jane, and pop into Lindford Parish Church. First, let us survey the lie of the post-watershed ecclesiastical land. The lifting of COVID restrictions has devolved responsibility on to parish clergy. No longer can they hold up holy hands and absolve themselves by blaming government regulations or the bishops. Anyone familiar with the good old C of E knows how much fun this is going to be. Any given congregation is likely to be a microcosm of the nation and incorporate the full Civil War spectrum, from daily-figure-checking ultra-compliant Roundhead through to 'bring on the shared cup, I've been double-jabbed' Cavalier. We all accept *in theory* that you cannot please all of the people all of the time. But when clergy are stressed – and what has the pandemic been but eighteen months of stress? – they sometimes lapse into heresy. They find themselves once again believing that if they only scuttle around covering all conceivable bases by pastorally placating the entire electoral roll, they will manage to keep everyone happy after all. Dearly beloved, this cannot be. The church is the body of Christ. It contains wisdom teeth. These may be small, bless them, but the pain they cause when they flare up is disproportionate. (Let the ordained reader understand.)

Father Dominic has been a clerk in holy orders for a very long time. This doesn't mean his heart is cauterized and he no longer gets hurt by angry emails and sharp words. It does mean, however, that he has devised a filing system for negative feedback. He has the serenity to accept his own shit and distinguish it from other people's, and the wisdom to leave impacted molars to the heavenly dentist. Sometimes he cocks up – Lord, does he ever! That funeral he forgot back in Renfold still haunts him. But he knows he's on the side of life and is doing the best he can. So he stands fast, Saddened and Disappointed of the Lindford Parish Church coffee rota notwithstanding. He no longer confuses trying to please people with the patient business of loving and serving them anyway. There is a redeemer, and it's not Dominic Todd.

He is in church this Thursday morning with some volunteers from the cleaning rota. Plainsong is playing, as if they are in a French cathedral. The scent of lime blossom creeps in through the open doors, reminding Dominic of his ordination all those years ago. Before you imagine all is peaceful, I'd better tell you that the limpid Gregorian chant is being rudely punctuated by the sound of mighty ripping. They are peeling the social-distancing tape off the pews, and removing the stuck-down laminated signs saying *You can sit here* or *Please don't sit here*. Ooh, it's like giving the church a leg wax! Everyone's wearing masks, although this is no longer mandatory, of course.

End of an era! Dominic peels off another sign and shoves it into the bin liner. His glasses keep steaming up. Quite why no entrepreneur has developed an effective solution for this, he cannot imagine. They would've made an absolute fortune! The tape brings a layer of Victorian varnish up with it. Oops! Well, if someone is saddened by the damage, Dominic will sympathize and invite them to set up a sanding-and-varnishing group.

He gazes at the pale lines left on the pew ends – like his bare feet after he's been wearing his holiday Birkenstocks! The legacy of the pandemic will be with them for decades, in the very fabric of things. Future generations will wonder what the ghostly stripes on the woodwork are. Eventually COVID-19 will vanish from living memory, like Spanish flu, like the First World War. And then it will be like people gazing round the sanctuary today, knowing nothing of boys of the parish who died at the Somme, in whose memory the lamps hang from their long brass chains.

He demists his glasses again. The PCC has voted for keeping the back four right-hand pews set up for those who prefer to maintain social distance. Hand sanitizer and QR codes will still greet people in the porch. Dominic has been urging Christian love of neighbour. Be considerate. Please wear a mask while moving about the building, though you can remove it when you're in your pew if you prefer. Communion will be in one kind and there will be no sharing of the Peace.

But – oh, glorious but! – this Sunday there will finally be congregational singing again (behind masks). Mother Gin has done the service booklets already and stacked them neatly in the vestry. Her last act before getting pinged on Tuesday evening, poor darling. It looks as though her neighbour in the terraced house next door has tested positive, and Virginia's phone was less than two metres away through the party wall during the night. A bit of a blunt instrument, the app. Fortunately, she's fine so far (and the neighbour's symptoms are mild), and her gag-and-sneeze lateral flow tests have all been negative.

Oh, but hymns! How Dominic has missed them. He was caught out by a rush of tears earlier at the sight of the front cover of the booklet. Eighteen months since he'd seen that utterly unremarkable Anglican thing: the photocopied text of the opening hymn. He hums as he tackles the next strip of tape, 'O worship the Lord all glorious above'. The first thing they'll sing together after eighteen months. If he'd stopped to think how momentous this was, would he have picked that? He can't remember the last congregational hymn back in March 2020. It ought to be engraved on his mind, the utter poignancy of it. Nor, come to think of it, can he remember the last service his mum came to before she went into the home. Oh help, oh dear!

No, it's no good. The tears are trickling down under his mask. He dumps the bin liner and scuttles to the Lady Chapel for a proper weep (the cleaners will think he's praying). He kneels in front of the flickering candles and looks up at the statue of Mary holding out her son. There's a vase of delphiniums blazing blue at her feet. Star must have been in before starting her day at the hair salon. She's carved out a niche for herself on the flower rota. The older members have finally ceded this little bit of church turf to her. Sometimes he worries about how much she must be spending.

He crosses himself and whispers a prayer behind his mask. Why can't he remember his last service with Mum? His pandemic memory's like writing on a shore – everything's being erased as fast as it's written. Was it only last week that we lost the footie Final? No, it must have been the week before that. The roar of fans in the centre of Lindford during the six o'clock mass. *'It's coming home, it's coming!'* Men with flags and no shirts, girls in mini-skirts and stilettos, white or red, the crash of recycling in nearby bars. Poor old football. Coming home at last, only to find the locks changed.

'O gratefully sing his power and his love.'

Yes. We can always sing gratefully. We're battered and exhausted, but we're mostly still here. And probably the worst is behind us now, he tells himself. Infection rates are going up, but hospitalizations and deaths don't seem to be. He's just so knackered. He can't keep up with life any more. Everything – the news and weather, the Olympics, Wimbledon – playing on in the background like a TV in another room. He feels so much, but he doesn't always know why. Tears soak his mask. His emotions are out of sync, lagging behind the action.

The monkish chant spools out in the church, up, up to the rafters, like incense smoke rising. *'O clemens, O pia.'* He hears voices of passers-by outside. Silence. It sounds as though the ripping is finished now. Someone else enters the chapel behind him. Eek! He tugs down his mask and blows his nose. Quick! Scramble pastoral face!

He turns. It's Madge. He relaxes. 'Hello, darling. How are you?'

The parish nurse sits, leaving a two-chair gap. 'Fine. How are you doing?'

'I'm gratefully singing his power and his love. Or trying to. How's your racist neighbour?'

'Jim?' She rolls her eyes. 'He came round to apologize. Says his daughters called him out. "You can't say that, Dad!"'

'"Your boys lost us the cup", quotes Dominic. 'Out*rage*ous! It never *occurred* to me people would think that!'

Madge pats his arm and gives him a tolerant squeeze. 'Mmm hmm.'

'What – you knew they would?'

'Oh yeah,' says Madge. 'The minute Saka missed, I thought: Great, here we go.'

Dominic slumps. 'Damn. I still have *no* idea, do I? I'm genuinely *trying* to get it right.'

'Relax. You can't get it right all the time. Nobody can. Nobody's perfect. Everyone's racist. I'm racist.'

'Yes, but—'

'*No*, but.'

'But I get *anxious* if I can't be right about things!' he cries. 'I want to be like God, knowing good from evil! What could possibly go wrong with that plan? Oh, wait . . .'

Madge lets out a whoop. 'Sorry!' She raises an apologetic hand towards the statue, as though she's just made the Blessed Virgin jump out of her skin and nearly drop the Christ-child. 'How's Mum getting on?'

'Well, she spends a lot of time dozing now.'

Madge nods. 'That's going to be the pattern.'

'Yes,' he says. 'She went through a bad patch last week, and for ages the staff couldn't get to the bottom of what was distressing her. It turns out she was scared she had a little boy, only she'd forgotten about him and he was starving to death somewhere . . . I know!' Dominic fans his tears back down into their ducts. 'So we've made a little photo album of me through the ages, so she can look at it.'

'Aw, nice idea. I'll pop in to see her this afternoon, after I've escaped from Miss Sherratt.'

'Bless you. Chloe told me you'd both been summoned for afternoon tea at Tinkerbell Towers. Have fun.'

'Will do. Look after yourself.'

He stays, praying for Madge and the rest of his flock. For the ones barely staying afloat. What will happen now the furlough scheme's being wound down? He prays for those still vulnerable, or caring for others. He pictures the huge liner, HMS *Economy*, setting sail from the docks. So many left behind! Tiny people in tiny boats bobbing helpless in the churning wake. '*Oh, after this our exile, show unto us the blessed fruit of thy womb, Jesus.*'

Later, as he leaves the church to go and prepare Sunday's homily and tackle his emails, Father Dominic passes a woman in a yellow dress hesitating in the porch.

'Is the church open?' she asks. 'I just wanted to . . . sit.'

'Yes, of course. Welcome, welcome.'

My tiny watershed moment has been and gone. Paver did not manage to go in and speak to Neil. Neil didn't go in search. It was Ellis who moved the plot on and revealed what we already know about his character – that he is kind; that he loves and understands his young cousin. Here's what happened.

As Neil was leaving, Ellis called across the yard. 'Paver? Come and see this. You'll like it.'

'*Like* it?' said Neil. 'Thanks, pal.'

Paver emerged from behind the barn and approached, like a heron stilting its way along a bank, gazing off to the side.

'Look at Neil's car,' said Ellis. 'There.'

Paver glanced at the bonnet of the Porsche, where Ellis was indicating. The black paintwork was dimpled.

'There you are: proof,' said Ellis. 'Hailstones the size of golf balls.'

Paver's eyes widened.

'You'd better believe it,' said Neil. 'I was down in Loughborough seeing a client and the heavens opened. I pulled over, because the road was like an ice rink, cars skidding everywhere, and for ten solid minutes, I kid you not, it was apocalyptic. Like being machine-gunned by God.'

'I thought God was meant to be on your side,' said Ellis.

'Och well, he is, but that's the hellfire upbringing for you. You can take the boy out of Sunday school . . . Anyway, ten minutes of that and the car's a write-off. Will you look at the state of it? It's got cellulite! I'm having a wee arm wrestle with the insurance guys, trying to prove the damage. I keep telling them, it's like a hen party in stilettos jumped on the bonnet. Photos can't do it justice.'

'Show Paver the hailstones pics,' said Ellis.

'Hang on.' Neil started scrolling. 'Aye, here we are. Look at those bad boys.' He held out his phone. 'Told you. Big as Frosty the Snowman's baws, they were.'

Paver glanced quickly at the screen, nodded, and looked away. There was a pause.

'Good. What time is it?' Neil checked his Rolex. 'Look at that. You'll be wanting to open shop. I'll get out of your hair.' He blipped the car. Inside, Bear leapt up and barked.

'Just quickly, while we've got you,' said Ellis, sliding between Paver and the dog. 'Neil knows the hymn on the sampler, Paver. The jewels one.'

'"Like the stars of the morning, his bright crown adorning,"' sang Neil. His voice filled the yard. '"They shall shine in their beauty, bright gems for his crown." I thank you.' He bowed. 'And thanks for coffee. I'll be in touch, Ellis. Nice to meet you, Paver.' He opened the car door a crack. 'Stay! I said STAY, you wee bugger. He's in disgrace. Chewed up one of Hubby's funeral shoes, right before the service. Heh heh! God's way of telling you to buy new shoes, pal. But they *are* new! says himself. I only bought them ten years ago! Parsons, eh? I don't know. Move!' Neil shoved the dog off the driver's seat and climbed in. 'Catch you later. Byesy-bye.'

The car roared away.

Ellis and Paver stood on the yard as the July stillness closed back in.

'So to my point, I think it's probably rubies triggering me,' said Paver. 'Like the associations with blood? Pigeon's blood, blood red, red alert, red button, emergency. Any time you actually see blood, it's got to be bad news, say an accident, a cut, self-harm. I mean, isn't blood only good when you can't see it?'

Ellis was silent.

'Um, Ellis? Are you mad at me because I didn't come in and talk to Neil, who incidentally I'm probably OK with, now I've met him. I mean, he's kind of loud, but. So I can probably manage if I can wear my headphones – or is that rude? Oh God, I really tried to make myself come and meet him, only—'

'Paver? It's OK, I'm not mad. Try this?' Ellis laid his hand on his heart.

Paver gasped and copied. 'Thanks, Ellis.'

'I was thinking about what you said, that's all. What about transfusions? I had one once. After my surgery, so we're talking years and years ago now. There were complications and I lost a lot of blood. I remember looking at the line going into my arm, barely conscious, and after a while, the strength – the life – was literally flowing into me. Oxygen levels going back up, I expect. Extraordinary feeling. Like a miracle.'

'OK, yeh, yeh, yeh – life blood, OK.' Paver was nodding. 'I get that. Thanks, Ellis. And someone somewhere donated it and saved you? Like, somewhere you have kind of a blood sibling, who you'll in all probability never meet, or never know you've met. Wow. So as well as biological family, there's potentially this whole other matrix, a blood network joining people, even if they never know? That's kind of joyous.'

'Well, I hadn't thought of it like that.' Ellis laughed. 'But now you mention it, yes. It's joyous.'

Up in his study on the Close, the canon precentor wipes away a tear as he proofreads the service booklet for the 10.30 cathedral Eucharist. He hums the first hymn the congregation will sing after their long silence:

> Thousands of thousands stand around thy throne, O God most
>   high.
> A thousand times ten thousand sound thy praise, but who am I?

All across Lindfordshire, wood pigeons croon their love song and an infinity of thistledown glides everywhere, everywhere, busy along pathways we cannot see.

AUGUST

Poppy and Peridot

'Ladybird Jeanie Cecilia Hardman Garner-May. Born 5 August 2021, weighing 5lb 2oz.' Mother, fathers, baby, dogs and chickens are all doing well. Let the champagne corks fly and happy tears be shed.

Those of you with a midwifery background may have been fretting. You doubtless spotted Chloe's fat ankles and anticipated the medical emergency – pre-eclampsia – that led to her two-week stay in hospital, followed by an emergency caesarean section at thirty-four weeks. If so, I hope you were consoled by the thought that we left Chloe in safe hands. She was having tea with two of Lindford's most formidable medical women on the afternoon when it all kicked off: Miss Sherratt and Madge the parish nurse. They looked at her and asked a few gentle but urgent questions. Madge whipped out her blood pressure monitor, and then Miss Sherratt dialled for an ambulance and arranged for Jack to look after the hens. Afterwards, there was the NHS.

Oh NHS! Underfunded, overstretched, simultaneously utterly brilliant and dismayingly crap. How shall we extol thee, we rosehip-syrup-reared fortunates who were born of thee? Miss Sherratt pre-dates you. Little Ladybird will outlive you – if I am correctly interpreting the blue hand as it writes on the nation's wall: *You have been weighed in the balance and will be stealthily privatized.*

Look at Ladybird, poor wee mite, fast asleep in nappy and eye mask under the UV lights that are treating her jaundice. Look at her little hand there, curled like a sea anemone, the plastic ID bracelets round ankle and wrist: *Baby girl Garner*. Baby girl, baby girl, with your fluff of black hair, your skinny arms and legs – you're here, you're actually here! You little miracle, I wish I could scoop you up and hold you to my cheek while Chloe dozes beside your cot in her hospital bed. I would bless your tiny eyelashes and fingernails, the veins on your eyelids, your baby-head smell, and marvel to think that in your tiny ovaries all your microscopic eggs already exist fully formed. Miracle within miracle. How can this be?

Outside Lindford General Hospital, the cars and buses still drive over the fading rainbow on the road, and the white letters spelling *Thank you*. Inside, babies are born, lives slip away. From the cradle to the grave, our alpha and omega.

Enough with your paean, the reader cries. Ladybird Jeanie Cecilia Hardman Garner-May? What the actual heck?

Names are never just names, either in novels or in real life. The choice encodes a complex package of information about personality, family history and social background. Do please remember that the parents are all millennials. If you think that it's not fair to call a little girl Ladybird, then frankly you should see the names that didn't make the final cut. She is called 'Jeanie' for Freddie's beloved Miss Blatherwick. Chloe flat-out vetoed Barbara as too old-ladyish, and fortunately Miss Blatherwick was Barbara Jean, rather than, say, Doreen or Gladys – names still kicking their heels in the comeback waiting room. 'Cecilia' is for St Cecilia, of course, patron of music. 'Hardman' is a third middle name, which avoids the triple-barrelled challenge I saw looming. Does this subtly signal some kind of dad hierarchy, you may be wondering? Freddie is the biological father and named on the birth certificate, after all. Is Ambrose cool with this? If he already felt sidelined, then Baby Girl's name might have formally enshrined that.

You may be sure that up on Cathedral Close people have hand-wringingly discussed all this at length. The poor child – that's not a name, it's a thesaurus! With the best will in the world, the Close community cannot really see how this can work out happily in the long term. How will the relationship/s survive? How will little Ladybird (*Ladybird!*) grow up well adjusted, with a mum and two gay dads in a sort of ménage à trois (do they *actually* share a house, or is it two separate flats; how does it work? – we need to know!)? Yes, Freddie has *mostly* settled down, he hasn't run away with a millionaire sugar daddy (and *apparently* Ambrose isn't too vanilla for him), but how will he handle the pressure of parenthood? What if he goes off on one of his legendary week-long benders and it all falls apart? And then there's the whole first cousin thing. (Vague icky incest taboo – are we allowed to name that?) True, it wouldn't contravene the table of kindred and affinity if Ambrose actually *were* the biological father – and not that it's any of our business – but isn't the whole dynamic a bit . . . *complicated*?

Obviously, we are hoping and praying it will all be fine. We are knitting little hats, and gift-wrapping *The Tiger Who Came to Tea* board books and non-gendered organic cotton sleepsuits from John Lewis. We are sending shepherd's pies, tray-bakes, plastic-free care packages of every kind, and offering to walk the dogs. Oh, but we worry, we *worry* for them!

As you can see, dear reader, worrying (and its evangelical equivalent 'Could I just ask you to pray about x?') is what we do instead of gossiping in Anglican circles. Just as well, because gossiping is a sin. The Bible is clear about that. Gossipers and slanderers will not inherit the kingdom of God. You can't be a Christian *and* a practising gossip, or adopt a gossiping lifestyle, any more than you can practise a greedy lifestyle and be a Christian. It is not enough to repent of individual acts of bad-mouthing and gluttony. You must acknowledge that slander and greed are not part of creation. They fall short of God's plan, and you need to renounce them completely. It's time to draw a line in the sand. We cannot remain in communion with those who continue to consume ten times as many natural resources as those in developing countries, or slag off their neighbours whose lives differ from their own.

It's 12 August. The weather is all rainy-sunny-thundery, with moors the colour of old bruises, and poppies everywhere. Over at Gray's, Paver has decided that the August garden is not confined to a single plot. All across Lindfordshire, *papaver rhoeas* dots and edges the wheat fields like blood flecks. It flourishes patriotically with corn-flowers and oxeye daisies in municipal verges. Petals fall and paste themselves to rainy pavements. *Papaver somniferum* petals flutter like silk rags in gardens. Pepperbox seed-heads ripen and dry out. The wind blows. Seeds fall the way seeds will, on the path, among stones and thorns, eaten by birds, and (take heart) some on good soil.

In Miss Sherratt's garden, Jack makes the most of a sunny day. He gathers the dead heads from the opium poppies to dry out in the garage. Later, he will tap the tiny seeds – tinier than grains of black sand – into paper bags. Madge, the parish nurse, wants some for her garden. So does the vicar. Thinks they're pretty, does Father Dominic, the mauve flowers and green-grey stems and leaves. Jack saw fields of the stuff, back in the day. Big industry. Especially in Afghanistan, of course. He shakes his head. Twenty years. And now we're pulling out. Same old. You go in thinking you can do good, make a difference. Do no harm? Fine and well for doctors. Can the government, the armed forces, stand by and *do no harm* in the face of evil? Here's the conundrum, though: how to look God in the face when it turns out your best was worse than doing nothing would have been.

He bumps his fist gently against his forehead. It's a stress trap, a sink hole, this train of thought. Best not to dwell on it.

He watches a pair of cabbage whites go flickering over the pond. Scent of roses. The sleepy *chook-chook* of the hens next door. A mouse darts between the hosta clumps. Now it's gnawing on something. Then Jack hears a burst of song from over the fence: 'We had joy, we had fun.' Jack smiles. They'll be heading up to the hospital soon. Little Ladybird, bless her heart.

Well, he'll walk the dogs for them as per the arrangement. Leave them some sweet peas in the kitchen. Can't touch sweet peas for scent. Time was when nobody would trust him with small change, let alone the keys to the house. Nice people feeling bad, not giving money to the homeless because they'll only spend it on drugs.

Later on, he'll walk the dogs down along the river; watch the sand martins skimming the water, spot a heron, or maybe even a kingfisher, if he's lucky. He'll mow the lawn if it stays nice, then do a bit more on the summerhouse. He's been replacing the rotting wood, new for old. No rush, just a bit at a time, as and when he can get to the builder's yard for the timber. The same summerhouse, but not the same, like Nelson's ship – was it Nelson's? Some ship or other, replaced plank by plank. Quite the poser, that. But this one's more your relaxing conundrum. Nice to turn round in your head.

For a moment, Jack stands with the dead poppy heads, watching the house at the end of the garden. A white curtain licks out through an upstairs window and flutters in the breeze. This year's sunflowers look over the tall fence. Where has the time gone? The blinds are down in the other half of the semi, the old weed house. Still standing empty. The landlord 'had no idea' what was going on in his property, so looks like he's got off scot-free, if we're allowed to say that. Scot-free. Welshing. Got to be discriminatory, like Irish jokes, when you stop to think. No sign of new tenants, so Jack's guessing the gang's lying low, and then they'll be back to start over, new kit, new slave. What can you do?

Jack wonders where he is now, that lad who came scrambling over the wall like a terrified animal, whether he's safe, whether he got leave to remain. Be nice to think Jack had made a difference to that one. Like the boy in the story. Throwing them back one at a time. Starfish on the beach.

Inside the house, Freddie has just taken a COVID test.

'Say what you like about latflo tests,' he says, 'you'll never be short of a baggie ever again. Your turn, dude.'

Ambrose goes through the familiar gag-and-sneeze routine, tidies up, re-sanitizes his hands, and starts poaching some eggs. Freddie is singing the Brahms ladybird song.

'"*Marienwürmchen, setze dich.*"' He breaks off. 'German's one crazy-ass language. That's literally "little Mary worm"?'

'But we're not going to call her that. Are we?'

'Naw! Course not.' Freddie reverts to 'Seasons in the Sun' instead. He hangs over the test strips. 'Come ON! Wanna go see my baby! *Our* baby.' He glances at Ambrose.

'It's fine, babe.' Ambrose watches the eggs seething in the water. And it is fine. It's pretty much what he'd anticipated. He loves Ladybird the way he loves his nieces and nephews, the way he would've learnt to love any child he adopted. He wasn't expecting to feel besotted, to have love exploding in his heart the way Freddie and Chloe seem to. He knows they hover, watch him anxiously, in case he's feeling left out. They're looking for more than he's got. He has to repress a spurt of annoyance sometimes. Just let me go at my own pace!

The toast pops up. He serves the eggs. 'They'll be home soon, Freddie. Her jaundice has almost cleared up.'

'Yeah. And then the ordeal by grandparents. Gah! I mean, not your folks or Chloe's, I'm cool with them. But . . .'

'Listen, *we* get to decide who comes when and for how long.'

'Hello? Dude, have you actually *met* my dad?'

'He suckered me once, but this time I'll defeat him like a mega boss and unlock your next level of happiness.'

'Ha ha ha! You're crushing it, dude. I mean, defeating Andy for me with your secret life-coach attack? Whoa! Guy's totally neutralized by lurve.'

'He's admitted it?'

'Nah,' says Freddie. 'Never in a million years will he admit it.'

Ah, little Ladybird. Sleeping, waking, feeding, sleeping in your tiny hospital world. All over Lindfordshire life goes on. Canal boats putter through locks. Children wait for A-level and GCSE results. Weddings with two hundred guests go ahead at last. There are roars from the stadium at Lindford FC on a Tuesday night. Dr Elspeth Quilter drives to Short's Cut Flower Farm with her heart singing. She's tending the shop while the owners are on holiday. The twittering laugh of the green woodpecker carries across Martonbury's golf course. Children paddle and swim in the Linden, where a man walks two labradoodles, and a heron waits on the opposite bank. Signs go up in pubs and restaurants: 'We regret that we are currently not serving food, due to staff having to isolate.' There are empty shelves in supermarkets. All the time, more people are vaccinated. We hold our breath, cross our fingers, light a candle. So far, our worst fears haven't been realized. Maybe it's the good weather, the school holidays – who knows? – but it's not spiralling out of control. Let's wait and see what happens in September, when universities and colleges are back, and Lindford fills with thousands of youngsters – that'll be the test, all right. And then comes winter.

This will be the world you grow up in, Ladybird Jeanie. The valley of the shadow of COVID.

Far away in Argentina, your grandmother drives into Salta again and lights another candle in the cathedral. Her little flame of prayer flickers among the others under the eyes of saints and angels. All the company of heaven. For thirty-one years, she's loved your dad, wept for him, feared for him. And now comes this double granny whammy of loving, weeping, fearing for you too. She is so far away, and who knows when she'll be able to visit?

Your grandpa May strides about his office under the Picasso sketch, the Sickert, the Moreau (all the company of Sound Investment). Right. He will sort out a trust fund for you, and lay down a case of top vintage Bordeaux, and one of port, like he's done for his other four grandchildren. Your parents just have to say the word and he'll get you on the waiting list for the top school of their choice, not a problem – he knows people, he can make it happen.

He sighs and looks out across the big sweep of gravel drive. Vintage Bentley, Land Rover, Steph's convertible, then the staff Range Rovers, housekeeper's 'cute' little Fiat (each to their own). If this nonsense carries on much longer, he will fucking get in the fucking Defender and visit, even though he's been told not to yet. No, he won't really, but he needs to know you're being looked after properly. Why the hell won't they go private? What's the big deal here? He's offered to foot the bill. (It's fucking Ambrose, isn't it? Why's he so fucking controlling?)

He can't stop looking at your photo on his phone. You have your dad's mouth. He remembers holding Freddie, the way the kid gazed up at him. Total trust. Freddie the heartbreaker, the mistake, the baby he'd actually paid not to have, except she couldn't go through with it, thank God (with hindsight). Everyone warned him. She's too young, Rory. It's too soon after Josie's death. Say what you like, he's always been a good husband and provider. (Not his fault she ran off with a fucking Argie horse breeder. You'd think she might've done better for herself, but there it is, water under the bridge.) He always did his best by Freddie. Always. Wanted the best for him. Supported him. Loved him. Tough love sometimes, but let's not confuse being nice with being kind – pro leadership tip right there. No father could've done better.

He sits at his big desk.

Let me know when it's convenient for Steph and me to pop down.

He deletes it and sighs again. For God's sake, is it too much to ask? To meet his new granddaughter?

Hope all's OK. Steph wants to know if you can send more pics. Cheers.

12 August 2021
So here we are on holliday in bishop Pauls house in the Peak District like last year once again. I for one will be glad when the pandemic is properly over and we can go abroad. NB it is nearly over finger's crossed, there are no restrictions now, choirs can sing again YAY!!! Me and the other girls and boys choirs will be singing Mendellsons 'Elijah' with the Community Choir, we will be the ripieno choir in the clearstory. It is good to be grateful and practise an attitude of grattitude, like for example, to enjoy this cottage because this could be our last holliday here. That is what dad says LOL, I am mearly quoting him. He told us that bishop Paul (aka dads ex-boss) and Susanna his wife are coming back to live here because he is retiring.

I am sitting on the window sill in the bedroom with a view of the moors, it is beautiful with the purple heather coming out like in the song ect ect. Don't get me wrong, I am super-grateful, it could be A LOT worse, but it is not Colorado. Why have you got this thing about Colorado (says guess who) do you have any idea of the air miles??? I went we could go by boat, and she went durr boat's are exactly as bad you moron unless they are solar powered like the one Greta went in to New York bla bla.

Tbf I stopped listening. I will cut her some slack because I know she is stressed out with climate anxiety, it is CODE RED FOR HUMANITY, there is this report. Plus she is missing Kai. She is proper mad at mum and dad because Kai's parents invited her to go with there family to France and they said no. I privetly whispered to dad (in case Leah went off on one) 'So are chanel ferries solar powered?' and he went no. Make of that what you will, at the end of the day we are all floored individuals who cannot be consistent all the time. ☺

So anyway Colorado, I will precede to tell you about that with alacrity. (NB that is my new word, it is pronounced 'ALACK-Ritty', not 'al-KRASS-ity'. We would do well to remember that if people say a word wrong they are not total idiots, it ACTUALLY proves they have learnt the word from reading thus proving they are INTELLIGENT fyi (mentioning no names). If you follow him you will already know last month Mr Hardman-May and his girls uploaded 'Rocky Mountain High' on Tik-Tok. I decided to research into it and lo and behold I totally fell in love with Colorado?

I am now composing my own score (SATB) of the aforementioned song (aka Rocky Mountain High) which I will dedicate to baby Ladybird Jeanie Cecilia Hardman Garner-May. OMG!!! I SOOOO want to meet her!!! The entire whole girls choir does too obvs, Daisy (head girl chorister) organised a money pool (well her mum did) and posted it to our FaceBook group to collect money, we are buying her a gift. We are all super excited for Ladybird and sooooo thankful for her safe arrival, mum says pre ickle eclams the thing Chloe had is very dangerous they both could of died so thank God all is well. Mr Hardman-May messaged dad a cute picture, he asked us not to share it anywhere, they are respecting Ladybirds privacy and not uploading images because identity theft and digital kidnaping?

So Rocky Mountain High contains the memorable line 'raining fire in the sky' which is a reference to the Perseid meteor shower which is happening RIGHT NOW!!!!! It is literally going on this minute only it is daytime here so we cannot see the shooting stars. I will be going out and lying under the stars for sure tonight, I will use mums yoga mat. (NB it is called 'a yoga mat' but she uses it for pillates, as Christians we do not believe in yoga.) Fortunatley it will be a clear sky, the 'grain moon' phase is 'waxing crescent (12%)' plus it sets at 22:33, thus it will not interfere with the Perseids. In my setting 'raining fire in the sky' has a super high soprano descant to symbolicise the meaning of the words, it will be awesome finger's crossed.

Dominic is in his smoking room when his phone rings. He's been tickling his bibelots with a pink ostrich feather duster, and feeling like Georgie in *Mapp and Lucia*.

'Janey! You're back! How was it?'

'Crawling with mead-quaffing fudge-munching tourists. With blessed lulls when the tide was over the causeway.'

'Didn't you walk in the footsteps of St Cuthbert and think holy thoughts?'

'I went and stood on his little island.'

'Oh! I did that once,' says Dominic. 'And I got cut off by the tide. I had to wade back up to my thighs, nodding and smiling at the tourists and pretending it was a devotional act.'

'You already told me that. In fact, I stood staring out to sea thinking what a numpty you were to get caught like that.'

'Oh, thanks. Love you too.'

'And then I turned round,' says Jane, 'and the tide had snuck in behind me.'

'Ha ha ha ha!'

'Exactly. So I ended up wading ashore up to my thighs as well, like a complete tit, mentally sticking two fingers up at the gawping tourists. Yes, I thought you'd enjoy that. How are you doing? Staying COVID free?'

'Yes, thank the Lord. You heard Father Ed's tested positive?'

'Matt said. How's he doing?'

'A bit rough, the poor darling. What about a quick lunch, then?' asks Dominic. 'Mister Bun's, or Gray's? What do you fancy?'

'Somewhere—' She breaks off. 'What the hell is that?'

'Oh, *that's* my vintage Black Forest cuckoo clock,' Dominic says. 'Ellis at Gray's warned me it needed an overhaul, but I like it the way it is. Apparently it got dropped and now it says "Ooh, cock!" instead of cuckoo.'

Jane lets fly her filthy laugh. 'Trust you to source the world's only gay cuckoo clock. And before it so rudely interrupted me, I was about to say let's go somewhere that doesn't serve cake.'

'Oh Lord. Bathroom scales being beastly again? I see you, darling. I see you.'

'A satanic barber's shop quartet has taken up residence in my brain,' she says, 'singing "Fat and Useless" to the tune of "Truly Scrumptious".'

There's a pause. Then Dominic shrieks. 'You've just sicced them on to me, you cruel woman.'

'What are friends for? Listen, it's still August. August is a separate moral universe, so sod the diet,' Jane says. 'Let's go to Gray's. I want to pick up a non-cutesy present for Ladybird, and I seem to remember they've got some steampunky birthstone stuff. Creepy little books in matchboxes, that sort of thing.'

'For a *baby*?' cries Dominic. 'You can't possibly!'

'Do I look like a set-of-apostle-spoons kind of woman to you?' asks Jane. 'I'm setting out my stall as evil fairy godmother, I'll have you know.'

'I think that role's already taken, darling. His Royal Dorian-ness will elbow you off *that* podium without creasing his Italian suit.'

'Sez who?'

'Sez me. "Fat and useless! You're truly, truly useless," sings Dominic. '"Useless as a chocolate barbecue!"'

'You're twirling round the room, you big ponce,' says Jane. 'I can tell.'

'I'm just dusting my fripperies. You've *got* to come round and admire the latest additions. I've got a pair of *perfect* Staffordshire china dogs.'

'Fine. Why don't I pick you up at twelve?'

'Perfect,' says Dominic. 'Toodle pip, then. See you at twelve pip-emma, useless.'

'Roger that, fatty.'

They ring off. Dominic flutters his duster over the cuckoo clock. Five past ten. He'll still have time to squeeze in a quick visit to Mum. Damn – lateral flow test. If he does it now, he'll have to wait thirty minutes for the result. Twenty-minute drive to the home, visit, then back . . . No. It'll be too tight.

Dust motes twinkle in the slanting sunbeam. This was her room. For a second, he senses the old iteration of the space shimmering behind his gentleman's snug, as if the two coexist: her bed where the chaise longue is, her Strawberry Thief curtains superimposed on the velvet drapes, her glasses and puzzle book on his footstool. He taps the duster gently against his leg. I can go tomorrow on my rest day instead, he thinks. She won't know the difference. Sometimes he thinks she's already slipped through to eternity, the eternal present where she is everlastingly surprised by joy each time a nice vicar visits to pray with her. 'Our Father, who art in heaven, hallowed be thy name.' Here's where our two planes intersect, he thinks.

It's fine, tomorrow will be fine. Even as he decides this, he hears the superstitious organ chords of dramatic irony sounding. He smiles and crosses himself. Yes, she might die tonight, and then yes, he'll wish he'd gone today. But there's no knowing when the last visit will be. It could be months and months away. He'd like to be there at her end, just as she was there at his beginning, but the truth is, they've already said their long goodbye.

'Are you sure this is OK, Ellis? Oh God. What if it takes too long and we're late back, and customers have to wait and they get mad?'

'Well, either we'll be back by eleven, or Cheryl will open up for us. No need to worry.'

Paver's leg jiggles up and down in the front seat of the van. 'Cool. OK. Cool.'

They buckle up, and Ellis starts the engine. They pull out of the gates, turn left along the lane and head towards Turlham Hall.

'Neil's partner is isolating because he tested positive, by the way. Neil's negative. Neil and I will be wearing masks. We'll maintain distance, and there's hand sanitizer, obviously. Will you feel safe with that?'

Paver nods.

'I've explained you're exempt.'

Paver nods again, and rocks back and forth slightly in the seat, counting something.

They pass under the horse chestnut trees. Conkers are falling already and it's dead squirrel season – juveniles misjudging their aerobatics and dropping in front of cars. Ellis drives round another spatchcocked corpse, its pale belly gleaming. It might be dead, but no point flattening it. Paver doesn't notice. Good.

The cabinet of curiosities is stowed in blankets in the back of the van, along with the carefully packed and labelled boxes of contents for the different compartments. Plan A is that they will unload it all and drive away, leaving Neil to assemble everything according to the detailed photos Paver has taken. A tentative Plan B – which exists only in the privacy of Ellis's head – is that Paver will discover that it's actually not so bad, and will feel safe enough to stay and spend the morning installing the contents. Ellis is relaxed either way. Beyond his control. It will likely end up depending on something he can't predict, like the number of telegraph poles between here and the hotel.

'Feels like autumn already,' Ellis says. 'There's usually a specific day in August when I think that. Rather early this year. I can never put my finger on it. The quality of the light? The wind making a slightly different sound in the leaves?'

Paver's knees are still jittering. 'Yeah, I guess. Listen, Ellis, you won't drive off and leave me there? I mean I know you won't, only . . .'

'I won't. Not unless you explicitly tell me it's OK. Don't worry. How's the August book coming along?' he asks. 'Oh, I meant to say, someone rang just now and asked if they can reserve it. I took a name but didn't make any promises.' Jane Rossiter. Ellis doesn't mention the lurch that gave him.

'Yes, cool, so as you know, August is poppy and peridot – pronounced either peri-dot or peri-doh, take your pick. Poppy is kind of double-edged to my mind. Remembrance Day, sure, but I mean the dual associations of opium production, which is kind of a both/ and situation. As in, before opium I guess there wasn't much pain relief, yet by the same token we have heroin addiction. I'm hearing Dumbledore's words here: "It's our choices, Harry." Interestingly, Dumbledore is an archaic dialect name for bumblebee, and to be fair, in the early books he does kind of bumble around? J. K. Rowling develops him over the course of the series.'

'You're . . . still OK with JKR?' asks Ellis after a moment.

'With the books, sure. I think you can still be allowed to honour what you experienced positively as a child, and not cancel the writer from your entire history. Because for me, it was like a paradigm shift, another possible take on reality, in which being weird and geeky might have this other spin? Easy to mock, I know. There was this mean girl at school who went through a phase of saying, "Sorry to break it to you, but the letter from Hogwarts is never gonna come, Potterhead." But I still never lost the joy? Second only to arriving at art college. The first week I was looking around thinking, Omigod, I'm not the only one? I have this whole tribe?' Paver glances across anxiously. 'Are you . . . OK with my take on JKR, Ellis? I was always kind of out on a limb with my uni friends here, so I can just not mention Harry Potter ever again if you prefer.'

'No, no. You're allowed to have your own take. Look, put simply, I enjoyed the books, but I'm not a fan of her latest pronouncements.'

'So we're still cool?'

'We're still cool.'

'Thanks, Ellis. So to my point, peridots, also called chrysolites, are green due to the iron content. They're formed not in the earth's crust, but in volcanic rocks in the upper mantel. And, get this – they're also sometimes found in pallasite meteorites, Ellis. Meaning they literally come from outside our solar system. I mean, how awesome is that?'

Ellis smiles. 'I'd say very awesome.'

'I know, right? Did you know we're currently in the middle of a meteor storm?'

'The Perseids? Yes.'

'So last year me and Corie and a group of us were going to watch them on Lindford Common, only I was in a bad place. I think there was maybe a thunderstorm, you know me and thunderstorms, but I can't remember for sure. Anyways, like an idiot, I didn't go.' Paver shrinks down, disappearing into the black hoodie, hands pulled into the baggy sleeves.

Ellis turns into the hotel drive. They pass the laurels and park by the huge monkey puzzle tree. 'It looks set to be clear tonight,' he says.

'Yes. Maybe I'll . . . Yeah, maybe.' Paver unclips the seat belt and takes a deep breath. 'OK. OK. We got this. OK.'

'Why not pop your headphones on?' suggests Ellis. He hoists his mask. 'Neil gets it.'

'He does? You're sure?'

The door of the hotel opens. Ellis sees Neil coming down the steps in a tartan face mask.

'I'm sure,' says Ellis. 'He admits he's a motor-mouth and says most sane people would wear earmuffs given the option.'

'Oh God, he's here.' Paver puts on the headphones, hands shaking. 'So meteors originate in outer space and if they make it through the atmosphere without burning up, and actually land on earth, they're called meteorites.'

Ellis nods. 'Let's unload.' They get out.

'OK. Cool. OK,' whispers Paver. 'Some meteors are tiny, like no bigger than a grain of rice or, say, maybe a big grain of sand.'

Ellis opens the back doors and Paver climbs in to hand the plastic crates out. Ellis and Neil carry them through to the hotel. As they walk up the steps, Neil looks at Ellis and raises an eyebrow.

Ellis does a hand wobble. 'We'll see,' he murmurs.

Behind them in the quiet of the van, Paver is still crouched, whispering. 'Even if things are small, they can still burn brightly. I guess that's my takeaway from this – my life hack, if you will. It's OK to be small, so don't worry. It feels like you're burning up, but maybe that looks kind of cool from a distance? I mean, someone already wants to buy your August book. So maybe a long, long way away, people see your life, what you do and make. People you'll never even meet could be thinking, Wow, that's actually awesome?'

Right now, Ladybird is awake. Freddie and Ambrose have given her her first bath, and now she's wrapped up snug in Ambrose's arms, gazing up into his eyes. He gazes back. Where have you come from, little time traveller, he wonders? Who are you? Something seems to be exploding in slow-mo in his heart after all. It feels as though the universe itself is on tiptoe and staring at him in wonder through those dark eyes. He realizes he's humming as he rocks her. Bowie's 'Star Man'.

'Aw, babe,' says Freddie. 'Look at her looking at you!' He takes a photo and wipes his eyes. He hesitates. Ah, why not? He WhatsApps the image to his dad.

Ambrose knows Freddie and Chloe are looking at one another, thinking *thank God*. But right now, it might as well be just him and Ladybird floating like astronauts in outer space. He smiles at her. It's a shitty world, and I have no idea what I'm doing here, he thinks. But I'll be looking after you.

SEPTEMBER

Michaelmas daisy and sapphire

It is 29 September, the Feast of St Michael and All Angels. Clouds of incense will hang in light slopes in the St Michael Chapel today. We have not visited the cathedral for some time, but the Burne-Jones stained-glass angels cast their coloured light on to the old stone again, now the repair work is complete and the scaffolding has gone.

All across the Diocese of Lindchester we can see the same mauve haze of Michaelmas daisies that greeted Bishop Steve's announcement seven years ago. Seven years! Where has the time gone? It feels like the mauve of half-mourning. We may have put off our black crêpe, but we are still only part-way through our long grief for all that we've lost in the pandemic. Mauve beside railway tracks, mauve on embankments, on wasteland and in neat front gardens. Swathes of mauve in Short's Cut Flower Farm. Mauve in the September flower bed in front of the wall at Gray's, where Paver has stencilled a huge pair of iridescent rainbow angel wings. You can stand in front of them and pose for a photo, trying the idea on for size. Who are we? What are we? What might we become? Are all things possible under the sheltering wings?

Jane glances at the stencilled wall on her way into Gray's this morning. She rolls her eyes. Notionally, Wednesdays are her non-teaching day, earmarked for research and writing, but today she's too distracted by Matt's important safeguarding meeting to focus. Some skeleton or other tumbling out of the vestry cupboard – she's not asked for details. With luck, it will turn out to be a storm in a Beryl Ware teacup, and the whole thing will be over by the time she gets home. She puts on her mask, goes into the craft barn and joins the queue at the till.

Jane is the only one wearing a face covering. Maybe it's fine. Big space, doors open. Besides, two weeks ago she was in a merry maskless crowd of a hundred and thirty for the long-deferred cathedral patrons' dinner, with all its gavel-banging 'pray silence' fuckwittery (the less said about which the better). Today's risk is low in comparison.

She gazes around as she waits. The walls are hung with bunting made from old dress fabric. Beside her, there's some Mexican-vibe furniture. Little chests of drawers, a bookshelf, spice racks. They're painted in vivid colours and stencilled with birds and flowers. Jane can visualize the charity shop originals before the wand of upcycling magic passed over them. The kind of things that graced the closed front parlours of her childhood. That little shocking-pink trolley with barley sugar legs – surely Granny Rossiter had one of those? Cute, but where would you put it? It'd stick out like a Teletubby in the inoffensive colour palette of the palace.

What if she were to take a leaf out of Dom's snuggery book, and do up her study like a hacienda? A project for when she goes down to point five. Is she going to do that? No. Even though her colleague Elspeth seems to be having the time of her life down at the cut flower farm. Oh well. Jane sighs out her longing into the craft barn's loveliness. She pictures her breath blighting everything like an evil east wind, withering the homemade clove and orange pomanders away to dust. Steampunk pterodactyl creatures hang over the till. Someone has constructed them from old bike parts. There's something about the barn that reminds her of a chapel. Ah yes – it's like the Wesleyan schoolroom next door to the library, she thinks, where Cousin Elaine went to Girls' Brigade. I wasn't allowed to join because uniformed organizations were 'stupid'.

The queue moves forward. Only one person in front of Jane now.

Those autumn evenings after the clocks went back. Little Jackie bored out of her skull, going to watch through the chapel schoolroom window, leaving Mum at her librarian's desk smoking, reading, stamping books. GB always looked like such fun from Jackie's Little Match Girl perspective. All those team games, the singing, the marching drills. Elaine kept her cousin Jackie up to speed on what she was missing. They did playground re-enactments: *Marker fall IN! Tallest on the right, shortest on the left, in single ranks SIZE.* But it wasn't the same as being there. *You can tell your mum from me it's not stupid.* Aunty Susan, sewing red and white braid on Elaine's GB blazer when she went up to Juniors. *I'll give her stupid.* Maybe it cost too much, Jane realizes now. The subs, the uniform. Like the ballet class in the room above the library.

Ha. Is this why I joined the Christian Union at Oxford? Jane wonders suddenly. Was I trying to fill that childhood belonging deficit? Yeah right, look how that turned out. Two years at theological college and a vocation that crashed and burned. Well, look at that – I've turned into Mum after all. Buried in books, cynical, pissing on other people's heartfelt enjoyment whenever I spot it. Yes, Jane – why *did* you roll your eyes at those angel wings just now? That's right: because you think the idea is *stupid*.

'Can I help you?'

Jane comes to with a jolt. 'Oh hi, yes, sorry. I've come to pick up an order. Jane Rossiter. It's paid for.'

'Ooh, yes, yes! One moment. Let me have a quick look.'

The woman bends and starts rustling about along the shelf below the till. Her flossy white hair is dyed pink, with red-framed reading glasses embedded in it. For a moment Jane seems to be staring down at a featureless furry face with scarlet-rimmed eyes, like a gormless Sesame Street puppet. If her son Danny were here, she'd nudge him and they'd both die of stifled laughter. Jane banishes Danny before she starts crying. The woman is wearing lavender tie-dyed dungarees. Jane can't see, but she's betting on purple vegan leather Doc Martens. I bet she's retired from some nice middle-class profession to this nice middle-class part-time job. Furthermore, I bet she grabbed her pink flag and yoga mat and went down to London the other week to glue herself to the Stock Exchange. Jane withers the picture with the east wind of her contempt. Because obviously, Extinction Rebellion is more absurd than climate change denial, global capitalism and the end of the world.

Yep. You are your mother, Jane.

'Here we are!' The woman straightens. She puts a brown paper gift bag on the counter, perches her glasses on her nose and double-checks the luggage label. She gestures *ta-dah!* as though she's created it herself out of sticky-back plastic for love of Jane alone. 'Do you want to check it's all there?'

'Thanks.' Something clicks: she reminds me of Susanna Henderson. The warm pastoral gaze. *That's* why I'm being such a cow. Well, she'll have time for amendment of life when Paul and Susanna return to the UK. She removes the tissue and lifts out the painted matchbox she ordered. 'Oh! A ladybird.'

'Is it OK? Do you like it?'

Jane checks to see there's a little book inside. Good. 'It's perfect.' She smiles. 'It's for a baby, who, improbably, is called Ladybird.'

'Yes!' The woman nods and clasps her hands, Susanna-like. 'Paver added it on purpose.'

'Really?' Jane feels a faint chill. 'How come?'

'Ellis will explain that when he . . . Let me just get him.'

Jane rewraps the gift swiftly and tucks it into her Poundstretcher cloth book bag. 'Don't worry, it's fine.'

'No, no, please. Ellis wants a quick word anyway. He's just in his workshop.'

'Actually, look, I'd better be off—' But the woman has disappeared through a door. Damn. Jane isn't quite rude enough simply to walk out. She shrugs apologetically to the people behind her in the queue and takes a deep breath. The cloth mask sucks against her face. Her heart starts thumping. Well, so long as it's only Ellis, not Coran's half-elven friend (presumably this Paver).

Ellis emerges, putting on a mask. 'Oh, hello there. If you've got a moment, come and see another August gift idea. Just a hunch.'

Jane follows him to the jewellery section and peers into the glass case Ellis is indicating. 'What am I looking at?'

'That.' He points. 'Suffragette necklace.'

'So it is!' She bends to look at the price: £195. Blimey. Do I love you that much, little Ladybird?

'It's Edwardian. Gold. All the seed pearls still intact, amethyst and peridot.'

'Clever sales pitch there!' Jane laughs. 'I'm a history lecturer, so spot on. This is my stomping ground. Late Victorian, early Edwardian.'

'I know.'

'Ha!' Jane bends closer over the case. She can feel the blood pounding in her ears. 'So my fame goes before me!'

'Yes. Freddie told us you were Ladybird's godmother,' says Ellis. 'My cousin Paver and I did some work for Turlham Hall, and Neil and Freddie—'

'Neil and Freddie! Of course.' Jane straightens in relief. Nothing to do with Coran and Poundstretcher. 'What the heck – I'll have the necklace. I've got to trounce my rival godparents, after all.'

Ellis unlocks the case. 'I can do you a ten per cent discount.'

'That's kind. Thanks.' Jane watches him reach in for the necklace. 'Presumably the Freddie connection is how – Paver, is it? – knew to paint a ladybird on the matchbox?'

'Paver. Yes.'

'Unusual name.'

'It crops up in our family tree,' says Ellis. 'Paver says it just felt like a fit.'

'Well, I'm all for people choosing their own name,' Jane hears herself saying. 'I segued from Jackie to Jane at Oxford. Not entirely sure my motives were honourable, but there we are.'

Ellis hands the necklace to Jane and relocks the case. They both stand, as though there's more to be said. Jane can feel an uprush, an imminent blurt-fest. What is it about this man? His calm presence, the dark eyes watching her over the mask. Some Aslan warmth is undoing all her White Witchery. She's crumbling at the edges.

'Actually, I knew Paver's friend Coran,' she says. 'I taught him.'

'Ah, did you.'

'Yes. I was here in the summer with a friend and I recognized Paver then, from the funeral, and . . . To be honest, I panicked a bit. I wasn't sure how Coran's friends felt about the university's role in all this. Or mine. Because basically it was me. Who dobbed him in for plagiarism.'

He puts a hand on her arm.

'Don't!' Jane lets out a bleat of a laugh. 'For God's sake, don't be kind to me!' She sniffs back the tears. Ellis squeezes her arm and takes his hand away. Too late. Jane covers her face. Shit.

'Come and sit down. Come.'

Jane lets herself be steered out through the door.

'Have a seat and I'll make you a cup of tea.'

Let us leave poor Jane weeping in the old captain's chair in Ellis's workshop among the dismantled clocks and broken crockery, while we go on a tour of Lindfordshire.

It's a perfect September day. Bright sunshine burns off yesterday's rain. For a few moments, all of Lindfordshire seems to smoke. Everything the sun touches – roads, playgrounds, roofs, backyards and wheelie bins, the skips and freight containers, railway sidings, all the old York paving stones and cobbles of Cathedral Close – it's as though the whole diocese is offering up Prinknash St Michael's incense. It rises to the blue heavens, to the sapphire pavement and the sapphire throne, to the impossibility that lies on the far side of our groping meta-metaphors (like unto the likeness of a likeness – how can human language sing that majesty?). It soars to the realm where the angels continually cry *Holy. Holy. Holy.*

The potagerie at Gayden Magna vicarage is steaming. Father Ed watches through the window. The ripe cardoon heads seem about to spontaneously combust. He's trying to summon up the courage to make himself an espresso with the new cherry red Gaggia coffee machine. It adds a pop of colour to the slate grey kitchen and matches the phone kiosk cocktail cabinet in the corner. Ed's trusty old stovetop espresso maker has been banished to the charity shop, because it's aluminium and will give him Alzheimer's.

I'm still not well, he thinks. Reduced almost to tears by the impossibility of picking a path through the espresso minefield. The Gaggia was a present from Neil to cheer him up. But Ed longs for the familiar routine of his stovetop maker, the soothing autopilot of filling the base with water, spooning in the coffee, screwing the top on. He misses settling it on the hob, then sitting down to wait for its hoarse whispering gobble. Radio 3 in the background. Coffee smell filling the kitchen. He still hasn't mastered the new routine, although Neil has demonstrated it at least four times – *See? Piece of piss. Now you try.*

Ed fills the James Bond stealth kettle, and furtively fetches out a cafetière. Then he goes to the fridge. He stands in front of it. What was I doing? He stares at the fridge magnet. The Taste Polis long ago decreed that all fridges shall be unadorned, because fridge magnets are naff. This one, however, is permitted. Why? Because it is grey and white, the typeface is acceptable (monospaced rounded Slab Serif) and the words are words to live by:

Do all the good you can,
in all the ways you can,
to all the souls you can,
in every place you can,
at all the times you can,
with all the zeal you can,
as long as ever you can.

Ed rests his forehead on the fridge. Judged by bustling old Wesley. I'd prefer to sleep, he thinks. In every place I can, as long as ever I can. It's the lingering effects of COVID. It will pass. He knows that. Each week he's a little better. He just needs to be patient with himself. Thank God he'd been double-vaccinated – what might it have been like if he'd got it before?

The kettle boils and clicks off. Milk – that was it. He opens the fridge and gets out the pint bottle. They have their milk delivered at the vicarage now, doing their bit, banishing plastic. The church carillon begins to chime like a giant musical box in the distance, 'When morning gilds the sky'. He can hear children's voices as they walk to the village primary school. That's probably where he got infected. (God's way of telling you not to take assemblies, big man.) Weird that he didn't give it to Neil. It's like the End Times. One is taken and one left. No way of predicting who will get it, and how badly. This has been the scariest thing about the virus from the start.

The doorbell goes. A delivery probably. Another forgotten gift ordered by the Ed of last week. He goes and opens the door. It's his neighbour from the Old Rectory, Mrs Logan. He stares. Then the penny drops. Shit! She's here to liaise about the autumn weddings she's got booked for clients. A surprise appointment booked in by the Ed of last week.

'Am I early?' she asks.

'Not at all,' says Ed. 'I'm afraid I'd completely forgotten.'

'Oh dear! Shall I come back another time?'

'No, come in, Mrs Logan. I was just having coffee. Will you join me?'

'Lovely. And please call me Carrie.'

They go through to the kitchen. He sees her looking around in amazement. She's only been in his study before, the tiny rebel state still holding out against Neil's benevolent dictatorship.

'Wow! *Love* the phone box. This is amazing! Not what I think when someone says "vicarage".'

'Neil's genius at work, obviously. And Neil's money,' he adds, in case she's thinking, No wonder the diocese is cutting clergy posts if vicarages all have quarry tiles and Welsh slate worktops. 'Coffee? Carrie?'

'Yes please.'

He eyes the Gaggia. 'Oh God. This thing intimidates me. It's new, but I suppose I could . . .'

'Ooh, let me!' She puts her handbag and iPad on the table and comes across. 'We've got one of those.'

'Thanks. Don't tell Neil.'

'It can be our little secret, Father,' she whispers.

There's a pause.

'Well, that didn't sound at all dodgy!' Carrie says brightly. 'Shall I froth some milk too? I can do fancy ferns and everything.'

'Please. Um. Look, sorry, I'm going to have to sit down.'

'God, yes, of course. You're still looking a bit knackered. Can I say "knackered" to a priest?'

'Of course you fucking can.'

She laughs, but he can see he's shocked her. It's as though she can't quite hit on the right register in his company yet, ping-ponging between deference and profanity. The frother hisses. She does something arty with the milk.

'Here you are, Father.' She hands him the little cup. 'I've done a sacred heart for you.'

'Look at that! You're so clever.'

She opens her mouth to say something, then shakes her head and smiles. 'Right. I'll just make mine. I really missed you for those

August weddings. Your stunt doubles did their best, but I prefer it when you're there.'

'I prefer it when *you're* there, too.'

'Because I'm your human shield,' she says. 'I stand between you and the Bridezillas.'

'Exactly,' says Ed. 'The wedding season always used to be a real headache pre-pandemic, but I was enjoying it this time. Probably because I've done so many funerals in the last eighteen months.' He shakes his head.

'COVID-related?'

'A lot of them, yes. I hated hearing the wedding bells from my sickbed.'

He shuts his eyes. Oh God. Here it comes again. Fever dread washes through him. It's like backdraught after you think a fire's out. The thickness and thinness of things is all wrong, the weave of the linen duvet cover vast as trawler nets, his hands are three miles away at the end of his arms. Mothers are passing babies over a high wall outside the vicarage. There's a gathering roar. It's the last planes taking off from Afghanistan. People cling to them, then they're falling, falling, and he's lying there, with the bells ringing and splitting his head open.

The milk steamer hisses again. There's a clink of coffee cup. He hears her come and sit opposite him at the kitchen table. The thing recedes. He opens his eyes.

'Are you OK?' she asks. 'We can do this another time.'

'Sorry. I'm fine. Just a flashback. Is that a thing? COVID flashbacks?'

'I've heard of people suffering from PTSD afterwards.'

'But it wasn't that bad. I wasn't in hospital or anything.'

'Well, COVID's a weird one,' she says. 'The medics don't really have the full picture yet.'

They talk for a bit about Carrie's daughter Rachel, who teaches at Queen Mary's grammar. How the older members of staff were inclined to be gung-ho about abandoning all restrictions the minute they were double-jabbed. Why in hell did the government drag its feet so long over getting teens vaccinated? It's underway now, but she's had death threats from anti-vaxxers. It's carnage. A third of the staff are off, and finding cover is a nightmare. And obviously the younger

113

kids who haven't been vaccinated yet pick it up at school and take it home to their parents. And now Rachel herself is quarantining after a positive lateral flow test on Monday. She's feeling fine so far. It could be a false positive. She'll have to wait for the PCR results.

Anyway, they need to crack on with business so poor Father Ed can go back to bed, and Carrie can go and sit in her husband's car at the garage and queue for petrol. Fingers crossed she'll be able to get him thirty pounds' worth. He's had to take her car to work today because she still had three-quarters of a tank. You'd think health care professionals would get first dibs. Crazy times, they agree.

Later, when she's walking back up the lane from new rectory to old, she curses herself. For God's sake, calm down about him being a vicar, and stop going all *Fleabag* on him! It's just that she still finds it ridiculous. A sensible grown-up in the twenty-first century taking the God-bothering seriously. Yet she doesn't get flustered by other kinds of cobblers – horoscopes and aliens, conspiracy theories. They don't get to her. Maybe she's scared, deep down, that the God stuff might be real. And that if it is real, it's a game-changer. Oh well, at least she managed not to say that the latte art also looked remarkably like a bum. Or call it the sacred arse. She snorts guiltily and gets into her husband's car to go and hunt for petrol.

All across Lindfordshire, all across England, people are doing the same. London is gridlocked round every petrol station. Crazy times. But we have become inured to craziness. Crazy is the new sane. The unimaginable has been all around us for so long that it's the sweet old ordinary things, those things we took for granted, that catch us out and make us well up. The first in-person meetings. The return to the office. All round the diocese, school and village fêtes are finally declared open. We make our first trip to London, and there's the Thames, its bright water, bridges and boats all wavering through tears – my city, my capital, oh, I've missed you.

Round greenish bales sit in stubble fields. There are pumpkins lying like school netballs in allotments. Red admirals flutter by. Here and there along the Linden, conkers drop with a sploosh into the water. The harvest moon is waning. Leaf blowers bellow. Then silence falls. Listen. Such waves of sorrow still washing in, in, in, shushing on the mind's beach whenever we pause. Infection rates continue to bubble along at around 30,000 new cases a day, and somehow this feels normal. Are we crazy? On the other side of the world, Sydney goes into lockdown again after one case of COVID. Are *they* crazy?

The furlough scheme ends tomorrow, on the last day of September, like the big ship sailing down the ally-ally-oo. Goodbye, goodbye. Will it sink to the bottom of the sea, with people trapped in the hold, drowning, while the foghorn mourns out one final sub-sonic boom of cognitive dissonance? There are always gaps on supermarket shelves now, gaps on pub and café menus. There is no food crisis, no petrol crisis. It's just supply chain problems. A shortage of HGV drivers. We mustn't blame Brexit. The captain said this will never, never do. We will get more drivers. Short-term visas will be issued. The army will step in. Poultry workers will be lured here from Poland and Christmas will be saved.

Meanwhile, gas providers fold. Food prices soar. House prices soar too, as wealthy professionals flee the big cities and relocate to picturesque villages. They are snapping up properties in Gayden Parva, in Carding-le-Willow, in Turlham.

And life blurs by. Lindford is full of students again. Crazy to think all those freshers were born after the Twin Towers fell. How can it be twenty years since 9/11? Look at them, with their full heads of hair, their bare flat midriffs; look at the bounce and insouciance of youth. How silent our streets have been without them, how old and weary the world has felt. But one day it will be twenty years since COVID. By the time little Ladybird starts university, perhaps.

Jane takes off her mask and blows her nose. Ellis sets down an enamel mug of tea on the table beside her. 'Thanks.'

'You're welcome.' He sits with another mug and takes off his mask.

'That chair's from a church,' says Jane, pointing. 'That's a hymn-book rest on the back. You only ever see them in coffee shops now.'

'You know why they're so popular?'

'Hipster trendiness?' suggests Jane.

'Because they're uncomfortable,' says Ellis. 'Nobody lingers over their coffee. Rapid turnover of customers maximizes profit.'

'Hah.' The air is full of polish smells. Polish and oil. A proper work-shop. She takes a sip of tea. Ellis has made a good old-fashioned brew. It looks as though he is in the middle of cleaning up and restoring a set of old brass scales. Duraglit, that's the smell. Granny used it to polish her copper kettle.

'You did nothing wrong, Jane,' says Ellis.

Tears rush up again. 'Oh stop it, you silly bag,' Jane mutters.

'Do you always talk to yourself like that?' he asks.

'That?' Jane laughs. 'That's mild!'

'No wonder kindness slays you, then,' says Ellis. 'You did nothing wrong.'

'Yes, yes, I know that, but—'

'You did nothing wrong,' he repeats.

Jane squirms. 'Well, *technically*, no. But—'

'You did nothing wrong.'

Aargh. She takes another mouthful of tea. Ellis is watching her. As if he knows her. He's going to carry on saying this until she gives in and takes it, accepts absolution. Suddenly, her head, ears, everything, feels strange, like loss of cabin pressure, or fever.

'You did nothing wrong,' she hears him say.

She nods, once. I did nothing wrong. Tears spill out again.

Ellis nods back. 'Good.'

Her head clears. She wipes her eyes and finishes her tea. 'Thanks. I need to pay you for this necklace.'

'Just take it to the till and say I said a hundred and fifty pounds.'

'That's not ten per cent.'

'Mates rates.' Ellis hesitates. There's a strange smile on his lips. 'We . . . overlapped at Oxford, actually.'

'We did? Same college?'

'Yes. I remember you from rugby.'

Jane shakes her head. 'Sorry. Long time ago. Probably concussed too many times.'

They laugh. Ellis turns his attention to the scales he's been restoring. 'There weren't many other state school pupils,' he says.

'God no! Wall to wall posh kids, mimicking my accent. Hated it.'

'Me too. You were in the God squad.'

'I was! And I apologize unreservedly if I was a dickhead. Sorry I don't remember you. Which team did you play for?'

'Um.' Ellis shifts the brass weights slightly along the workbench. 'Same as you, actually.'

There's a pause. 'Oh!' says Jane. 'Weren't you . . .'

Ellis starts to stack the weights up carefully in order.

'. . . our hooker?' says Jane. 'No – prop. You played prop.'

'Tight-head. Yes.' He adds the final quarter ounce weight to the top of the pile. His hand trembles slightly. Then he looks at Jane and smiles.

'Yes, sorry, I remember you now. Sweet bird of youth,' says Jane. 'Well. Good to meet up again after all this time, Ellis. You seem very happy here.'

'I am.'

'Good for you.' She puts her mask back on. 'Well, better make tracks. Thanks for the tea. Do say thanks to Paver for the ladybird box.'

'I will.' They both stand. 'Be kind to yourself, Jane.'

Jane drives home to Martonbury. She is trying to be kind to herself, but you can't shake off nearly six decades of habit in a fifteen-mile journey. It astonishes her, now she stops to listen, the savagery of her inner chiding. Even now, it's accusing her of crass blundering back there. *Weren't you . . . our hooker?* Yes, very subtle mid-sentence swerve there, Jane. Idiot.

Come fly with me up among the angels this Michaelmas. The sky above Jane's car is busy with them. Thistledown, and pigeons on flickering wings of light. We are heading for the Close. The four-by-fours have been and gone, delivering children to the cathedral school. The cathedral clock chimes eleven. We swoop down to land on the gracious gravel drive of the palace. Bishop Steve is across in William House in a meeting. His EA Kat is at her desk in the office.

If we peep in through the window, we will see her. At the other desk, the one that used to be the chaplain's (back when the bishop had a chaplain), sits a lawyer. He is patiently working his way through blue clergy files of clergy new to the diocese since 2009. This is for Past Cases Review 2. He is also cross-checking other files with any information the safeguarding team has gathered from parish churches. A letter from a bishop in 1987 that says 'X's ministry ended at St Botolph's in some disarray' might take on a whole new meaning in the light of PCC minutes about parental complaints from that era. Doubt might now be cast over the 'fresh start' the bishop was so confidently predicting X would make elsewhere.

The lawyer is called Hugh Bartlett. Because this is the Close, he has acquired a nickname: Mister Blue Files. Hugh doesn't know that, of course; but he has noted that the bishop's office is surprisingly informal, and people tend to greet him with 'Hey there' rather than 'Good morning'.

'I'm about to make coffee,' says Kat. 'Want one?'

'Well, yes please, if it's not too much trouble,' says Mister Blue Files. He blinks at her through his little round glasses. 'You're very kind. You must be longing to get your office back to yourself!' He laughs. It's a strange laugh, louder on the in-breath than the out, thinks Kat. Like someone sawing wood backwards.

'Not a problem.' Kat goes to the little kitchen and fills the kettle. Damn – missed the golden opportunity to say 'It's so nice to be with you'. Probably freak him out, poor guy. He reminds her of a little Sylvanian Families figure, beavering away at the files.

She checks her watch and stares out across the palace drive. She wonders how the meeting's going over in William House – if they've decided yet whether they have to suspend Bishop Matt. Matt's working from home today. That's what she'd do too. She'd want to avoid the walk of shame, packing up her stuff and leaving, with people knowing and not meeting her eye.

She makes two coffees and takes them back through. They'll suspend him, she thinks. While they investigate. Her hunch is there won't be a CDM, but she's not the safeguarding expert. She doesn't actually know the details, either. But you don't get to be in her role and not hear the Close goss. This is about Freddie and the previous bishop. God, poor Freddie. Seems harsh to rake it all up now, just when he's got his shit together and is loving being a dad. Let's hope they turn it round quickly. How will it affect Jane? she wonders.

Kat shakes her head. Jane's a weird one. Kat can't make her out. Not once in the last seven years has she got eye contact from her, the shared look that says 'I see you, sister'. Latest example – the patrons' dinner during the speeches. Kat was already outside having a breath of fresh air. She could still just about hear Lord Numpty of Numpty Hall, Lindfordshire, spouting at high table that we should not apologize for our history, we should be proud of what Britain has achieved, when out stormed Jane. You go, guurrl. Kat would have offered her a sneaky ciggie too, but Jane carried on walking. 'If anyone asks, I've got a migraine.' That was it.

Oh well. With a shrug, Kat goes back to her emails. Good – here's one from someone wanting the pope's mobile number, so they can pass on a message from God. Kat spends a happy moment running through the list of people in the diocese who have annoyed her, and whose number she has in her database. But how to choose, how to choose?

Matt is driving out to the cut flower farm to pick up a bunch of flowers for Janey. He's got lunch booked with an old mucker from the force, the one who retired to set up in the organic flower business. Lovely day for it. The sunroof is open and he's got 'Free Bird' playing. But it's not helping, to be honest. He sighs and turns the music off. The phone call will come any time. Could go either way. They might investigate and resolve it quickly. Or he might be in for the CDM long haul – anything up to eighteen months. He's braced for suspension – pretty much a foregone conclusion, that. Might as well treat it literally as gardening leave. He's planning ahead for that eventuality. Doesn't want to be hanging about getting under Janey's feet, doing her head in. Hence the trip out here. He'll have word with Shorty, offer his services.

He pulls into the car park. Five minutes early. He switches the engine off and settles himself to wait. Bad calls all along. Bad calls seven years ago, more bad calls this summer from a process point of view. He's still guilty of taking matters into his own hands. He chose to wait another three months before contacting the Diocesan Safeguarding Adviser. First he was waiting till he was sure Bishop Paul was coming back to the UK. Then he was waiting till the timing wasn't so bad for Freddie – all the stress of Ladybird arriving early. He wanted to give Freddie time to enjoy being a dad before upending this can of old worms. He meant it for the best, but that's not his place to decide, is it?

Freddie, Freddie, Freddie. It's going to feel like a bombshell, an utter betrayal. Their friendship mightn't survive this. Matt's heart tightens at the thought. He can see the knock-on effect for Janey, trying to navigate being Godmother if Matt's not welcome at the baptism. Could he have kept schtum? Was he prioritizing his own safeguarding record, and what this would look like if it came to light, over Freddie's wishes and wellbeing? Matt rubs his hands over his face. Not his place to decide. If only he could just pop round to Freddie and give him the heads up, though . . .

Come on, just ring me! Why is it taking them so long?

Cool your jets, Tyler. No point reading anything into this delay. Maybe one of the safeguarding team was running late, maybe they've taken a break for lunch. Could be anything. He dangles his phone between thumb and forefinger, swinging it gently to and fro. He sees a tall red-haired lad go by, pushing a wheelbarrow. For a time-warped second he thinks it's Shorty. But it'll be his son, of course. Kai. Young Leah's boyfriend. Quarantining? Or has he actually finished school now?

No, the delay is irrelevant. The facts of the case haven't changed. Freddie was not underage at the time. It was consensual. It was a breach of pastoral trust, for sure, but not part of a wider pattern of offending on Paul's part. The safeguarding team will contact Freddie. They will contact Paul. They will need to know who knew; what was put on the record. Then they will probably follow up and want reassurances from the theological college in South Africa . . .

But now he's trying to second-guess it all again. He gets out of the car and sticks the phone in his pocket. He'll hear when he hears.

In gardens and old orchards, damsons and plums and apples ripen. Leaves drift from the ash trees at Shotton Hall Farm, and little by little the heron nests become visible again in the branches. The alpacas play-fight. Lesley, the farmer, feeds the white geese in the field.

It's midday. Incense rises in St Michael's Chapel at the Eucharist. The girl choristers will sing at Evensong, and Freddie will be there to introduce them to baby Ladybird. He doesn't know that tomorrow the

Diocesan Safeguarding Adviser will ring, and the bottom will drop out of everything.

How odd, this life we lead, never knowing what lies ahead. If only we could shout back a warning to our yesterday selves: *Enjoy it now!* But instead, we stumble through the hurdle race, hanging on till the end of the week, the term, saying we just have to get through *this* and we'll reach the imagined time where everything will be OK.

'So sapphires are basically the same mineral as rubies,' says Paver. 'As in corundum. I didn't know that, Ellis. I've just finished the September book. Did you know there's such a thing as star sapphires? They literally look like there's a star inside them, shining. How magical is that? The phenomenon is called asterism. Do you think maybe there's a human equivalent? I mean, don't some people, like, shine when you meet them, and you could just watch them for ever?'

'You're thinking of Coran?'

'You got me. I am, Ellis.'

They are both in the kitchen. Gray's is closed for the day. Paver is painting another matchbox, tiny brushstrokes, viewing it through the vintage magnifying glass.

'Jane says thank you for the August gift, by the way.'

'She liked it? Cool.' Paver focuses, adds another brushstroke.

Ellis waits until Paver pauses, then says, 'She knew Coran. She was his tutor, it turns out. For that assignment. She's been feeling bad.'

'She has?' Paver looks up in surprise. 'To my point, asterism is caused by inclusions. Remember inclusions, from emeralds?'

'Faults. Yes.'

'I kind of love that,' says Paver. 'Like, something could be your fault, or maybe it's *not* your fault but you still feel like it is. Jane would be an example there, I guess. It's so not her fault, Ellis. Did you say that?'

'Repeatedly.'

'People make mistakes. Everyone does. You do things you feel bad about afterwards, and bad stuff will happen to you and leave scars, because life's like that. So altogether, that's like your inclusions? Does that make any sense to you?'

'It does.'

'But is it too, like, trite, Ellis? I really hope not, because here's what I wrote in the September book. Look.' Paver opens the tiny book and holds it under the magnifying glass.

Ellis bends close and reads the minuscule writing: *Your faults and scars are part of you, part of your history. There is a star in your heart. So don't be scared. Let it shine.*

'Thank you.'

Ellis goes and stands at the sink, looking out of the window at the golden late September light. He can see the wall where the rainbow wings arch above the bed of Michaelmas daisies. He puts his hand on his chest. Maybe there is a star in your heart, Ellis, not just a bag of broken fragments. He's still feeling something – bruised, tender at any rate – after his conversation with Jane. He almost wishes now he'd kept quiet. But there was something in that moment – in Jane's abandonment of all defences, perhaps – that he needed to honour with an equivalent soul-bearing.

His eyes wander to the framed sampler on the wall.

> Like the stars in the morning,
> His bright crown adorning,
> They shall shine in their beauty,
> Bright gems for his crown.

If there's a star, it seems to take a lifetime of patient polishing to make it shine, he thinks. Before you dare call it a star and show it to someone.

OCTOBER

Marigold and opal

Bishop Matt is picking marigolds at Short's Cut Flower Farm. It's a Thursday in mid-October, and he is now in his second week of suspension. Good word, suspension. Suspended animation. Living in a pocket outside time, here in the garden. Blue sky. Wasps and bees still busy investigating. Butterflies. He lays the marigolds carefully in wooden trugs on the barrow. Some for the shop, and others for this week's bouquet for those who have an online subscription for a fresh flower delivery.

Matt's in the swing of things here now. He's cooled his jets and adjusted to the low-octane pace of the farm. Those pesky inner calendar alerts have tailed off. They're no longer pinging every five chuffing minutes, reminding him to get on to stuff. He trundles his cargo of marigolds down the path. First stop for these beauties is the conditioning room, where they will join the other stock in the cold and dark for a nice long drink. Later on, he'll be laying three blooms in each of the long flat cardboard boxes, as per instructions, along with some golden rod, dark red-brown mums, and those blue thistle jobbies – what are they called again? Not eurythmics. Elspeth will print the labels, and off the bouquets will go, to bring joy and colour into homes across Lindfordshire and beyond. Joy, colour and the odd creepy-crawly, but that's the organic lifestyle for you.

I don't know what you picture when I say 'cut flower farm', reader. Rows and rows of industrial planting, like the tulip fields of Holland, perhaps; or acres of lavender on a Provençal hillside. Well, it's nothing like that. Short's is small and intimate. If you ever decide to go there to buy flowers, I suggest you don't set out with a clear idea of what you want. Each week is different. Prepare to be delighted and surprised. It's more like a charity shop than a high street chain. You never know what treasure you will find.

The heart of the enterprise is a walled garden and old glasshouses. These were once part of Hopewell Hall in East Lindfordshire. The marigolds Matt picked today grow in a long bed with sunflowers, rudbeckia, cosmos, salvias and I know not what. If you, reader, can picture it, it's there. Knock yourself out and let your horticultural imagination run riot. After all, the banquet of fiction has something of the bring-and-share about it, a spirit of collaboration between reader and writer. I invite you into my invented walled garden and you chip in with anything from Granny's hollyhocks to those espaliered Serbian gold quince trees in a stately home you visited in June.

Beyond the walled garden lies the wildflower meadow. It's enclosed by ancient nest-cluttered hedgerows and rich in species all but eradicated elsewhere by intensive farming. Help me here – corncockle? fritillaries? orchids? Down at the bottom of the gentle slope the field gives way to marsh, where kingcups shine by a stream in the summer. A heron hunts here from time to time. This quiet acre has been left to its own devices for generations, never grazed, just mowed once a year in midsummer.

This, then, is Short's. The family live in what was once the gardener's house. Flowers are conditioned in the former dairy, while the old stables are now the shop and workroom. Davy Short stumbled upon the place back in 2017, like the man in the parable. He was out on a recce for somewhere to set up business and live his long-cherished retirement dream – and there it was. He took out a loan and sold everything to buy it.

Some of you will remember Davy from years ago. It might not surprise you to hear that during the first lockdown, when the shop was shut and there was no wedding trade, Short's gave their flowers away. They donated armfuls of tulips, narcissi, anemones to NHS staff at Lindford General Hospital, to GPs and health visitors, to care homes, funerals and foodbanks, to the police, to village shops and post offices, to any frontline workers they could think of. And still their borders weren't empty! They went out into the highways and byways and compelled people to have flowers.

That's the Short family all over. You may perhaps have wondered over the years how Davy was doing. Did he ever recover from his broken heart? Why aye. Relocated south shortly after, to pastures new, which is where he crossed paths with Matt. He laughs and shakes his head at his daft younger self. If there's a parallel universe where him and Isobel got hitched, he'll not be visiting. (Except mebbes with a SWAT team, in case his parallel self was wanting out.) Is Kai repeating family history with that lass of his? By, she's a handful that one. Well, there's no short cut to graduation in the school of hard knocks. Kai will have to figure it out himself.

It might strike you as a curious career jump from policing to flower farming. It certainly surprised Matt when he heard. But the roots of Davy's dream go deep into the soil of childhood. He has vivid memories of the gardens and allotments of grandads and uncles up on Tyneside, of prize flowers nurtured alongside giant leeks. He remembers pressing his way through dahlia forests as a toddler, staked flowers taller than him, shaggy heads bigger than his own. Later on, he earned pocket money helping dig up and store the tubers, or tying paper bags over blooms to protect them from late frosts.

Matt unloads the trugs in the old dairy. He could get used to this. Pootling around in the garden. Fresh air. No chuffing inbox. No naughty priests, no bonkers prophecies about Pfizer being the mark of the Beast, no handwringing grave concerns divorced from practical solutions, or conspiracy theorists accusing him and Bishop Steve of turning the diocese into an HTB mega-plant. No. Life's peachy now that his biggest challenge is deciding which marigolds to pick, rather than which vacancy he can afford to fill.

He wheels the empty barrow back out of the dairy. He can hear Shorty whistling in the distance. There's no knowing how long this palaver will drag on. Well, it'll just have to run its course. Not like this is the only case on the diocesan books, not with Past Cases Review 2 still grinding on. How's Bishop Paul taking it? he wonders. He'll understand why Matt was obliged to log this. Well, he ought to. If Paul doesn't get it by now, he needs to pull the old finger out and get himself some safeguarding training pronto. Can't have retired bishops rattling around still not up to speed on current good practice.

But Freddie. Ah, the thought of Freddie always feels like a misstep on a slippery rooftop. Matt's heard nothing. Let Freddie be all right. Let him be getting the support he needs.

Life plods on. How can we be in the last quarter of 2021 already? Another of those subliminal memos has gone round, this time saying we can abandon face-coverings in shops and on public transport. The last valiant mask-wearers feel increasingly like the kind of pedant who waits for the green man before crossing a deserted street. Infection rates haven't shot up exponentially, so perhaps it doesn't matter. We've been double-jabbed, mostly. Some have had boosters. We're winning. Fingers crossed. True, there are thirty to forty thousand new cases a day, but fewer than fifty deaths. Of course, fifty deaths is fifty tragedies, but back in January the figure was up around eighteen hundred.

So ye-e-es, it looks as though we're winning this long battle, we tell ourselves in Lindfordshire. Touch wood. We are winning our generation's equivalent of the Second World War. But will there ever be a day when COVID surrenders, and we can take to the streets to celebrate? Or will it be winter boosters for the rest of our days in a world that's learnt to accommodate the virus? What if COVID is just the first in a series of pandemics, and 2020 was the start of the Hundred Years' War? We block the thought out, but even as we do, we get faint echoes of February last year, when we watched them singing opera from balconies in locked-down Italy, and still thought it wouldn't happen here. Do we feel a *Game of Thrones* chill? *Winter is coming . . .*

But for now, it's all mists and mellow fruitfulness across Lindfordshire. September weather. August, even. No frost yet, and too hot for a coat in October! Forget winter – summer is coming! We're looking the wrong way, fighting the wrong war. Just ask Leah Rogers. She was bending Davy Short's ear only last week. This is literally humanity's last chance to keep global warming to under 1.5 degrees. Protesters glue themselves to motorways, and everyone gets pissed off. Yeah, what about if the same motorways get closed through catastrophic flooding? Nobody's arresting the fossil fuel lobbyists, are they? The state of people!

Leah is in double Maths right now. How's she meant to focus on past fucking papers when the world's literally on fire? *George is planning a holiday for seven people for five days. Here are the costs for each person. Flights: £150. Hotel: £60 each day. What is the total cost of the holiday?* 'George is a terrible person and an irresponsible global citizen. He obviously has an unsustainable lifestyle if he is flying seven people abroad on a five-day holiday,' writes Leah. 'He should investigate holidays in the UK. I refuse to calculate the financial costs of George's immoral trip. The costs to the environment if humanity fails to meet the 1.5 degree Celsius target are as follows: droughts, wildfires, extreme rainfall events, floods, landslides, rising sea levels, displacement of people, mass migration, hunger, homelessness, human suffering on an unimaginable scale.'

Leah grinds her teeth as her eco bamboo pen gouges the practice paper. How long will everyone COMPLETELY MISS THE POINT? She still hasn't forgotten the guy in the BMW two years ago, who screamed at her to fuck off when she was blocking the road in Lindford, because it was making him late for work. Boo hoo, you're late for work. How about being LATE TO SAVE THE WORLD?

She puts her pen down and stares out of the window. The cherry tree still has all its fiery leaves. The signs are everywhere. Yeah, that's right, sheeple. Getting harder to pretend, isn't it? Too many extreme weather events in your own back yard, that's why. Denial is morphing into delay – the exact same tactics the tobacco companies used. Leah's packing her bag ready for COP26 in Glasgow at the end of the month. She'll be there with Kai, even if Mum and Dad flat out ban her. This, *this* is our generation's war. Wake up!

'Leah Rogers, if you've finished already, why not check over your answers?'

'Did you know marigolds are also known as "flowers of the dead", Ellis?' Paver has just arranged a bunch of twelve in a stoneware jug and set it exactly in the middle of the kitchen table. 'As in *flor de muerto* in the Day of the Dead festivities in Mexico? People put either real or paper marigolds on crosses and graves and altars. Sometimes they lay whole marigold petal pathways leading up to the altar. Back when I was planning the October garden, I was all for doing that, making a pathway leading up to the chimney pot. Only then I couldn't, you know? Pull apart loads of flowers like that.'

'We probably wouldn't have enough anyway,' says Ellis. 'I love the orange against the blue Formica.'

'Me too. It sings, doesn't it? If you can say a colour combination sings, which I think you can. As in, each colour has its own note, a resonance, if you will, equivalent to a specific sound wavelength, and put together they make visual harmonies. But to my point, it seems counterintuitive that a flower that's so bright and cheerful is all about death in some cultures. In other cultures it's all about life, which to me makes more sense. I mean, how bright are they?'

The flowers seem to emit fiery light in the kitchen as the cousins stand contemplating.

'They literally shine,' says Paver. 'Like when you're little and a grown-up puts a buttercup under your chin to see if you like butter. So marigolds as birth flowers symbolize fierce love, passion and creativity, which would be more aligned to life, not death.'

'Another both/and situation, then.'

'Sometimes I think everything is, Ellis.' Paver adjusts the full daylight spectrum lamp and sits back down at the table to continue work on the October book. 'I'm loving opals. I guess you know they're in a class of their own? As in, they're not crystals; they're comprised of tiny spheres of silica, and they form when silica-rich water seeps through cracks in the rock? Sometimes they fill up actual shapes, like for example crab claws, or plants, or wood?'

'Aha, like the petrified forest, you mean?' says Ellis. He actually knows a great deal more on this subject, but as always he's trying not to get his encyclopaedic know-all-ery over everything.

'The petrified forest – yeah. Have you been there? Me neither. I once had an opalized ammonite, but I don't know what happened to it.' Paver sighs. 'So there are two kinds of opal – well, there's actually loads, but to make things simple, let's say two kinds – common, and precious. Precious opals have "play of colour". I know, right? Like they play music in colour form, see above. Common opals, aka potch, are opaque and kind of boring in comparison, some say, but get this, Ellis: you can make doublet opals, where you stick a thin layer of precious opal on to a dark layer of potch, and the dark backing makes the play of colour brighter. You know where I'm going with this for the book, I guess.'

'Both/and?'

'Both/and,' agrees Paver. 'Plus patience. Did you know it takes five to six million years for a one-centimetre opal to form? We are so small, Ellis. Ever think that? I do. We are so, so small.'

Little Ladybird is asleep. It's mid-morning. Chloe is asleep too. She sat on the edge of the bed intending to put her shoes on, but then she lay down. Just for a moment. Neither of them will wake for two hours, at which point Chloe will rear up with a shriek. She'll have to feed and change Ladybird, then scramble the baby kit together and race off to her hair appointment, hoping she's remembered everything, that she hasn't left the baby on the drive, the front door open or a bosom hanging out. Oh, she used to be so organized!

Odd how peacefully Ladybird sleeps during the day, considering that for the last six weeks on the dot of 7 p.m. she's launched into a five-hour scream-athon. Her parents take shifts pacing and jiggling her in their arms, trying to find the magic position that will ease the racking pain. It's colic, poor mite. Chloe, Freddie and Ambrose have been spammed with unwanted advice and theories. Have they tried anti-colic drops? Baby massage? Cranial osteopathy? It's because she was premature. It's because Chloe has been eating onion and garlic. Their personal favourite is that infant colic is caused by parental stress. Yay. Closely followed by people saying, 'If it's any help, all mine had colic.' Thanks, but know what, guys? Nope. Not a help. Naturally, the Rules of Englishness forbid saying this aloud, but that hasn't stopped Freddie on occasion. Go Freddie.

But Ladybird is thriving. All the evidence points that way. She's putting on weight, she's outgrown her first set of sleep suits and vests. Those reusable nappies no longer look vast on her. Reusable nappies? My older readers may be picturing the drudgery of terry towelling squares soaking in buckets, of catastrophic leakages and those scary great nappy pins capable of puncturing a Zeppelin. You may relax. Nappy technology has come on in leaps and bounds. It's all cute fabrics with Velcro fastenings these days; double gussets and tri-fold organic inserts. Kind to skin, kind to the environment!

It's quiet in Chloe's little apartment. Just the soft breathing of mother and baby and the faint tick of the new window frames expanding in the October sun. A car goes by. There's a leaf blower bellowing down the road, but it won't wake Chloe. Round the back, the hens burble very gently in the coop as they scritch and scratch. All is silent in the former weed house. It's a relief to think there are no neighbours to be disturbed by a crying baby. For now, anyway. A *For Sale* sign went up last week. Viewers have been coming and going. If we look down from Chloe's window, we will see a magpie swooping down to land on the sign in a whirr of black and white wings. One for sorrow – but not to worry. There's probably another nearby. Joy is never that far off. Two sorrows or one joy, who can say? It's hard to tell where these things shade over into one another in the plague years we are trudging through.

The magpie is off. There it goes, over the rooftop, across the back garden where the hens burble, over the fence, across Miss Sherratt's chamomile lawn, to land on one of the fancy chimney pots of her Arts and Crafts mansion. The old weathervane swivels in the wind with the sound of a mournful donkey. Jack has yet to figure out a way of getting up to the pointy witch's hat rooftop to give it a drop of oil, so all night comes the soft rusty braying, like strings of mules in the distance.

All around Lindford and out across towns and villages, the blank round eyes of chimneys stare up at the sky. Thickets of tall chimneys on the Georgian terraces in Lindchester's lower town, fancy coroneted Victorian chimneys on the red brick rows, metal cowls on cottage chimneys, flashing as they turn. Trumpets raised heavenward in fanfare to the good old days of coal. For every dwelling a hearth, for every hearth a chimney, all across Lindfordshire. Remember the smell of a coal fire? Remember the coalman coming to deliver a load to your shed, your bunker? Why are those houses so black, Grandpa? Why are all the cathedral saints and martyrs dirty, their robes, the books they hold, the niches they stand in? Why is our past engrained with soot? What can wash away our stain?

Many miles away, just over the border of the Diocese of Lindchester, another *For Sale* sign has just gone up. It stands outside the little bolthole of the former Bishop of Lindchester, which I expect will be snapped up in no time by yet another young professional relocating to a beauty spot to work from home. How the pandemic is redrawing Britain. The interior of the cottage looks gorgeous in the estate agent's photos. There was no need to whip through with a coat of white emulsion. It has always looked perfect, like something from *Country Living*. Look – there are Paul and Susanna now, standing outside as the estate agent drives off. End of an era. They look at the sign tearfully, then go back inside. Smoke rises slowly from the cottage chimney. Coal smoke. The smell of the past. It rises vertically, until it slopes on the wind and sidles away.

It turns out that the Hendersons had always planned to put the house on the market and move down to the southwest to be near the grandchildren. Paul was never going to ask for permission to officiate in the diocese. I wish Susanna had explained this in that birthday card she sent to Jane back in June. Bishop Matt will be kicking himself when he finds out, I fear. It will plunge him back into turmoil. All this hassle and grief for nothing! (Is it for nothing?) His regret isn't for himself. Matt can plough on up to his axels in hassle and grief. Par for the course. But Freddie. That poor kid. Would it have been better to spare him? Take a hit on the outside chance of it all coming out later and making Matt's safeguarding record look dodgy?

These will be Matt's thoughts. But what of Freddie? Yes, the bottom did drop out of everything when the Diocesan Safeguarding Adviser got in touch and raked up the unhappy events of August 2013. But not in the way Matt anticipated. There was no meltdown and histrionics about betrayal, followed by a spiral of self-destruction. That was the default mode of a much younger Freddie. Matt is carrying around an outdated mental image of a troubled kid.

Freddie's first thought when the DSA called was, Shit! Now what have I done? Weirdly, it was a relief that it was just the old Paul thang, not some accusation about the girls' choir, parents complaining, some misreported banter he's forgotten even happened? Because, major *major* flashbacks to the time Marty and Leah dumped him in it? He knows how innocent things can get twisted, and next thing you're suspended, everyone's whispering, No smoke without fire; he must've done *something* inappropriate?

133

So, basically, relief?

Plus panic. He was all, RED ALERT! Close this down, close this down!

He'd stepped out into the garden to take the call. 'No problem, now's fine to talk . . . Yeah, that's correct. Him and Suze took me in . . . Yeah, driver, office help . . . That would be June 2012 . . . Uh-huh, that's correct. Till I moved to Barchester in August 2013 . . . Wow! Sorry, you know this how? . . . From Matt. OK. I see. Fine – we were "intimate" . . . Lemme think. Sooo, maybe over a coupla days, right at the end of my time there? That's literally *all* . . . What? . . . Oh God yeh, definitely. Totally consensual . . . No. No complaints . . . Yeah, sure I felt looked after. Matt was a star. Listen, I do not, and I mean really NOT, want to take this further? This is so not an issue for me. I am so not a victim? I've totally moved on, got my life on track, husband, baby daughter, you know? So can I ask you to please respect that and keep my name out of this?'

Man. He was shaking when he hung up. Deep breath, back inside.

'Everything all right, babe?'

'Yeah. Issue about an employment record . . . thang? From back in the day. All sorted.'

'You're sure? Happy to talk.'

'Nope. I officially declare everything's cool.'

The kitchen was silent. Dogs asleep in their basket. Clock ticking.

'OK.' Brose came over and kissed him goodbye. 'Everything's cool, then. Have a good day. See you at rehearsal.'

Freddie listened to Brose's footsteps walking off along the road. His heartrate was still crazy.

Whoa.

I mean, *whoa.* Did that ever feel like shoving the skeleton back in the closet and leaning on the door! Jesus. Scanning, scanning – any stray metatarsals lying around? So yeah, obviously in an ideal world you'd give it a proper burial (what would that even look like?), but so long as you're – what? Skeleton-aware? Long as you know not to open that particular cupboard in company, you can be self-accepting? Hey, it is what it is. You just gotta live with it. We've all done stuff we regret, no?

I'm not a victim. End of.

134

Except, turns out that wasn't end of. Nuh-uh.

Freddie is ruminating again today, a couple of weeks on, as he drives out to Rosemary Lodge to belt out his cheese repertoire for the oldies. Another rough night on the colic coalface. New record: screaming till 1 a.m. and poor Chloe crying too. Freddie's head's fuzzy with sleep deprivation. Probably why he gave himself a scare with the lat flow test back there. Lost the plot and got the letters backwards, thought it was a positive. Brose shaking his head. How many of these have you taken, babe? But in Freddie's defence, C for Covid and T for test would be logical, right? Right?

So yeah, he's been blanking the Paul thang out, la la la, so Brose and Chloe don't worry. But when he's by himself, he can hear another narrative running alongside the 'I'm not a victim' story. To be fair, this version has been there all along, but since the bombshell phone call, it keeps breaking the surface, it just keeps on coming up for air, and Freddie hears himself blaming Paul, thinking, Couldn't you see I was breaking up inside and all I needed was for you to hold me?

There's no drowning it, no matter how hard he shoves it back down and holds it under. It's not like this is a new thought even. I mean God, didn't he literally say this to Matt? Years back, that time Paul came out as so-called fucking 'same-sex attracted'? Freddie literally said something like: Paul was out of order – why did he do me when he knew my head was all over the place?

So what's the problem now? Why can't he sit comfortably with this narrative? As in: Paul Henderson, an older guy in a position of power and pastoral responsibility, took advantage of my vulnerability?

Gah.

Freddie knows why he can't give this head space. Because if he admits it's true for more than, like, thirty seconds, then suddenly it's not just one manageable skeleton in one manageable closet? It's an entire fucking loft rammed with skeletons. If he opens that trapdoor even one inch, the whole shit show of bones will come raining down on him and bury him alive.

Because won't he have to reframe *everything*? Like, where does it leave his pre-Brose career, back when he was living his best life of off-his-face non-stop partying and out-and-proud slutaciousness? Like, revelling in it, and don't anybody DARE slut-shame him? All

135

the clubs, the whole scene, drugs, lovers, casual partners, amazing fucks? Are they all of a sudden *not* lovers, partners, amazing fucks after all, but just a bunch of mainly older guys who used him when he was in a really bad place? Is *that* what's going on? Freddie can sense the ceiling above him groaning with the weight of whatever it is. Shit, there's something else; he's still missing something. What's he missing?

Oh man, if only he could offload all this, talk it through with someone? But the only person he ever confided in was Matt, and probably he shouldn't contact him while the process is ongoing? He can't talk to Brose. Just can't. Because Brose will be all, How come you're only telling me this now? Don't you trust me, babe? Shit, if he'd told him right at the start, this would be history now, just part of his neediness and emotional shit, like that box of bills and demands he handed over when Brose first did his tax? Now it's like, Oh yeah, so I forgot to mention this million pound debt?

He could talk to his former mentor, maybe? Andy gets him. Reads him like a fucking Batman comic. *I won't let you add me to the long list of father figures who have betrayed your trust.* But no, Freddie can't bear the thought of talking to someone else ahead of his husband. Plus he doesn't one hundred per cent trust the intergalactic emperor of head games to not enjoy the power of having one over Brose.

But here he is at Rosemary Lodge. His heart does a little flip. He's driven on autopilot. Anything could've happened. Gotta stop doing that. He's a dad now. He parks up and gets out, humming to warm his vocal cords up. Back you go in the closet, Skeletor. Deal with you later, dude. He heads for reception, hooking his mask behind his ears as he goes.

Ambrose knows. Of course he knows. He heard the rumours on day one in Lindchester. That particular skeleton never made it as far as the cupboard. It hung unofficially from a rather high gibbet, for the edification of the Close and the wider choral world. But time marches on. Familiarity has rendered it almost invisible.

Ambrose is between appointments. He's staring out of his office window across the accountancy firm's back garden. Being good at sums, emotional as well as financial, he's put two and two together.

His husband's white face after that phone call + Matt's suspension over a historic safeguarding issue = the ancient bishop-and-chauffeur scandal. And being as good at playing the long game as he is at sums, Ambrose is waiting. He's giving Freddie space to process this one himself.

The lawn below is silvered with rain. Drops blaze on all the shrubs. He remembers autumn mornings like this as a boy on the farm, crossing the sparkling garden to go and let the geese out. He opens the window a crack. An emergency siren wails in the distance, and he can hear someone mowing. There's a sycamore hedge at the end of the garden, and beyond that, a small park. There goes the guy with the mower, shadowy, just visible in tiny flashes of light as he walks to and fro, as though he's mowing in the life of the world to come. As Ambrose watches, other faint shapes cross the hidden park. A woman pushing a buggy. Someone walking a dog.

Here we go, he thinks. It's happening again. Depression approaching like a weather front. He sees the tiny cobwebs tremble in the corner of the window frame. It will pass, like it always does. But maybe this time he'll contact his GP before Freddie and Chloe stage an intervention. That would be good. For Ladybird's sake. For all their sakes. And maybe it's time to help Freddie out. To say, Talk to me, babe. You know there's nothing in this world that could ever make me stop loving you. Either talk to me or talk to Captain Fuckwit. I don't mind which. Ambrose watches as a slow arrow of vapour trail makes its way down the sky, falling in slow motion like some remote Icarus nobody cares about. And in the hidden park the shadows pass to and fro in the light. Life goes on in that other realm he can't reach right now. But this too shall pass.

Funnily enough, Jane has just thought the same thing as she enters Hair Works. It will pass. She now knows the ins and outs (as it were) of the safeguarding case. *Officially* knows, rather than just having a pretty good idea based on intuition and observation. Poor Freddie. Poor Paul? Yes, him too. And poor Matt. It will pass, this limbo of gossip and speculation – in all probability without her having to punch anyone, though she reserves the right to contemplate that possibility. The investigation will conclude, and then there may be another CDM against Matt to endure. After that, what say we jack it all in, and go and open an organic cut flower farm in New Zealand?

Jane wrenches her thoughts away from that bright vision, and the son she hasn't seen for over two years now. She's got her head tilted back over the sink, and her shoulders are covered with some kind of giant kitchen roll, in the absence of proper salon towels for COVID reasons. Star has begun to massage her scalp, and Jane is barely managing not to moan with pleasure. Her whole being wants to whimper with gratitude. This is just what I needed. Oh, *this* is what I needed! Jane hasn't yet finished thinking about Ellis's words: *No wonder kindness slays you.* She's been starving her poor self of tenderness for decades. Part of her wants to trump up a reason to go back to Gray's and have another conversation with Ellis. But she can't think how to engineer it.

What Jane doesn't know is that Star is working magic. Star does this every time she's washing a client's hair and unknotting their worried scalp for them. Love, love, love, she thinks. There you are, that's right, you are loved. May you know you're loved, may you know you're safe. Sometimes hair amazes her? It's got your DNA in it, all your ancestors, like microscopic fossils. Well, something like that, anyway. Star's not a biologist, ha ha! But a single strand of your hair will tell you where you come from, who your people were. It won't tell you everything, but the code is all there and you can try and read the message sent from all the ancestors who live in heaven now and are looking down and loving you. Every single hair could be a love letter. That's what it seems like to Star, anyway. Which is why it's so crazy, sweeping hair up from the salon floor and thinking, All those people, wow. It's in the Bible. Every hair on every head and every grain of sand. Something like that. She kind of wishes she could respect the clippings more, and not just put them in the bin. She wishes the birds would all come and carry the hair away to make their nests. All the birds of the air, sparrows, robins. She rinses off the conditioner, and pats Jane's wiry hair dry.

The next client will be Chloe. It's all been arranged. Chloe will enjoy a baby-free cut and finish. Jane will enjoy a little stealthy practice at playing grandma (in case that's useful one day) as she pushes Ladybird away in her buggy for an hour to have coffee with Dominic in Mister Bun the Baker's. I hope nobody undoes all Star's magic by making waggish jokes: You kept *that* quiet, Jane! But for now, all is perfect. Jane pushes the buggy through the little park, where the smell of fresh-mown grass fills the air. Little Ladybird has her eyes open, gazing at the sky, and all the golden and green leaves, the dog on a lead – Look! a doggie! What does a doggie say? She's gazing with her big dark eyes (she has her mum's eyes) and marvelling, marvelling, while Jane burbles a stream of tender doting nonsense, half to her poor starved self.

Meanwhile, Ellis is hunting through a drawer in his workshop. He's got one somewhere – a fossil with what looks like traces of iridescent mother of pearl clinging to the grooves and ridges. Ammolite, technically, rather than opal proper. This is probably the type of thing Paver is talking about. He searches through devil's toenails and shark teeth, fragments of mammoth tooth, and bivalves. Aha, there it is. He holds the fossil up and examines it. Beautiful. How long and random the process is, he thinks, that sorts out what survives of us. And what ends up precious.

NOVEMBER

Topaz and chrysanthemum

The November garden is indoors. Ellis and Paver planned ahead. I'm glad they did, for today – at the end of November – the country is blighted by weather worthy of St Stephen's Day. The rude wind's wild lament that you can hear in trees and chimney pots is Storm Arwen. Not Arwen in the book, who barely gets a narrative look-in; Arwen in the film, riding bareback, breakneck, to the Ford of Bruinen, with the Nazgûl on her tail. The gale has brought down big trees and power lines across Lindfordshire. Polythene sheets on new builds have been shredded to ribbons. Litter dances five storeys high on the Abernathy estate in Lindford. What chance would Paver's poor chrysanthemums have stood?

If we press our faces to the window of the craft barn at Gray's, we will see the flowers grouped there. Paver planted them in an assortment of vintage containers hunted out by Ellis: milk churns, old zinc pails, jerry cans and bathtubs. They stand there in the eerie blue stillness of this snowy dawn. You can just make out the shapes of spider chrysanthemums, pompons, anemone, quilled – all the varieties that were on offer in Short's glasshouse when Ellis and Paver drove across to choose. All the varieties – provided they came in white. Fixing on a single colour was Ellis's suggestion. It offered an escape from the multiverse of choice where Paver was trapped and panicking. This morning it's as though the craft barn window had stood open all night, and drifts of snow had blown in over the plants.

I am pleased to report that the display won the approval of Neil Ferguson himself (self-appointed taste tyrant for the Diocese of Lindchester) when he popped in before opening hours at the start of the month to collect some teak panelling. (What on earth does Neil need teak panelling for? That's for him to know and Ed to wonder.) Ellis's best guess is that the wood came originally from a gutted Victorian bank. Someone in the 60s or 70s must have known it was too good to sling out, but they had never got round to doing anything with it. Ellis rescued it from a skip outside a house in Martonbury. He took the lot away for a tenner, then charged Neil the proper reclaimed vintage price. I daresay the panels will join the parquet flooring in the vicarage garage until the last trumpet.

There was a tense moment, I can tell you, while Ellis and Paver waited for Neil's judgement on the November garden. They crossed from car park to barn with Neil talking sixteen to the dozen as usual. He declared himself not a fan of chrysanths, and shuddered at the thought of supermarket dyed monstrosities, or red ones dipped in glitter for Christmas. Ellis unlocked the door and deactivated the alarm. He flicked the light on.

'There. What do you think?' asked Ellis.

The three of them stood in silence, apart from the sound of Paver's knuckle-cracking. It was like that pounding wait in *Strictly*, just before the winner is announced. The scent of chrysanthemums hung like green light around them.

'Fair enough,' conceded Neil. 'That works. Understated. The combination of white blooms and dark foliage against the dull silver tones there. Very well. White, I'll allow, but coloured? I think not. Too garage forecourt for me.'

'Chrysanthemums are one of the four gentlemen,' whispered Paver. 'Aka the *junzi*.'

There was a moment of tense wonder, as though a robin had flown in and landed on a milk churn handle right in front of them.

'Plum blossom, orchid, bamboo, chrysanthemum. As seen in Chinese painting. Chrysanthemums are also renowned in the Double Ninth Festival, as in the ninth day of the ninth month, when Chinese people visit the graves of their ancestors or climb a high mountain and drink chrysanthemum liquor.'

Silence. Neil raised his eyebrows and turned to Ellis.

'OK bye.' Paver flitted out through the barn door and vanished.

'Well, that's *me* told,' said Neil.

'No, no, that's just Paver making conversation.'

'Hmph.' Neil leant forward and pinched a leaf. The fresh spiky odour intensified. He scowled. 'No disrespect, honourable gentleman, but you smell rank.'

'Really? I like it.' Ellis leant forward and sniffed. Out of the corner of his eye he saw the kitchen light going on and off, on and off. 'Reminds me of my grandad's potting shed.'

'Reminds me of cat's piss,' said Neil. 'Well, if you could give me a hand loading, I'll be out of your hair.'

Paver was pacing in the kitchen and counting, counting, when Ellis came in.

'Oh God, Ellis, was I spamming him with trivia? He didn't answer. Is he mad at me? Why can't I ever get this right, talking to people like a normal person?'

'Paver?' Ellis waited until his cousin looked at him, then he placed his hand on his chest. 'It's all fine.'

Paver took in a gulp of air and copied the gesture.

'OK? Good. Why don't I make us some tea?' He filled the old whistling kettle and set it on the hob. 'I'd say Neil arrived already mad.'

'Truly? That's a relief, Ellis. But what was he mad about?'

'No idea.' Interesting! And I'm a bit mad at *him*, Ellis noticed. That was Paver's first attempt at conversation with you, you pigdog, and you just stonewalled. 'Anyway, it's his shit, not yours.'

'How do you know?' Paver sat at the table, knees jiggling, jaw clenching, unclenching. 'How do you even know this stuff, Ellis? Because when I register negative feelings in the atmosphere, I'm like, it must be *my* shit. That's always my go-to explanation.'

'Well, sometimes it will be you,' said Ellis. 'But not on this occasion, I'd say.'

'Yes, but how do you *know*?' pleaded Paver.

Ellis put two enamel mugs on the table for Paver to move into the correct places. 'It's a question of gauging whether people's reactions seem proportionate, I suppose. If they don't, then there's probably more to the story.'

'OK, so I'll need to process that, Ellis. Time out?'

'Of course.'

Ellis dried the breakfast bowls and put them back on the shelf. He stared at the cross-stitched sampler rather than at Paver, who sat rocking, narrow arms around narrow torso. *Alice Greatrix, aged 12.* What was your story, Alice? There might be something about the New Orphan House in the county record office. Maybe he could ask Jane. If they ever went for another pint.

The kettle began its soft whiffling. He moved it off the heat. Slowly, Ellis dried the cutlery and put it in the drawer, six of each, spoons snug as sleeping lovers, knife tips and fork tines all level so Paver wouldn't freak out. Ellis went back over that pub visit last week. Something had been off. But what? It seemed to end on a wrong note. He couldn't tell whether he'd overdone the self-care advice. Jane was clearly a woman with her own shit. But it bordered on Ellis's shit and that seemed to be complicating things.

He called his thoughts back and refocused on the sampler. I wonder how long it took Alice to finish it? Maybe it was a chore. To Ellis's eye, it looked like something made with love, though. *All His jewels, precious jewels.* He could hear Neil's voice singing, but couldn't quite remember how the tune went. We all get polished, thought Ellis. There's no escape in this mill of life. Cut and endlessly tumbled.

He hung up the tea towel. Suddenly he remembered that 70s craze of pebble polishing. Hah, how jealous he was of Caroline Maxwell, who got a machine for Christmas and made chunky pendants! 'You don't need a machine,' Dad said. 'Just shake them in a tin of grit and water. It takes longer, but it does the job.'

Tumblestones. Tumblestones . . .

Paver was looking at him.

'Sorry. Did I say that out loud?'

'Yeah. Five times, Ellis. Could you maybe—'

'Tumblestones!'

'Thanks.' Paver relaxed. 'I'm all about even numbers, as you know, Ellis. I get that I can't control anything by counting, but my OCD says

146

it's got to be even numbers all the way so that the topaz will arrive in time for Coran's birthday?'

'I hope it will.'

'I went with blue topaz. Did you know that not all topaz is yellow? I didn't. But to your point: proportionality and there being more to the story. Here's the thing, Ellis. If your own reactions are mostly way off, if they're always *dis*proportionate, how can you gauge other people's?'

'You think your emotions are off?' Ellis warmed the teapot. 'I'd say they're spot on. Entirely proportionate to what you've been through.'

'You mean Corie? True, true – in that any- and everyone would find it traumatic to lose a loved one like that. Grief is just part of being human.'

Ellis held the milk jug over the table, waiting for Paver to indicate where it should go. Paver pointed. Ellis put down the jug. Paver made a minute adjustment.

'But to my point, Ellis, my entire life before I even met Coran, I had people telling me my reactions were off. You're overreacting. *That's* not scary! Taking a bus isn't scary, so why are you scared?'

'But for *you* it *is* scary,' said Ellis. 'So when everyone tells you it's *not* scary that just makes you doubt your own judgement. Maybe this is why you find it hard to read the atmosphere.' A tremor of Jane-related doubt quivered through him. Was he overdoing the self-help guru again?

'Yes, but nobody else thinks it's scary, Ellis.'

'Nobody else is you.'

'But I'm an outlier. Doesn't there need to be a consensus? About how things actually are?'

'Yes. But a consensus isn't fact. It's more a working theory.' Ellis sat down. 'If enough things don't fit, then it's back to the drawing board to rethink the theory. Not all topaz is yellow, for example.' He smiled. 'And that concludes today's lecture.'

'You're not lecturing, Ellis; you're trying to help. You don't have to self-deprecate.'

Ellis bowed his head. 'Fair point. Thanks.'

'So maybe the story I don't know is that Neil associates chrysanthe-mums with funerals? Maybe someone died.'

147

'Maybe. But we don't know what's going on in Neil's head, remember.' Any more than we know what's going on in Jane Rossiter's head.

'True, true. So probably you shouldn't second-guess other people's story and put that story on them, because it might only be *your* story, not theirs?'

'Wise words.' Ellis poured some tea for them both.

'Thanks. Because it can be so damaging, you know? Like when people are convinced they know you're one thing – a boy, say – when deep down, you've always known that's just not true, you're something else, but who can say what? I mean, it's not like you're a girl either.' Paver sighed. 'But people just lay their biological narrative across you regardless.'

Ellis sighed too. 'Don't they just!' He raised his tea. 'But here we are.'

'Here we are, Ellis.' They chinked their mugs together. 'Here we are.'

Yes, here we all are, with our harps still hanging in the willows by the waters of COVID. A year ago, it would have broken our spirits to know we would still be in exile; that we would still not be back to normal despite restrictions being lifted and everyone getting boosters. Wander with me through the streets of Lindfordshire on a weekday afternoon and you'll see a sad emptiness where once there was bustle. Shuttered shop fronts. Debenhams boarded up. Streets of little eateries and vape shops and hair salons. How are they still in business? Where are the people?

But what *is* normal any more? November never used to be this beautiful, with sweet peas and roses still blooming, and postmen in shorts. Where are the chilblains and frosty windows of yesteryear? It's taken Storm Arwen to strip the leaves from the trees.

The clocks have gone back. The days draw in and the Christmas lights have been switched on in Lindford. It's a year since that second lockdown; the one that was meant to save Christmas. The Eleventh Session of General Synod has happened. It was the inauguration of a whole new Synod this time, postponed from last year, with the Earl of Wessex standing in for Her Majesty. In the run-up there were the inevitable schemings and manoeuvrings, of course. Colours were nailed to a variety of masts in statements and at hustings, and there was a high turnover and many first-time members. This prompted much Googling of 'convocation robes' and ironing of tabs. Chloe did not stand. Father Dominic was duly re-elected under the rainbow flag and declared himself appropriately #humbled on social media. You may check the diocesan website to see who the other Lindchester reps are, and gauge for yourselves the extent to which the precious ointment of unity is likely to run down Aaron's beard even unto the hem of his garment.

We wish Synod well as it sails the choppy sea of love and faith in battalions of small opposing vessels, or attempts to save the parish without recourse to anything as vulgar as return on investment. When did Jesus ever talk about return on investment in his parables, I ask you? We now retract our authorial claws and leave church politics to other pens. If you want any more, you can sing it yourself.

All Saints' and All Souls' have been and gone. COP26 has been and gone too. Leah Rogers did not attend, for with a snicker into his hood the pale rider took a little detour past the door of the Rogers' house again to leave another calling card. Leah's last-minute lateral flow test came back positive. Her backpack and banner were standing in the hall! Their train tickets were bought! Kai was on his way! His aunty Julie in Glasgow had the beds made up ready in her spare room!

Poor Leah wept with rage and despair in isolation. Her chance to save the planet had gone. There would be no turning this clock back. Becky and Martin stood helpless outside her bedroom door. They promised to join the Lindford march on her behalf, bearing her banner proudly. But what could they say to make it right? There, there, don't worry? It'll be fine? What can any of us say to our children, our children's children, that would console them in their grief, or absolve our generation from guilt?

Saturday 27 November

You totally wont believe it but its literally THE CURSE OF THE JACKS ANTHEM STRIKES AGAIN!!! I opened my eyes this morning and knew befor I even put my glasses on. NB I have new glasses, mum went are you sure, aren't they a bit heavy for your face? Personally I think they are cool, they make me look like a serious musician and FYI Leah they are <u>not</u> cheugy. I get that she only said that because she was devasted over missing COP26 when she didn't even have any symptoms, but that is no excuse for being mean is it, when I literally went on the Lindford climate march and carried her banner with COP IS A COP-OUT when it was raining really hard? But I forgive her, I understand we are all just trying to be our best self. Plus it is illogical, how can I be cheugy, when I am objectively Gen Z??? PLUS plus people are not stupid if they have only just worked out that it is spelt Gen Z not jenzy!!! But like I said I forgive her, I do not require an apology we will draw a line under it.

LOL I totally forgot what I was writing for a bit there, I must of got carried away!!!

Sooooo ANYWAY before I put my glasses on or opened the curtains I could tell it had been snowing. Like the light was different? Normally I'm all YAY! SNOW! But this time I was oh no your kidding me, because it would be soooo ironical if Advent Carols tomorrow got snowed off just because we were premiering the new Lindchester Carol by Jacks. I mean obvs its not <u>because</u> of that, it is because of climate change and extreme weather events e.g. Storm Arwen. It is still snowing. It is quieter now but trust me it was scary in the night, I thought the roof would blow off, it was RED warning of wind which never happens.

But finger's crossed, it will stop snowing. The Lindchester carol was specially written for the girl's choir and dedicated to baby Ladybird by her godfather who is non other than Doctor Jacks himself, he will be taking our rehearsal tomorrow afternoon and conducting us in the service! Mr Hardman-May says you better CONCENTRATE girls and COUNT, because trust me, he is Professor Snape, he can be super sarcastic. Then he said but don't worry deep down he's like totally 100% Baymax. Then because the carol is super syncopated and tricky we played Big ~~Booty~~ Daddy (NB we have to call it big daddy now because Laura Jellico's parents complained to Mr Littlechild that big booty is inappropriate???!!! Laura was so mad, I heard her say to the other Jessica 'I mean it, I am SO divorcing my parents, can you believe how embarrassing they are?')

So anyway, long story short it is a clapping song where everyone gets a number and it goes Big Daddy, Big Daddy, Big Daddy (2 beat rest) OH YEAH (2 beat rest) Big Daddy! Then, Big Daddy Number 3!

Number 3 Number 5! ect ect. It gets faster and faster and if you make a mistake you have to go to the end and everyone points at you and goes Down you go, to the lowest of the low! To start with Mr Hardman-May is always Big Daddy and we all try to get him out so we can be Big Momma, I'm telling you we are all literally wetting ourselves. Some of the girls have a poor sense of rhythm I am sorry to report. A word to the wise, I have a good sense of ryhthm and do not make mistakes or not often. If you do make a mistake in practice you just put your hand up and move on, it is not a big deal Mr Hardman-May says.

Sound advice from Big Daddy. How is Freddie getting on? We left him standing on a metaphorical stepladder, holding the loft hatch shut against the skeletons of his chequered past. He couldn't figure out a way of putting his hand up to that mistake with his former boss without bringing an avalanche of bones raining down into the present. There was some aspect to this shit he still didn't *get.*

Part of him wanted to pick a massive fight with Brose, see if that flushed it out, this thing he could only ever see from the corner of his eye? Fighting was totally part of Freddie's language of love, but he reined it in, cos Brose had his own demons right now, mood indigo, the pandemic, politics, avian flu, LGBT rights and crazy ass bishops in Ghana (say *what*?) and migrants drowning in the Channel – plus a shedload of other stuff all probably amplified by the house. I mean, what kind of a house *was* this for a depressive? Fucking literally blue from top to bottom! Freddie couldn't even remember if Brose had signed off on the idea, or Freddie just went right on and painted it without consultation? Man, was he ever selfish? (So bite me, I'm selfish! Wanna fight?) Nobody to fight, just himself. He couldn't fight Chloe, cos aw, who could fight Chloe? Even over where to have the baptism – cathedral or Lindford Parish Church? So they kind of rumbled on, these pass-agg non-fights, like the fucking pandemic, like Ladybird's colic, just one long endless fucking angst. Or it felt like that. Looking ahead, it felt like this was never going to end now he was a dad – shit shit shit.

Freddie held his breath. He could feel the creaking overhead. Nobody move. What the fuck? Ladybird was, like, his whole life? No. No way. He was not going to let *that* be the thing?

Poor Freddie. Life is hard. We are tumblestones. That's why we will all shine in the end. Or, to put it more Anglicanly, 'many a blow and biting sculpture polished well those stones elect'. There's no exemption. Even Simeon Stylites had to engage with the village boys who brought his flatbread and goat's milk, to say nothing of the endless succession of pilgrims and sightseers climbing up his ladder to ask questions every blessed afternoon. All of us get churned in the long rumbling grit and grind of life – in the small private tumbling machine of the family, or in the bigger machines of workplace or institution; the grind of region against region, nation against nation. And not forgetting the special instrument of abrasion that is General Synod, which testifies to the sorry truth that sometimes the most biting blows are dealt us by our fellow pilgrims. And the sorrier truth that we too deal them out. Through ignorance, through weakness and through our own deliberate fault. 'Blessed city, heavenly Salem, vision dear of peace and love' indeed. Maybe it will look different on the other side. Maybe it will be worth the pain.

Paver's tumbled blue topaz arrived in time after all. This morning, in the eerie light of dawn, the topazes shine like pebbles of glacial ice. There are sixteen of them on the sill of the round window of the Old Barn's sleeping platform. Paver lies looking out across the garden. So it's your birthday, Corie. I got one birthstone for each month I knew you on this earth. I thought I'd be broken today, but strangely not? Maybe it's the snow. Isn't it awesome? This is the blue hour – you told me that. Like someone has put a blue filter on the world. Or like looking through one of those porthole windows in an aquarium, and there might be penguins or seals flying past, with air bubbles clinging to them like diamonds. Have you ever seen that?

Paver can almost feel Corie there, right alongside, lying with his chin propped on his arms, looking out too. He's saying, Anyone can fly in their right element, Paver. Penguins and seals only look comical and weird on land.

Jane has concluded that her element is not running. Or at any rate, it is not running with other people. For 'other people' read 'Matt'. Matt is still suspended, as you will know if you've tried emailing him during the last month and had a reply from his PA instead. The long weary safeguarding investigation continues. Jane reminded herself that the pain of being investigated was a mere airy nothing compared with the pain experienced by the myriad victims whose story had not been believed.

She said something of the sort to Ellis over a pint. 'But that doesn't invalidate your own suffering, Jane.' To which Jane did not reply, 'I KNOW!' Ellis queried her habit of derailing herself by rationalizing everything away, thus not attending to her own needs. To which Jane did not reply, 'Fuck off.' Because in all fairness, wasn't this precisely the kind of self-helpy guff she'd dished out to Elspeth over coffee that time? Clearly dishing it out was a different skill set from taking it, and not transferrable in Jane's case. Elspeth was more receptive – she'd cut her hours at Poundstretcher and gone to work at Flobbadob Flower Farm, as smiley and chirpy as Little Weed, according to Matt. Elspeth had taken to turning up at Lindford Parish Church as well, after Jane's suggestion. *And* going for coffee with the vicar! Obviously this was just Dommie being his lovely pastoral self, not Elspeth stealing Jane's gay best friend. Argh, what if Elspeth ended up living Jane's best life, while Jane carried on treadmilling away till she dropped dead at seventy, still telling herself to emigrate to New Zealand one day?

This was the grumpy train of thought going round Jane's head as she plodded 'companionably' round Martonbury Reservoir with her beloved a week ago. His suggestion had been: 'Let's make the most of the opportunity to do more together.' They ended up doing more together than Matt had anticipated; namely, tripping over and landing companionably in a deep muddy puddle. Words were exchanged. It was pointed out to Matt that as a former rugby player Jane knew how to fall, thus there was no need for him to grab the back of her shirt to save her when she stumbled. His misplaced gallantry not only prevented her from tucking and rolling, but had brought him down too.

No injuries, just bumps and bruises, and looking back, Jane was able to find their tumble hilarious. What was less amusing was her embarrassing meltdown in the car afterwards, when she couldn't stop sobbing, nor for the life of her work out what was wrong. No, Matt, it wasn't delayed shock! But she was crying too hard to yell this at him. It was *everything*. Cumulatively. It was all so hard, so sad.

The pandemic. The safeguarding bollocks. Missing Danny. Losing a student to suicide, the relentless slog of simply carrying on at work. And now this new variant scare. It was completely understandable. And yet she couldn't understand it.

But this morning – this seventh anniversary morning – something drifts into place. Matt has already snuck downstairs to rustle up breakfast in bed. There's a curious quality to the light. Jane gets up and opens the curtain. Snow! After a night of ferocious winds, it has settled down into this. This is a lull, Jane knows. Arwen hasn't finished yet. There's more on the way. But right now, the world is magical.

Downstairs she hears the muffled pop of a champagne cork. Coffee, buck's fizz and croissants. Is that what she actually wants? She's not sure. In a flash, she sees why she doesn't know what she wants. I want winter boots. I want more pocket money. I want straight hair. I want a Pippa doll like Elaine's.

I want doesn't get, Jackie.

But here's Matt coming up the stairs. Jane twitches the curtains shut, leaps back into bed and feigns sleep. In her half of the big IKEA wardrobe is her present to Matt (she remembered this year, thank God): a heron garden sculpture wearing a pair of socks – seven being copper and wool. The bedroom door opens. Would her life have panned out differently, she wonders, if her mum had said, just once, 'I know, darling. I know you want that, and I'm sorry we can't afford it. It's hard, it's really hard'? If her mum had been kind.

We will leave Jane and Matt to enjoy their breakfast and unwrap their presents and discover that they have hilariously bought one another the same thing. They now own a matching pair of copper herons to stand companionably beside the little pond constructed by Janet Hooty all those years before.

Come with me now and we'll cross the Diocese of Lindchester to join our other anniversary couple in the vicarage at Gayden Magna. Can you believe it's seven years since Ed and Neil got civil partnered (and *still* no possibility of getting married without Ed being rebuked and/or losing his permission to officiate)? The landscape passing below us is like a black and white film. White fields and roofs and roads, black tyre tracks and footprints, black railway lines and twigs and crows on the wing. Swoop down closer and notice the way the snow has high-lighted the windward side of everything till each detail stands out. We discern the individual shape of every holly or ivy leaf where the eye would normally see a generic mass of green. The detailed structure of different trees, their specific twig formation. Every broken bit of knackered rubbish in every skip 'selves – goes itself', like Hopkins' kingfishers. We spot the diamond pattern in chain-link fences. The ancient laid heritage of hedges becomes visible in their lowest sloping branches. We realize now that sheep are not truly white, but creamy yellow. How the snow has revealed the truth of things by paradoxically covering them. Like love, maybe; accomplishing what was purposed, never quite returning void, if you take the long view.

Close up, it's not all black and white. There are holly berries, Santa red, and bright hats and coats on the tobogganing and snowman-building children. Red brake lights as cars slither cautiously through the streets, blue lights on emergency vehicles. There are the high-vis jackets of workers already out to restore the fallen power lines and take a chainsaw to the trees that block country roads. Lindfordshire has got off lightly. Arwen trounces the 2018 Beast from the East three times over in Scotland, with catastrophic damage. A major incident is declared. Schools will be closed and tens of thousands will be without power for days to come.

Here's the Gayden Magna vicarage now, where we will encounter nothing as tacky as a pair of garden ornaments. That said, I have just realized that Neil has had Ed's favourite dog-chewed funeral shoes cast in copper at huge expense, and mounted on a wooden plaque with a little commemorative plate saying *Well done, good and faithful shoes, 2015–2021, R.I.P.* I withdraw my earlier statement.

You will see that the vicarage drive has already been cleared. Neil was out early, channelling his inner Wesley by shovelling all the snow he could with all the speed he could, tragically unaware that one of his anniversary gifts from Ed was an industrial supply of grit salt (because Ed wrongly thought this was their eighth anniversary). Salt that would have melted the snow away 'as wax melteth before the fire'! Neil was mightily pissed off to learn this when he appeared in the kitchen glowing with entire sanctification. Fortunately, he was mollified by his second present: a bronze-coloured cashmere turtleneck. Bronze was wrong, obviously, but by a stroke of pure luck it came under the heading of 'wool', thus qualifying as an appropriate seventh-anniversary gift after all.

Ed had been quietly confident this choice would prove accept-able because he had checked the label inside Neil's other cashmere sweaters and ordered the same thing in burnt orange. Still, it had been dizzying, the effrontery of deciding *all by himself* that something was luxe. Not *quite* as dizzying as the price tag, mind you, for a poor parson whose M&S V-necks last him a decade, but Ed was consoled by the thought that Neil had apparently never heard of vicuña wool.

If you look around the vicarage kitchen you might notice a small change. The red Gaggia coffee machine is still there, but the Wesley fridge magnet has vanished. This is the result of a compromise reached after negotiation. Ed has mastered the new coffee machine, and the Wesley magnet is now on the mini-fridge in Neil's unit at the Britannia Business Park, where he keeps his quinoa salad cool while he goes to the deli for a big greasy burrito instead.

I say negotiation. It was actually a row. It preceded Neil's trip to pick up the teak panelling. There was only time for the opening salvos of 'Why do you always/never?' but not for making up. Neil had to head out to Gray's with the matter unresolved. So Ellis was right: Neil had brought his bad temper with him that morning. Paver was also right, but Neil doesn't know that. Ed could probably hazard a guess. He's held Neil and soothed him when the night terrors strike. But as far as Neil's concerned, the past has 'Gone, gone, gone, gone . . . buried in the deepest sea, yes that's good enough for me'. He doesn't realize that the smell of chrysanths is in the nostrils of a six-year-old squatting outside a crem on a raw Glasgow morning beside a yellow floral tribute spelling *MAM*.

Tomorrow is Advent Sunday. We look from afar. The new candles stand ready in Advent rings across the diocese. Carols both new and old are brought out of the choral treasury. 'Go ye out to meet him' and say, Is it you? Is it really you at last? What must we do to inherit eternal life? Become like little children. How hard it is; how hard it is to enter the kingdom of heaven. Kindness always slays us. It feels like gentle hands untwisting us, and there inside is a littler version of ourselves. And then another, and another, until at last we are matryoshka-ed down into a tiny baby again. Kindness does this if we let it, and it kills.

The way it killed Freddie to see his dad holding Ladybird when he visited a fortnight ago. They were all in the kitchen trying to get a meal ready, but it was colic o'clock. Freddie took Ladybird through to the lounge, but Dad came after him, all: 'Give her to me, son. Trust me, I'm the baby whisperer.'

OK, Dad, whatever.

So there was Dad, walking up and down jiggling her, and Freddie could hear him going, 'Ssh-shush-shush, whoa-whoa-whoa; it's OK, Grandpa's here.' Freddie could one hundred per cent predict what would happen – Ladybird would fall asleep for, like, five minutes, because that was her pattern, but Dad would be all, Told you I'm the baby whisperer! Like, BOOM, out-dadded you there!

Yep, there you go. Ladybird was quietening down.

His dad caught his eye. 'I'm winning.'

Right. You always are. You always have to. Freddie said, 'She'll probably start up again.'

'I know. You were the same.'

'I had colic? Hmm. Did not know that.'

'Oh God, yes.' Ladybird tensed up again and screamed. 'Whoa-whoa-whoa. This was the only thing that worked. Holding you. Must've clocked up hours. Ssh-ssh-ssh, whoa-whoa-whoa.'

Freddie felt his mouth twisting. His chin was trembling. He turned to the piano and played a soft chord. Tried to get it together and say he'd go fix some cocktails? But a sob got out.

'Aw, what? You big girl's blouse. C'mere.' Dad made a scooping sweep with his arm. 'I'm serious. Come on, trouble.'

So Freddie blundered over and there they were. It was all, 'Ssh-ssh-ssh. I've got you. I've got you.'

God, you were such a shit dad. But at least you held me, I guess?

DECEMBER

Holly and turquoise

It's Advent 2021. All across the Diocese of Lindchester, traditionalists dust off their copies of *Carols for Choirs* ready for community singing or church services. Let us turn to number 39, 'The Holly and the Ivy'. You might be forgiven for wondering why it's not called 'The Holly and the Holly', given that the carol elides all mention of the ivy's attributes. Blossom, berry, prickle, bark, it's all about the holly. Of all the trees that are in the wood, the holly bears the crown.

There's another holly-and-ivy song you probably won't hear. It celebrates the fabled contest between the two trees. 'Holly standeth in the hall, fair to behold:/Ivy stands without the door; she is full sore a cold.' I can picture them singing it, the blokes in the warm tavern with their ale, trolling the womenfolk: 'Nay, Ivy, nay, it shall not be, I wis./ Let Holly have the mastery as the manner is.' Did the women come back with ripostes? Songs about the slow, patient endurance of the ivy, its twining growth and eventual throttling of its victim? We may never know. What we *do* know here in deepest Lindchester is that significant artistic work of a high standard always survives to become part of the canon, because the canon and its gatekeepers are neutral and our green and pleasant cultural playing field is level.

The cost of living rises this December. More energy companies go bust. Storm Barra brings high winds and heavy rain again. The new COVID variant has long since stowed away from South Africa into the UK and the white horse has been caracoling round all our major cities. Once again there's a risk that the NHS will be overwhelmed. Quite why, nearly two years into the pandemic, it still falls to the general public to pick up the slack for a decade of underfunding, we do not pretend to say. The word 'irreversible' undergoes a Humpty-Dumpty semantic shift from its July meaning. Whatever. It's just a word. Plan B is activated, with the threat of another lockdown cracking its knuckles in the background like a mob enforcer. You know the drill. Work from home where possible. Masks in shops, classrooms and on public transport. Regular lateral flow tests. COVID passes are required in night clubs and major sporting events. Heigh-ho the holly.

We wait in long queues for our boosters as reports emerge of rule-breaking Christmas parties in number 10 Downing Street last year. Far off in Westminster, pages are snatched from the Trump playbook. First, we deny any parties happened. Second, if parties did happen, they were work events, so no rules were broken. Third, we understand the public's anger and apologize if anyone feels that parties happened, but in our defence, nobody told us the rules. Fourth, we must wait for Sue Gray's inquiry findings to establish whether parties happened. Fifth, and most importantly, the government and the prime minister are doing an excellent job, so let's focus on the world-beating vaccination programme instead, while we wait for a bigger news story to eclipse this one.

Sing with me: Let posh boys have the mastery, as the custom is. Do you remember last December? All the loved ones we didn't meet. The children we tearfully told not to come home for Christmas. All the festive work gatherings that didn't happen. The carols we never sang. Those pared-down weddings and funerals. If we pause, we can hear it: the vast sea of sorrows, always breaking, breaking on the shores of the mind. But the rules don't apply to the holly, standing fair inside the Bullingdon Club. We remain outside, made a monkey of, full sore a cold. Perhaps the ivy will have the last word. The slow relentless throttling continues as each day more photos seep out, more rumours are leaked.

It's the 15th today. Jane and her mother are in a big old house, and further upstream (Jane somehow knows) the dam has burst. A great wall of white water is crashing towards them. They cling to one another. Her mother feels so small and frail. 'Well, Mum. Here we are,' says Jane.

Then Matt's there too. 'Cup of tea for you, Janey. I'm heading off to Short's.'

Jane clambers awake, fighting the dream off like tangled sheets. 'Thanks. See you tonight.'

'I'll cook. Shepherd's pie OK?'

'Perfect.' She checks her phone. Just after eight. Last week of term and her final day on campus. And possibly Matt's final week in the sin bin. The results of the investigation are due any time. Pray God there's no CDM waiting at the end of it.

She sips her tea. She'll head in mid-morning, as she only has an afternoon seminar with Level 6 students. Unless she tests positive. They'll all be in masks in the classroom. Will that be enough? Like everyone else she knows, she runs a swift calculation to see whether she'd be out of the woods in time for Christmas if she got infected by a student today. The sun rises golden, and the curtains glow.

It's another ordinary extraordinary day in December. It's both/and, like all our days. There's no teasing the good out from the bad. A day of first and of final breaths; of birthdays, weddings and funerals; of lottery wins and eviction notices. Some life events are planned and eagerly anticipated. Others (in the true spirit of Advent) come upon people unawares.

These are the early weeks of Omicron. It's not clear yet how to pronounce it. Those of my characters who studied New Testament Greek at theological college cling to their O-MIKE-ron pronunciation, while the rest dither between OMMY-cron and OH-me-cron. It's even less clear how serious this wave is going to be. Will it evade our immunity, get past the vaccine defences? Is Christmas safe? Nobody wants a repeat of last year's crushing disappointment. We hold off buying the turkey, and hang over our lateral flow tests, praying there won't be a second line. The pub and restaurant owners of Lindfordshire watch in dismay as their December bookings vanish. People are playing it safe. If they have that luxury.

New daily cases stand at 59,610 and they're rising. Omicron infections are doubling every two and a half days. Since the start of the pandemic, there have been 11 million recorded cases in the UK and over 146,000 deaths. How many more will this variant claim?

The early signs are that Omicron's more infectious but less deadly. We can only wait and see. This might just be a bump in the road. Even so, swathes of the Greek alphabet wait in reserve for further variants. Please don't tell us that the roadmap passes through more gridlocks; that we're not nearly there yet after all. The World Health Organization tells us to cancel our Christmas plans. We wait like voles in the grass when the hawk's shadow sweeps the hillside.

But today the sun is shining. Flocks of birds fling themselves up into the sky as the London train heads south. Ivy-lagged trees stand silhouetted on the rims of hills. Sheep lie in tussocked fields beneath pylons. The turfy bumps look like more sheep waiting to emerge, as though God has commanded the fields of Lindfordshire to bring forth livestock. Or perhaps this is resurrection morn, when the grave gives up its dead and all the sheep of Lindfordshire rise to be judged. Have you enjoyed the green pastures and still waters, dear sheep? Then enter into my bliss.

Have we enjoyed our life? A monstrous inflatable Santa is switched on and rears up jerkily beside the Tree Kings Christmas tree shop in Lindford. Ho ho ho. Children walk to school or wait at bus stops out in the sticks. Shop shutters rattle up and the homeless sleep on in their cardboard and duvet nests. A magpie pecks at the moss in the grooves of an ancient corrugated-iron shed.

All across Lindfordshire fallen trees have been chopped up and dragged away. Fresh sawdust powders the dark tracksides and woodland paths. Everywhere today holly leaves reflect the sky. You'd almost think they were blue if you didn't know better. Perhaps baby Ladybird thinks they are. She gazes wide-eyed at the big bushes beside the Linden, riding along in her sling when she's taken out for a walk. Her world brims with wonder. She's four months old now, and over the worst of her colic. This afternoon she will be meeting her godfather for the first time. Storm Arwen prevented him coming on Advent Sunday, but today both Andrew and Theo will be visiting.

Which is not a big deal obviously? All the same, Chloe and Freddie tear round screaming, and cleaning the entire house the minute Ladybird goes down for her first nap. The dogs are going crazy.

'Aaaaaaargh!' Chloe docks the cordless vacuum and starts furiously wiping the kitchen counter ready to bake a batch of Granny Gno's coffee cookies. 'Remind me why we're screaming?'

'Aaaargh! Mentors are coming?'

'Aaaaargh! The mentors!'

'Plus Brose isn't here to tell us to calm down? Listen, I'ma take out the recycling then shoot across to Short's for fresh flowers that look cool, not supermarket-y?'

'*I'll* do the recycling. Go, go, go!' she yells, as if this is a war movie and he's parachuting out of the plane. 'God speed!'

He races out and leaps in the car and guns the engine. As soon as he's on the road, he drives responsibly, because yeah yeah, *technically* Brose is correct – red lights and speed limits are not advisory? Plus he's a dad now. He sings as he drives. One of Ladybird's favourites: '*Funiculì funiculà*'! For all the screaming, Freddie is actually chill here, he's happy; he's just amped at the thought of Andy and Theo coming? Him and Chloe are just messing. He just loves, loves, *loves* her. Loves how this is all coming together, this crazy family, and Christmas is coming, and he's gonna buy his baby girl ALL THE THINGS. Aw, Ladybird's so smiley no and Brose is coming back from whatever Gulag he's got going on in his psyche.

And finally, finally, Freddie has located the missing piece in the whole 'loft full of skeletons' scenario. Turned out to be this: what if Ladybird, aged fourteen, starts acting out the way Freddie did? Going with any guy, letting them do whatever, drugs, self-harm. The whole self-destructive dangerous fucking works? Whoa! She makes one single step down that road and he's gonna be *distraught*. Even the thought of it literally *killed* him. God, he'd literally crack open his own ribcage, hide her away safe inside him right in his actual heart safe safe safe? His tears fell on to her little head as she slept on his chest.

Unfortunately/fortunately, Brose walked in the exact same moment Freddie got this worked out? He was all: 'Babe! What's wrong?' Turned out, doh, Brose had always known about the Paul thang. (Why's Freddie so dumb?) And he had this life-coachy advice, like, 'Babe, maybe you need to say to your fourteen-year-old self what you'd say to Ladybird if she was headed down that path?' The things he needed to hear his dad say, only he never did? You're loved. You're worthy of respect. You're acceptable. You're safe. How cliché was that? But oh, my sweet baby Jesus. Cue an avalanche of old skulls and bones bouncing round and smacking him on the head, with Brose holding him and going, 'I got you, Freddie, I got you'? But hey. That old loft's clear now.

Sometimes he thinks it's down to Miss B, up in heaven still praying for him? (Five years! How's that even possible?) His dad's all, 'You can come home to me if it doesn't work out.' Say *what*? 'Son, it's not fair on Ladybird; you've got two conflicting lifestyles in one household, children need stability.' Hello? Like, what, the two psycho older stepbrothers followed by acrimonious break-up you gave me – *that* stability? (Can the guy even hear himself?) Yeah well, no. Freddie smothers a laugh. To be fair, there is the *occasional* conflicting lifestyle moment. Gah! Memo to self: never let Chloe clean down the back of their sofa. Ohhh, *there's* my . .|. c – URTAIN RING! Thanks, I will just put this in the garage in the curtain ring box because yep, this here's definitely a curtain ring? Moving on. '*Jamme, jamme 'ncoppa, jamme jà*'!

We too will move on, reader. Over at Gray's, there's a choice of two gardens this month. Holly is not the only birth flower for December. Paperwhite narcissi is your other option. You will find the holly – a pretty, variegated variety – not standing in the hall, but in the far corner of the grounds, beyond the concrete pipe that forms the June garden. The paperwhites are in the reclamation barn. They stand on the windowsill growing on a bed of pebbles in an old glass aquarium. Ellis began forcing them back in October. It's part of what makes his Christmas – the scent of paperwhites combining with the smell of grated nutmeg as he mixes his mincemeat in the kitchen. But Paver was icked out by the sight of the wormy white roots, so Ellis relocated them. Admittedly they're less overwhelming in a bigger space. It's the indole – stink of death and desire. Ellis could explain the chemical formula, where it occurs in nature, why it smells both flowery and faecal, its role in the perfume industry. For him, knowledge always extends empathy and acceptance. But he knows that an info-dump will not persuade everyone to relish paperwhites.

There are paperwhites in the kitchen in Lindford, where the new/old Mr and Mrs Rogers sit holding hands across the table. They've just got back from the registry office. Today would have been their seventeenth wedding anniversary but for the seven-year hiatus of heartbreak. Later, they'll go to Lindford Parish Church for a blessing of their wedding vows with Mother Virginia, but before that they've booked a special afternoon tea at Turlham Hall, with a ridiculous five-tiered stand of scones, sandwiches and all the fripperies of the pastry chef's art. Leah has granted permission for a responsibly sourced, ideologically sound takeaway family meal tonight to celebrate the fact that she has not been forced to attend a cringe ceremony or made to wear a bridesmaid's dress. Right now, Becky and Martin are enjoying a couple of hours' downtime they built into the schedule in case Martin felt wiped out. Mostly he's fine, and today is a good day, but long COVID lingers on.

'We were so young,' says Martin.

'We were!'

Martin shakes his head. 'And I felt so grown up at the time.'

'Me too. Remember my mum's stand-off with the photographer?'

'I certainly do.' He picks up a Tesco receipt and begins to concertina it into a fan. 'I ended up keeping the album, by the way. You know, just putting it in the bin seemed wrong. Anyway, I thought one day the girls might want to see it.'

'Well, I'm not ready to look at it,' Becky says. 'Is that bad of me?'

'No, no, I wasn't suggesting we did.' He crumples the paper fan and tosses it towards the bin. It lands on the floor. They look at one another.

'Uh oh. You're OK with that?' asks Becky.

Martin shakes his head. 'No. But I haven't got the energy to put it in the bin.'

Becky gets up and with a flourish drops the paper in the recycling. 'There. A place for everything, and everything in its place.'

'Thanks. Sorry I'm so anal. I'm working on it.'

Becky reaches out to the paperwhites and slides one up out of the vase until it's standing three inches higher than the rest of the bunch. She grins at him.

'Noooo!' Martin grips his hands together. 'You're evil! Listen, what would you say to "young us" if you could?'

There's a long silence. She's scowling in concentration. 'Is it just me, or do these flowers smell of poo?'

'That's what you'd say?'

'Ha ha.' She stands and grabs the vase. 'I'm putting them in the hall.'

He waits. Outside he can hear someone with a leaf blower. Is the smell really bothering her, or has he said the wrong thing? He scans the conversation. His chest tightens. What if they're back to treading on eggshells, now they're officially married again?

Becky comes back and sits down. 'That's better. Right, so two years ago I would've screamed, "Don't do it, you idiot!"'

'Sorry, I shouldn't have—'

'It's fine, Martin. Anyway, I wouldn't have listened. That was always my life script – marriage, children, grandchildren, happily ever after.'

'And as good evangelicals, that was the only way we were going to get sex, of course.'

'Yeah, that felt like such a big deal. People did warn me, to be fair. Aren't you a bit young? Are you sure? But I would not be told. Ever.' She catches his eye. 'I *know* what you're thinking.'

'So Leah's not a changeling after all!'

Becky laughs. 'She's got half your DNA too, Martin. So anyway, now I'd maybe say something like, "I can see you're sure, but this is going to be hard. Really hard. Because Martin is not actually the solution to your problems. And it's not fair to act like he is."'

Martin squeezes her hand. For a moment they sit quietly. The smell of the banished paperwhites lingers. She's not asking what he would have said. He waits. Has she forgotten? If he tells her, it might sound like a rebuke, an accusation that she's self-absorbed. But what the heck.

'And I'd probably tell the young me to relax,' says Martin. '"Stop trying to solve everyone's problems and prove you're right about everything all the time."'

'There. What did I tell you? Half your DNA.'

'Yes, but Jess has half our DNA too, remember.' Good. Worrying about nothing. 'She must get her sweet nature from one of us. My money's on you.'

'Maybe she's the changeling.'

'Or maybe you're lovely, Becky? And kind? And sunshiny?'

'Maybe *you* are, Martin.'

They both pause, as though they're trying to identify a strange noise. Becky starts laughing again. He loves that sound. It softens the edges of things.

'What?' he asks.

'It's like playground insults. You're a good person. No, YOU'RE a good person!'

'YOUR MUM's a good person!'

Later, Martin will sneak down the hall to slide the rogue paperwhite back into its proper place, only to find that Becky has done this for him. But for now, we will leave them giggling helplessly at the kitchen table, trying to allocate their daughters' personality traits to one or the other of them. As though that were possible. As though there might be a big old DNA pie chart to explain the mystery of us. Pie indeed! We are all soup; a random beakerful of ancestor soup. That is all we know on earth and all we need to know. Jane is in the middle of voicing this kind of opinion. It's lunchtime, and she's FaceTiming her son Danny in New Zealand from her office in the Fergus Abernathy building. We join her in mid-disquisition.

'You've been suckered, kid. So you have a seventeen per cent chance of inheriting male pattern baldness? Fer feck's sake, Danny, do your research. It's not an exact science. There's a limited data base and all they can do is check for similarities and offer approximations.'

Danny is currently manifesting one hundred per cent of his dad's DNA by sitting there and letting her rant wash over him, like an elephant seal waiting for the tide to go back out.

'It's invented!' says Jane. 'Leaving aside the whole problematic question of using "ethnicity" as a euphemism for "race", these DNA testing companies artificially create geographical boundaries round clusters of people with genetic similarities when the picture is always much more nuanced. Communities mix and everything blurs all the time.'

He's still just sitting there, conserving his energy, with a 'Yes, Mother' thought-bubble floating over his head. Jane's betting that Danny's dad Mickey is somewhere out of shot doing yackety-yack hand motions.

'They're bastards,' Jane continues. 'Their ads cynically target the groups most likely to be desperate to know their roots – i.e. people descended from enslaved people. Did you think to check whether they store your DNA, by the way, and whether some rapacious global corporation now owns the information as part of their intellectual property? Great, thanks for that, Danny. They now have information about *my* DNA, which I never consented to!'

Mickey appears on her screen, leaning over the back of the sofa. He squeezes Danny's shoulder. 'Leave it, mate. Your mum's not interested, eh?' He grins at Jane.

Jane grins back. 'You can fuck off, Mickey Martin.'

'She doesn't care if you're twelve per cent West African,' says Mickey.

'You're *what*?' Jane catches herself. 'Whatever, but for the record that would mean one of your grandparents was African, Mickey.'

'Or yours, babe.'

'Well, that's clearly cobblers. I knew all my grandparents. White as Mother's Pride sliced bread. You're the one with, I quote, "mongrel genes".'

'Or you could both be, like, an eighth African?' suggests Danny.

'Or *you* could do five more tests with five different companies and get five completely different breakdowns,' says Jane. 'Better still, save your money and read your tea leaves. Why were you even doing a test anyway?'

Danny shrugs. 'My girlfriend's mum won it in a charity prize draw? They've all done theirs, so—'

'Whoa-whoa-whoa, back up, matey Joe. Girlfriend? What girlfriend? Is it serious? Quickly. I've got a seminar in two minutes.'

On the other side of Lindford, Chloe and Freddie contemplate the vase of flowers on the round IKEA kitchen table: holly, winter honeysuckle, dogwood stems, rosemary, amaryllis. Is this cool enough for Mr Dorian? His standards of taste make Neil's look bourgeois.

Behind them, the cooling rack and all the cookies crash to the floor. They whip round. Chloe shrieks. Cosmo and Alfie stare up at them as if a big dog did it and ran away.

'Oh my God, you bad boys! Basket! NOW!'

'Seven-minute rule!' shouts Freddie.

'It's seven *seconds*, dummy!'

'Whatever!' They frantically gather the cookies and heap them on a plate.

'Phew. I'll just blow the dog hairs off and dredge them in icing sugar,' says Chloe. 'Nobody will know.'

'Plus I guarantee he's eaten worse shit in his time,' says Freddie.

'Sorry what?'

'Oh God yeah, for sure. He's one hundred per cent the kind of dick where waitrons will spit in his starter? Or, you know, worse.'

'Ew! Please tell me you've never done that to anyone, Freddie.'

'I have never done that to anyone. Nope. Not me.'

Let us summon our energy for a final flight of 2021 across the diocese. We will launch ourselves from the empty heronry and fly over the alpaca enclosure towards the walled garden at Short's, where the Bishop of Barchester has just parked his wheelbarrow to take a call from the Diocesan Safeguarding Adviser. On we go, across the reservoir, where the wind sings for joy *whee! shee!* in the ropes of the little boats, and the masts tonkle like bells. There's the dual carriageway below us now, embankments festooned with old man's beard. See the lorries, lorries, lorries, overtaking one another ponderously on hills and pissing off the other road users. A silver Tesla takes the Lindford turn and follows the old Roman road to town. Is everything ready in the cerulean blue house?

There's another household in Lindfordshire where anxious preparations are taking place this afternoon. Today is Paver's birthday. Ellis has baked a cake. Paver's parents and brother Josh are coming for a party. And because that makes five, and five is problematic, Paver asked Ellis to invite Neil. Never one to stomp on someone else's hard-won social courage, Ellis has done this.

'Why are you taking the sampler down, Ellis?'

'I decided I'd prefer it in my bedroom.'

Silence.

Ellis sighs. 'Sorry. That's a lie.' He hangs the sampler back on its hook. 'Moment of weakness.'

'That's OK, Ellis. You're allowed that. Everyone is.'

'Thanks.' Ellis comes and sits at the table where Paver is working on the December book. He's careful not to disturb the mussel shells of paint or the ordered paintbrushes. 'I'm not sure I can face being ambushed by a conversation about the name coincidence in front of Neil. Sorry – that sounds like I don't trust your family to be sensitive.'

'I get that, Ellis. Josh will be cool, but Mum and Dad – sometimes they are, sometimes they're not. They're doing their best, I guess.'

'I know. We all are. So how's the book coming along?'

'Slowly. Here.' Paver looks up from the magnifying glass, puts the brush down and passes the tiny book across. 'Crazily, I'm doing a border of holly round each page, which is super-time-consuming I now realize, but I'm something of a completer/finisher as you know, Ellis, so I'm locked in. Hopefully I'll get it done by the end of the week.'

Ellis puts on his reading glasses and begins looking through the book. 'This is amazing, as ever. I like the fairy. And the owl.'

'Thanks. I'm going to add in the turquoise glass bird you gave me, which I totally love. You know, sometimes I get this weird feeling they're looking back at me while I paint them, and to them I'm just this humongous eye staring down, and that's like an intrusion on their privacy?'

'But you're looking with love.'

'Looking with love. I am, I am. Do they know I'm painting them? It's a question. Anyway, Ellis, you know your holly tree? Have you noticed how most of the leaves are variegated, as in dark with a pale border, but some are one hundred per cent pale? How does that even happen?'

'Something to do with recessive and dominant traits, maybe?'

'I love how you always do that, Ellis. I'm guessing you know a shed load of facts here, but you don't ever download it on to me when I'm just wondering out loud about stuff.'

'Well, I try not to,' says Ellis. He carefully turns another page in the book. The minuscule script comes into focus: *Turquoise is neither blue nor green; it combines the blue of the sky and the green of the earth. It represents protection, wisdom and enduring love.* 'Turquoise is probably my favourite colour. Especially when I see a kingfisher.'

'I know! It zips through your heart – if that makes sense?'

172

'Perfect sense.' He closes the book and hands it back. 'Well, I'd better ice your cake.'

Paver's hands start flapping. 'You remembered about the candles, Ellis? I'm hoping my family don't make this massive thing over my age. I get that it's traditional, the keys to the door, and the olden-days coming of age, all that, but . . .'

'Got it. Just one candle. Don't worry.'

'Thanks. I know it's dumb to get freaked out every other year, like: Oh no, I'm an odd number old, so bad stuff will happen. That theory would be totally falsifiable based off this year alone, when the shittest thing you can imagine – sorry, Ellis – aka your best friend taking his life, happened when I was an even number old, as in twenty?'

'Did you know the Chinese calculate birthdays differently? Your first birthday is the day you're born. Which means you're twenty-two today.'

'It does? Cool. Cool.' Paver nods. 'OK, so in a sense I'm twenty-two. Calming down now. Thanks. You're the best, Ellis. And to your point, I think you can give yourself permission to take the sampler down. You're entitled to protect yourself from people dead-naming or accidentally outing you. You get to set the boundaries for discussion about your choices and your body. That was something Corie taught me. I can't always hold on to that, Ellis, especially when my family keep asking what I'm going to do next: When are you going to finish your art degree? What's your plan? Will you come home for Christmas? Did you ever reach out to your other uni friends? You can't stay with Ellis for ever.'

'Well, you can as far as I'm concerned.'

'Thanks. I love you, Ellis. I feel seen, as in you see me, looking with love. You get that it's not a case of one linear heteronormative life route everyone has to follow; queer temporalities are outside of that, which can be joyous.'

'We can all use more joyous,' agrees Ellis.

As he spreads the cream cheese icing on the cake, he glances at the sampler. *Alice Greatrix, aged 12*. Maybe he'll leave it there. His own act of social courage. Let things unfold as they will. Ellis stands the single turquoise candle exactly in the centre of the cake. He found his way here alone thirty years ago with no maps, and dug himself in

173

deep. Drew up the drawbridge and lived unseen. *Thou God seest me.* A gigantic eye looking down with love? He shakes his head. He's glad for Paver's generation that they have a shared language – dead-name, queer temporalities. And company along the way. But even that's not always enough. Dear Coran, whom Ellis never met. All these beautiful lives, like glass birds in a sharp-edged shattering world. Or is that fair? Ellis looks at Paver, head bowed again over the little book. What looks fragile might turn out to be endlessly resilient, and bulletproof at the last.

It's dusk now. Ambrose looks out of his office window as he clears his desk. The light takes on an uncanny mauve tinge over the garden and hidden park. He's humming yesterday's anthem: 'Of one that is so fair and bright.' He hears the ghostly response echoing across the nave: '*Velut maris stella.*' He's been facing down old ghosts at last. Talking to Theo. Pulling up the floorboards on his family history. Great-great-grandfather, great-uncle, second cousin, every generation, someone. Men who knew about guns, and took that way out. The indigo DNA running in his veins; an underground stream breaking the surface here and there. He finally located it: the fatalistic fear that in his generation it will be him. And now something has turned, like the turning of the year. Imperceptible at first, but it makes all the difference. His days are beginning to lengthen. 'Darkest night, then comes the day.' He switches off his computer and heads for home.

Jane is heading home too. She's on the train enjoying the rail company's state-of-the-art ventilation technology, otherwise known as open windows. It's like being on the deck of a ferry. The carriage is fairly empty. She's picked a seat away from the young maskless couple, feet on seats, sodcasting some chat show on a phone.

She looks out at the back gardens of Lindford, the football stadium. A crane high over everything, with some Christmas lights on. That's that done, she thinks. My last teaching of 2021. God, a year ago we were still all online, with no vaccine, Christmas about to be cancelled and another lockdown looming. How did we survive?

She gets that spurt of dread: we didn't all survive. If I'd been teaching that final session in an actual seminar room, would I have spotted that Coran was so close to the edge? If I'd insisted they all put their cameras on in Teams? Stop! No way would she be pursuing Elspeth with this kind of question. Therefore she won't subject herself to it. She will follow Ellis's advice and try to be kind. To say something like: Dear Janey, this is so hard, but you did your best.

Nope. Toes still curling. She watches the houses with their twinkling Christmas trees, then fields, an empty paddock with half-dismantled jumps. Mauve light lies reflected in standing water along the strip of canal. I'm so rubbish at this kindness malarky. Ha! – there you go again, Jane. Always down on yourself. Oh great. Now I'm criticizing myself for criticizing myself. Jesus, it's like that story. What was it? *My Naughty Little Sister*, maybe. A little girl drew a picture of her classroom, then added a picture of her picture on the classroom wall. Jane remembers how much this bothered her as a child. Did the girl then have to draw a picture of her picture in the picture in the picture, getting never-endingly tinier, like corridors of reflection at Granny's dressing table when you angled the side mirrors? Mum just brushed her off when she asked, of course.

God, I hope I was kinder to Danny than she was to me! Yes, I was. I *was*. (Wasn't I?) Well, Danny seems to have turned out OK, whether by luck or good parenting, nature or nurture. She can safely tie a ribbon on him and hand him over to this girlfriend, Nell. Mickey Martin can do one, though, saying he'll take a DNA test if she will, and what's she scared of?

Jane's not scared. Now Mickey's not looking, she can admit to being curious. She's a historian, for God's sake. Show Jane a family with no skeletons in the closet and she'll show you a bunch of people in denial. In any given family, you probably don't have to go back more than a couple of generations to find cuckoos in the nest. Take Mum, for example. Dark wiry hair, when Aunty Betty and the rest of the Allsop clan were mostly fair-haired – what's going on there? Shame and scandal in the family?

According to her cousin Elaine, who's been interviewing older relatives before they pop their clogs and the stories are lost for ever, there are family legends about Romany blood on the Allsop side. Maybe that's where the dark hair comes from? And it might account for the minuscule percentage showing up as Southeast

Asian in Danny's results. But to imagine that any of her Allsop or Rossiter grandparents were African – no. Got to be Mickey's heritage. Either that, or one of her grannies had a bit on the side. Dammit, Danny! I wish you'd never taken that test. This is doing my head in.

She gets out her phone and WhatsApps Elaine:

Hi there. Hope all's well and you're dodging omicron. Just a quick one re your family tree research. Danny's had his DNA tested and it's come back with 12% African. Prob from his dad. Assuming there's no reason to think there's anything going on in our side of the family? Ta. Jane xx

The train goes through a tunnel. No signal. The open windows rattle. *There's light at the end of the tunnel.* That's what we were starting to think, and then bang – Omicron. More tunnel. On and on. The flickers of light nothing more than ghost stations.

The train bursts out at the other end. Jane's ears pop. She checks her phone:

Hi Jane. I'm on a Zoom call till 5.30. Can I call you after? Xxx

Jane's heart squeezes. Shit. There *is* something. Some bombshell Elaine doesn't want to put in a WhatsApp message. Her hand starts shaking.

OK. Thanks xx

The train is approaching Martonbury now. It's almost 4.30. An hour to wait. It hits her: what if it turns out Mum was mixed race, only she never knew? Or she *did* know, but never told me? Never told me that *I'm* mixed race!

The train stops. Jane gets off. She can hear Matt telling her to cool her jets. No point getting your knickers in a twist till you hear what Elaine's got to say. She walks down Station Road and heads for the cobbled square with the quaint butter market. Is any of this real? She passes the picturesque cottages, where tasteful wreaths hang on Farrow & Ball painted doors, and tree lights twinkle through leaded window panes. She might be a bishop's wife these days, but deep down she's still Jackie Rossiter, outside looking in.

This would make sense of it, wouldn't it? That feeling of being odd. Different. Mum said as much too, once. *I always knew I wasn't like the rest of my family.* Reading reading reading, the ladder up and out.

It's no good. Jane stops under a streetlight and gets her phone out again.

> **OK, guessing there's something. Any chance you can quickly give me the headlines? Ta xx**

The wind blows. Jane hears an owl calling somewhere in one of the big gardens. There's a sweet smell in the air. Some kind of winter-scented shrub.

Elaine is typing . . .

Jane grips her phone and starts walking. It vibrates. Shit! But it's just Matt.

> **All sorted. No CDM, no case to answer. Fizz in the fridge xxx**

She sends him a thumbs-up emoticon and carries on walking past the houses with their trees. All these families behind closed doors, all these secrets. Her heart pounds. There's the moon, almost full over the bank of trees. A fox slips across someone's drive. She checks again.

Elaine is typing . . .

The dream comes back. Holding her frail mother, with the wall of water heading towards them. *Well, Mum, here we are.* Her footsteps sound in the empty street. Her phone buzzes again. She leaps. It's Matt:

> **Everything OK Janey?**

She checks. Shit. She only sent him a middle finger.

> **Argh! Sorry. Meant to be this.**

She sends a thumbs-up and adds a heart. He sends a pulsing heart back.

> **Love you xxxxx**

The owl calls again.

Elaine is typing . . .
Elaine is typing . . .

Well, Matt loves her regardless. Whatever the secret is that her cousin is sweating over – writing and deleting, and rewriting – whatever is about to happen, it will be OK. It will be OK.

She walks on and the lights start flashing. Bugger. Migraine aura. Jane knows that when the message arrives, she won't be able to read it. Matt will have to read it for her.

'Darkest night, then comes the day.' Love is still holding things together.

JANUARY

Snowdrop and garnet

I t's 2022. Twenty is an even number. Twenty-two is an even number. The year sits right. Paver felt it happen at the stroke of midnight when the fireworks were going off. The calendar app went to Sat 1 and everything clicked into place.

And weirdly, January sits right too, it turns out. Obviously, January is month one, and one is OK, but you'd think *this* January, a year on from the day that punched a hole through your life, there'd be flashbacks and triggers everywhere. Because you know the anniversary date is getting closer and closer and there's literally nothing you can do about it. You'd expect that thought would be like a really hard-to-handle noise getting louder all the time, car alarm, clock ticking, the kind of thing NT people can just screen out, but which drives you crazy. Instead, this January's noise has been like the wind blowing. Sometimes it's sad in the trees, like waves on the seashore, but most times it's more like this vast *something* beyond everything – God, if you will – just gently stroking stuff, from the lowest moss up to the highest mountains, and breathing kindly on the world. That's how Paver experiences it, anyway.

And now the day has finally come and here's Paver, walking down the lane to Turlham Church! Would not have predicted *that*, for sure. But just letting the day go by would feel all wrong. And this afternoon Tay, Ben and Lovatt are coming over to Gray's and they'll have tea together, and celebrate Coran's life, but Paver's not thinking about that, not thinking about that. To Ellis's point, you've got to eat the stress elephant one bite at a time! To be fair, each mouthful is like snow, it melts away, generally stress melts on contact.

Church was Neil's suggestion. The wind's stroking the trees right now, and it's sunny. Paver's hand grips the two blue topaz pebbles, Corie's birthstone, which will be like an offering to the universe. You'll be OK. You did a dry run yesterday evening – Ellis's suggestion. Along the lane, in through the lychgate, up to the door, twist the big handle. It's all good. Today the door will open. Paver's channelling Ellis, talking gently, soothing, validating. You're allowed to feel what you feel.

There's that vanilla smell again, winter heliotrope (according to Ellis) growing all along the road edge. It's invasive, says Ellis, but who wouldn't want to be invaded by sweetness? Invaded by sweetness. That works, that works. Last night there were robins singing in the dark on all sides, in all the trees, till it was like walking through a robin a cappella competition, and the vanilla scent rolling and rising till you thought you were wading synaesthesiacally – is that even a word? – through mauve; you could swim in it, almost. Both auditory and olfactory sweetness, if you will. And then an owl called right above the lane *ke-wick, ke-wick*, and in the distance another one answered *hoo-hoo-hoo*. You hear owls all the time in Turlham, but you hardly ever see them. But this time – there! It took off silently. Paver saw its wings and the head, round like a baby animal's, as it flew over. And maybe the owl was looking down at Paver standing in the lane looking up? Cool thought. Night is always so intense. Like night's the full oil canvas reality and day is pale, a quick watercolour sketch to remind you of it.

There's the church now. Paver's heart jumps. In through the lychgate, up to the door. We got this. There are cars parked and lots of people, but don't worry, they're going into the parish rooms because it's Mums and Tots, so-called. Neil's explained everything. Neil knows, because his partner is the vicar. But Paver's heart is thumping all the same. Gravestones, too many to count, stretching away on both sides. Paver grips the birthstones tight. Snowdrops just coming out under the trees, like in the January garden. Paver let go of the idea of trying to grow carnations, just let it go, which was liberating, as per Ellis's motto: When in doubt, simplify.

Paver remembers Neil's voice: 'True, it's daunting first time. I'm telling you, I sat outside church in my car for forty minutes trying to grow a pair . . . No, there's no entry fee. You live in Turlham – it's your church, not a private club . . . You don't have to cross yourself . . . There's a service at twelve, but you'll probably have the place to yourself until eleven-thirty. Nobody's going to say, "And where d'you think *you're* going, pal?" If they do, you just say, "I've come to light a candle for a friend." Och, it'll be fine. Don't worry.'

Here's the porch again, the worn flagstones underfoot. There's the round-arched doorway, Norman, with the zigzag pattern Ellis said to look out for. Notices pinned to the board. Crooked! Not my problem, not my problem. Don't count them, but too late. Five. No no no no. Paver looks away, grasps the big round metal handle, twists. The heavy latch lifts with a clack and sure enough, when you push, the door slowly opens. In you go. Breathe. It's OK. There's nobody here. Paver closes the door gently, gently, but the clack of the latch still sounds like a gunshot. Paver winces. Silence closes over again. Nothing. Just the wind outside.

'I've come to light a candle for a friend,' Paver whispers.

Go down the centre, then the chapel is on the right-hand side. Paver tiptoes up the aisle and hesitates outside the chapel. Empty. Someone's already been here, though. There are flames flickering. One on each side of the wooden carving of a mother and child aka Mary and baby Jesus. Two smaller candles in the tiered stand, which has a name, but Paver doesn't know what. Everything here has a name, technical religious language. Paver smiles. Ellis will know even though he never goes to church, because Ellis is objectively Google.

Imagine if you *did* go to church though, and this was normal, not niche. Paver hasn't been much since that time in Infants when the vicar did a christening with a plastic baby doll in the . . . Paver wants to say font? But mainly that experience of church was about sitting on the floor rocking, because of the statue. You could literally see the nails going right into his hands and feet. Oh wow, all coming back – I really lost it. The school had to phone Mum. She did her best, but you could see her problem. Like, as an atheist having to whisper, 'It's OK, he came back to life, sweetheart.'

'He did?'

'Well, in the *story* he did.'

'So he's, like, magic?'

'Um, yes. In a way.' (Side-eye at the vicar.)

'So how come he didn't use his magic powers to escape?'

'I don't know, darling. That's just the story.'

The story is what the story is. You can't argue with the story. Like, there's no point asking why Harry didn't magic himself 20/20 vision so he wouldn't need glasses.

Outside, a car door slams. Voices. Let it just be kids super-excited for Mums and Tots. Don't let anyone come in! Paver gets a spurt of panic and starts counting. Chairs. Six. Three rows. But that's OK. Eighteen in total. Eighteen blue cushions to kneel on, tapestry with a white logo MU and lilies. Light's coming in through the window. Three panels! – but they make a whole window, just one. One is safe. Candles. Two by the statue. Two on the stand. OK.

Focus. I've come to light a candle for a friend. There's the metal box in the wall with the coin slot, just like Neil said. *Donations.* He's right, you can't pay with your phone. Paver posts in the pound coin from Ellis. It lands with a clash. And here's the box of white candles. Paver selects one, and that's when the problem leaps out. The minute this one's lit, there's going to be three candles.

Hey, we got this! (But have we?) The Gollum/Sméagol program launches in Paver's head. *OK, so you can light two.* But I don't have another pound! *It's a donation. They don't literally cost a pound, idiot.* I can't. *Who cares? Nobody will know.* It's stealing. *So come back later and pay!* Paver tries to channel Ellis again, to drown out the Gollum voice saying, *You're so lame! Why do you have to make a song and dance about everything?* You're allowed to feel what you're feeling, Paver. *Weirdo! Freak! Nobody likes you!*

And now someone's coming!

Paver sits quickly, head bowed, knee jiving away uncontrollably. Don't let them look at me, don't let them talk to me, oh God help me.

Paver sees the hem of a long black robe. Black shoes. It must be Neil's partner. Probably they've been in some church office or something the whole time. Paver can't look up. They're getting a candle. There's a faint hiss of the wick lighting and then the sound of the candle being fixed in the stand. After a long moment, there's a rustle of cloth and Paver knows the figure's crossing themself. Then they go. Paver feels the faintest of cool draughts as they pass, and breathes out a long sigh.

The third candle flickers. Paver wonders who it's for, what Neil's partner was praying about. World peace or the situation in Ukraine maybe. Problem solved, though. In a moment, Paver will light the one for Corie and scroll through the prayers Neil texted, and maybe say some of them.

Paver stares at the three candles. Then at the window. The wind outside is still sad and kind up in the tall trees and down in the small snowdrops. Then this weird thought occurs: Suppose everything is all one? Then everything would be OK. Wow! Paver almost laughs. That would be wild. You wouldn't have to endlessly count and count and count and straighten things and line them up and level them off the whole time. Hey, but wait – what if *everything's already counted*? Wow. Paver almost laughs again. Another cool thought. That's a Corie kind of thought. Wish so much he was here to think it.

Paver lights the candle and puts it on the stand, then scrolls through the prayers. 'Bring us, O Lord God, at our last awakening into the house and gate of heaven.' The word jumps out as if it's high-lighted all the way through them. *One* equal light. *One* equal music. *One* equal eternity.

The little candle stands there with the others. All four flames flicker in their different ways. Paver tiptoes to the window and places the topaz pebbles on the stone window ledge, exactly in the middle. One for Corie, one for Paver, leaving an even number back at home. They gleam pale aqua, glassy, sad like Arctic ice, which Paver knows is melting away so, so fast. There's still a hole punched right through Paver's life because Corie wasn't magic and he's not coming back – that's just not the story. Humanity could for sure use a bigger story. For sure. One big story, one equal eternity everywhere. Where maybe Corie already is. And where Paver *kind of* already is too?

The wind blows where it wills across the Diocese of Lindchester this January day. How I long to gather up all these little imagined lives in my story and show you everything, ransomed, healed, restored, forgiven. But all we have is twelve random days. We fly on our heron wings and alight wherever the kind wind blows us. Who can say any more what a novel looks like? I offer you an impossible bouquet. Twelve flowers from one equal reclamation yard where snowdrops and carnations, roses and daffodils all bloom together. Or else I offer you a string of twelve stones with the thread of passing time holding them together. All my jewels, precious jewels, my loved and my own. Sometimes I can't believe I made these characters up. They all come out of my head, and now they live in yours, as if they're real people, and we care about what happens to them. Even now I sense you clamouring to know what happened to Jane. What was Cousin Elaine typing?

You'd think by now the mysteries of Jane's family tree would be unlocked and your questions answered. Not so. Like Jane, we are still left contemplating that cut-in-half photograph from the lockdown album she made. Who was in the other half of the picture? Duh. Jane's biological father. Thanks for that, Mother dear. Thanks for never once mentioning that fact. Thanks for taking your secret to the grave.

When she finally spoke to Elaine, Jane learnt it was an open secret. It turned out that everyone in the family knew that Mum had returned home unexpectedly from her library job in Toxteth and married 'confirmed bachelor' Ray Rossiter smartish. Great. A lavender marriage? Now she felt like a complete idiot. She wished someone had mentioned all this. *We weren't sure you knew, Jane, and you never asked, so we didn't say anything.*

Obviously Jane instantly recalled that deleted email from a stranger in Liverpool way back in the first Zoom-and-Zumba lockdown. But can Jane find it? Can she bog roll. She's searched every which way through her work account. Presumably it's still languishing some-where on the Poundstretcher server, there to remain until Judgement Day, when the secrets of all inboxes are laid bare. Or when Sue Gray delivers her report on the Downing Street parties – whichever is sooner.

If you were feeling brave, dear reader, you might venture to suggest that Jane contacts Poundstretcher IT to see if they can help her retrieve it. However, you would be told roundly that there's no point. How can IT possibly find an email the title and sender of which she cannot remember? Nobody would be foolhardy enough to suggest that there's something funny going on in the fact that she can't remember; or puzzle aloud over the fact that she, a professional historian and researcher (married to an ex-copper with who knows what resources a mere phone call away!), is drawing a blank on this fairly straightforward bit of detective work.

Matt isn't foolhardy enough to raise all this, anyway. He knows Janey is going at her own pace, getting her head round the fact that the man she always thought was her dad turns out not to be, and that she's potentially got a whole other family she's never met. If she wants help, she'll ask for it. He did accidentally notice out of the corner of his eye that she's been searching the 2020 funeral and death notices in the *Liverpool Echo*. Probably hoping that if she sees the name it'll jog her memory.

Jane knows he's waiting patiently, reining in his mansplainy problem-solving skill set. It makes her want to punch him. And now, delightfully, she's forced to query whether this punch-happiness of hers is inherited from her biological father rather than Ray, lovely gentle Ray, her childhood champion and, let's be clear, *still her real dad*. What *else* has her biological father – who may or may not be mixed race – bequeathed her?

Jane has the faintest recollection that the woman who emailed – her putative half-sister – had an Irish surname. But if she's married, the surname tells Jane nothing, of course. She remembers the phrases 'reaching out' and 'these strange times'. But Jane's inner redactor has been so thorough that she's left herself with nothing useful to go on. Anyway, she's waiting to hear what Mickey's DNA test throws up.

Before doing what, pray?

Before tackling the work of reframing. Of interrogating what it might mean to discover that you have not in fact been a chippy working-class gal struggling your whole life on the iniquitously unlevel Oxbridge playing field. Instead, you've sailed through life illegitimately festooned with white privilege, deploying your bogus white swipe-y card to open the doors to power that would not open as easily for your (putative) Liverpool family.

Anyway, that's all on hold because it's probably Mickey's heritage, not hers, showing up in Danny's results. Elaine would've heard if that particular shame-and-scandal-in-the-family rumour was circulating, surely? Jane checked, and apparently, 'Nobody would've *dared* asked Aunty Eileen that, for God's sake! We were all terrified of her!'

Jane can't stop thinking of her mum and the shit choices she had back in 1960, pre the Abortion Act, and when the pill wasn't available to unmarried women. She's assuming her biological father was already married but he'd neglected to mention this. Jane can picture Mum's rage. I bet she burnt the other half of the photo. Ground out her fag on his cheating lying face, packed her bags and left without looking back. Cutting him out of her life in every possible way.

Did he ever wonder about me? Did he drive over from Liverpool and sit outside my school and wait to catch a glimpse? When did his wife and child (children?) find out? Or have they always known about me?

That oddly prophetic dream comes back in the wee small hours: Jane and Mum in a strange house with a wall of water bearing down on them, all the more vivid since news footage of the tsunami in Tonga. Jane can still feel how small and frail that old body felt in her arms. She feels a tenderness she never felt when her mother was alive. Did you spend your whole pregnancy scared of what I'd look like? Steeling yourself to protect me and face down the raised eyebrows, the 'touch of the tar brush' whispers. Ah, you poor old thing. No wonder you were always so hard, so closed down and sardonic. I ruined everything when I came along. Maybe your only remaining goal was to fire me from the trebuchet of academic success over your community's narrow walls, so I at least could escape.

Round and round go these thoughts and questions as Jane lies awake at 3 a.m. Sometimes Matt lies awake too, pretending to be asleep but ready to talk whenever she wants to. Outside, the owls call and the wind blows in the trees.

Jane is not the only one lying awake with doubts, discomforted, these January nights. Houses all across the Diocese of Lindfordshire sigh and weep. The cost of living rises at the fastest pace for thirty years. Hundreds struggle with the price of the weekly food shop. Can things be eked out, or will one more price hike spell ruin? Churches Together have opened a community grocery in Lindford where for £3 people can buy goods that would otherwise end up in supermarket bins. A small beacon of hope in the iniquitous absurdity of hungry people on the one hand and £60 Norfolk Bronze turkeys chucked in the trash on the other. How can this no-brainer be so hard to fix? Is the world drowned in sleep? How fragile the borders around comfort, where the principalities and powers of hostile market forces have been massing for decades. One redundancy, one illness, one broken washing machine and the invaders break through.

COVID hospitalizations doubled in two weeks at the start of the month, and Lindfordshire Hospital Trust joined the list of those forced to declare a critical incident because of staff shortages. It's the 19th today, and true, the worst of the Omicron wave seems to have passed. The temporary Plan B restrictions are set to end next week, but still there's no unclenching, no end to our doom-scrolling. The habit is hard-wired now. Current events splat on the mind's wind-screen, then slide away – Prince Andrew, the Djokovic/Australian Open saga. We can only eat this impossible winter elephant one mouthful at a time, scratching off each day on the prison walls of January. And all the time we watch numbly as Russian troops mass on the border of Ukraine. Sweet Spirit, comfort us.

Gratitude, thinks Father Wendy as she plods to Cardingforth Church with Pedro. Her spiritual director is right: gratitude is the answer. Well, gratitude and Wordle. She and Doug are hopelessly hooked! As she walks, Wendy tries to come up with a five-letter synonym for gratitude. (Thank? Not really. Credit?) Then she catches herself. Oh dear, oh dear! She can already see what her Lenten discipline is going to be this year. She tries to focus. What am I grateful for today? Well, for health and strength and daily bread. For Doug. For my sons and grandchildren. For a stipend and a roof over my head. For the fact that I'm living in a democracy, flawed though it is. For the NHS and the government's defeat in the House of Lords over the Police, Crime and Sentencing Bill. For Pedro.

'Oh Wendy!' she sighs. She can tell she's just grimly going through the motions and trying to tick the gratitude box. As though God's standing over her like a strict teacher saying: 'Nobody leaves until all the blessings have been counted!' It's just January, that's all. On top of almost two years of COVID. 'Oh, I've been so good for so long!'

a little voice inside her wails. Pedro limps along beside her as they approach the church. Lulu would have whimpered for Wendy's pain. But here we are, Pedro, here we are.

She could do with that sabbatical, postponed first by her cancer treatment, and again by the pandemic. Yes, she should revive those plans. It will give her something to look forward to. But even this feels like too much work. Come along, Wendy – gratitude! At least the sun's shining. Cardingforth didn't get flooded in the storms this year. She sees two rooks waddling like beadles on the lawn in front of the church. The first daffodil spikes are coming up already in the grass. Yes, the earth *is* charged with the grandeur of God. There *is* a dear sweetness deep down things – or is it freshness? Her brain feels fuzzy. She'll have to reread the poem when she gets home.

She goes into church and heads for the vestry. Pedro settles in his basket under the table. Dear Val, the churchwarden, is already there in the chancel getting things ready for the service. I'm just so weary, Wendy thinks. But probably everyone is. Probably that's what they need to hear her say at this lunchtime Eucharist, the dear faithful ones who come: it's very hard and it's very sad. But there's still a sweetness – or freshness – deep down things. Spring *will* come. And the bright wings of the Spirit are still brooding over everything.

It would surprise – and cheer – Father Wendy to learn that not everyone is tired. Some of her parishioners are raring to go. They're retired, cheery extroverts, who are triple- or quadruple-jabbed. The restrictions of COVID have meant lonely boredom and frustration. They are not plodding wearily through the days like Wendy. They have a spring in their step as they volunteer at charity shops, attend services, visit the elderly, run committees and rotas, sit on boards of this and that, organize events, sing in community choirs and dress up for long-postponed posh do's. They've endured a string of unplanned unwelcome sabbaticals, thank you very much. Now that the winter of COVID is almost over, they brim with life and gratitude. (Wordle answer: VERVE.)

This is true across the diocese. Miss Sherratt, for example, is on tip-top form. She's poised to resume her bustle of activity the minute Plan B regulations are discontinued. Tally-ho! She'll be back supporting the parish nurses on their stall in the covered market and saying a weekly rosary for them in church. She'll be volunteering at the community grocery and inviting people round for high tea at Sherratt Manor just as soon as it's deemed safe. In the meantime, there's plenty one can do via the telephone.

For some, the frustration has amounted to an infringement of their civil liberties. They have been in touch with the bishops at various points during the last eighteen months to tell them off for their lickspittle kowtowing to the powers that be and lack of strong Christian leadership. Matt, back at his desk now, is up to his axels in disgruntlement again. He reflects on the strange similarity to his time at Short's Cut Flower Farm. It's all about the transferrable skill of shit-shovelling. But at least he's not facing a CDM.

Far away, just over the border of the Diocese of Lindchester, a *Sold* sign has gone up outside the bolthole of the former Bishop of Lindchester. We commend Paul and Susanna Henderson to the wideness of God's mercy as they settle somewhere in the South West near their grandchildren. I assume his blue file has been updated to reflect the recent investigation and that everything from the summer of 2013 is now duly on record. He might ask for permission to officiate in his new diocese. But that lies beyond the scope of our narrative. I cannot tally up the nation's sparrow population or count the hair on every head.

But here's what I can do: I can tell you that Paver is not the only person lighting a candle for Coran today. Jane and Elspeth met earlier in the Lady Chapel of Lindford Parish Church with Father Dominic. They all lit candles, and Dominic said some prayers. This was at Elspeth's request. Jane went along with it because it would have felt churlish to refuse. Furthermore, she feels vaguely responsible for Elspeth's sudden religious phase. Argh! Jane has accidentally done the work of an evangelist!

Elspeth drove off to her afternoon shift at the flower farm, and Jane went back with Dominic for a bit of lunch at the vicarage. We will join them as they finish their Middle Eastern couscous and chicken salad.

'Pomegranate seeds are scary,' says Jane. 'Each crunch makes me think I've lost another filling. Can I give mine to Lady?'

'No!' But the dog pricks up her ears at the sound of her name and trots over to the kitchen table. 'Aw, sorry, Lady! Did the Wicked Witch get your hopes up?' Dominic pats her head. 'Basket!'

Lady trots back to her bed and lies down again.

'They look nice, I admit.' Jane shovels another mouthful in.

'Exactly!' cries Dominic. 'Like gems! I always—'

'The word "garnet" derives from the medieval Latin for seed, as in pomegranate seed,' interrupts Jane. 'Interestingly.'

'Thanks, Hermione. Talking of which, can you bear to help me with Mum's jewellery? I've decided to sell it and donate the money to the Alzheimer's Society, but I don't know where to start.'

'Happy to try. I know zip about jewellery, mind you.'

'Thanks. I'm gently starting the offloading business now, so I don't have it all to do when she dies.'

'Good plan. How's she doing?'

'Oh Jane! Can you believe it – she's caught COVID? There's been an outbreak in the home.'

'Bummer.'

'That's not as bad as it sounds. Apparently two cases constitute an outbreak. Anyway, she's symptom free so far.'

'Well, that's something. Can you still see her?'

'They arranged a window visit,' says Dominic. 'I stood there in the beastly wet drippy horrid yesterday afternoon, bellowing the Lord's Prayer through the crack in the window. She's bedbound now, but the carer assured me she could hear. She said amen, apparently.'

'Good. Does she like her bed jacket?'

Dominic flings his hands up. 'Who knows? She was wearing it, anyway. Thanks for finding her one.'

'You're welcome.'

Dominic gathers the plates and fills the kettle. 'Oh Janey, my photo stream keeps trolling me! Look!' He opens his iPad and shows her today's 'featured photos'. Mrs Todd beams out at her, modelling Dominic's 'More Tea Vicar' tea cosy as a hat at a parish pancake party in 2016. Dominic is gurning in the background with his frying pan and 'Our Lady of Guadeloupe' apron.

Jane laughs. 'You're both as mad as hatters, you know that?'

'Guilty as charged.' He laughs too. 'Her transition to dementia was a seamless one. Promise you'll come and visit me when I'm completely doolally?'

'I will, sweetums. And I'll source you a scrumptious bed jacket from Etsy too.' She squeezes his arm.

He puts a hand on hers and squeezes back. 'Are you doing OK, darling?'

'Yep.'

'Any progress with the detective work?'

'Nope. Just a whole bunch of questions. And a grudging sympathy for Mum. Surprisingly. In the sense that when Danny was on the way, there was no shame involved.' She eyes him. 'And I didn't have to compel you into a lavender marriage to save my reputation.'

Dominic crosses himself. '*Deo gratias*.'

She swats him. 'Come along then. Let's see the gewgaws. Then I need to get to my marking.'

There's a pause.

'Shit,' says Jane. 'It all came flooding back. That Turnitin Similarity Report.' She draws a long breath and blows it out slowly. 'OK. Interesting. So, not as doing as well as I thought.'

They sit in silence for a bit. Lady sighs in her basket by the French windows.

'This is always going to be shit,' says Jane. 'Isn't it?'

'Yes. It is,' agrees Dominic. 'Can't you take the rest of the afternoon off, darling?'

Freddie is visiting a different care home today for a mini-recital followed by a community singalong. There's a piano in the communal sitting room, but no accompanist, so he fires up his phone and syncs it with the manager's speaker, humming to keep his vocal cords warmed up. Man, breaks his heart sometimes, these care home gigs. Don't get him wrong, Luscombe Court is high end, but still, it can never have been, like, the plan, can it, to end up here? Probably everyone's plan is literally: I wanna die peacefully in my sleep in my own house, so la la la, not gonna think about it? Until suddenly, shit happens and you gotta think about it, and then it's too late to plan.

Freddie rolls his shoulders, does a couple of facial exercises. OK, so what are we doing today? Maybe it's an *An die Musik* kind of moment? Dark hours, for sure. Grey hours. Time to give his and Chloe's English translation a premier? He scans round. Some eye contact and smiles, but mainly heads lolling forward or back in the armchairs. Lot of dementia patients this afternoon, he's guessing, but hey, never ever prejudge it; anything can happen when you start singing. Literally?

The manager gives him a thumbs-up and he hits play. The piano chords thrum softly from the speaker. Freddie fills his lungs and begins to sing: 'Beloved art, when dark is all around me . . .'

Cool. Someone's humming along. His eye roams the sitting room until it lights on an old guy in the corner, sunk in blankets. The carers are grinning and biting their lips. Freddie sings on. The old head rises up, like a tortoise coming out of its shell, and the voice sings with him, in literal perfect German? All ri-i-ight, maestro!

Freddie crosses the room and squats in front of the chair and looks into the guy's face, because this is it, this is literally what the music is doing – transporting them to a better world? My. Actual. Heart? Because maybe fifty years from now, there'll be some other singer calling me back from a great dark distance into the light?

There are tears streaming down Freddie's face as the two of them sing together: '*Du holde Kunst, ich danke dir!* Beloved music, my thanks to you.'

After Evensong tonight, Freddie will relate this story and discover his fellow singer's name – Edwin Greatrix – and learn that he was a tenor lay clerk at Lindchester Cathedral in the 70s and 80s. His great-nephew Thomas was head chorister a few years back. Perhaps Edwin and Thomas are from the same Greatrix clan as the Alice who embroidered Ellis's sampler. I cannot say. That would require some genealogy work by a keen family historian to establish. Greatrix is a common Lindfordshire name, and it crops up nationally under various spellings: Gratrix, Greatrex, Greatorex. Alice Greatrix of Lindford New Orphanage may have married and dropped from view behind her husband's family name. Names shift and mutate. People up sticks and move on. How hard it is to know who we are and where we come from.

Anyway, what's the big deal about ancestry? We are all humans. Isn't that enough? We are all 99.9 per cent identical in our genetic make-up. Does that 0.01 per cent make so much difference? This was the rhetorical question posed by Jane to Danny's dad Mickey when they last FaceTimed. His reply: 'Yeah, and cucumbers are ninety-six per cent water. But you wouldn't want one up your backside, eh.'

In the end, Jane followed Dominic's advice and took the afternoon off. After half an hour of rummaging through Mrs Todd's jewellery box, it became clear that neither of them had a clue how much any of it was worth. Dominic had a funeral visit to do, so he turned the lot over to Jane to sort out, with the one stipulation that she choose a piece for herself to remember Mum by.

Jane walked home from the station with the jewellery box in an Aldi bag for life bumping along at her ankle. There was the *pat-pat-pat* of a basketball from a yard as she passed. Probably a child off school isolating. This term was an Omicron car crash. Jane had already clocked up twelve hours of cover for colleagues with COVID. The government seemed to have thrown up its hands and said, 'We give up. You're all going to get it.' This morning she was half hoping to see that second faint line so she could farm out her marking to someone else. No dice. Knowing her luck, she'd go down with it in Reading Week, which would put the kibosh on her and Matt's trip to the Isle of Wight.

Two years on and everything's still so shite!

Oh well. Over halfway through January now, with Blue Monday behind us for another year. She walked down her drive. There were masses of snowdrops and crocuses coming up among the first daffodil spikes. Thank you, previous Mrs Bishop of Barcup. Jane let herself in and put the bag down on the kitchen table. Right. Cup of tea, then marking.

Marking. The spectre of Turnitin reared up again. The wash of dread and guilt. Oh shit.

Jane drew another long breath and blew it out slowly again. OK. Let's do what the nice vicar says. Why don't we take this little stash across to Gray's and see whether Ellis can value and sell it? And have a nice coffee in the garden and hope that, like the PM, we get ambushed by a big fat wodge of cake while we're at it.

It's twilight now, at quarter to five. Ellis glances out of his workroom window. He can see that the kitchen lights are still on, where Paver is showing the January book to Coran's other friends. *In Ancient Rome, garnets offered protection in battle and safety on long journeys. Today, garnets stand for loyalty and unchanging affection.* They will be taking it in turns to look through the magnifying glass and spot Corie himself in his bowler hat, sitting under the snowdrops on the final page.

Ellis picks up the garnet bee brooch again from the box Jane brought, and angles the lamp at it. Late Victorian. The wings glint with dozens of small cut stones. Probably Bohemian. The thorax and abdomen are cabochons, glowing in the light like sucked boiled sweets. He turns it over. The catch is broken, but probably still worth a couple of hundred, plus a bit more to pay for a repair. Jane's apparently supposed to be choosing a piece for herself, but she seems set on making a donation. Paying it forward for when she's a mad old bat herself. Her words.

There are voices outside. Goodbyes. Paver's friends are leaving. It sounds as though this day that Ellis was dreading has treated Paver kindly. He lays the brooch down on the bench and goes to lock up for the night.

Before long the full moon will rise above Lindfordshire. It will shine through the stained-glass windows of Turlham Parish Church, lighting up the topaz pebbles. Robins are already singing as Ellis sets the alarm and crosses back to the lit-up kitchen. And all across the diocese the winter heliotrope breathes out sweetness. In every town and village, wintersweet, sweet box, mahonia, viburnum. Dark is all around us, but we are still invaded by sweetness.

FEBRUARY

Primrose and amethyst

Wild primroses emerge in the woods and hedgerows of Lindfordshire. Father Wendy was among the earliest to spot them, as she walked along the Linden with Pedro. Fragments of Cicely Mary Barker's verse tumbled from her lips. 'Something something "petals pale and clean".' She was too creaky to bend down and sniff, but she knew they would smell of 'every happy thing'. In gardens and municipal flowerbeds, their multicoloured cousins blaze flamenco-ruffled. Prime rose, the first flower of spring. Many a heart leaps to greet them. Longer days can't be far away now.

Miss Blatherwick loved primroses. She pointed them out to generations of choristers on nature walks in the decades when she was Matron at the chorister school. Every spring she'd call back her charges from their rampage along Lindchester's steep wooded banks. 'Notice, boys, that the petals are all heart shaped.' Poor little Freddie May, that boy pinball ricocheted between divorcing parents, always picked her a bunch. She accepted it with a tender smile, even though the picking of wildflowers was discouraged by the 90s.

Her ashes rest now in the far corner of the cathedral lawn near the old battlements, where an ancient copper beech spreads its branches. Primroses grow round her memorial stone. Freddie planted them five years ago, and they have spread, popping up between plaques nearby. Maybe the whole plot will be a field of primroses fifty years from now. This is where former residents of the Close, Chapter clergy and members of the choral foundation are entitled to have their ashes interred. Miss Blatherwick sleeps out her days till the general resurrection as she lived – in mixed company. Sheep and goat, wheat and tare. Impossible for mere mortals to tell the difference, as we stand here gazing across the field of stones.

Barbara Jean Blatherwick
1935–2016

This late February morning Freddie squats in front of her resting place. He can't kneel: the ground is waterlogged, although the sun's shining now at least. 'Pray for us, Miss B,' he whispers. 'Pray for us left behind in this shit-hole of a world. Man, you got out just in time.'

It's surreal. Primroses, sunshine, and here he's drenched with terror. And we thought 2016 was bad! Maybe for a moment he, like, forgets, but then the truth roars past like a truck through a puddle and soaks him again. Ukraine. There's this crucible of molten fear he's got to carry, trying to not drop it, to keep it level, stop it spilling over? Maybe it's not just him – maybe everyone's the same? The invasion jogged the entire political landscape, slopping every little crucible, and it's spilling out everywhere, toxic fear, burning everyone and everything. Like, this could finally be it? The nuclear option? Fuck. Suddenly that's not just a dumb phrase you say; it could literally be on the cards? Mariupol could be Hiroshima?

'Shit, Miss B, I can't do this, coz now I'm meant to be the grown-up? I mean, how am I meant to take the girls' rehearsal when I'm in bits? Going, "OK, ladeez, Walmisley in D Minor"? Trying to not transmit *Aaaargh, the world's on fire and we're all gonna die!* and freak the shit out of them?

'All this on the back of a global pandemic, Miss B. Two years wasted! Two whole years since things started dropping out of the diary? Career's still not back on track. Plus Brose has COVID,' he tells her. 'And *man*, is it ever lonely in the spare room! (If that's not TMI?) Chloe's over at her folks' with Ladybird and I miss my baby so much it *kills*? Testing negative so far, but what's the betting I go down with it just in time to balls up the half-term trip? Plus my dad's being a dick over the baptism? He's not coming if Mum and the quote Argy horse dealer unquote are invited? Asshole neighbours anonymously hating on us. I know I know I know, my shit's so small. I'm literally so privileged I have no idea?'

Freddie's mind flickers with footage. Kids sheltering in the underground. Like this is literally World War Two all over again – 'Which you remember, Miss B, I guess? You were evacuated. Yeah, you always got it – what it felt like to be suffocated and drowning with homesickness, and all the time your mum and dad are, like: "It's for your own good, son; we're doing this because we love you?" Say again? Like, exactly *how*? *How* is being abandoned good for me?' He shakes his head, as if this will shake away the images. Brose is right. Step away from the newsfeeds. Brose can handle it; he's always been able to, it's how he copes. Like, if he can only read everything and watch everything and listen to every podcast, he'll be across it and then nothing bad can happen to us?

But for Freddie, he only has to see the words 'all men between the ages of 18 and 60 must remain to fight', and boom, it's happening here? Suddenly Chloe's trying to leave the country with Ladybird, not just heading on over to the rellies till Brose tests negative again. Him and Brose are getting, like, three days' training then given a fucking machine gun? Shells are pounding Lindchester, the cathedral's bombed out, and God knows if he'll ever see his little girl again!

Miss B says nothing. Freddie stares at the primroses, their crinkly leaves, their heart-shaped petals, and tries to channel her, what she would've said. But to be fair, mostly she just sat and listened and loved him while he emoted, so . . .

On the other side of the Close a chainsaw is bellowing. Then comes the clattering gobble of the woodchipper. It's the tree surgeons dealing with the cedar in the palace garden. Freddie saw it when he passed. A huge chunk – omigod, like fully one third of the tree – has fallen across the lawn? Brought down by that crazy trio of storms last week: Dudley, Eunice and Franklin.

Man, he so shoulda been a tree surgeon. Awesome job. Monetizing those parkour skills. He'd be crushing it. That tree, though. Hundreds of years old, easily. Used to climb that bad boy back in the day to scare Suze, and hey, coz it was there? Used to look at the top of it from the palace roof, too, same height almost, see the birds landing on it at eye level while he was laid there stoned. Insane. You'd think a tree like that would outlive us all – it's always gonna be there. Suddenly Freddie remembers Miss B's apple tree that fell over symbolically right after the referendum. 'Hey, maybe I'll swing by later and look over your old fence, check if it's still there?'

The cathedral clock chimes the quarter. Gah! Knees are killing him. He stands and hobbles, shakes his legs out to unlock them. The wet ground mushes under his trainers. Jeez. 'Getting old, Miss B.' A bird starts singing in the copper beech. Song thrush. He knows this because of her. Man, all those 'nature walks' in the woods. 'Listen, boys! That's a song thrush.' Then reciting a poem for them – he wants to say Browning? But mostly they didn't listen, too busy playing Power Rangers or Pokémon round the trees.

He feels the crucible slop again in his chest: 'Ah, God, Miss B! All the guys in Ukraine! Grown up now and not playing any more, shit scared in the woods IRL with their literal fucking machine guns. One day you're in uni, the next . . . Anyway, gotta run.' He kisses his fingers and stretches his hand out over her resting place. 'Love you, Miss B.'

Freddie walks back round the Close to the Song School. The limpid phrases of the thrush follow, follow, follow, until the chainsaw drowns them out. Somehow, he feels calmer. Like when you sing the gloria after one of the 'WTF, God?' psalms. As in, what are you *playing* at? Arise, dude! What happened to setting Putin in slippery places and casting him down? You pour your heart out and no answer. Except the silence kind of *is* the answer and you sing the gloria into that, into the nothing, and the vast space of the cathedral absorbs it? Like it knows, it feels you, it gets it, and you are so gonna run out of psalm before it runs out of listening. Ha, like him emoting to Miss B back in the day.

Freddie punches in the door code for the Song School. Above him flutters a strand of blue and yellow bunting. *As it was in the beginning, is now, and ever shall be, world without end.* He signs in, points the electronic thermometer at his forehead, and records his temperature. Yesterday he asked the girls not to pretend-shoot themselves in the head any more, even though he was the one who started it way back. Not so funny right now. Probably there was never not a time when it felt like this, he thinks. Like the world's ending. Yeah, and probably all grown-ups down history everywhere have thought: 'Shit, how can *I* be the adult? I'm literally only six years old inside?'

Friday 25 February

You won't believe this but after all this time . . . I've got Covid!!! SMH. Don't worry I am feeling fine. I am isolating in my room, mum is bringing me food. So I did a test this morning as per usually (I do 2 per week) and lo and behold there was the legondary second line. I was NO!!! Leah looked and she went I bet you used orange juice (NB coke and orange juice make you get a positive test). I regret to inform you I yelled 'DID NOT, some of us actually LIKE school it will surprise you to learn, plus I was meant to be soloing this Sunday!!!' (I yelled because I was super disappointed, normally when she goes low I go high like Michele Obama). Obviously she yelled back 'DON'T YELL AT ME I WAS ONLY SAYING!' Then mum yelled WILL YOU TWO STOP YELLING and dad came in and went 'is the moon godess paying us a visit by any chance, I will get my flack jacket' so we all yelled at him to shut up but then we were laughing. When Leah was leaving for school she said 'hope your not too ill, sorry about your solo Jess, are we good?' and I went yeh we're good.

Finger's crossed it wont be to bad. My head is a bit achy but tbf that could be 'the moon godess' LOL. So I have to isolate and test every day till I get 2 negatives then I can go back to school god willing, but not in time for Sunday ☹. On the bright side next week is choral half term so I wont miss much. APART FROM THE PANCAKE PARTY!!! ☹☹☹ Dad said you are in good company Jess, the queen has covid! She got it from Prince Charles, I do not know where I got it, probs from choir. It is 'ripping through' the proverbial back row, Mr Bennet and the other Mr H-M have gone down with it, it is literally everywhere and next month restrictions end, it will be carnidge says mum. We are all so relieved dad has had his 4ᵗʰ jab but I am isolating from him, I would never forgive myself if I gave him covid again. For what its worth mum has a low opinion of this goverment. She said lucky Russia invaded Ukraine, that has diverted attention from partygate and Leah went you can't say that, and she went I just did.

OK so I just got a text off Ellie and she's positive too surprise surprise. We have vowed to use our time prophetably, we are super aware how fortunate we are to be living in England not Ukraine, it is Day 2 of invasion, it is all so sad and scary. So we will get our mum's to plant the sunflower seeds Mr Hardman-May gave us all yesterday, sunflowers are symbolical of Ukraine and of hope, we will keep them on our bedroom windowsills and do mindfullness meditations. I will then precede to revise my 'Rocky Mountain High' score. NB Mr H-M has given me some proffessional feedback, he says it is very promising but maybe think again about how it sits in the tenor voice (he is a tenor) atm he's going 'should I chest it or head it?' because of the whole passaggio deal? Plus he says he gets why the descant is super high but you don't want the trebles/sops thinking oh crap, here comes the high bit all through the entire whole thing so maybe transpose it down?

Obvs Ellie and me will do our homework and practice our instruments (clarinet ((me)) and violin ((her))) Then tonight we are both going to watch the movie Don't look Up because it's on Netflix not Amazon Prime. (Amazon Prime is a hard no from guess who.) It is a wake up call for humanity and everyone should watch it even if its depressing (says guess who). The ending is surprisingly moving and Christian by all accounts alegedly. This morning when we would of been at rehearsal me and Ellie are going to listen again to Nina Simone singing 'He's got the whole world in his hands'. We will sing it 'largo' like she does, the way Mr H-M had us singing it yesterday, it is hauntingly beautiful IMO, not allegro like when you sing it at Infants when you clap.

Bishop Matt hears Freddie and the girls singing as he passes the Song School on his way to William House. He's had to park on the palace drive today, because the diocese is having a couple of electric car-charging points installed in the staff car park.

'He's got the little bitsy baby in his hands.' These days Matt can't un-hear what Jane told him; how her son Danny always thought it was 'He's got the little bits of baby in his hands'. The plastic bunting rustles in the wind. Yup. All the broken bits of this poor world, thinks Matt. Good to remember God has it all in hand. Ultimately. Despite appearances. The sinner man, the gambling man, gambling with millions of lives. Matt shakes his head. Everyone's spooked, glued to the news, helplessly trying to help, praying, fundraising and whatnot. Mushroom clouds from Cold War childhoods popping up in the old imagination again. What a mess.

He's off to a sesh with the four archdeacons now, to discuss training for spotting the signs of spiritual abuse. Important stuff, but not what you'd call a mood-lifter. Probably won't escape getting his ear bent about this open letter on conversion therapy either. Matt's never been a huge fan of open letters. Not without a very clear agreement over how and where it will be published, and that no additional material's going to get bunged in without consultation.

He passes the deanery. More blue and yellow bunting flutters along the wall top. Matt's prepared to bet Dean Marion has already sourced a Ukraine flag for the cathedral pole. The lawn beside the cathedral is thick with crocuses. But before Matt can smile at the cheery sight, along comes another worry – his poor Janey, still swinging in the DNA wind, waiting to hear from Mickey. In Matt's view, Mickey's been a tad cavalier about Jane's feelings throughout. Treating the whole thing as a bit of a joke.

February is almost over now. Golf courses are closed. Everything's waterlogged. The fields of Lindfordshire can absorb no more. The people of Lindfordshire can absorb no more. And yet they must. Omicron rampages unchecked. Food costs rise and fuel bills are set to double. There are long queues at petrol pumps again as oil prices surge and people panic-buy in case the Russian invasion disrupts supply chains. War has now joined the other apocalyptic horses grazing the pleasant pastures of Lindfordshire and clopping virtually through its towns and villages. Yes, we know there has always been war somewhere. Invasions, atrocities. But this time the victims look like us. They could be us.

Fly with me over this poor storm-trashed landscape. Below us lie lakes of floodwater and fast-seething streams, sand-bagged streets and houses. Let us swoop down and see the low winter sunshine blinding off rainy roads. Blue wheelie bins lie on their sides in polite suburbs. All that scrupulous recycling, those cardboard sleeves pedantically peeled from organic yoghurt pots – all, all is scattered! It's like Lindford town centre on a Sunday morning. Domestic spending secrets are broadcast like knickers from a burst suitcase. Already the volunteers are mustering for the big clear-up with their bin liners and grab-and-grip tools. In the fields beyond, broken trees lie felled, their live wood demonstrating why doctors use the term 'green stick fracture'. Sunlit polythene tugs and flutters in hedges, snagged on thorns like scraps of luminescent plasma after an alien invasion. Oh, when will it be over, this season of storms?

Spring cranks up, regardless. Trains may be cancelled. There may be *Road Closed* signs and widespread travel chaos, but until further notice, spring will continue to operate a normal service. The cherry plum blossom is almost out, and look – catkins, pussy willow. Later, as he walks back round the Close, Freddie will see that buds are forming on Miss Blatherwick's heritage Lindfordshire pippin. Birds are singing. Robins, wrens, thrushes inscribe their musical calligraphy on the air, while from thickets comes the hasty scrawl of dunnock song. Rooks tumble and play round church spires.

Our fictional year is almost done, reader. Herons gather once more in the heronry by Shotton Hall Farm, where the foam-rimed Linden races and Freddie's alpacas scream horny songs at the little short-neck ladies in the field nearby. On every ledge in Lindfordshire male pigeons strut on little pink legs, turning in tight circles, bobbing and bowing to unimpressed females. The first buds burst on the hawthorn. And everywhere, primroses. Primroses like our photo stream, mocking us with memories of every happy thing.

It's almost Lent. Next Tuesday evening the deanery air will be thick with the COVID-breath of excited boy and girl choristers, even though it will be half-term. Gene decides to accentuate the positive (though this word has experienced a perverse semantic shift during the pandemic): not so much a health risk as an opportunity to don his *Silence of the Lambs* face mask. There may no longer be boarders at the cathedral school, but the deanery pancake party is so fixed in the choral calendar that – heavens to Betsy! – to omit it would be like Barchester abandoning the Buff Run. And nobody wants *that*. Well, apart from the po-faced safeguarding gestapo. What is the world coming to, wonders Gene, if a group of off-their-tits stark-naked men cannot innocently sprint round the Close at midnight any more? *Eheu fugaces*.

He looks out of the kitchen window and sees – talking of safe-guarding – Matt going past. The resurrected bishop/chauffeur brouhaha, about which Gene officially knows nothing, has apparently been put to bed. (Ooh, Matron.) The lid is back on that fermenting copper of Close scandal. Gene enjoys a slug of scandal gin as much as the next man, but he's relieved the story hasn't belatedly escaped into the tabloids or ended in discipline and defrocking. He never warmed to Mary Poppins, but Gene has always had a soft spot for that scamp Mr Hardman-May. And for old Buster Barcup, who was probably doing his best.

As are we all! Doing our best in a world of knaves, pettifoggers and tinpot tyrants. Gene sighs again, because here comes the beekeeper with her trailer, pulling into the deanery drive. She'll be making the necessary apiarist preparations on this saddest of mornings. Gene has bowed his acquiescence. He aired his views fully and frankly last week when the outrageous demand was first made. In Gene's opinion, Beatrix the Bedlamite ought to have exercised due diligence before enrolling little Anna Phylactic at a school in the shadow of a cathedral famed for its honey. Be that as it may, Marion temperately pointed out, to have three hives, each containing thirty thousand bees, right next to the school playground, might justifiably be a cause for maternal anxiety. Besides, it all pales into insignificance in the current context. Beloved, let us love. For God's sake, said Marion, let us try to love.

'Beekeeper's here,' calls Gene.

Marion comes through from her study. 'Thanks.'

'I know you are all godliness and equanimity, Deanissima,' says Gene. 'But it will stick eternally in my craw that the bedlamite has won.'

'Ah, but has she though?' asks the dean. 'Did she really want us to get rid of the bees? I think she was looking forward to months of energy-wasting nonsense by mounting a campaign and filling everyone's inbox with ten-page emails full of nebulous micro-queries.'

'That's her modus operandi, is it?'

'Yes. You should see the correspondence file the Head has already. It's attention she wants, not solutions.'

'Ooh, well in that case, do let me help you hone your message down to a single line: "The cathedral beehives have now been relocated outside the Close."'

'"Every blessing".'

Gene claps his hands. 'Brava! I take that to be a godly synonym for "and off you fuck, sad little person".'

For once, Marion does not bother to look back sternly at him as she goes out to meet the beekeeper. Gene's proposed solution – moving the hives to the palace garden – proved unviable. Apparently, you must move a beehive either three feet or three miles, otherwise the bees get lost and die. Another cherished notion bites the dust. All the fabled cleverness of bees – their satnav waggle dances and spatial map memory – can be stumped by a mere two-metre relocation of their home. And there goes eight happy years of cathedral beekeeping.

Oh, the art of losing things! Gene can out-lose the poet here. Lost first wife, lost house, lost country, lost continent. Lost pregnancy, lost chance of ever being a bishop's spouse – ah, those cabochon amethyst cufflinks he will never sport! Lost referendum, lost political hope. Two years lost to a global pandemic. And four years ago, why, he was a whisker away from losing his very life! What are three hives and ninety thousand bees?

He blows his nose. Tilly-vally. Not a disaster. Marion comes back in. They stand by the Aga with their arms round each other.

'I've left her to it. She's doing something with the frames,' says Marion. 'Making sure they don't move in transit.'

'Did you tell the bees what's in store?' he asks. 'You're supposed to notify them of significant events.'

'Yes. I've said my goodbyes,' she says.

'Me too.'

'Fortunately, I'll be at Evensong when they finally go.'

'Well, well. Never mind. We'll go and visit them at the flower farm in June, Deanissima,' says Gene. 'We must picture them living their best little bee lives carousing on nectar in the wildflower meadow.'

'We must.' She hugs him tighter. 'Listen, there's going to be a scheme to take in Ukrainian refugees. I'd like to register. If you're OK with that.'

He thinks of tanks rumbling down suburban streets. Keeperless hives in every sunflower field. 'Of course.'

The other Mr Hardman-May is at home feeling like shit. He's not feeling so shit that he can't get showered and dressed and work from home. He is an ox, remember. He too misses his baby. Misses her sunbeamy smiles and cheeky dimples, so ridiculously like her dad while simultaneously managing to look ridiculously like Chloe. He misses her head-banging dance in her high chair and getting a pea puree facial as he tries to feed her. Above all, he misses the way her presence fends off the dark. Freddie is not entirely right to think Ambrose can handle 24/7 doom-scrolling. It helps him if he can understand what's going on, for sure. That way at least he won't get blindsided. But today, he's admitted he needs to ration himself. He's got to, or he won't be able to keep his cosmic pessimism in check. He learnt back in 2016 not to lay any Armageddon forecasts on Freddie.

So he's at his desk, phone out of temptation's way in the bedroom. He's got his study window open. The first breath of spring is in the air. He can hear the hens, and the flutter of the rainbow flag they hoisted in response to that anonymous note about their 'lifestyle'. Chloe talked Freddie out of banging on every door in the street demanding to know who sent it. You've got to hand it to Chloe. She put the letter in a rainbow-glitter heart frame and stuck it on their gate. Result: lots of love and support from shocked neighbours and delivery guys. It still kills Freddie not to know who the perpetrators were. Ambrose smiles. He's waiting to see if there's a repeat before he lets on. The moral of that tale, people, is always check for hidden security cameras before posting hate through someone's letterbox. Ambrose is looking forward to testing negative so he can call round at number 39 with a carton of eggs and heap burning coals on their homophobic heads.

A car drives past. He can see Jack on a ladder in Tinkerbell's garden. Looks as though he's fixing the storm damage to the summer-house. Ambrose is amazed that thing's still standing. Jack'll be round to walk the dogs later. The dogs who – dude! – have totally not been illegally sleeping in the spare room with Freddie? Hmm. Ambrose strokes his chin. Would the world's shittest liar lie to me? The windchimes he bought in the first lockdown still ring like distant church bells. It should all be soothing, but his throat's raw, his head's thumping and he's jittery from newsfeed withdrawal. He's using work to distract himself.

Work, and Googling the regulations governing the demolition of semi-detached houses. Turns out it's legal. It doesn't even require consent of the neighbours you share a party wall with. Great. Ambrose is really hoping the guy booming into his phone just now in the garden next door – property developer by the sound of it – doesn't put in an offer on the old weed house. Another thing not to scare Hubby with.

The WhatsApp message from Mickey lands as Jane is speed-walking back to the station from her morning lecture, hoping to catch the 12.55 to Martonbury. She finished ten minutes early, because she didn't want to kill an hour in Lindford. And yes, she's aware she should have stayed and talked to the students about Ukraine. But dammit, it wasn't even her unit! Yet more cover, busking her way through a set of 'Commerce and Conflict' slides this time, because Elspeth has COVID now. Jane steps into the cycle lane to overtake a bunch of dawdling students and gets sworn at by a cyclist. Fair enough. Should've checked first. But you can fuck off too, matey, and WEAR A FUCKING HELMET.

That's when her phone buzzes. Mickey. Her heart does a caper. He's forwarding his DNA report. Afterwards, Jane will think of it as an out-of-body experience, watching herself filmed from above, skittering this way and that, bouncing off lamp posts and passers-by, with the *Benny Hill* theme tune playing. But in the live action moment, she's plunging down into that chasm between imagining something in advance and having it actually happen to her.

Looks like it's YOU who's a quarter W African, babe.

There's a shrugging emoji. Before she can absorb this, another message pings in. It's a screen grab from Danny's results, with a clumsy red arrow and exclamation marks: *Links to communities in Jamaica!!!!!*

Jane grabs for the fence, leans against it. So it *is* me! Shit fuck. Now what?

She rings Matt. It goes through to voicemail. Shit, that's right – back-to-back meetings. She rings Dom. He doesn't pick up either. She tries to remember what day it is. Maybe Dom's got a service? What time is it now? She stares at her watch, trying to decode it. Think. What time is it? Her whole arm is shaking. A quarter black! How can I not have known this about myself? Oh God, what am I going to do now?

Right. She walks briskly towards the station again. No, you won't make it. She wheels round and heads for Dom's church instead. OK.

Right. OK, this is fine. This is nothing to cry about. Communities in Jamaica. Mum's Toxteth job. OK, that fits. Falling into place. She sniffs back the tears. Smears them away with the back of her hand as she walks. Even if Dom's not there, she can sit quietly in the Lady Chapel and get her head round this. It's fine. Not a problem. A shock, that's all. She just needs a moment to process it. Work out what she's feeling.

Wait – it's Friday. Dom's day off. Maybe he'll be at home? She veers past the lychgate and heads down the vicarage drive under the lime trees. A bullfinch toots softly. She presses the doorbell, but there's no answer. Now what? Jane stands in the spring sunshine with literally not a clue. Then a car comes down the drive. Dom! Thank God. But it's not Dom. It's Madge, the parish nurse.

Ah, I like this development. I take this to be the right person at the right time. What a blessing in a world that currently seems to deliver a constant stream of the wrong people at the wrong time, pissing us off and eating into our COVID-depleted supplies of Christian charity. I'm optimistic that Madge will be a friendly sounding board for Jane's first bogglings over the DNA surprise WhatsApp has dished up.

Madge has just been to Costco for supplies for the parish pancake party, which will happen in the parish hall where ventilation is better, rather than the vicarage. Dominic hasn't *quite* accepted this yet, which is why Madge is delivering the stuff here. But she will talk sense into him. Failing that, she'll unleash Tinkerbell to spank him for his reckless attitude to Lindfordshire's current infection levels.

'Hi Jane. Looking for Dom? He's out visiting Mum,' says Madge. 'He'll be back any time now for lunch. Stay. Stay and join us. Come on, give me a hand with this lot and we'll put the kettle on.'

Jane stuffs her emotions down and carries in a box of pancake mix and bottles of Quicklemon Juice *Not from Concentrate*. 'Mrs Todd would skin you alive if she saw this.'

Madge just laughs.

Is that where my laugh comes from? Is it genetic? Do I have a Caribbean guffaw? Jane stands in the middle of Dom's kitchen with the box. Oh God, everything about her is up for grabs now!

'Um. You can put that down, Jane.'

'Sorry.' She parks it on the work surface.

'Everything OK? You look kind of dazed.'

Jane draws a deep breath. She essays the thought of confiding. Will she blub? Would that matter? Unclear. 'Hmm. Dazed. Yup. Just had a bit of a DNA bombshell go off on me. My son got tested before Christmas, which threw up some anomalies, so his dad got tested, and . . . well.' Jane shrugs like Mickey's emoji.

'Sheee-*it*.' Madge puts a hand on Jane's arm. 'Those tests. People don't think it through. They treat it like a party game and suddenly here come the family skeletons.'

'No no no, it's not *that*.' Jane laughs. 'God no, he's Danny's dad all right. It's *my* dad that's the surprise.'

'Oka-a-ay. Cup of tea?'

'Thanks.' Jane sits down.

Madge puts the kettle on. She sits opposite. They look at one another, until Jane looks away. She sighs and stares up at the ceiling in case the tears brim over.

'So.' Jane clears her throat. 'Interestingly, and somewhat to my surprise, Danny's dad's test results do not explain the anomaly in Danny's results, which is what I'd assumed. Therefore the explanation is, the logical . . . In short, it appears that around twenty-five per cent of my genetic heritage must be West African. With strong links to communities in Jamaica.' Jane blows out another long breath and looks at Madge.

Madge looks steadily back.

'So there we are.' Jane shrugs again.

Madge nods. 'Yeah, that counts as a bombshell. When did you find out?'

'Just now. My ex WhatsApped me.'

Madge rolls her eyes. 'In the middle of the working day. Nice one.'

'He lives in New Zealand. Never remembers the time difference.'

Dominic's cuckoo clock calls from his snug. *Ooh cock!* The kettle boils. Madge makes two mugs of tea. 'Milk and sugar?'

'Milk, please. I found out before Christmas that my dad wasn't my dad. That was bombshell number one. My cousin tells me the entire family knew. Might have been nice if someone had thought to mention it, but there we are. Bombshell number two is going to be news to everyone, though.'

Madge puts the mugs down and sits. 'Oka-a-ay.'

'Yeah. I checked with my cousin when Danny's results came through. Not a whisper on the family grapevine. Basically, everyone always said I looked like my mum, but with my dad's eyes. Except he's not my dad.' Shit.

'Of course he's your dad, Jane.'

'Thanks. I know.' She blows her nose. They sit in silence for a bit.

'So, what, your biological dad's mixed race, then?'

'Yep.'

'But your mum never said?'

'No. I do know she left school after A-levels and got a library job in Toxteth,' says Jane. 'Then came home out of the blue a year later.'

'Ah!'

'Yes, ah. I'm guessing he was married and she was livid when she found out. Anyway, she came home, got married to an older guy she knew from the WEA, and six months later there was me.' Jane tells Madge about the email she now wished she hadn't deleted.

'And you never wondered at all, ever?'

'Nope. Not once.'

'OK.'

Silence.

'What?'

Madge just grins at her.

'No! You could tell? Oh my God! How?'

'Girlfriend!'

'Oh my God!' Jane starts to laugh. 'You mean it's obvious?'

'Mmm-hmm.' Madge is laughing too. 'Well, not *obvious* obvious. But I saw you.'

'You did?'

'For sure.'

Jane bursts into tears.

'Aw, Jane.' Madge comes round the table and reaches out. 'Come here. Come on.'

We will leave the pair of them laughing and hugging in Dominic's kitchen while their tea goes cold. Later, as Jane tells Matt all about it, she will find the right word for the feeling: relief. Relief that although

213

she didn't have the full picture, at least she knew that the scene stuck on the puzzle box lid of her life had always been fake – and that this made sense of why the pieces never quite seemed to fit. They will talk long into the night, and Matt will finally be permitted to bring his mansplainy solutions-oriented skill set to bear on the problem of tracking down Jane's Liverpool family.

Jane will eventually fall asleep emotionally wrung out at 2 a.m., with the owls calling and the chilling screams of vixens tearing the night. When she wakes the following morning, however, Matt's help won't be needed. During her sleep, the long-deleted email title will have been miraculously restored to the inbox of her consciousness: Family History.

Such are the consolations of fiction, reader. Now and then, the author will sustain your flagging spirits with a swig from the hipflask of prolepsis. I intend this as a pious analogy for faith which, as every good Sunday school pupil knows, is the substance of things hoped for, the evidence of things not seen. Jane's rebooted memory lies in the narrative future, but I trust this little glimpse of it acts like a light to surprise the Christian when comforts are declining. We will need it. We haven't got through today yet. There are still ninety thousand bees to sort out.

As it happens, only two of the three cathedral hives are bound for Short's Flower Farm. Ellis is taking the third. I think a reclamation yard is the perfect place for rehoused bees. It's due at Gray's at dusk, after the yard has closed for the day. There were no near neighbours to consult, and any vexatiously litigious choir mums planning a visit will be duly warned by the safety signs. Ellis does not anticipate a drop in customer numbers, and he's looking forward to having 'cathedral' honey to sell. He's consulted with the beekeeper and chosen the site. It's in the far corner of the garden behind the high fence that screens off the compost heap and the shed full of gardening paraphernalia. Level ground, south facing, some shade, all the flowers of Gray's garden, and acres of farmland stretching all around. Bee heaven.

'So many primroses, Ellis,' says Paver, as they close up at five o'clock. 'It's the same situation that we ended up with for the August garden, remember, with the poppies?' Ellis nods. 'In that this month's garden is any- and everywhere you look, if you have the eyes to see. To my point, some primroses have come up in the April garden among the daisies, so it's like an April slash February mash-up, which I kind of like. The little gravestones are hidden now, and I kind of like that too, in a "nature heals" kind of way. Do you believe nature heals, Ellis?'

'Well. I believe it consoles.' Ellis switches off the lights. 'Like music.'

'Like music. For sure. I'm guessing when I dug the daisies up, I collected some primroses at the same time. Did you know it's technically illegal, Ellis? As in, apparently, you can pick wildflowers but it's illegal to uproot them.'

Ellis steers Paver gently over the threshold without ever seeming to hurry. They step into the porch and Ellis sets the alarm.

'Well, considering people are forever digging daisies out of their lawns and trying to eradicate them, I wouldn't feel too bad about it.' He locks the main door.

'So maybe another way of looking at it is to say I rescued the daisies, and this is like a daisy refuge? Cool, cool. Oh, I meant to say, Ellis, I'm more relaxed now about the whole violet situation, as in, I'm OK they aren't in bloom yet, even if violets make a perfect pairing with amethysts, colour-wise, and part of me will always regret that.'

They walk back to the house.

'Look how light it still is,' says Ellis.

'The sun sets at seventeen-forty-three today. That's thirteen minutes later than last Friday. Which might not seem like a lot but every little helps – if that doesn't sound too much like Tesco. You know once, Corie saw that slogan and the E had gone? Very little helps? That totally resonated with me after he died. But if you get enough very little things cumulatively then I guess it does help. A little. Like thirteen more minutes of daylight helps, is all I'm saying.'

'Who hath despised the day of small things?' asks Ellis.

'The day of small things. Cool. Bible or Shakespeare?'

'Bible. There will be masses of violets where the hive's going, by the way.'

'So violet honey? Wow.'

Ellis laughs. 'It will be rape honey mostly. With some lime blossom thrown in.'

They go into the kitchen. The table is still laid out with Paver's painting equipment.

'The last page is just drying, then I'll clear up. Are you OK with that, Ellis? I'm not invading your space?'

'No rush.' Ellis fills the kettle and begins their end-of-the-working-day tea routine. He glances at the sampler. *When He cometh, when He cometh to make up His jewels.*

'Thanks, Ellis. You're the best.'

They go through this anxious ritual every few days. Probably Paver's dealing with some endless loop of thought in which Ellis is about to blow his top and evict his cousin. And the situation in Ukraine isn't helping anyone's anxiety levels. When the moment is right, Ellis will float his idea. He will venture something like: 'We could plan towards creating you a proper studio space. Long term. A converted container, maybe. Anyway, have a think.'

Paver bends over the table, still talking. 'Looks like it's dry now. Next up, daffodils and aquamarine, meaning seawater. The daffodils are nearly out for the March garden. Can you believe that's the last one?' marvels Paver. 'Plus obviously, the March book will be the last one too. I'm kind of hoping it will feel like closure if that's not too simplistic. Things coming full circle, if you will. And maybe we've made some progress over the year, and maybe not, because life can still have value and meaning even if you haven't made progress in the sense capitalism expects.'

'I could drink to that,' says Ellis.

'Ha ha! Well, you should wear an amethyst ring or have amethysts on your drinking vessel,' says Paver. 'Look. I literally just wrote that this afternoon. Here.' Paver switches on the daylight lamp. The tiny book lies on the table in the circle of light.

Ellis peers down at it through the vintage magnifying glass. *Amethyst derives from the Greek word amethystos meaning 'not intoxicated'.* 'Ha! I'll remember that next time I'm out on the lash. May I?'

'Of course.'

Ellis carefully turns the pages. He finds the little figure in a bowler hat, sitting under a primrose parasol with Robin Goodfellow and assorted insects. 'Is Coran in all the books?'

'No. I only thought of putting him in last month, sadly. But I can always make more books. It's not the end of the world. Did you know that until the nineteenth century, amethysts were super-rare and then they discovered them in Brazil as well, which devalued them?'

Once as rare as ruby or emerald, amethyst was suddenly in abundance. 'Yes, I've just read that bit,' says Ellis.

'I find that so weird,' says Paver. 'They are literally the identical same thing as they were before, only suddenly they're ubiquitous so they're not precious. I mean, how wrong is that as a value system? Do you enjoy something less, Ellis, just because everyone else can afford to enjoy it? Just because it's everywhere?'

'Well, I hope not.'

'I know you don't, Ellis.'

Tomorrow morning, Ellis will go out first thing to check on his new beehive. Sunlight will blaze through the raindrops that tremble on every twig and leaf. He will pause to stare. It will be as though the world is hung with a thousand fairy chandeliers. If he had to choose between trays of Tiffany solitaires and the sight of his garden right now, he wouldn't hesitate. This is my treasure, he will think. His loved and his own – his own, because he has noticed it. He will bend over the hive and whisper to the bees that they are welcome here. They are safe. He cannot solve the conundrum of how it's possible to be happy when others are suffering. But at this moment, his spirit will flash joy back at every flashing drop of water. He will brim with love at the thought of the bees sleeping in their hive, and of the promise of honey to come, and all the small things that are not to be despised.

MARCH

Daffodil and aquamarine

We began this tale, dear reader, last April on bank holiday Monday, and we are concluding halfway through Lent. That's a whole year with no Easter. Perhaps this resonates with our current experience, though. The last COVID restrictions may have gone in England, but the virus still sputters away like a dodgy firework that no one can approach and officially declare that it's gone out. Limbo land has always been our theological terrain. The church exists between two resurrections. In the midst of wars and rumours of war, the grand prolepsis glints through when we pause to look for it. Apocalypse means revelation, not disaster, after all. Any- and everywhere an edge might curl back to remind us that we are accompanied by heaven.

The spring equinox has passed. So too has the second anniversary of that first lockdown announcement. How fast the weeks slip by now, compared with the treacly pace of January. The clocks go forward. It is Mothering Sunday. There have been suitable cards and bouquets and breakfasts in bed. If we fight back through the fog of memory, we will recall that a year ago it was all red lists and roadmaps. We were only just getting our first jabs. But today we may travel the length of the country to visit our mums and crowd mask-less in unventilated rooms. Meanwhile, China puts whole cities back in lockdown as their zero-COVID policy buckles under the pressure of the Omicron onslaught. The fat lady has not sung yet on the global stage. She's still in her dressing room touching up her rouge.

This week has seen many autocorrect errors – Mithering Sunday, Othering Sunday – most of which were intercepted before they appeared on service sheets or data projection screens. It is the secular world punishing us for refusing to say Mothers' Day like normal people. But this is a hill we are prepared to die on. Or rather, upon which we are prepared to die. It lies in a low range of similar hills where we may be united in death with fellow pedants, on elevations such as correct apostrophe usage, different *from*, and unsplit infinitives.

It's the end of March. Lindfordshire blazes with daffodils. From your classic Dutch Master down to the tiniest dwarf Tête à Tête, they cheer every border and verge. If you want to encounter all thirteen official categories of daffodil, why not visit Short's Cut Flower Farm? Trumpet, large-cup, small-cup, doubles, tazettas. Time would fail me to tell of petticoat and butterfly daffodils; or to list all thirty-two thousand registered cultivars. Angel's Breath, Bell Song, Minnow. Even Short's cannot stock them all. Ice Follies, Daydream, Bantam and Rapture. Jack Snipe. A great multitude that no man can number. There are more ways of being a daffodil, Horatio, than are dreamt of in your ecclesiology.

All across the Diocese of Lindchester, clergy experience the usual daffodil distribution angst. How to pick a path between the devil of motherhood-related trauma and the deep blue sea of not celebrating our mums? Poor little bunch of daffs in foil! Complex it was and complex it shall remain, until we find a way of separating the weft of joy from the warp of woe without unweaving life's cloth altogether. Or until God makes us and our mothers of some metal other than earth. We are but dust, even though we wiped the ashy reminder from our foreheads three weeks ago.

'Well I never.' Ellis stares at his iPad. 'Well, well, well.'

Paver looks across the breakfast table in the Old Barn. 'What's wrong?'

'My childhood home is up for sale. I'm just doing a virtual tour. Look at this.' He turns the screen round to face Paver. 'This is my old bedroom. These are the stairs. I wonder if the seventh step still creaks. Sitting room. Hallway. And here's the kitchen. They kept the quarry tiles but, apart from that, unrecognizable. This is the outside now. Honestly, I could've driven past it and not known.'

Paver studies the screen. 'Isn't this kind of corrupting your memory files, Ellis?'

Ellis turns the iPad round again and stares. They blandified it, he thinks. All the quirks are concealed under laminate flooring and fifty fashionable shades of grey. This could be any house. 'No, I've got enough distance on it. Anyway, I carry the real thing up here.' He taps his temple. 'I'm just a bit wistful. But people are free to do what they like with their houses.'

'True, true.'

'At least the daffodils are still going strong. Mum planted them. Look.' He enlarges the image of the drive.

'Is that why you planted so many daffodils by the gate, Ellis?'

'Ha! Maybe it is.'

'We should go and pick a bunch and put them on her table here,' says Paver. 'And honour her memory on Mother's Day. Or is that complicated? I don't want to second-guess your relationship with her, Ellis.'

'No, it was good. I can certainly honour her.' Ellis flips the cover shut on his iPad and finishes his tea. 'We'll pick some on our tour.'

We will leave Paver and Ellis to conduct their tour of the birth month gardens. Gray's is closed, as it is every Sunday morning. They will go round with Paver's draft treasure trail map, to check that everything is in order before making copies for visitors. Paver is creating a virtual version too, with embedded hyperlinks and tiny animations. It will appear on the new website that Paver's friend from art college is developing.

The website is not the only project in development. Ellis has commissioned Neil to create a studio from an upcycled freight container. The studio is not *necessarily* for Paver, so there's no pressure. But Paver will have first refusal. That's the way Ellis left it. Thus, it is Ellis facing the blunderbuss discharge of Neil's micro-queries. Paver has been advising from a safe distance on the kind of thing an artist might prefer. A spot that will offer the all-important north light, for example. In the far and peaceful corner of the grounds, perhaps, near where the beehive stands.

I am happy to report that the relocated bees are doing well, both at Gray's and at Short's. They have survived the lean months when starvation threatens. The queens are busy laying, and there is a reliable supply of nectar and pollen now. Already this morning the workers are foraging in the March sunshine. The blackthorn is out in all the hedges. There are dandelions, cowslips and a hundred other wildflower species we don't notice because we're not looking for them and don't know their names.

Yes, there will be honey yet for tea in this idyll of mine where the honeybees are thriving. Let us edit out the fate of parasitized bumblebees, their poor brains requisitioned, driven to dig their own grave in sandy banks along the Linden, where they will be eaten alive by the wasp larvae they host. In fact, let us edit out all of Britain's six thousand-plus parasitic wasp species. We will pick and choose from Mother Nature. Emperor penguins. Focus on the emperor penguins. Let's keep this traditional and stop the clock for an eternal afternoon tea with nostalgia wafting in the background like a threadbare Union Jack.

All across Lindfordshire the blue and yellow bunting flutters. Charity shop windows are styled with mannequins dressed in yellow and blue. Blue wheelie bins stand on grassy verges among daffodils, as though even our recycling yearns to express solidarity with Ukraine. Once again, we rack our souls with the eternal question of how we can be happy while others suffer. Sunflower seeds germinate on the girl choristers' windowsills. The good people of Lindfordshire sign up in droves to house refugees. Prayers are said. Candles are lit. Funds are raised. The first razor edge of terror has grown dull, as Ukraine fights back and sanctions against Russia start to bite.

This is Day 31 of the invasion, and we have almost stopped counting in days. It is becoming weeks, just as it did with lockdown and COVID. Weeks that drifted into months. And now it's years. Even when it's finally over, it won't be. The effects will still ripple out from that specific moment in a far-off province of China, where in one human body the virus first jumped over to our species and made us its unwilling host. Variants give way to ever more sub-variants. We may never shake it off. We never really shook off Spanish flu either. Our seasonal flu viruses today are descendants of the 1918 pandemic.

And so, here we are at the end of my tale, still in the desert of Lent with temptations on every side. My characters are mainly targeting booze, carbs and social media. Father Wendy has renounced Wordle. Such things are theoretically possible to resist. They don't prowl about like a roaring lion seeking whom they may devour. They're more like slugs in among your hostas. You could scoop them up with a fish slice and fire them into your neighbour's garden. But ultimately, how can we resist a force that's threaded through everything? It may depart, but it's just waiting for the opportune time, this behovely thing that lurks in our mitochondrial DNA, handed down by every mother, to every mother's child. This is what it means to be human. It hurts. With the best will in the world, stuff will go wrong. Things will wear out. We will break things, sometimes on purpose. And in the end, we will all die. But hey, maybe it's not our fault. If we are born with it, we can't be held responsible for our crimes and failings.

In far-off London town, Partygate limps on. In the end, the prime minister will 'take full responsibility' for what happened. What! you cry. He will resign? Don't hold your breath. In current political circles, 'taking full responsibility' is a playground-truce phrase. It operates like crossing your fingers and shouting *Fainites*! You can't tig the prime minister now – he's in the den. Theologically speaking, taking full responsibility for something looks rather different, as a quick glance at any church crucifix will remind you. You have to level down before you can level up. But by all means let's keep the church out of politics.

Talking of temptation, I am sensing my readers' urge to skip ahead and find out how Jane is faring with her newly discovered family. Patience! Bright skies will soon be o'er us. I have not forgotten that today is also Refreshment Sunday, Laetare Sunday, the midpoint in our Lenten fast when we don pink socks and allow ourselves a little tipple. Let us rejoice, joining with Lindchester Cathedral choir as it sucks, in Latin, at the breasts of consolation, as per today's introit. Our rejoicing will stop short of the H-word, of course. As sticklers will remind you (braced for martyrdom on the low hill of liturgical pedantry), hallelujahs are banned in Lent. Nevertheless, our hosannas can still clap their way up to heaven like feral pigeons at every gunshot or champagne cork. Save us! Hooray! Both/and, inextricably tangled together.

And so, rejoice! I am here to tell you that the sun is shining. It's all blue sky in Lindfordshire. There are lambs in fields and larks in the clear air. The first cow parsley leaves are coming up. Everywhere the wood pigeons croon their patient woozy love song to the human race. Celandines and coltsfoot flowers stud each bank and path side. People are wearing shorts and planning BBQs in accordance with Home Office guidelines on How to be British.

There goes Jane, jogging round Martonbury Reservoir in her knackered sportswear and new sunglasses. She's finally found a pair that don't slip down her nose when she sweats. The sun keeps pace beside her in the water and the polarizing lenses turn it into a glinting blue disc. Fizzing blue sparks flash on the ripples. She hears the metallic *plink-plink* call of a coot. All around, hawthorn and horse chestnut buds are bursting. Then a swan goes spanking across the reservoir to get airborne. Jane stretches out her arms as though she's also going to lift off and fly away into the blue, like the fucks she doesn't give.

Everyone knows.

Jane accepted that there was no point trying to control a story as juicy as this in the C of E, where 'in strictest confidence' means that you tell people one at a time. She suspects everyone and their dog is now saying, 'It's obvious. I mean, you only have to look at her!' Each morning she examines herself in the mirror. She analyses skin colour, lips, nose, hair. It's the same old face. Nothing has changed. Except everything has. Which just goes to show you can't see what you're not looking for. But she sees herself now. Or does she? Yes. No. Yes *and* no.

Galling to admit that *they* saw her – the jeering kids in the play-ground. Jane is retrospectively seared by racial slurs that, at the time, bounced harmlessly off the carapace of imagined whiteness. Interesting to discover that it's not as simple as getting her *head* round this. She needs to get her body round it. All these years she's been living in the wrong narrative. Thanks, Ellis, for that phrase. Jane burst into tears over him a second time when she went to pick up the repaired garnet bee brooch. Ellis gets it. He understands about the importance of bodies in this whole identities shebang. How nothing in the world of colonial studies could have prepared Jane for

226

the sudden drenching moment of realization that her own flesh and blood was once literally enslaved. She carries this knowledge, this abhorrent history and injustice, in every single cell. What does she need to do now? What does she need to undo?

In all fairness, Mum never actually lied. She didn't say, 'What a load of old rubbish, Jackie.' No, she just said, 'Sticks and stones. Ignore them and they'll stop doing it.' She left Jane to believe it was nonsense. Protecting her? Lying by omission, anyway. Had Mum started lying to herself as well? Editing Elliot Robinson out of her memory, as well as her photo album?

As you might imagine, reader, Jane has been doing more than her fair share of wrestling with thoughts of motherhood this year. She's not expecting to be remembered by Danny today, because Mother's Day is not till May in New Zealand. But she is remembering her own mum as she slogs on along the reservoir bank through sun and dappled shade. There's no grave to visit. Jane can picture the local churchyard where Mum isn't. Many a game of tiggy-off-ground played there. Not to mention twilight visits after the clocks went back, scaring one another with the art of levitation. Instead, Mum was cremated and her ashes scattered in a patch of woodland not far from the village. There is no bench commemorating *Eileen Rossiter who loved this spot*, although she had loved it. She knew what to look for in spring and even managed to din a love of nature into her counter-suggestible daughter. Imparting knowledge was her best approximation of maternal love. Jane doesn't need to drive back and visit. Any patch of English countryside will do. Like this one in deepest Lindfordshire. Mum would have loved it here. Jane crosses the bridge at the halfway point of the 5k loop. She glances down at the riverbank and glimpses a yellow flash. *Look, Jackie – king cups.* Jane grins. It was years before she clocked they weren't kink-ups.

Just to fill you in, patient reader, Jane has spoken several times on the phone to her half-sister Sandra O'Brien. She's learnt that far from being an only child, she has two other half-sisters, Michelle and Tessa, a half-brother, Titus, and nieces and nephews innumerable. To say nothing of half-aunties and -uncles and -cousins. It's beginning to feel like a Gilbert and Sullivan song. They only found out about Jane three years ago, when her biological father (a widower) was dying of cancer. Since then, they've been longing to meet her, but respected her firm rebuff back in the first lockdown. But now, oh now, they've spammed her with love and photos of themselves and her dad. And yes, she can sometimes glimpse herself in their brown and black faces. She has the full picture these days. Literally. Elliot kept his copy of the photo that Eileen cut him out of. Jane has it on her phone. 'My parents,' she repeats to herself. Oh, there's so much love waiting for her. Too much, to be honest. Which is why she's glad she can't go to the big Mother's Day clan gathering in Liverpool this lunchtime. Not ready for that yet.

Apologies for contacting you out of the blue like this, but I think we might be related. Jane knows that retrieved email by heart. She can't believe how quick she was to bat it away. Actually, she can believe it. Not much got through the curiosity-repelling wall her mother had constructed. That is how Jane has come to picture it: a false wall concealing what was too painful for either of them to contemplate. Namely, that Jane had ruined her mum's life. In all fairness, not once did Jane's mum say this. Not in words.

Jane passes a fisherman on the bank. There's a whiff of garlic. Jack by the hedge. Poor man's mustard. Now that the metaphorical wall is rubble, Jane is frankly in awe of how smooth the papering-over job was. There was not a single edge you could get your nails under. Why, for example, had Jane never before done the maths and calculated that when they married, her mum was twenty and Ray was fifty-six? Mum's voice comes tinnily from the rubble like a buried radio: *Oh, you don't want to know all that rubbish, Jackie.* Actually I do, Mum, because what the holy heck – a *thirty-six-year* age difference? No wonder everyone in the family knew it was a marriage of convenience and assumed Jane must know as well.

Apologies again, because I have no idea how much you know already about your father. Next to nothing, it emerged. About either father. With hindsight, Jane can say that when Sandra's email landed, Ray Rossiter was as unknown to her as Elliot Robinson. Both men were concealed behind that false wall.

Jane approaches the muddy patch where she and Matt took a tumble. No companionable jogging any more. His diary has cranked back up from leisurely to insane. Jane successfully avoids the villainous tree root this time as she interrogates the unknown-ness of Ray Rossiter. Not many memories of him at all, really. Just a sense of his warmth. His smile. His subversiveness. Buying her *Twinkle* comics (*I don't know why you waste your money on that rubbish*) and teaching her naughty songs. Yes, he slipped her contraband kindness wherever he could.

Jane rounds the final bend. Her sporty black mini is in sight. There are more cars parked along the roadside now. She jogs round open doors and people getting out with dogs and buggies. A chiffchaff calls from a bare ash tree, chipping away, chipping away at the morning.

Done! Jane slumps against the car to get her breath. She checks her watch. Comfortably inside her Personal Worst, which is all she aspires to these days. Good. Plenty of time to get showered and have a sartorial meltdown over what to wear for the fairy godparent lunch at Freddie's with her oppos. Tiresomely, the idea of Mister Dorian seems to be reactivating her historic Oxbridge shoulder chips. But as Freddie himself so cogently remarked on the subject, 'Fuck that shit, Jane. You're awesome. That's why we asked you to be Ladybird's godmother.'

Jane gets into the car and heads for home with the windows down. Chiffchaff song comes in on the spring air and her thoughts keep on chipping away at the mystery of her parents' marriage. Did Ray somehow learn of her mum's situation and offer? Maybe she went to him and flat out asked. Possible, knowing Mum. Well, however it came about, Ray rescued Eileen from the choice between ruinous shame and illegal abortion. Was it love? Was it lovelessness? If she could understand this, maybe she'd be able to understand why she can hardly bear it, the thought of all that love. A house full of birthday presents with her name on, waiting for her to arrive.

I'm happy to say that Jane has not been trying to process all this on her own. Matt has been a rock, as have Dominic, Madge and Ellis, of course. This morning Matt is on his way to St Margaret's, Thrapton, to offer cover in the interregnum and get a right handbagging from members of the congregation. St Margaret's has always had a vicar, and they should therefore get a new vicar. QED. The Church Commissioners should stop pouring money into all these ghastly church plants that are ruining the real C of E and stump up for a priest in every parish. Matt will point out that *the diocese* funds stipends, not the Church Commissioners, and there's currently a hole in the old diocesan bucket. With what shall we pay them, dear Liza? With what? And it's not as though St Margaret's was beamed down from heaven like the New Jerusalem. It was itself a Victorian church plant from nearby Risely.

After the service Matt will head to Lindford to join the lunch gang at Freddie's (shooting up a quick 'thank you' prayer that the safeguarding fiasco apparently hasn't sabotaged their friendship). There will be a bunch of three daffs in foil on the dashboard for Janey. Matt's route will take him past Short's Cut Flower Farm, and I'm afraid our good friend will let out yet another sigh for that brief career window when the only shit he shovelled was literal.

All across the diocese, Sunday worship is underway. The ancient homing device still faintly calls Anglicans back to mother church, like servant girls of yore with the day off heading home to Mum with a simnel cake and gathering wildflowers on the way.

In Lindford, Star places a little bunch of violets in front of the statue of Mary, just as she did two years ago. She kneels and crosses herself. To be the literal mother of God – what must that've felt like? Especially when you lost him in Jerusalem, wow. I bet you thought you'd blown it and lost God for ever! Three whole days. Star got lost once in IKEA for like twenty minutes and Mum and Dad were in bits. So, I guess although you're perfect, you still sometimes got things wrong? Probably Star's not allowed to say that. But part of her thinks maybe that's why Mary knows how to pray for us sinners. She crosses herself again and slips out, as Miss Sherratt (still resolutely wearing a mask) enters to light her customary candle.

Madge glances in as she passes the Lady Chapel on her way to set up the post-service Prosecco table. Her and the BVM are not besties, the way Tinkerbell is. ('We pray and then we serve, Nurse Williams!') But Madge and Mary are on nodding terms these days. They've got a bit of rapport going. 'Tss,' says Madge. 'That statue looks nothing like you, girl.' 'Tell me about it,' says Mary. And they both roll their eyes.

Miss Sherratt genuflects creakily and leaves. The organ is playing softly. Already a rumour of incense is sneaking out from the sacristy.

Here comes Chloe with Ladybird. The service is about to begin, but they have to do this every week – go and look at Mary holding out her son to the world. Ladybird reaches out her hands too and shouts, 'Buh! Buh!' Baby! Someone little like me!

Bells are ringing for the morning service all over the diocese. The carillon in Gayden Magna tinkles out 'Jerusalem the Golden', and Mister Dorian, driving his Tesla to Lindchester Cathedral with the sunroof open, catches a phrase in passing and makes a mental note. Later he will arrange this hymn for the Dorian Singers, and years from now, unimagined audiences will hear it and catch a faint echo of the shout of them that triumph. And so the ripples quietly spread, radiating out beyond the measure of our mind. Foolish hearts, don't give up. We know not, oh we know not, what joys await us there.

Over in Turlham, Paver and Ellis hear the church bells as they follow the birth garden trail round Gray's.

'Right, so here's the July garden. Look, Ellis. The delphiniums, aka larkspur, are just starting to come up. So that's good.'

'Should we discard the hard old heart?'

'Ha ha – you remembered that! Not this year, I'm thinking. But probably we should start using the garlic drench. Did you know metaldehyde slug pellets will be illegal from April first? I'm so glad about that.'

'Me too.'

'So, from July the trail goes to September, because August is everywhere, like February. Oh, cool new fact vis-à-vis primroses, Ellis. Did you know that ants are responsible for dispersing primrose seeds? I know, right? Don't you just love nature, Ellis?'

Ellis edits out the six thousand-plus parasitic wasp species and says, 'Yes, I do. And I like the way you've used bird footprints on the map.'

'Thanks. I went with pigeon tracks because of the way pigeons wander around – they don't do linear from A to B. They're more in the moment, like, A to G, taking in K and D, depending on happenstance.'

'Ah yes, "Bannockburn by way of Brighton Pier".'

'I've not heard that, Ellis, but I'm guessing it's a saying?'

'A poem. About the rolling English road being made by English drunkards.'

'Cool. I'm totally here for pigeons,' says Paver.

'Well, they do love you, after all.'

'Ha ha! You're never going to let me forget that, are you? I love them back to be fair. People stigmatize them as vermin, flying rats if you will, but have you ever watched them in the sunshine? The light on their feathers – iridescence – it reminds me of the Schiller effect in gemstones. Ha ha! Why am I even telling you this, Ellis? I bet you already know. Yeah, you do, you're smiling. I want to say refraction?'

Ellis laughs. 'Yes. The refraction of incident light on the microscopic structure of the feather.'

'Ha ha! OK, so here's September.'

They stand in front of the wall where the stencilled angel wings shimmer.

'I was basing those on pigeon feathers, to be fair. Can you tell? Anyways, I may introduce some other varieties of Michaelmas daisy so that we get a whole range of different purples this year.'

'Gray's is all signed up to variety.'

'We so are. My friends think it's awesome here. And now here's March.' They walk to the entrance where the gates stand open. 'I can't believe we've come full circle and that's the full set of birth flower gardens we've made? I for one never thought we'd get here. I'm so grateful for my life, Ellis.'

'Me too. I've just spotted Coran on the map.'

'Yeah, I wanted to pay tribute. I began all this for him.'

'Has it helped? You seem happier.'

'Up and down, Ellis, up and down. It's been like a torch app, I guess is how I'd put it. As in, yes it's dark, but you can at least see the next bit ahead and keep going forward? And morning's got to come in the end, if that doesn't sound too cheesy?'

'Something to hang on to.'

'Totally. So I just need to finish the March book and I'm done. Did you know aquamarine grows in six-sided crystals and they can be – wait for it – a foot long? Awesome, right? The name means seawater. Bloodstone is the other March birthstone. Tradition says the first bloodstone was formed when Christ's blood dripped down from the cross, which turned ordinary jasper into bloodstone.'

'Presumably the red flecks are iron oxide?'

'Iron oxide inclusions, that's right. And there's iron in blood, so a connection there maybe? I don't know. Bloodstone's other name is heliotrope, meaning sun-turning, like sunflowers.' Paver checks the map. 'Cool, so the pigeon tracks end here, at the March garden, which is also the entrance, the gateway in. Alpha and omega, if you will. I got trapped in a scary mental loop or sinkhole, if you will, over was it weird to start the year in April? But then I thought: the tax year starts in April, the academic year starts in September, not a big deal. I'm saying here, I got out of the sinkhole for once. So there's that.'

Both sides of the gate are thick with the daffodils Ellis planted thirty years before. The scent whispers *Easter*. They stoop and begin to pick, counting as they go so it comes out even. Ellis puts the bunch to his nose. He breathes in and gets catapulted back to childhood and Mum. He pictures her old whiteware jug full of daffs on the Formica table.

'Full circle,' says Ellis.

'Full circle. To my point, I'm thinking in the end we're all heliotropes, Ellis. That's in the March book. Even when it's night, we're still sun-turners, always turning to the sun and round the sun.'

We too have come full circle, dear reader. We will pay a final visit to the heronry at Shotton Hall Farm, where the chicks have hatched and are clacking for food. Perhaps these very birds are descended from the lucky herons whose fate was not to end up on the banquet table of the medieval bishops of Lindchester. The less fortunate young birds were filched from nests and raised in special barns. Not a pleasant job, nest-raiding, given the herons' trick of regurgitating their last half-digested meal down on to intruders below. Ah, regurgitation! Full circle indeed. I daresay you were wondering whether I would bring that up again (*badum-tish!*).

Come. Let us wind our necks in and unfurl the heron wings of this narrative and take to the sky. Beloved Lindfordshire lies below us now. All things bright and beautiful, along with all the dull and ugly things that never made it into the hymn. Pretty hamlet and down-at-heel high street. Farmland and urban waste. Artisan ice-cream parlour and foodbank. Gated communities and tented communities. What To Look For In England as the cost of living climbs: the rich man in his castle, the poor man at his gate. We no longer believe God made them high and lowly. It's the economy, stupid. Market forces ordered their estate. What virtue-signalling woke blasphemer dare question it?

Oh, landlocked Lindchester! Perhaps you foreshadow the new heaven and earth when there will be no more sea? That's a hard vision for us Brits to stomach, with vestigial Ruler of the Waves DNA lurking in our every cell. We love the silver sea our precious stone is set in. To us, it is not the Scriptures' untamed forces of chaos; it is Arnold's bright girdle of faith. And by faith, we mean of course the historic formularies of the Church of England. Why, even now as I write this final chapter, I can almost hear through my open window the melancholy long withdrawing roar of people who cannot bear to engage with SDF bid paperwork. Listen! It's the note of eternal sadness that comes from collapsing the distinction between the C of E and the heavenly city. Of believing it all revolves around us when we are really just pebbles, teeny tiny pebbles, tumbled smooth against one another in a sea without a shore.

Here we are in Lindford, where this narrative terminates. Let us alight, legs all gangly-dangly, on Miss Sherratt's terrace where she is enjoying her after-mass glass of sherry. Jack has arranged a jam jar of spring flowers on the patio table for her. His relationship with his own mum broke down decades ago in the hell of his addictions. She died before he could mend it and make it right. But Miss Sherratt has mothered him since he first trespassed in her garden at the start of the pandemic to make his home in the falling-down summerhouse. I cannot count the number of others Miss Clarabelle Sherratt has mothered in her time. Nor can she. Her life is a carillon. There's no telling who has picked up her tune in passing and gone away with an earworm, humming about some sweet and blessed country they can only dimly intuit.

Music comes today from the garden beyond her fence, where the rainbow flag flutters from a tall pole. Dogs bark. A baby screams. There are champagne corks and gales of laughter. Ambrose is chan-nelling his inner Fats Waller again, reinterpreting Walt Disney's 'So

This Is Love'. Freddie and his ex-mentor start duetting in smoochy harmony, getting it on musically with rather a lot of sighs and quivering glissandi. Heavens. I don't know where to look.

Miss Sherratt smiles in a sherry haze. Bless them. She recalls the day Freddie and Ambrose moved in. And those early thrilling glimpses through uncontained windows. (Behave yourself, Belle!) There's a *Sold* sign outside the old weed house now. She sends a blessing wafting across in that direction, to alight upon whomever the buyers are. Not, she devoutly trusts, the chappie planning to demolish the house. Perhaps it's been bought by the pregnant woman who rang the Sherratt Manor doorbell to enquire about the neighbourhood.

'We saw the rainbow flag and wondered if this is the kind of area we want to bring our child up in.'

Did you, indeed! 'Apart from the occasional bad apple,' said Miss Sherratt frostily, 'I think you'll find this is a very inclusive and accepting place.'

'Thank God for that,' came the reply. 'I'll tell my wife.'

And let that be a lesson to you, Clarabelle. Judge not that ye be not judged.

The partying in the heavenly blue house will continue into the evening. Both Freddie and Ambrose have got someone depping for them at Evensong today. This is a sneak preview of that bigger party that will happen in Lindford Parish Church on Easter Day, when Ladybird will be baptized in the afternoon. All three family clans will gather – Garners, Hardmans and Mays – to say nothing of members of the congregation, Lindchester choral foundation and other friends from all over and way back. Freddie's dad is insisting on footing the bill, but nu-uh, not gonna happen, dude. Like Mum and the, quote, Argy horse dealer, you are welcome to the party. But put your credit card away, coz your money ain't legal tender in my world. (And hey, what is even the point of asking two ridonculously loaded guys to be godfathers if you don't let them bankroll shit?)

We will fly the short remaining distance and perch on the henhouse roof (ducking to avoid the hawk-scarer). From here we can see in through the window to where Jane is jiggling Ladybird while Chloe and Freddie fly around the kitchen. (Aaaaagh! The mentors are here!) Chloe tosses salads. Freddie bangs a tray of bread rolls into the oven.

'No no no. Sharp! Ouchy!' Jane closes her hand over the garnet bee brooch. 'You don't want to eat that! I've got a nice vintage suffragette brooch for your very own when you're bigger. Yes, I have. Oh, yes I have!'

A waft of bespoke cologne creeps up on Jane as she burbles. She turns and takes in the full vicuña-sweatered suavity that has manifested itself beside her. The vision raises a chilly Oxford eyebrow and reduces her to thick Jackie, the comp girl. She feels herself blush. Great.

'You must be Andrew.'

He inclines his head. 'And you are . . .?'

'Jane Rossiter.' Arsehole. 'Your opposite number.'

He surveys her like a Regency nonesuch with a quizzing glass. 'So, Jane,' he drawls, 'what do you bring to the godparenting table?'

'Awesomeness, Andrew. You?'

'Where to begin, Jane? Where to begin?' But then he melts and smiles. 'Actually, I bring fathomless depths of besottedness for this little girl. Give.' He reaches out.

'No way.' Jane hugs Ladybird tight. 'I saw her first.'

'Ah, but she loves me more. Watch this.'

He begins to sing 'Funiculì, Funiculà'. Ladybird's eyes widen in astonishment. She looks round for Freddie.

'Omigod, baby girl!' Freddie comes over from the stove and spreads his oven-gloved hands in wonder. 'Is he singing our song again? How's he doing that? How's he even *know* it? Is he *magical*?'

Jane laughs. 'Oh, go on then.' She hands Ladybird over and watches while Andrew dances and swoops her round the room. '*Jammo, jammo 'ncoppa jammo jà!*' Ladybird lets out roll upon roll of fat chuckles, the way Danny used to when she danced him. Why is Jane practically crying? She has no idea. Maybe she's aching to be a grandma? Maybe she's already pissed on Theo's vintage champagne?

'Aw, Janey. C'mere.' Freddie tosses the oven gloves aside and gathers her in for a hug. Then another pair of arms circle them both. It's Matt.

'Guys! Guys!' shouts Freddie. 'Group hug!'

'All pile on, all pile on!' Matt chants.

A moment later, Jane is in the middle of a playground scrum of love. Ambrose, Chloe, Andrew and Ladybird, Theo, Father Dominic (back from visiting his mum). Matt gets flashbacks to the episcopal bundle of his consecration. Even the dogs leap up on their hind legs and join in, barking. Jane is laughing and sobbing, 'Oh, piss off, the lot of you!' They only hug her tighter, as they join in Ladybird's song, or some bold approximation of it. 'Oompah! Oompah! Umty-tumty-tee!' It ends on a triumphant Pavarotti high C from Freddie.

So, this is love, reader. It goes straight to our head, undoing us and frankly making us ridiculous. We cry for no reason and laugh when babies burp formula on to our thousand-pound sweaters. Because who cares? Before we know it, we're piling on the little funicular of faith and trundling up the volcano to the fiery heart of everything. We don't get to choose our company. Everyone's a heliotrope here, a bloodstone. We are all riven with holy DNA and grace flashes off our flaws.

It's evening now. All across the Diocese of Lindchester there are little daffodil bouquets in foil. In Martonbury and Carding-le-Willow, Turlham and Risely, on Cathedral Close and the Abernathy estate. On graves, on windowsills. There's one on the bedside cabinet in the care home where Mrs Todd sleeps. She spends most of her time sleeping now. She didn't even wake when Dominic visited. She smiled though, as if his voice and the smell of daffodils reminded her of something.

In the Old Barn, Paver puts the final touches to the March book. *Aquamarine brought ancient mariners safe through the storm to their destination.*

Ellis leans forward and sniffs the daffodils in the whiteware jug on the blue Formica-topped table. No real regrets. Just wistfulness, like he felt for his childhood home sanitized on the estate agent's website. He will always wish he'd found a way to tell her before she died. But he knows she probably knew anyway. Ellis straightens and looks across at his framed sampler. He places a hand on his heart and breathes. Here's where the real thing is stored: in the heart, not the head. *Thou God seest me.* Dear old namesake, Alice Greatrix. Was it OK in the end? I hope you felt seen. I hope you felt loved. The way I do.

The story isn't over yet, but the time has come to say farewell to our Lindchester friends. I haven't told you everything. How could I, in just twelve random days? It's all there, though, like bric-a-brac in Gray's reclamation yard. Twelve baskets full of broken fragments. Nothing will be wasted in the end. Nothing will be lost.

Jane is dozing on the sofa in the palace, wrung out and happy-sad. Her daffodil bunch is also a little the worse for wear, having languished forgotten in her handbag until ten minutes ago. She stuck it in a beer mug and the flowers will probably perk up. Maybe tomorrow she'll pick some more from the garden. There are enough to choose from. Her predecessor planted about a thousand all along the drive. Jane yawns. What a day. Knackering. She's still not back up to her full pre-pandemic partying speed. It's as though she has social long COVID. God, imagine if she'd gone to the Liverpool bash instead!

Jane cannot imagine this at all. Nor can your author, really, any more than I can imagine heaven. I can only tell it sideways, refracted through the feathers of fiction. Here's what I can imagine. In a few minutes Jane's phone will buzz. It will be a text from her half-sister Sandra on her way home from Liverpool to Northampton, where she lives. Sandra will offer to swing by Martonbury, if Jane is in and up for a meeting.

Yes, I can picture it: Jane waiting on the doorstep, trembling. She will hear an owl call. A car will stop on the road. In a moment, she will spot her sister's torch app bobbing towards her along the dark drive. And the night will be sweet with the scent of a thousand daffodils.

THE END

CHANGES AND CHANCES

A Lindchester story for Christmas 2018

'Tis the year's midnight. The winter solstice. Back in John Donne's time, the shortest day was 13 December, the Feast of St Lucy. Blame the slippage on the Gregorian calendar, imposed on us in 1752 to bring Britain into line with the rest of Europe. Bloody Gregorians. Coming over here, nicking eleven days off us.

So today, 21 December 2018, is the year's midnight. Let me take you by the hand, gentle reader, and lead you once more through the streets of Lindfordshire, in the mild hope that I can show you something that will make you change your mind. About what? you ask suspiciously. Well, anything really. We should never be *too* certain we've got right and wrong nailed, here in the time of this mortal life. Let's not forget our primal blunder – falling for the scam that we could be like God, knowing good from evil, when all along we were nothing but dust.

Before we begin our journey, we pause to acknowledge that there may be those who have never heard of the Diocese of Lindchester. To them I say, Google it. You will be directed to a trilogy of such hardcore, full-frontal Anglicanism as will have you fanning yourself with a pew sheet and needing a little lie-down.

The lands of this fictional diocese lie in the very heart of England. They border on Lichfield to the south and Chester to the north. In our earlier sojourns, I confess we spent rather too much time wafting about in the stratosphere of the Close, and too little with our feet on solid Lindfordshire ground. Our business, by and large, was with the Pound End rather than the Penny End of the diocese. This tale seeks in its small way to redress that balance.

And so, beloved in Christ, let it be our care and delight to go even unto Lindford indoor market and hear again the message of the angels. This is the *new* indoor market. It was opened only last year by a Royal Personage. Aficionados will already have deduced this from the perishing rubber security seals that still adorn every drain cover in the vicinity. After declaring the new market open, the Royal Personage went on to Lindchester Cathedral for a Lindfordshire Regiment service. Security was tight there too. But happily, the feckless lay clerk who shinned over a high wall into the Old Palace garden (having been bounced by the police at the gatehouse when he failed to produce any ID) was not gunned down by marksmen as he emerged, black-clad, from the shrubbery, carrying a sports bag. He was later released without charge, though I'm afraid by then he'd missed the service.

But that's enough about the Close. Come with me into the new market. I don't know about you, but for me it just isn't the same as the old market, in that the old market was leaky, vermin-infested and miles from the bus station, and the new market is none of those things. Yet, somehow, we hold fast to the old market in much the same spirit that we testily resist upgrades to our mobile devices, because they make things different.

There ahead of us, as we enter the bright and airy new market, is a priest. Huzzah! It is our old friend Father Dominic, slightly more silvery, slightly tubbier than when we last saw him, but let those of us who have not aged a jot in the past two years cast the first stone. He is wearing his clericals, because he regards a cassock as overalls, not dress uniform. He is also wearing red fuzzy antlers, which I admit is a liturgical solecism as it is still Advent. He shouldn't really wear antlers until the midnight mass.

A small brass band is oompah-ing carols in the entrance. Trombone and euphonium twinkle with tinsel. 'Up! good Christen folk, and listen!' The air is merry with voices and tradesmen's calls. 'Three for a fiver! That's all they are now, girls!' Breathe in the aroma of fried onions, of vinegar, mingling with acetone from the Infinity nail bar.

As you weave your way through the crowd there comes another scent – stealthy and sweet on the air, like rumours of heaven. Oud, sandalwood, attar of roses, wafting from Osman's stall, where glowing bottles line the shelves like gifts of the Magi.

There goes Father Dominic ahead of us, past fruit stall, bakery, haberdashery. He is distributing Christmas service invitations to shoppers, and inadvertently frightening the bejesus out of lapsed Roman Catholics who can't tell from looking that his orders are absolutely null and utterly void. He works his way along the crowded market aisles, past Wood's Family Butchers, where people are queuing for their pre-ordered legendary Wood's pork pies, without which it would not be a proper Lindford Christmas.

As he walks, Dominic prays. He prays for the shoppers, the traders, the screamers in buggies, the grouches in mobility scooters. He prays for the local council, and the market managers with their headache over empty retail units. Lindford FM plays from Lee's Workwear. A news bulletin. Dominic catches enough to register it's about Brexit, but not enough to grasp what's going on. O hideously apt metaphor! He can't grasp any of it. There are no good alternatives, and he cannot even identify the least worst with any confidence. What, oh what, will it be like this time next year – for these small traders, for their customers, for *any* of us? Don't even *breathe* second referendum. It's a *gilets jaunes* movement waiting to happen. Jesu, mercy.

Ah, goody-good – here's the Lindford Cheese Company. He admires the nativity under the glass case. (Look! Baby Cheeses in his Camembert-box manger!) Dominic orders his festive cheese stash. Then on past Dale's Vac and Electrical Spares, where you can still buy bags for the ghosts of Hoovers past.

He draws level with J&L Hot Tubs. A middle-aged woman catches sight of him and leaps up. She dodges through the crowds and taps his arm. 'Excuse me.' He turns with a kindly smile.

I can tell you that Dominic does not know her from Adam. He, however, can't be a hundred per cent sure of that, because he might have encountered her under who knows what pastoral circumstances. He deploys one of those omni-functional lines that wise clergy keep in the tool kit: 'Hello! How are things?' (where 'things' might range from 'your exciting new business venture' through to 'the hideous protracted death of your beloved').

'Oh! Fine, thanks. Listen, sorry to bother you, but have you got a moment?'

Dominic does not have a moment. No clergyperson in the run-up to Christmas has a moment. And yet he has all the time in the world. 'Of course.'

We will leave Father Dominic to have his pastoral conversation, and skip to his destination in the middle of the market. This is where the café area is, with its mismatched chairs, ash tables and silk flowers in empty IPA bottles (the first signs of hipster trickle-down). The central space is surrounded by stalls. See that giant logo *#FollowTheStar*? It rests over the unit that has been let, rent-free, to the parish church of Lindford for the month of December. (The market is in Dominic's parish, after all.) The ox and the ass are already standing by, but it is otherwise empty of its nativity cast. At noon there will be a short carol service with a tableau of figures. The participants are on their way.

The stable occupies the back half of the unit. At the front there's a table of leaflets and Christingle marmalade (made by an entrepreneur who gathered up the discarded oranges once the dolly mixtures had been scoffed). Plates of mince pies are being set out. On the opposite side there is a big bright red sofa, ex-showroom. A freebie blagged by Father Dominic's clergy colleague, Virginia. You may sit on it beside whoever is on the rota (currently it's Pauline, one of the church-wardens), pour out your heart and get yourself prayed for, under the banner *Free Prayers & Christmas Blessings*. If that's a bit touchy-feely, you can write on one of the prayer stars and hang it on the tree instead.

A Christmas CD is playing. Oh dear. It sounds to me like the Dorian Singers' latest offering. I expect Virginia will swap it for something more godly when she arrives. The album contains all your favourites, from Slade to 'Santa Baby', and is by far and away the campest thing you'll enjoy in the holiday period – unless you happen to be reading this in your Gammarelli biretta, with a unicorn mimosa in one hand and a mauve Sobranie in the other.

And now look next door, please. You will find something here to rejoice your heart. It's a pop-up barbershop, offering free shaves and haircuts to homeless people, to the poor and helpless, the cold, the hungry and the oppressed. It is staffed by rotas of volunteers from the barbers and salons of Lindford. The idea was the brainchild of Kaz. I wish I had time to tell you about Kaz. In fact, I wish I could tell the story of every soul in the Diocese of Lindchester, but even the world itself could not contain the books that should be written, so we must choose, and I have chosen Star.

Star is seventeen. She looks younger. She looks about twelve – such a little slip of a pixie, with hair like turquoise candyfloss and almost translucent skin. She's shampooing an ex-serviceman, Jack, who fell through the gaps when his last tour of duty ended. Star was the first to volunteer from Hair Works, and so surprised were the rest of the staff that they had no option but to volunteer too. She began her training in September, and can cut under supervision, but mostly it's washing and scalp-massaging, and sweeping up the fallen hair. But somehow she makes drudgery divine, as Herbert paternalistically put it (did he ever wield a broom in his life, I wonder?).

Star doesn't say much. 'Temperature all right for you? . . . Got any plans for this evening?' There are those (the wife of the Bishop of Barcup, to name but one) who infer from the soft Lindford drawl that the speaker is not the sharpest pair of scissors in the salon. I concede that Star did not shine at school, although she worked hard. But now she's doing what she always wanted to do since she was a little girl. Maybe this is why she glows. That, and the fact that she knows she's loved. Loved for what she is, not what she achieves. Was there ever a little scrap loved with such fierce and tender love?

Over on the other side of the market, at J&L Hot Tubs, Lynne is finishing her tale to Father Dominic.

'By rights, she shouldn't even be here. Came on Christmas Eve – twelve weeks early! She's our Christmas miracle, isn't she, Jez?'

Jez nods. 'That's why we called her that.'

Lynne blows her nose. She shows her pendant to Dominic again. 'So what do you think?'

'Yes, that's Our Lady, with baby Jesus.'

'A woman at work gave it me. For a safe labour, she said. I thought it was just a lucky charm. But then that night . . . '

Although Father Dominic has all the time in the world, it is now nearly midday. He gently heads off a repetition of the story about the mysterious nurse, Maria, who came at night and sat by Lynne's hospital bed and told her the baby would be fine, when it turned out there was no such nurse in the whole of Lindford General Hospital.

'Yes, that does sound like Mary. Shall I bless this for you?'

'Oh, if you would.'

He improvises a prayer, gives them an invitation and a *#FollowTheStar* booklet. Then he scuttles off, with shouted promises of a good deal on hot-tub hire following after him.

He arrives, panting, to find it's all kicking off in the stable. The Blessed Virgin Mary is stuck in traffic on the ring road. Dominic's mum offers to go and find a stand-in, but Dominic does not want Mum wandering off. Lord, he needs a 'Find my Mum' app on his phone as it is.

'No. Virginia's looking. You stay and guard the mince pies.' He burrows his way into his stripy Joseph robe.

'I'd offer to do it myself, but I'm a bit old.'

'You're a bit old for St Anne, never mind Mary!' he tells her.

'Sarah was ninety when she had Isaac, I'll have you know. And your tea towel's on crooked.'

The crowds are gathering in the central area. A pop-up barbershop quartet – they popped up from the cathedral – are in next door, already singing 'O Holy Night'. The musical among you will be aware that when a group harmonize perfectly, a strange phenomenon occurs: it is as if an eerie fifth voice joins in, singing a high note. Listen! There it is. On this occasion it's Alfie, the golden labradoodle, who likes to join in when his masters are singing. Dude! Go Alfie!

Virginia reappears in a flap. Nobody's willing and she can't volunteer, as she's leading the act of worship. Dominic scans the crowds, sticks his head into the unit next door – aha!

There's a last-minute scramble and the day is saved.

It's nearly over now, this saved day, this shortest of days. The traders have packed up. Shutters have rattled down. All across the town of Lindford, people are heading home. Schools have finished. We make our way towards the town hall, past the library, the former banks. Such stout Lindcastrian civic pride. It is still visible, if you look up, past the Primark trappings of this generic rundown high street. The town hall carillon is just finishing its Christmas medley. *Sweet Chiming Bells*.

Look, you can buy bratwurst and Glühwein at the Christmas market to cheer you on your heavenly way. Judging by the giant reindeer head, fixed like a trophy to a chalet front, these traders have come from Germany. The reindeer flutters its eyelashes and croons 'Chingle Belse' with Bavarian bonhomie. *Auf wiedersehen. Adieu.* Will we see you again next year?

We just don't know. Eleven days. Eleven days and we will be in 2019. You, dear reader, have already recycled 2018 and hung up the new calendar. But do you or I have a clue what lies in wait? Brexit/ no Brexit. Deal/No Deal. Referendum? General Election? We are suspended in mid-air, like a cartoon character who has run off a cliff edge, pedalling furiously, not daring to look down.

Walk with me towards the station, where trains rumble by at roof height and people bed down under the viaduct. The derelict station hotel is still for sale. The wind hisses through the ash keys as if through clenched teeth. Old leaves and litter blow along the gutter. Everyone is going home. Everything is closing.

Dominic and his mum bicker gently as they drive to Sainsbury's for their Big Christmas Food Shop.

'What on earth is War Use? Are they bringing back rationing?'

Dominic glances at the giant fiery letters. '*Warehouse*, Mother. Some of the letters have gone out.'

'Oh, I *see*! I thought it was a slogan.'

'You're right!' cries Dominic. 'The E for Europe has gone! And the ho! The festive ho ho ho! Prepare for War Use. Goodbye, Cool Britannia. We're all doomed.'

'Well, aren't you the cheery one,' she says. 'People are stockpiling, mind you.'

'Don't say it. I *know* what you're going to say. No. La la la.'

But she says it anyway. He should never have chucked them out, those tins of hers.

'Mother, that corned beef was sixteen years old! You'd die of botulism.'

'Pish and tosh. Don't come running to me in a food shortage.'

'I'll *always* come running to you. You're my mum.'

She pats his knee. 'Well, fingers crossed, this will turn out to be another storm in a teapot. Like the millennium dome.'

'Bug.'

'That's what I said.'

'No, you didn't. You said dome.'

'Well, same difference.'

People, look east. The night sky is ribbed like a beach at low tide. Above the trading estate, the moon glows in its sepia halo. Tomorrow it will be full. The Cold Moon, the Long Night Moon, with the Ursids flashing across the sky. Flecks of dust, smaller than a grain of sand, but how brightly they shine.

Star is walking home. Her back aches. It's better than TV, walking past people's windows. More like Instagram. Like they're all posting selfies #Crimble #yay. You get to see into their lives. There's an old lady in her kitchen. There's a boy in his bedroom with a guitar. All the trees! Every house. Aw, it's magic.

She turns down her street. First thing she's going to do is get into the hot tub, even if Mum's got tea ready. She can see herself already. She's going to lift the cover, see the steam rush out at forty degrees. Breathe in the chlorine smell. Then she's climbing in – ah! That's *the best*, that moment. Cold air on her shoulders, then sliding under. She'll turn off the jets and it will go quiet. And after a moment, the security light will go off and the back garden will be totally dark. She'll feel all the aches melting away. Maybe she will be thinking about kneeling in the straw like that, and that Cabbage Patch Kid doll, the exact same one she had when she was little. And the people singing.

She hums as she walks down her parents' path. *I love thee, Lord Jesus. I ask thee to stay.*

And maybe there'll be shooting stars?

ONE MORE RIVER

A Lindchester story for Easter 2019

I t's 29 March, when something was supposed to happen.

That day came and went. Did you wake and check your diary, wondering why 29 March rang a bell? Or were you on the train (booked months in advance to get a cheap seat), heading for London to celebrate our national freedom?

I propose a new term: Brexchatology. Our exit from the EU recedes before us, always imminent, never actually happening. When, Lord, when? Of that hour no pundit knows – not even the angels in heaven. I have no expertise, no answers for you. Two-and-a-half years have passed, and we are still shaking it all about in the political hokey-cokey unleashed by the referendum.

By the time you are reading this, who can predict which playing field we will be on, let alone where the goalposts will be? All I can do is lift the lid once more on my little experiment, and see what's going on in the fictional Diocese of Lindchester.

Lindchester! Its imaginary lands lie between Lichfield to the south and Chester to the north. It is Erewhon. Utopia, in the strict sense of that word (pedants, rejoice with me!), which comes from the Greek: *ou* ('not') and *topos* ('place'). Utopia, literally *no place*. Ah, but there's no place like home! So let us click together our heels – everything from tatty trainers to burnished brogues (we are a Broad Church yet!) – unfurl our Anglican wings and head for home. We will zoom back to that very day (calm was the day. . .) of which we spoke at the start of this tale: Friday 29 March 2019.

See how the diocese lies spread out beneath us! Lambs frisk

in green fields below the cooling towers. Hedges are snowy with blackthorn. Every twig is dotted with buds. They look like those magic-painting books of childhood: a swish of wet paintbrush and lo! colour everywhere. Turbines turn, turn. There goes a heron, loping in pterodactyl stateliness. We wheel over village and town. Feral pigeons explode from a derelict factory, and light winks off every windscreen, every reservoir and puddle, every tower block. There's the River Linden below us. Sweet Linden, run softly, till I end my song!

Where shall we land? 'The Close, the Close!' you urge. No. It is still Lent, you sybarites. (Or it is where I'm writing this, at any rate.) We are heading somewhere more down-to-earth, more down-at-heel. There it is now: Martonbury. But not the Martonbury of quaint butter markets and artisan cheese shops. Not posh Martonbury, where suffragan bishops live with grumpy wives in Tudorbethan mansions. I am taking you down to the edgelands, to that mish-mash of trading estates and abandoned works where Martonbury struggles briefly to become countryside, before giving up and slumping into the outskirts of Lindford.

And through it all runs the River Linden.

Today, as I weave my own Spenserian Prothalamion for that Brexit bridal day (which is not long), we catch up with an old friend as he strolls along the bank with his golden labradoodle. A carrier-bag festival is being held in the trees.

Our friend whistles as he walks. *Shall we gather at the river, where bright angel feet have trod?* Sunshine flashes on his Ray-Bans and diamond ear-studs. The dog finds a ferocious plastic bottle and sets about subduing it. *Gather with the saints at the river . . .* Then – how rude! – the path runs out.

PRIVATE LAND. NO TRESPASSERS.

Private? I'll give you private. There's a padlock on the gate, but he tries it anyway. Open! *Yes, we'll gather at the river!* They go through, and cut across the car park of Cardwell's electrical engineering works. What's he supposed to do – scramble along the bank among the nettles and shopping trolleys? I think not. Do you have any idea how much these trainers cost?

Uh-oh. A security guard has spotted them. 'Oi, mate!'

Our friend turns.

The guard strides across. 'You're trespassing.'

'I *think* you'll find there's a historic right of way through here, pal.'

'No there isn't. This is private property.' He points to the sign. 'Can't you read?'

A pause. 'I'm partially sighted, I'll have you know. This is my guide dog.'

'What?' The guard sees himself twice, tiny and dumbfounded, in the Ray-Ban lenses. He blinks. Looks down at the doodle. The doodle, daft as a loo-brush, grins through a mouthful of Lucozade bottle. 'Look at him! He's not much of a guide dog, is he?'

'I don't know,' Neil says. 'I can't see him, can I?'

The guard makes a helpless gesture. 'Well. I'm telling you: you're trespassing.'

'And I'm telling *you* – historic right of way. Come along, Bear.'

Oh, dear. It looks as though Love's redeeming work is not *entirely* done in the life of Neil Ferguson, Reader-elect in the Diocese of Lindchester. Oh, he's a bad man. He knows it. His Big Day looms – the Licensing service in Lindchester Cathedral – and he's fretting more about his bespoke, hand-tailored-on-Savile-Row cassock than the state of his soul. *I, Neil Ferguson, hereby promise to endeavour, as far as in me lies, to promote peace and unity, and to conduct myself as becomes a worker for Christ . . .*

Yes, he's a sinner. But he's also a saint. (Aren't we all?) He will somehow find the grace not to send the cassock back a third time for alterations. (We must thank the Lord that nobody has told Neil about Gammarelli's, or he'd be making weekly trips to Rome to test their promise to 'meet any kind of request or need'.)

In a moment, Neil will reach the far edge of the car park, repent and turn round. (What is repentance but the act of turning round – turning round and heading home?) He will apologize to the guard for telling whoppers. Then he'll introduce himself, explain about his church's planned community litter-pick, and his project to clean up the riverbank, lay proper paths, maybe establish a wee nature reserve?

The guard will be more interested in a slobbery game of wrestling the plastic bottle than in capturing the Ferguson riverbank regeneration vision. But later – as the hours yawn past and nothing happens in his crap job, and he aches for his Friday night to begin – his thoughts will keep drifting back to Bear and the way that gobby little Scot turned round and apologized. And he'll smile.

I sometimes wonder whether the C of E should introduce a licensed dog ministry. Which English heart is not open to a daft dog? How naturally we enthuse to strangers about Duke and Daisy, when to enthuse about our faith would be *death*.

The 29 March meanders by. There's chiffchaff song, and the first swallows are swooping. Stand under any cherry tree and feel the air thrum with bees. The glass of blessings has been upended on us once more. Spring runs a finger round our souls, and everything hums.

All the while, in far-off London town, parliament debates and votes, up against the wire, striving to deliver the impossible to the implacable. Day after day, our MPs have stayed at their posts against a backdrop of ridicule and haranguing, of death- and rape-threats, while placarded tribes roar at the gates. And, this afternoon, crowds will gather in Westminster, like storm clouds banking up, and there will be thunder in the air.

Still the sun shines. It's shorts weather, sunblock weather. Meteorological irony, or a care package, parachuted in just when we most needed cheering up? Which is it? If we put it to the vote, we will be divided. We are divided on everything in the United Kingdom. We cannot even decide how to pronounce 'scone', for heaven's sake! Sometimes I wash my hands of us.

All the same, I'm generally glad of fine weather on a Friday, because clergy frequently choose this for their rest day (aka their 'I know it's your day off, but [insert footling problem]' day). A sunny Friday therefore maximizes the chance of encountering our clergy friends strolling along beside the Linden with their beloved hounds.

We will go looking for them. Up, once again, into the trembling air. We will follow sweet-breathing Zephyrus along the silver streaming Linden to Lindford. The river path is better cared for here. I wouldn't claim that Lindford has a vibrant café culture exactly, but there are pleasant places to stroll, clematis trained over iron arches, and so forth. You'll find a handful of bars and restaurants with terraces overlooking the river. This area is popular with the students of ~~Poundstretcher~~ Linden University.

Come with me, to the spot where the river passes through a tiny parcel of urban woodland, where you might even hear a woodpecker, if you are lucky.

There below us now, entering the trees in a state of high excitement, is a second golden labradoodle. Yes, yes, there are other breeds of dog in the Diocese of Lindchester. But a happy accident back in 2016 produced a litter of five; so please re-suspend your disbelief.

This dog is out for walkies with the Rector of Lindford, Father Dominic, and his mum. He stoops to unclip the lead. Off bounds the dog on squirrel patrol. She's called Lady (short for Lady Day, of course). This is a choice of name that Father Dominic has had occasion to regret. He had not considered how female passers-by might react to an angry priest bawling: 'Hey! Lady! COME HERE!'

'Oooh! Are those flags?'

'No, Mother. They're carrier bags.'

'Shame. They look like flags. I thought it was a celebration.'

It is, Dominic thinks. We haven't crashed out of the EU today with no deal. Huzzah. 'Enjoy it while it lasts. When you get your eyes done, you'll see litter in its full glory again.'

'If I'm still here and compost mental,' she says.

He squeezes her arm. 'As you so wisely said yesterday, we can burn that bridge when we get to it.'

'So we can!' She laughs and begins to sing: '"One more river, and that's the river of Jordan!"'

He joins in: '"One more river, and that's the river to cross!"'

'Oh, my son used to love that song when he was little!'

His chest goes icy. 'And I still do, Mother mine.'

'That's what I mean,' she says quickly. 'You love it.'

Last week, for the first time, she hadn't recognized him when he came back from mass. She made light of it, the way she'd made light of getting dressed at 3 a.m. to go shopping that time. But that 'Who on earth are *you*?' look jolted him out of denial.

The assessment is set for the week after Easter. What horror lies on the other side of it? Oh, Lord. This is so crap. Please spare us this horrible, horrible crumbling away, this eradication of all we love.

They pass the place where skeletal bouquets still cling to the fence. A drunken stumble after a student binge? Suicide? We will never know. Dominic remembers the candles lit in his church; the desperate nine-day vigil before the poor body washed up by Martonbury's weir. Twenty years old.

They lean on the fence and look down at the sparkling water. From the opposite bank, out of sight behind high brick walls, Dominic can hear clashing and bleeping from the scrapyard. Above that rears the brutalist cliff-falls of the university's Fergus Abernathy building.

He gazes downstream. Buddleia sprouts out of abandoned stacks. He can see sky through the roofs of empty factories. There are more students than industrial workers in this town now.

'I could always just end it all,' Mum says.

'That's cheating,' he says. 'Like sneaking a peep at the last page of a thriller.'

'Tiddly-widdly! I do that all the time.'

'I *know* you do, Mother, and it ruins the dénouement the poor author has sweated blood over.'

'Well, hard cheese. It helps *me*.' She gets out her hanky and wipes her eyes. 'The tension's more bearable if you know how it ends.'

'We do know how it ends, darling.' He puts his arm round her and rests his head on hers. How tiny she is these days. 'It ends with us going home.'

'Oh, get away with you. I know it does. I just get frightened about . . . You know.'

'I know. The verge of Jordan.'

The cellophane on the faded bouquets rustles in the breeze. He can smell the conditioner in Mum's newly styled hair. First solo cut by Star, bless her. He'll be baptizing Star and her mum at the Easter vigil.

In a moment, he'll whistle for Lady, and they will totter to the Rising Sun for a nice, spoil-y, day-off lunch. Light flashes off the ripples. He prays for the repose of the student's soul. Two swans glide into view. Mum will spot them any moment, and he'll pretend they're carrier bags to wind her up.

Oh, don't be frightened, dearest Mum. I'll bid your anxious cares subside. I'll be with you on the verge, even if you have no idea who I am. In the distance, he hears Lady barking at another squirrel she will never catch. And just for this moment, even though it's crap, everything is perfect.

Everything is crap and everything is perfect in this no-place of mine. Maybe some blueprint still shines through whenever we hold our experience up to the light. Plans for the Holy City, the New Jerusalem, the No Place behind and beyond all our no-places. Small wonder we can't picture it, we who can think of eternity only as time going on interminably.

Star thinks everything is perfect. You remember Star? Star from Hair Works salon, the last-minute, stand-in Blessed Virgin Mary at the Lindford indoor-market nativity. Being chosen like that (by a frantic Father Dominic) flicked on a dormant homing device in her, and she slips into the parish church whenever she can.

She's finished work and she's heading there now, along the banks of the Linden. She's got a bunch of forget-me-nots to put in front of the statue. She'll write some more prayer-request slips – for the world, and Brexit, and for Mum and Dad; for her baptism; and not forgetting Jack, the homeless guy whose hair she cuts for free (the salon lets her).

She has to write it all down because she doesn't know how to pray properly yet. She doesn't really get how it *works*. Like, can you just ask for anything and it will happen? That doesn't sit right, or nobody would ever get cancer or starve or be homeless, would they? But you've got to try.

Sometimes, she thinks it's like your prayer is just a tiny cog. It goes round, and then there's another huge, huge cogwheel that turns, only you can't see it? You just get the feeling something big is turning too. Ha ha, like the ancient toy from the 70s Dad got down from the loft to cheer her up that time she was poorly. She'd forgotten about that. Spirograph? Yes. The big wheel going round and round, and you're making flower patterns with your pen? Except, ha ha, it always slipped and you did a massive scribble. But probably if you practised it would get easier.

Look! Kingfisher! She holds her breath.

Hey, that dream last night – that was so weird. So she's standing in a big circle, miles and miles wide, with a ring of mountains in the distance going all the way round, whichever way she looks. There's other people there, maybe Mum and Dad and Father Dominic? And suddenly she's all: 'Wait – this is a volcano, everybody! We're literally standing on a volcano!' And she's panicking, because a cloud of smoke is rising up behind the hills. Only, when she looks again, it's not smoke

– it's birds. Thousands and thousands of birds. And as she spins round, there's more and more, swirling up, till the whole sky's full of them.

'A murmuration of starlings,' Star whispers. She wrote them all down once, in Juniors. Pride of lions. Murder of crows. But *murmuration* was her favourite.

She watches the river a little longer to see if the kingfisher will come back. The late-afternoon sunshine lights up her candyfloss hair like a turquoise halo.

The sun is going down over the Diocese of Lindchester. Nothing much has happened here today – this red-letter day stamped on our brains, when everything was going to change. We'd hoped that at least we'd know what we were in for by now. Do we have to go on endlessly trying? Can't we just get it over with, even if it's a disaster?

Hate spews out in London, and across our screens and timelines. We are living on a volcano. If it blows, what will become of us? This terrible waiting. We can't even ignore the whole thing. Oh, what can possibly lie on the far side of catastrophe?

Blackbirds are singing. Magnolia candles gleam as darkness falls. Streetlights flicker on along every street. No, nothing much has happened to my characters. They have walked their dogs, worked, shopped, cut hair, told fibs, repented, prayed, wept. What lies in store for them? I can't tell. Sweet Linden, run softly as I end my song. Even now, your water brims with light, while all around darkness falls.

Yes, we'll gather at the river. What lies on the far side? Come, we know the answer. Hate will not have the final word. We are Easter people. Turn, turn your little wheel of prayer. Hate will wear itself out. The heavens and earth will wear themselves out.

An owl calls as we make our farewells and head for home. The Linden runs, as all rivers run, towards something bigger than itself. Perhaps we are living on a volcano. But, if we look up, we will see that all around us pulse the murmurations of love.

ONE THOUSAND
CHRISTMAS LIGHTS

———◆◆◆———

A Lindchester story set in December 2019

A full moon sets behind a stand of trees. The Cold Moon, the Long Night Moon. And now, just before dawn, it's finally dark. Or what passes for dark these days. It's never pitch black here in Lindfordshire. A dirty orange smear hangs over every built-up area. LED necklaces link town to town. Even when you're out in the sticks, security lights blaze in alarm at every stirring branch or trotting hedgehog.

Listen. High above the sleeping landscape a cathedral clock chimes. Five. Six. Seven. On the dot, the doors open in all the little sports halls and community centres, the parish rooms, primary schools, libraries. All the venues gatecrashed when the General Election circus came to town. The returning officers have been there since 6.15. They sit braced behind their trestle tables with their lists and ballot box. It'll be a long day. Tyres crunch on gravel. Car doors slam. Here we go.

It's 12 December 2019. The good people of Lindfordshire go to the polls again, and they're not happy. This is really inconvenient, to be honest. December is rammed enough as it is. And tonight's the office Christmas party. I'll have to vote early on the way to work.

What time is it? Hands grope for phones. Lights go on in upstairs windows. Lindfordshire is waking up. Office cleaners ply their Henry vacuum cleaners. In bus shelters and doorways, the homeless stir under mounds of old duvets. Out in the hills, farmers put down their mugs, stick feet in boots, call the dog and leave the warm kitchen. Up and at it. They head out in the dark for the Landrover, the quadbike. Check the stock, the drainage ditches. They'll find time to vote later.

Self-employed delivery guys load up at the depot and check their impossible schedules. *Your driver Matt will toss your parcel over a nearby hedge between 12.18 and 13.18 in despair.* Uber drivers fire up their apps and check for requests. They'll just have to vote as and when. If they get a moment. The long trudge begins for the zero-hours workers. Walk, bus, walk, clock in at the vast hangar, walk, walk, walk the aisles all day, cough, ache, throb. Should be in bed, but they're already on three penalties and they daren't take the day off. Every nerve strains to make ends meet as Christmas approaches. Get fired, and the ends will twang apart like bungee elastic. So it's walk, walk, walk. They pass the night shift walking home at last after their ten-hour stint. And then they have to remember to vote.

This is all the time we have: 7 a.m. to 10 p.m. Today is where the road forks. We will look back and see clearly what went wrong. But first we've got a busy December day to get through as best we can.

'Jess? Jess! Come *on*. We're going to be *late!*'

Jess rinses and spits. Then she leans so close to the bathroom mirror she can see her voice misting the glass.

'"Now light one thousand Christmas lights."' She's singing as softly as she can, because soft shows real control; anyone can sing loud. But no matter how softly she sings, the toothpaste-y mist still forms. '"Ten thousand, thousand also shine . . ."'

'I'M NOT WAITING FOR YOU!'

Leah could really damage her vocal cords yelling from her throat like that. You have to yell from your diaphragm.

'Coming!' Jess wipes the mirror with her blazer sleeve and runs downstairs. She grabs her coat and hat. 'Bye, Luna!' she calls.

'Dad's taken her to the hub, you idiot.'

'Wait, I haven't opened my Advent calendar!'

'Oh, for God's sake.' Leah storms out into the dark.

Quickly! Jess picks the window open on the Climate Extinction Countdown calendar Leah made for her. Today it's bush fires in Australia! Which is important. (But boo, no chocolate.)

'JESS!'

'Coming!'

Purse, keys, phone, train pass. Jess shoulders her backpack. The door clashes shut behind her. A berry drops off the wreath. Keys, phone, train pass. Train pass! Phew, here it is. She scampers to catch up. Leah's only grumpy because she's got to walk Jess to the station today. But there has to be give and take; they all have to play their part in a crisis.

To make the dark earth— Jess breaks off from humming, because it's a bit tactless – Leah can't sing. Or she *can*, but it's in her own individual way.

'Leah?'

'WHAT?'

'I'm really pleased you're Santa Lucia?'

'Pah.'

Jess has to scuttle the whole time to keep up. They pass the cemetery where logically zombies can't be waiting to get them, because they don't exist. (Or ghosts.) The sky is just starting to turn paler in the east. Last week it was amazing red sky and frost, but today everything's grey and it's raining.

But look, look! Everyone's got their trees up! Lights twinkling in bushes, and lit-up icicles with actual dripping lights! And a snowman all shining from the inside. Yay, Christmas! Then they pass the garden with a *VOTE LABOUR* sign, and someone's put tinsel round the pole. Her and Dad noticed last week that literally *right next door*, there's a *VOTE CONSERVATIVE* one! Jess almost says, 'Look, we are a divided nation!' to prove she *is* thinking about the important stuff in life. But to be honest, she doesn't want to get Leah started on politics again.

They go under streetlamps and her breath comes out white in puffs, like a steam train. And now her glasses are fogging up, because she's hurrying into her own breath. This is the inconvenience of glasses, but it's *so* a price worth paying for that amazing moment, like an actual miracle, when you step outside Specsavers in your first ever glasses, and WOW! Who would of ever thought *this* was what the world looks like? Like it's all 3D CGI. Pigeons with sharp edges, not fuzzy; the rooftop looks like it's been sliced with a craft knife.

'Stop it!' shouts Leah.

'What?'

'You're singing "Thomas the Tank". God, you're so *embarrassing*.'

'Sorr-ee!'

They cross the bridge over the Linden. A bus goes past with its windows all steamed up and white. Jess stops to look over the wall. You can still see the snapped trees and rubbish tangled in the branches from the flood.

'Come ON!'

Jess has to full on run now to catch up. Her bag bounces on her back. Maybe in two years she'll have a growth spurt too, then she'll be as tall as Leah, which would be so cool. Everything would look small, like when you go back to Infants, and all the desks and chairs look cute, like doll's house furniture. Unless it's gradual, so you don't notice, like gradually going short-sighted, and you just think that's what the world looks like to everyone.

They're outside the station.

'You're so unfit,' says Leah. 'If you were fit, you wouldn't get out of breath.'

'I know. But actually, in another way, I've got quite good breath control?' she mentions.

Dragon smoke comes out of Leah's nostrils. 'Look, I'm not mad at *you*, Jess. I'm just not a morning person.'

'I know. Thanks for walking me.'

'Right. I'm going. Don't talk to any weirdos, OK? Not everyone's nice in this world, Jess.'

'I know.'

'Meet you after school. Bye.'

There are eyes everywhere in Lindfordshire. By the time the sisters reach the station, nine cameras have tracked them. If ill were to befall them today, the grainy black and white footage could be played back by the police. We could view clips of their last moments on the BBC website, and get in touch if we had any information. Even now, another camera watches Jess as she waits on Platform 4, tiny among the potential weirdos, in her chorister hat, with her backpack. Yet another (for her safety and security) will keep watch on the train.

Nobody will meet Jess at the other end, but she will be stalked by a tag-team of electronic eyes as she makes her own way from

Lindchester Station and toils up the steep cobbled climb to the medieval gatehouse, where the cathedral security cameras will pick up the baton.

Back in Lindford, cameras track Leah. Out of the station, along the High Street under swaying festive lights, through the village of garden sheds that form the Christmas market, then past the construction site with its gnash and bleep of heavy plant. More student accommodation going up. It's almost light now. Men in hard hats watch her pass. They don't wolf whistle in this age of considerate construction. They don't tell her to cheer up, it might never happen. But they watch, and she feels their gaze. All the livelong day, eyes and cameras are on her, framing her, capturing her.

Fuck you.

Her stare is lethal. Any second, she could unleash her signature shark-tooth knuckle-strike and take an eye out. Fuck you, creepy old guys looking at my chest, who are literally *older than my dad*.

And *now* she's got to wait in the rain, because the fucking café isn't open yet. Fuck everything. Well, not Dad, although she's properly mad at him for making her get up early and walk Jess to the station. There goes an hour of sleep she'll never get back. Oh, but we *all* have to pitch in when there's a crisis, Leah. Give and take. Blah blah. Fine then – if I've got to *take* Jess to the station, you can *give* me £5 to get hot chocolate and cake before school. Which, fair play, he did.

Leah cups her hands round her face and peers in through Diggers' window. There's someone moving about in the kitchen. Come ON.

Fuck Mum for not getting the whole give-and-take aspect and being all, 'My boundaries are clear: the girls are your responsibility in the week, Martin.' Except . . . Nah, forget that. Mum has issues.

Leah scans for another target.

Fuck the stupid flood relief hub? Probably not. But fuck the big landowners burning off the grouse moors and causing the flood. And the big polluters and deniers, and all the so-called 'adults' who are stealing our childhood and our future. Fuck *them*, definitely. And fuck everyone who can't be arsed to go and vote, when young people who ACTUALLY CARE about the planet aren't allowed to! Kind of fuck Mum here for going, 'I'm not voting, because I don't know who to trust any more.' Duh, vote Green then, moron. Issues are no excuse. Hello? Wake *up*, idiots! Like this isn't the last possible moment when the human race can do something to avoid climate extinction.

And more than anything, fuck the guy in the white BMW who roared 'Fuck off!' right in her face, because he got trapped behind the barrier last week in the School Strike for Climate and had to wait. Oh, boo hoo, he had to wait! Leah feels her face go hot. The world's on fire, and you're whinging because you're being *inconvenienced*. She should totally have said that. Or even, 'No, *you* fuck off, old man!' If it happens again, she'll react for sure; not just stand there frozen and nearly crying, like she was some kind of *baby*. Like she couldn't take a punch, like she wasn't a junior black belt, for God's sake.

She blinks back the tears. Fuck him.

Not as in literally *fuck* fuck, obviously. Leah self-identifies as asexual. Like St Lucy, aka Santa Lucia, who Leah will be acting tomorrow night and, to be fair, turns out is pretty kick ass for a saint when you Google her. Back in June when Father Dominic asked, Leah was all, 'You've got to be fucking kidding me. I think not,' because he was showing her these puke-inducing images of girls with long blonde hair dressed like angels. He just laughed and said, 'Well, why don't you research St Lucy of Syracuse, have a think and get back to me?'

So, she'll be riding on the float tomorrow (tomorrow! stomach lurch, like it's going to be a karate grading), which is like a mini-conservatory on the back of a truck, custom made for the occasion. She'll be with a bunch of other girls, and they'll all be in long white robes with red sashes. Red sash means martyr. St Lucy literally died for her beliefs. Leah would totally do that too, if it came to it. And it might. She might easily get run over one day by an angry boomer in a BMW. She'd just calmly stand there, resisting, and get run over, and then she'd be globally famous, because someone would get it on their mobile and it would go viral.

Anyway. The Santa Lucia carol will be playing, pre-recorded by the cathedral girl choristers, and they'll drive all along the One Thousand Christmas Lights route, which is part of the old pilgrim route to the cathedral, except they'll end up at Lindford Church. The girls on the float will all carry candles in jars. Leah will wear the special Santa Lucia headdress of candles, but hers will be LED, not real, for health and safety reasons, in case her hair catches fire. Right, Father Dominic. Like *that's* going to happen when you've got a buzz cut. Sadly, she won't be holding a gold dish with fake eyes from Partymania glued in. Father Dominic vetoed that, even though he took her point it would be authentic and part of St Lucy's iconography.

The lights go on in Diggers. Finally!

High above on a roof corner of the nearby Unite Students block, a camera captures a tall skinny girl as she shoulders through the door into the glowing café and vanishes from view. Pigeons watch from the town hall roof. At pavement level, the homeless guy watches from under his umbrella. And way out of sight, the orbiting satellites look down too.

Rain falls over Lindfordshire. It falls on sheep in muddy fields. It falls on the apples that still hang like ornaments in neglected orchards, and on the sodden fields of winter wheat, where a pair of pied wagtails flit. It falls on the little wood, where a woman walks head down, weeping, because her project is falling apart and there's nothing she can do to make it right. There are only wrong options and she's bone weary, but she has to see it through. Then a group of muntjacs surprise her, and for a moment the dripping wood is bright with wonder.

Rain speckles the windows of Lindford General Hospital, where another woman is in labour. Still only four centimetres. Here it comes again. Dear God! Make it stop. She can see the clock. Another hour has passed. She's just a tiny boat in a giant storm. Wave after wave. I can't take it. I just can't take it!

Rain drums on the hospice roof, where a man sits by his father's bedside. He's got nothing left. Can't even wipe his tears. They drip from his running nose. Just die. Please die. I can't take it any more.

Rain falls on a white BMW caught at a level crossing. The driver looks at the dashboard clock. Shit! He'll have to vote after his shift now. He bangs the wheel. Come *on*! Drops crack down on to the windscreen from the tree above.

Breathe.

He lets his head fall back against the rest. Sees the girl's face again. Her shock. Is this what he's turned into – a monster who yells at children? The justifications start up in his head again. Look, I was half dead from my Pakistan trip, where I did over a hundred cataract ops for charity, then I was straight back into the insanity that is the NHS, late for my afternoon clinic, where whingers whinge and entitled gits get their way, because I can't tell them where to stick it, or they'll lodge a formal complaint against me. No, I have to smile and say, 'Hi! My name is Mr Logan and I'll be operating on you today!'

I'm sorry. I'm a good person, truly I am.

The train trundles through. Rain drips from the barrier. I just can't take much more of this, he thinks.

It's mid-morning. Rain patters on the flood relief hub, where Martin, the girls' father, stands in his dog collar and navy blue raincoat. The hub is no more than a gazebo, held down by sandbags. Luna is off for a walk with Kathleen. Martin thanks God for that dog, and for his girls twisting his arm into buying her. Luna is notionally their responsibility. They had to promise faithfully to walk her and feed her. Ha! It took about three minutes for Martin to lose his heart to that wriggling bundle of joy. She's done more for morale post-flood than anything he has to offer.

One month on and there's not much to see. Here and there you can still spot front gardens stacked with house contents, everything turfed out, carpets, flooring, furniture, the lot. But mostly the wreckage has been carted off to the distant landfill, where gulls circle and scream.

The drama has died down. Rescue has a certain glamour, with boats and bacon baps, and heart-warming stories of bravery and community spirit. Recovery is grey and dull and relentless. It's two steps forward, one step back. Rescue is when the TV crews come; and lord lieutenants, bishops, high sheriffs and prospective prime ministers all visit to listen, push a mop around and pledge support. Perhaps they will be back when it becomes a story again: *Two years on and still in temporary accommodation*. Or, God forbid, *Lindford floods twice in twelve months*.

Recovery is what you see now. Rain falling on a gazebo. A clergy-man making a cup of tea for Maureen, who has come out to get away from the noise of the dehumidifier, which is doing her head in. Recovery is Bob, whose gas-fired cooker, the one he uses on fishing trips, has been burning from day one to keep the hot water coming.

Recovery is Virginia, networking and liaising, accessing the council fuel voucher scheme so that people can afford the £15 a day in electricity that it costs to run a dehumidifier. It's Kaz, offering to drive people to the mental health support hub a mile away, because a mile away feels like another planet right now. It's Jez and Lynne of J&L Hot Tubs, opening their premises opposite the gazebo to store all the donations. To start with it was food and clothes. It's mainly cleaning stuff now, supplies for the heart-sinking job of clearing up, so people can move back in or stop having to live upstairs with no kitchen.

Recovery is fragile. The Linden could flood again, any time. Any day there could be severe weather warnings. Rain like buckets of water dashed at your windows. Soldiers sandbagging the streets. The river rising in the dark, and all through the night the war-zone sound of Chinooks dropping ballast on the banks. And you're waiting for the evacuation order. Stay? Go? And you're still not insured, couldn't afford it in a million years; or you are insured, but you've just discovered the £5,000 excess in the small print. And on top of everything else, it's General Election Day. Maybe now's the chance to vote. To get things done. A fresh start. There are so many promises. There have been so many lies. Even if you manage to raise your eyes from the next metre of mud on the path ahead and look around you, it's still not clear who to vote for.

The rain is still falling at midday. By now the country lanes are rivers. Puddles like lakes spread across junctions. The gargoyles on Lindchester Cathedral are projectile vomiting. Water crashes from leaf-clogged gutters. In Lindford, the gum-pocked pavements are slick, and the Christmas market is snarled up with umbrellas.

In his study, Father Dominic sends out an email reminder:

> Don't forget – St Lucy's Day tomorrow! Light your candle and put it in a front window, then look out for Santa Lucia as she rides past your house (see attached schedule)! Join us in Lindford Parish Church for our Festival of Light and Hope at 7 p.m.

There. There's nothing else he can do today. Other than pray Santa Lucia's conscience doesn't suddenly forbid her to ride on the back of a diesel truck. If it does, he'll have to press-gang another more pliant maiden into the role at short notice. Leah. He laughs. Like St Lucy herself: there's no budging her when her mind is made up, even if you hitch her to a team of oxen.

He turns his computer off. It will be fine. He heads to the kitchen, where his mother is filling in the Sudoku with arbitrary numbers, because it wards off Alzheimer's. That stable is empty and the door's swinging in the wind. But he lets her get on with it.

'Right then, Mother mine. Let's be having you.' He holds up her coat for her to post her arms in, the way she did for him when he was a boy.

'Ooh, where are we off to?'

'To the polling station.' This is perhaps the tenth time he's told her. He could tell her anything. Anything at all! We're off for a balloon ride over the Serengeti, Mother dear. But knowing her, this would be the one answer that lodged in her brain, and he'd never hear the last of it.

'Oh yes, you said. There's an election.'

She's pretty good at speed-papering over the memory cracks. And if she flails about a bit with the standard questions, who can blame her? We might all have to relearn the name of the current prime minister tomorrow. Lord, have mercy. Who will it be? If Dominic could tentatively identify the least worst option, even, that would be something. Praying for a hung parliament – what times we live in.

'And Lady's coming too. Here, girl!' A labradoodle comes skidding across the kitchen floor, tongue lolling.

'I'll get my bits and bobs,' says Mum. 'Where's my bag got to?'

'Here. And here's your polling card.' She takes off her glasses and peers closely with her good eye at the pink Post-it he's stuck on: *The Labour candidate is Jenny Ashe. Jeremy Corbyn is the leader of the Labour Party, not Michael Foot. Today's date is 12 December 2019.*

'Jeremy Corbyn? Is he the one that hid in a fridge?'

'No, that's Boris Johnson, Mother. Corbyn is the one with the cap.'

'Oh yes.' She puts her glasses back on. 'Well, let's do our civic duty, then.'

He gets Mother and dog safely stowed, and they set off. The wind-screen wipers thresh.

'Where are we off to now?'

We're off to Armageddon with our four horsemen pals. 'To vote in the General Election. For Jenny Ashe, the Labour candidate.' He pulls out of the vicarage drive. 'There's a reminder on your polling card, in your handbag.'

'Really?' She checks. 'So there is.' She takes another quick close-up of the Post-it. 'I really must book an eye appointment. This is getting ridiculous!'

Well, it's cheering to know that age can delete that litany of outpatient cancellations and delays. Her cataract op is scheduled for tomorrow at 2.30 p.m., at Mr Logan's clinic. What a lovely guy he is. Endlessly patient with poor old Ma's eccentricities. Still, they can worry about all that in the morning. Sufficient unto the day is the amnesia thereof.

'Look at all the Christmas trees!' she says. 'It's like a painting by thingummy-jig.'

There are more Christmas trees than election posters. If Santa were standing for the Vote Christmas Party, he'd have a landslide victory. They reach the library. He parks up. Well, at least she's having a good day. She knows he's her son, not her long-dead husband. But how long will it last? Long enough for her to remember to look at the Post-it? Will she recognize the Labour logo? He can't exactly follow her into the booth and hold her hand as she makes her cross.

Sorrow ambushes him. He can stand in the next booth, but she'll have to go in alone. It's yet another little death rehearsal. Oh Lord, don't let him start crying!

Dusk. Dusk at 3.30 p.m. The stopping train from Lindford trundles towards Martonbury. It enters a tunnel. All Jane can see is the reflection of her fellow passengers and the faint silver gleam of the rail beside the carriage. And her own eyes, staring back at her. She'll vote on the walk home. Normally she'd have been out canvassing all day and running old biddies to the polling station, squeezing every last precious Labour vote out of Toryfordshire. But normally you don't get a General Election dumped on you in the last Thursday of term.

Half her students hadn't bothered to show for their tutorial. Too weary. Too ground down. I feel you, comrades. She badgered them all to register, those who hadn't already. Even made time at the start of her lectures. 'You might think your vote makes no difference, but wake up. You're students of history, are you not? Surely the referendum told you your *failure* to vote makes a difference? Do you want the boomers deciding your future? We won't even be here to see it!'

And then some massive cock-up, and a whole Unite Student block were told they were ineligible because of an 'incomplete address'! She could weep. For the whole human race, but the young ones most of all. For her son in far-off New Zealand. Thank God he wasn't on that volcano. If she was a praying person, she'd pray. She'd repent. We've let you all down. And now we're looking to our children for hope. How dare we? Greta Thunberg rightly lambasting us. Not forgetting Lindford's answer to Greta – Leah. God, how Jane loves that girl. Fierce and brittle as a glass spear. Pity they hadn't had time to stop and chat at the station back there.

Her ears pop. The train bursts out of the tunnel. It's like her morning in reverse. What a dismal dawn that was, a sepia photo with half-hearted tints laid on. Ghostly glimpses of sheep. And now it's dusk. The whole day's been like dusk, as if the sun didn't bother to rise, just slouched along under the horizon in a dirty dressing gown.

She glimpses a stream rushing over rocks. Acres of standing water. Please, not more floods. Probably her house will be safe. God alone knows if she'll ever be able to sell it. Insurance has doubled. Tenants are staying put for now, sandbags at the ready.

Jane shakes her head. She has a fairly good sense of where the world is heading. Even if some freak youthquake reconfigures the political landscape overnight, this here is looking remarkably like a handcart to her. Floods in Lindford and Cardingforth! Unheard of! What's happening to the world? Ooh, now let's see. Could it possibly be (a) that against all the odds, ninety-eight per cent of scientists turn out to be right after all, or (b) the posh toffs in Lindchester finally got the city's flood defences in order (part-funded by those bastards in Brussels – bye-bye, you're welcome!) thereby shunting the problem down river?

That's what we always do, she thinks. Shunt the problem down river. Ship our recycling to developing countries. Well, it's coming home to roost now, isn't it? Your shit. You deal with it.

She stares at the passing landscape. It's like watching a grainy black and white film. The only splashes of colour are the lights: traffic lights, tail lights, festive lights. They're approaching Martonbury. She gathers her personal belongings. It keeps coming back to her. That couple watching anxiously at their front door, praying the sandbags would divert the river down the street, while all the time the water was pouring in the back door.

We're looking the wrong way, she thinks. We've focused on Stop Brexit/Let's Get Brexit Done, and all the time the flood is rising behind us. We are all tourists on a live volcano.

The cameras watch. Two girls leave Lindford Station. The smaller one scurries to keep up. They pass out on to the forecourt, where another camera picks them up. They are both in school uniform, though from different schools. Men in passing cars glance, reflexively. Water rushes down the roadside gutters. The camera on the bridge watches them cross, and then the Tesco petrol station camera clocks them passing. And so on, and on, until they're home. Safe and sound.

There should be better watchers than this; kinder eyes than these that watch but never intervene. Eyes that can only show us, with hindsight, the moment when it all went wrong. There should be guardian angels, one for each child. But who believes in that any more in Lindfordshire?

Early evening now. The rain pauses, and for a moment the Long Night Moon looks down through its wide halo, and sheds silvery light on all the little sports halls and community centres, the parish rooms, primary schools, libraries. The after-work voters arrive. They hold the door for one another, they chat, admire one another's dogs and children. The returning officers cross off names. Been busy? Not bad, a steady stream. Only three more hours.

Farmers splosh across muddy yards, not liking the look of this rain. Deliveroo bikes toil out to the suburbs. Seasonal workers clock out of the vast hangar and walk, walk, walk, bus, walk.

And now it's night. Father Dominic takes Lady out for her bedtime walkies. It's raining again, but a soft rain. Water murmurs in gutters.

Deep below the road some hidden river is rushing. He hears the muffled roar under the drain covers. Then in the distance he hears the town hall clock chime ten.

'That's it, Lady. Polling's closed. Nothing more we can do. We'll just have to wait and see.'

He could stay up all night, but he won't. He knows in his bones already. The exit polls are the flood warning. Jesu, mercy. What will we do now? The whole nation's going to fall apart. The poor will get trampled further into the mud. There it goes, our last chance in my lifetime to elect a government that cares about the common good.

He knows there is hope. Of course there is. This is Advent. The people who walk in darkness have seen a great light. There *is* hope. He squats down and grabs Lady to him. 'Oh God, I just don't know what to do, girl.'

The dog cries, and laps his face. As if love is the answer.

'Good girl. Come along then.' Dominic straightens up and wipes his eyes. Blessed Lucy, pray for us. He tries to picture the pilgrim route through Lindfordshire lined with candles. And his ridiculous truck full of light-bearing maidens, coming through the dark.

'I'm pinning my hope on a mere child!' Then he hears himself and half laughs, half sobs. They walk on through the night, with Lady bounding ahead. Her light-up collar blinks red, dancing in the puddles.

All over Lindfordshire the tellers are counting, like recording angels, preparing for judgement day. What will we rise to tomorrow? A glorious heaven? Or an ever-deepening hell?

In a hospice room, a man finally sleeps in his chair. In the bed beside him, softly, like the first snowflake feathering down, his father lets go of his last breath.

And in Lindford General Hospital, a mother stares into the eyes of her newborn child. 'It's you,' she whispers. 'You're here.' The babe stares back, full of wonder.

And in a bedroom window, a tall girl glares through her tears into the dark garden. The grown-ups are in despair. But there's still hope. *There's still hope.* She raises her fist in a warrior salute, rehearsing for tomorrow. This is how she will come through the streets. Her reflection blazes in the night, radiant, candle-crowned.

And in the room next door, another girl looks out too, and sings softly. Her breath mists the glass. "'Now light one thousand Christmas lights, on dark earth here tonight.'"

High above, behind the clouds, ten thousand, thousand stars also shine, although we cannot see them.

THE END